A Risk of Rain

Dar Tomlinson

Genesis Press, Inc.

Love Spectrum is an imprint of
Genesis Press, Inc.
315 3rd Ave. N.
Columbus, MS 39701

A Risk of Rain

ISBN: 1-58571-025-3

Manufactured in the United States

First Edition

To Bobby, whose continuous patience,
expert teaching, and encouragement
allowed me to love all aspects of the
game and the world of golf.   In yet
another way, you have enriched my life.

CHAPTER 1

The staccato echo of metal golf cleats on the concrete path announced familiar footsteps, shooting a frisson of panic up Perri Hardin's spine. Excited murmurs from the Nissan Open's mostly female gallery made her want to bolt and run. Instead, she squared her shoulders.

Above the waiting crowd, she glimpsed rust-colored hair. Then the sea of bodies parted, ushering the last member of the golf threesome onto the first tee at Riviera Country Club.

I wouldn't caddie for Beau St. Cyr if I were starving, she vowed, while the flat wallet in the hip pocket of her coveralls reminded her she might very well be starving. Soon. Perri turned away, continuing to slather lotion on her forearms. The two waiting golf pros greeted the late arrival with banter.

"Any time now, Beau Jangles. Where were you? On the phone with Paine Webber?"

"Yeah. He was taking care of the green."

Beau's retort, "I knew the bus wouldn't leave without me," floated on the crisp California-spring air. Unlike his walk, there was nothing staccato in his voice. Just a refined drawl that honed every word to submission before releasing it. His laugh, sounding as if it harbored the punch line of an off-color joke he was too genteel to tell, barbed Perri's spine.

Her hand moved to the gold locket hanging between her breasts, palming the trinket for an instant. Gathering resolve, she stuffed it inside the neck of the T-shirt she wore beneath a pair of blowsy coveralls and tugged the long-billed Nike cap lower onto her forehead.

1

Turning her back on the male threesome, she began polishing the blade of a three iron, grateful that Pete Jacoby, the pro hiring her for her first day on the PGA tour "liked Halle Berry look-a-likes." Taking a new sleeve of balls from his bag, she initialed them with a red permanent marker. Then rifling in the bag she wasn't sure she could carry for eighteen holes, she withdrew a driver and handed it to him as a PGA official addressed the gallery.

"Please welcome Peter Jacoby from Fort Worth, Texas."

"Play well," Perri interjected into the smattering of applause. She smiled at her temporary boss and stepped back.

The ball sailed. The crowd applauded again and Pete Jacoby stepped aside, his squint trailing the ball in the low-hanging seaside air. The official announced the second pro, a rookie Perri visualized being in the tournament by special invitation, most likely issued by some old friend the pro's father had leaned on to give his kid a break.

Whap. Frowning, mumbling expletives, the rookie took his place beside Pete.

The announcer's voice split the subsequent hush. "From Anchorage, Kentucky, please welcome last year's leading money winner, with twelve tournament wins—including three majors—to his credit. Ladies and gentlemen, Beau St. Cyr."

A grizzled, stooped, black-as-pitch caddie extracted a Cobra driver from a big leather bag. He passed it across the distance to the sun-bronzed warrior who strutted to the tee amid applause. With a look of grim determination, he planted his feet and waggled his butt. Perri stood close enough to recognize the scents of Kouros and Coppertone. A shiny bead of sweat clung to the auburn thatch at Beau St. Cyr's left temple.

His image swam before her eyes. Her mouth went dry. The light and dizzy feel of her body tempted her to fly away, admit defeat. But she was earthbound. This man was part of her life, had once been part of her soul. Today was reality. Rejuvenated anger nagged her into giving the bag she held upright a calculated knee nudge. It veered forward, toppled, but she made a show of catching it before it hit the ground. Clubs rattled. Clanked. Beau's head snapped up to reveal those lauded amber eyes. They locked gazes.

A breeze ruffled squiggles of curls at the base of her neck and stirred his logoed shirtsleeve. His auburn-lashed eyes narrowed like those of a hunter sighting down the barrel of a gun. She tugged the cap lower, but not before his gaze burned with recognition. He straightened to his full six foot-one height, then backed away from the ball.

Overhead the Goodyear blimp hummed; on a distant green, Tiger Wood's gallery roared approval. Beau St. Cyr's gallery shuffled their feet, murmured speculatively, coughed. Cleared their throats. Satisfied with her ploy, Perri watched Beau regroup with familiar St. Cyr finesse.

"Give me my one iron." His voice carried over the hush.

The faked composure could cost him a par. Possibly a birdie. Possibly the tournament.

With furrowed brow, the old caddie pulled the iron from the bag, then stuffed the scorned driver in its place. Beau re-addressed the ball, re-waggled his slender hips. He set his jaw, hard lines forming around his mouth. His forearm muscles bulged as he gripped the club; he swung it back and down with precise fluidity—and drove the ball into the rough, far right of his target.

A verbal wave of empathetic disappointment washed through the gathering. Beau allotted his dazzling signature smile, passed the one iron to his caddie and with a cursory nod to Perri strode off

3

the tee and onto the fairway, head high, shoulders back. His caddie wrestled Beau's bag onto his aged shoulder and scurried in his wake. Pete and the rookie trailed behind.

The gallery shuffled collapsible stools and crumpled programs as they surged along the sidelines, keeping pace with the threesome.

Perri eyed the mammoth black bag beside her, breathing in the scent of leather and steel, tasting the threat of failure deep in her throat. But if Fanny, Nick Faldo's long-time caddie and right-hand woman, could do it, so could she. Fanny was taller and brawnier, but her need couldn't be greater. Indigence would see Perri to victory.

In one motion, she bent her knees and grasped a strap, then heaved the bag up, yawing to the side under the weight. Emulating Fanny, she planted her feet and swung the load to a horizontal slant behind her. She staggered with the first step, then regained her balance, grateful now she'd had the good sense to train in preparation for today.

Eyes on Beau St. Cyr's broad shoulders, she marched determinedly down the fairway.

Calvin pulled up, waiting, a grin lighting his ebony face. He leveled a rheumy gaze on her. "Couldn't you get you no heavier bag to carry, sugar?"

"Mr. Jacoby believes in utilizing the club limit." She risked giving the old man a brief, one-armed hug, then grasped the bag again. "This is my first day. Beggars can't be choosers."

He shook his head, eyes wary. "Well, caddies is valuable for sure, and soon's they see how much you knows 'bout golf, they'll be doggin' you. But what you doin' here, chile? Mr. Beau knows 'bout this? He ain't said nothin' to me."

"This doesn't involve Mr. Beau." Her tone derided the homage that Calvin, a St. Cyr family employee since before Beau's birth, paid his boss.

4

"It's a big tour." Yet, for some reason the gods had chosen to place Beau and her in the same three-some on her launch day. At least their initial encounter was behind her, or it would be in seventeen more holes. If she lasted.

She stopped, swung the bag down, relieving the burden. She would last with pacing, unless repeatedly lowering and hoisting the bag expended more energy than simply biting the bullet.

She studied Cal, faking a congenial tone and smile. "I can't believe he's got you here—caddying for him. What happened to that bag-toting golf guru *Links Magazine* said he was traveling with? You mean he traded in that spiritual experience for you?" Cal was too old for this job, but she wasn't really surprised. Because the St. Cyrs had taken care of his family, Cal felt he owed them his life. Her question reaped silence. "What gives, Cal?"

His red-rimmed, tarpaper eyes trailed down the belt of emerald green fairway to his worshipped charge. Inside the halo-like circle of curly white hair, his bald crown glistened with sweat. "His granddaddy thought he needed some lookin' after, that's all. I don't mind."

His granddaddy. The answer touched raw nerve. "Nothing's changed, I see."

Across the fairway, the rookie addressed his ball, the shortest of the three drives. Behind him, Pete Jacoby ambled toward his own ball. Hastily, Perri shouldered the bag again, making ready. She lunged forward, and Cal caught up.

"This what you been doin' since I seen you last?" The perennial rattle in his chest, the residue of unfiltered Camels on his breath snagged a memory of better days. "Carrying these big ole bags around, stuntin' yo growth?" He flashed her a weak, dingy-toothed smile.

"Not at first. I tried lots of things." Her mind ran a rapid gamut of her various endeavors, peddling cosmetics door to door, and telemarketing among them. "But I know more about golf than anything else. I tried playing the women's tour for a couple of years."

Cal's dark eyes turned empathetic. "I bet you showed up like a raisin in rice pudding."

She shrugged. "When I couldn't finish in the money and snag TV time, my sponsor lost interest." No reason to confess the career-ending injury. Or voice her disappointment.

Down the fairway, in line with where his ball had plunged into the rough, Beau waited, staring at the two of them, mouth grim, hands splayed on hips. Perri's spine prickled in unison with her stomach knotting. "Last year I caddied the women's tour."

"I reckon them girls' bags ain't so heavy as these." Cal's tone held the emotion she had seen in his eyes, understanding that edged much too close to pity for her comfort.

"No." The year scuttled across her mind. "But there were other pressures." Subtle and yet weighty enough to be troublesome.

"Uhn," he grunted, an instant of agreement passing between them. Then he insisted, "Well, for sure, a good caddie is a pro's best club, but totin' these here bags is man's work."

Gripping the bag, she mustered strength to do a soft-shoe, a twirl to reassure him, then walked backward a few paces, striving to keep her balance, her pride. The clubs shuffled in the bag, rattled, then settled in place. "I'm stronger than I look. Caddying pays better than anything else I can do— if I get the right pro. And I need money." She tamped down images of how much she needed and why. A few yards ahead, Beau's stare turned to a glare. "You'd better help the master find his ball."

Whirling an about face, she cut across the fairway to where Pete stood eyeing the remaining dis-

6

tance to the green. Mentally, she measured the same distance and the pin placement, calculating the breeze fanning the legs of her coveralls. She pulled a six iron from the bag and held it out to him.

"My sentiments exactly," Pete murmured. "Who ever said girls can't count?" He took a languid practice swing, addressed the ball in earnest and deposited it pin-high on the distant green. Grinning triumphantly, he handed the club back to her. She wiped the blade with a damp towel, secured the iron in the bag and shouldered it, determined not to grunt—or drop it.

Pete squinted into the emerging sun, watching Beau take a penalty drop from the rough and then blast the ball into the bunker right of the green. A look bordering on amusement crossed Pete's freckled face. "Got any plans for tomorrow?"

Her heart thudded. She smiled. "I'm hoping to caddie for a winner."

"If I finish today in the top ten, you've got a deal." He started walking.

She matched his stride, attempting to shift the weight of the bag off her hips without his notice. "Deal." Damn it. She sounded breathless.

He eyed her skeptically, grin tolerant. "If I don't wind up carrying that bag myself, it'll surprise me."

"Prepare to be surprised." Gulping air, she fastened her gaze on the green.

By the end of the first nine holes, Perri decided Beau hadn't changed much in eight years, except for the hard lines that now framed his mouth. He still relied on the guileless, boyish grin for effect, but it didn't line up with the jaded look in his eyes. He played with the same economy of motion, calculated, unrushed movements, but the past two hours assured her he had honed his no-nonsense approach to winning. Tenacity that had earned him the title "St. Serious" his first year on the tour appeared to have evolved to obsession.

His second-glance good looks had matured into angles and planes underlined by a proud stance and regal carriage. He still drew scantily clad groupies vying for his attention. Unlike them, Perri had never considered Beau to have the kind of beauty that struck like lightning, but she wasn't sure she was a fair judge. Throughout their childhood his good looks had descended on her like gentle rain, almost undetectable, until the metamorphosis had left her soaked with awareness. Captivated. Committed. Until the day she had come to detest him and all he stood for, the day he altered the course of her life by ordering the stroke of a pen over a checkbook.

✳

Once Beau recognized Perri in body-skimming coveralls, her hair shoved under a cap, anger fired his reluctant memory. He regressed to that day eight years ago at High Meadow Farm, his grandfather's Kentucky estate, discovering her gone. Today's disbelief hinged on her re-entry to his world. Today's pain came from knowing she'd be in his presence for five hours.

Luckily, he hadn't whiffed the ball on number one. Instead, he and his fickle one iron had set up the worst round he'd played since he found his father's rusty clubs hidden in the barn when he was ten years old. Today's game had gone in the tank the minute Perri rattled those clubs on number one tee, and he looked into her deceitful eyes. His breath had snagged in that moment of fusion, an instant of swift connection that meant he was not completely immune to her. Not immune, but a hell of a lot smarter.

Seeing her in the caddie role shocked him. There had been a time when a caddie was a glorified pack animal, but the term didn't apply in today's technical game. An excellent caddie could make a pro as fast as a bad one could break him. Perri's golf expertise was a given; her caddying ability remained to be seen. But she was tiny, and watching her hustle Pete's clubs roused protective instincts he'd considered dead and buried long ago. That scared him.

Curiosity got the better of his wrath as he and Cal approached the fifth green—or the sand trap bordering the fifth green, since that was where he had dumped his fairway shot. Again.

When they reached the green, Beau forged into the sand bunker. Digging his feet into sand, he practiced taking the wedge up and out from the piss-poor lie. Something had better work soon or else tonight he could count on one of those good-ole-boy pep-talk calls from Richard Braden St. Cyr, Senior.

"What did she say?" Getting no answer, Beau lowered the wedge to half-mast. Frozen in place, he stared at Cal where he stood on the bank of the waist-deep trap, rake in hand. "Well?"

"'Scuse me?" Cal screwed up his forehead, all innocence.

"Perri. I saw her hugging you. What the hell did she say?"

"'Bout what?" Cal glanced around, locating the rest of their party. "You best be hittin' that ball, boy. They's all waitin' and dark comes early this time a year."

Beau opened the face of the club and positioned it behind the ball, a fraction of an inch above the sand. He screwed his feet in deeper. If this sand shot was as wimpy as the others had been, he might just claim he was stuck and stay here.

"You know about what. What's she doing here? She's too little to carry a man's bag. Especially Pete's, for Christ's sake." That mental picture made him lift the club and back away from the ball.

9

Twenty yards away, Pete and Perri stood watching, Pete grinning encouragement, Perri stone-faced. The rookie had already walked onto the green. The gallery milled on either side of the fairway and filled the newly painted wooden bleachers circling the green. "Maybe I'll take an unplayable lie," Beau mumbled.

"You gonna let her root under yo skin, boy?"

Beau had heard that cajoling tone all his life. "You mean like for the last eight years?"

Now Cal mustered as much assertiveness as he was capable of. "Just hit the ball, Beau."

Not trusting his swing, Beau opened the club-face too far. The ball lit as gracefully as a butterfly with sore feet . . . ten feet short of the pin.

"Ump ump uhn." Cal rolled his eyes and began to rake trounced sand.

For the next two holes Beau seethed. Had the gallery not moaned over the frigging errant sand shot he would've sunk the putt for bogey. But by the time he trudged up number eighteen, failing to make the cut, he knew where to place the blame.

No golf course between Anchorage, Kentucky, and hell was big enough for Richard Braden St. Cyr, III and Ms. Perri Rae Hardin.

CHAPTER TWO

In the company of a few die-hard fans, Perri
warmed the bleachers behind the Riviera practice
range. Wishing for the coveralls she'd turned in
after the round, she pressed bare legs together and
raised the collar on her jacket to ward off the early
evening breeze,. She dragged her gaze away from
Beau, working his way through a steady stream of
practice balls, and attempted to concentrate on her
newfound roommate, Teddy Ridgely, at the far end
of the range.

Finding Beau practicing when she'd come to
wait for Teddy had been a surprise. Since today's
round had shut him out of the Open, she'd
assumed he'd leave posthaste on his jet for High
Meadow Farm, or report early for the Doral-Ryder
Open in Miami. She pictured him toiling at
unneeded practice there. In fact, he had occupied
too many of her thoughts since he'd trudged off the
green, only to be swallowed up by a horde of kids
waiting to receive the candy he always carried in
his bag. A TV journalist and a cameraman had
recorded the ritual.

As she watched his fluid swing again, her memory reconnected to the way his shoulder muscles
hardened in the club take away, then eased on the
down swing. Those arms exuded strength and gentleness. She had once found refuge there.

Forcing her gaze away again, she stuffed the
locket inside her tank top and buttoned her jacket
to the neck, hoping Beau hadn't spotted her. She
willed Teddy's pro to finish practice before Beau.
Timing loomed paramount. Five hours on the
course in Beau's presence had been punishment
enough. Relieved, she saw Teddy's pro winding up,

while Beau appeared entrenched. As Teddy wiped clubs with a damp towel, her eyes sought Perri. Somberly, Teddy nodded toward the clubhouse and the straggling line of buses that would take them back to the outer parking lot and Teddy's vintage Mercury Cougar, Sheba, left only God could remember where that morning.

Perri arched her back as she rose, fingers digging in to massage screaming muscles at her waist. As she descended the bleachers, her hope of escape waned. Beau handed the wood he'd been hitting to Cal and stood watching, so still he could have been a statue if not for the latent energy he emanated. On the range next to him, Freddy Couples and his caddie stopped to watch her descend. She elevated her chin, aiming brisk steps toward the clubhouse.

Beau cut her off, insinuating his body between her and her destination, his pricey golf shoes slightly spread, hands on hips. Muscled forearms shone coppery beneath the baggy sleeves of his shirt. His eyes were cold as a pond in winter, his expression boasting composure a bullish stance and pulsating temple denied. The strength of his ire scared her. With nothing more than a derogatory comment on her golf expertise, he had the power to deny her access to this kingdom, a domain where he reigned and she needed a foothold.

His gaze stole down her body, settling on her ankles just above the stained and tattered Doc Martins. Her legs pimpled with goosebumps, mind seizing on the bag-inflicted bruise she'd discovered on her shin when she'd taken off the coveralls.

"What's this all about, Perri?" Dark-amber eyes drilled hers. "What are you doing here?" Beyond his shoulder, Freddy addressed a ball while his caddie gawked.

12

"I'd think, after five hours on the course, you wouldn't have to ask that." When his invasive stare held steady, she added, "I'm working. Although not as glamorously as you."

His eyes narrowed. "Knowing what I know, I assumed you'd never have to work again."

The last thing she wanted to discuss with him, ever, was her finances. "Never assume." She folded her arms over her breasts, staring back harshly at Freddy's blatantly curious caddie.

A heated pause broadened into agonizing silence. Flustered, she took a Carmex tube from the pocket of her short wrap skirt, and glided balm over her lips. His gaze settled on her mouth. Unnerved by the memories she read in his eyes, she pocketed the tube and skittered sideways. He angled his powerful body between her and escape, saying, "I want to talk to you."

Lightly, his hand grasped her arm, fusing a longing ache through her that she had prayed was healed. She shrugged away. "What's to say that you couldn't have said years ago?"

Those gold-rimmed-in-brown eyes quickened. "I want to hear your story."

The bastard wouldn't live long enough to get the details of how she'd felt when he tromped her heart. "That's noble of you, but no thanks."

"Since I got the news second hand, I kept calling to hear it from you." His gaze measured her. "You were never around."

"Not to hear you gloat, you're damn right."

His sun-darkened brow corrugated, drawing her attention to a hairline cowlick. "What the hell does that mean?"

A few yards away, Teddy stood combing her spiked yellow hair, staring at the two of them somberly. Beau torqued an auburn brow when Teddy closed the switchblade style comb, shoved it in the back pocket of her coveralls, and then fished out a cigarette and a box of matches. She struck the match with her thumbnail, lit the cigarette and snuffed the flame with her fingertips, eyeing Beau through a smoke curtain. Abruptly, Perri wished she hadn't shared with Teddy her dread of running into Beau. Teddy detested men, Perri had discovered on the drive to the course, and she appeared even more capable of holding a grudge than Perri.

"I have to go," she murmured. "Teddy's waiting for me."

"Theodora Ridgely? You're kidding." He sounded incredulous, rather than amused.

"Not at all. She's teaching me survival tactics for a man's world."

Beau looked sick. "Perri, I don't think you should—" He looked back to where Teddy shouldered the pro's bag, ready to stow it for now. "Are you sure you know what you're doing?"

His meaning stung. "I know what I'm doing." The only thing she could at the moment. "And I don't give a damn what you think." Eyes denouncing, she whirled as gracefully as her Doc Martins allowed.

"I want to talk to you." He grasped her arm. His voice sliding deeply and smoothly into her ear tempted her.

She shook him off. "Go to hell, Beau."

Trembling and half blinded by scalding tears, she strode toward Teddy.

✳

"You through crying?" Teddy scowled across the ragged seat to where Perri scrunched against the passenger door. The glower lacked validity, and the question smacked of sympathy.

"Finished." Perri smiled feebly, cramming a damp tissue into the pocket of her scuffed eight-year-old Louis Vuitton backpack. "Again."

"It really burns my ass that you let him get to you like that. It's gonna be a long tour, you know."

Teddy watched for reaction, then added, "Apparently, you two were pretty involved."

Perri sifted the term through her mind. She had been and would be for the rest of her life. She leveled her shoulders, as she'd done mentally all day, and released a pent-up breath. "Today was the hardest. It's plush fairways and no wind in my face from now on."

"I coulda told you he was bad news." Teddy squinted through smoke from a cigarette dangling between her lips, as she checked the rear view mirror for a chance to change lanes.

Perri lowered her window. "Where was your wisdom when I was twelve years old?"

"That's when you fell for the son of a bitch?"

The label hadn't fit Beau then. He had been a brash fourteen-year-old who reminded her of an Irish Setter puppy, overly eager, full of restless energy and unlimited self-confidence.

"We met when my family moved to Kentucky so Dad could get a new job—he headed up course maintenance at Owl Creek, in Anchorage. Beau's great-grandfather founded the club."

"Your father was the greens keeper at that bastion-of-old-money club?"

Perri had known Teddy vaguely on the women's tour and reconnected with her at the motel. But Teddy's interpretation of the golf club led Perri to believe there was more to the girl than switchblade combs and a possible alternate lifestyle. "You know about Owl Creek?"

"I drove out there when the tour was at Valhalla in Louisville." She grinned. "Security wouldn't allow this clunker in the lot, so I parked out on the road and peeked through the fence."

"Dad was an employee, nothing more, in charge of course maintenance. There's a big difference between that and greens keeper." A job they'd never trust to a black man, a fact her mother never let Lee forget. "I hung around helping him in the summer." She could still feel the sun baking her shoulders and the bunker sand between her toes, smell the mowed grass and hear the crows calling out warnings of rain. "I couldn't go inside the club house, even to get water. He'd take me in on the days the club was closed and show me off to the clean-up help." She faked a smile. "He'd bend their ears about how I was the boy he always wanted but never had."

"Great way to learn your place in life, huh, scrapper?" Teddy hiked untweezed brows.

Perri had been too naïve then to recognize social or racial structures. For a while she had left that world behind to live in his. She had believed he loved her enough to overlook their cultural and social differences. Their unity had lasted a decade before being annihilated in one night. Or had the unity been real? Had it ever happened? Her hand stole to the locket beneath the tank top. A relationship had existed all right, even if it hadn't been real. "My years at Owl Creek shaped my life."

Jerking the wheel, Teddy shot into another lane. "You met Mr. Brain-In-His-Crotch."

"Actually, I learned to love golf there. That's how Beau and I became friends. We played junior golf together."

The brows hiked again. "They wouldn't let you in the club house, but they let you play golf on their fancy course with their white-bread kids?"

"Special dispensation."

"Who was the Pope?"

"Beau's grandfather, Richard Braden St. Cyr, Sr." Along with the bitterness in her voice; bile rose in her throat. "Beau and I went to the same school, although we lived miles apart. He grew up on Braden's horse farm in Oldham County. When Beau found out my name was Perri, he used to tug my ponytail and call me Pericardium or Periscope—

all kinds of things." At age fourteen, he had switched to calling her Periwinkle "because you always smell flowery," and she had begun to fall in love. "Beau was two grades ahead of me, a big difference at that age. But he'd seen me working on the course with Lee and talked his grandfather into letting me play on the junior golf team."

"Cool." Teddy's grin bared pristine, perfect teeth.

Perri ran her fingers through the ponytail hanging from the back of her cap, remembering how Beau's eyes had lingered there only a few minutes earlier. If she let herself, she could remember his hands in her hair, how he'd talked her into letting it grow, how he'd claimed he loved to brush it, the time he'd dried it with his shirt when they'd sneaked to the cool, dark creek for a swim after golf. The first time she'd felt that he—

But he had never felt for her what she had imagined and craved.

Shivering inwardly, she pulled back. "Junior golf is where I learned how to caddie, carrying my own bag. One of Beau's old bags, actually, and his old clubs. I caddied for the Ladies' Auxiliary, too."

Seeing the respect paid to big money pros, frequent guests at Owl Creek, convinced her she could share their glory when she grew up. Share as a caddie. She should have stuck with that plan and omitted those grueling years trying to play on the women's tour.

"So you played gratis golf with his hand-me-downs? Generous bastard, wasn't he?"

Perri gave in to a smile. Remembering the good times were all that had kept her sane that first year after they parted, through all the lonely, fearful nights. Then bitterness had moved in and recolored her memories, setting up a barrier of resentment. Seeing Beau today had almost chipped a hole in that barrier.

17

"We were children." She reluctantly allowed herself to go all the way back, to engage in less tainted memories. "Beau watched out for me, made sure I got to play and no one mistreated me because . . ." Her throat broadened. She swallowed around the lump.

"Because you're black, right?" Teddy raised a brow. You are, aren't you?"

"My father's black. When we grew up, Beau realized I never belonged in his world."

Teddy shrugged, the way Perri wished she could, with finality and disdain. "He's an ass." The old car shuddered a mutinous threat as it gained another lane. Teddy drove, looking into the mangled side view mirror. "He fits the mold. I read a spread in *People* that gave the full scoop on all his engagements. It hinted at an early marriage. One that got swept under the rug." She flipped the cigarette stub out the open window.

Perri had read the article, then burned it.

Teddy cast her a measuring glance. "According to Pete Jacoby, St. Serious is engaged for the third time. Apparently he has trouble sticking to a plan."

A *Town and Country Magazine* Perri had found in a laundromat contained a picture of Beau at the Kentucky Derby with last summer's fiancée. The woman also graced the cover in a riding habit, holding the reins of a million-dollar racing stud. Perri used her lunch money to run the magazine through scalding water on heavy-duty cycle. Afterward she had been ill for hours.

"Ms. Current Favorite appeared a while back— a regular show-pony." Teddy had used the industry term for the exceptionally beautiful women the players inevitably wound up with, as though that, too, was a competitive feat. "She came to be seen, not to see golf. I hear she spent most of her time with the pregnant wives, sipping mint juleps. She won't be around long."

"Probably. Beau's women have to pass inspection." Braden's judgmental face rolled across Perri's mind. "Acceptance by the St. Cyrs ranks even with getting into Owl Creek."

She had striven for flippancy, but as traffic came to a crawl, Teddy eyed her perceptively, fingers drumming the wheel. "The article accused him of trying to play all the courses while he still has the moves, but without buying a membership."

Perri gazed out the window, hugging herself. Aching.

"No comment?"

"No comment."

Beneath the locket resting coolly against her breasts, her heart scabbed over again.

CHAPTER THREE

In the Riviera men's grill, Beau pulled out a leather-upholstered chair and slid into it across from Pete Jacoby. He caught the waiter's eye and pointed to Pete's Michelob making sweat rings on the highly varnished table. "Well, Nick Faldo's the one to shoot at tomorrow. You've got your work cut out for you."

"Yeah, but better him than Tiger." Pete slouched in his chair watching rerun highlights of today's round on television. He nodded at an image of Tiger Woods dumping an approach shot into the water on the back nine. "The kid couldn't get it together today, though."

"Neither could I if I had a hyped-up gallery and a throng of photographers following me."

"I like your gallery. Ninety percent real women and the rest girls hell bent on donating their virginity, if they can get their phone numbers to your caddie." Pete tapped his bottle with the one now sitting before Beau. "My kind of action."

Beau had met Heather like that. She had given her number to Cal, and Beau felt just lonely enough to call her. When Braden got word and nixed the relationship, Beau was too indifferent to argue. So far, his grandfather approved of Stephanie Kane; but what would marriage be like with a woman who hated the game? "Quantity means nothing, if the right woman's not in the crowd."

"Another Beauism for my memory bank." A sardonic laugh jiggled Pete's shoulders. He eyed Beau over the top of his beer. "What happened to you today, anyway? Every time I looked up, my idol was in the Kikuya grass. Seeing you self-destruct kind of tested my mettle."

"I've had better rounds in nightmares." Beau gazed across the room, mind far from the companionable chatter resting on the smoky air. He pictured Perri's thick mane—sun-bleached tobacco— swinging from the back of her cap. No way to phrase what happened today, short of a dissertation the length of *War and Peace*? He detoured. "For starters, I didn't get to warm up."

"Why not? Warming up is your religion."

"My tires had been slashed." Aftershock of sabotage remained on his mind, entangled with the rest of a day he was glad to see ending. "I spent my warm-up time calling the Hertz agency and talking to hotel security, got here too late to hit practice balls."

"Punks. Destroying property for the hell of it escapes me."

Beau couldn't envision either one. "It gave me the willies."

"Don't take it personally. The little bastards couldn't know it was your car."

"Want to hear the rest?"

"You've got the tee."

"I played the round minus my pitching wedge." The one Braden had custom weighted in his workshop at High Meadow the year Beau won the National Amateur. "Cal swears it was in the bag when we finished yesterday. Maybe some kid working club storage wanted a souvenir."

Pete swigged his beer. "You need a new keeper, Beau. Cal's too old for the job."

Beau decided against mentioning that the five cases of promotion balls Titleist had given him were now missing from his temporary locker. That would sound like whining.

He lapsed into silence, sipping beer, thinking of Perri's tawny, smooth-as-a-club-head legs under her short skirt. Her legs weren't long. But they were the most perfectly proportioned and shaped of any he'd ever had wrapped around him. He shifted in the chair. Thank God for those Riviera regulation coveralls covering her legs on the course. Though how could he have played any worse, or be floundering any deeper in memory now? Hard to believe that within his rage, gut-grinding sexual greed had reared up like a racehorse at the starting gate.

Christ! This beer smacked of the cold-hot taste of Carmex. He shoved Perri's mouth out of his mind and the nearly empty bottle away, signaled for another beer, then changed the subject. "I'm going to wait for you instead of going on to Miami. I'll hang around for the weekend and watch Nick maul your rear, then we'll go together."

"Decent of you. You can coach from the sidelines, and the lift will save me a bundle."

"No problem." If he didn't hold the plane for Pete, he'd feel obligated to go home for the weekend and listen to his grandfather's rendition of how to survive the cut. But Beau doubted Braden had ever played under today's conditions.

When he signaled for his third beer, Pete grinned wryly. "You're a two-beer man, at most. Something stuck in your craw?"

"Yeah. Your caddie." So much for deciding not to talk about that either.

"I thought she did all right, for her first day. I hired her to see me through the finish."

Great. Abruptly, High Meadow Farm looked appealing. "I hope to hell you plan to take some clubs and balls out of your bag. She can't carry that tanker three days in a row."

Pete grinned, hiking his chair until only the back legs were on the floor. "She's no hoss," he admitted, "but I'll bet under all that camouflage, she's a show-pony."

Perri had hated that term. "She is. You can drop the speculation."

Pete's grin turned conspiratorial. "No shit? Been there, done that one, too? Well bless your liberal soul."

Beau twirled the beer bottle between his palms, confronting his demons. Again. Her laughter, her warmth, descended on him, along with recall of how she came into his arms and settled, fitting him as perfectly as a supple golf glove, so sweet and giving he could think of nothing but burying himself inside her. And staying forever. "She's my wife."

Pete's chair clopped to the floor, propelling him forward. "Get outta here."

Beau nodded, mouth grim.

"That proves it. You're a member of the Lucky Sperm Club."

"Ex-wife, if you count an annulment." He hadn't, but that's what Perri had dictated.

"So Star was right about the secret marriage, all those hints of the bride being black."

Beau wallowed in silent memory.

"If you want to get technical, an annulment means you were never married."

Beau pushed that aside. "She traveled the Nike tour with me my first year out." She'd been a partner rife with golf knowledge and love for the game, a buddy to laugh away grinding pressure with, a lover who journeyed to Elysium—her interpretation—beneath him every night, clinging to him, whispering his name. That year had been the happiest of his life. Apparently, she'd only been biding her time.

"What happened?" Pete urged.

"Hell if I know." He shrugged granite-heavy shoulders. "After a year, we got married between tournaments and detoured by High Meadow to break the news to Braden." The memory of spending their wedding night in his childhood bed clung like a leech. "I left her sleeping the next morning and went to practice my one iron. When I got back she was gone."

"Even God can't hit a one iron, Beau Jangles. You proved that today."

"Or satisfy Perri Hardin, apparently."

The surprise had rocked him. Since they were children, through all the separations, the protests from Braden and Perri's father, Lee Hardin, Beau had considered her connected to him, his other self. For the last eight years, he had longed for revenge, longed to destroy her as swiftly and cold-heartedly as she'd killed their love. He could do that now by keeping her off the tour, not allowing her to work, which for some mysterious reason seemed vital to her.

He had intended to level his threat on the range, in exchange for answers. But when he'd seen fear spark her eyes, followed by her effort to hide it, guilt coursed his spine. He no longer sought revenge. He wanted closure, the kind she'd obviously found. He wanted freedom from loving and hating her all at once. Freedom from caring why she'd stopped loving him.

Then he could find someone else, settle down and get on with his life.

Pete broke into his ruminating. "You know, Beau, a wife can saddle a man with a permanent slice on the ball. You showed signs of that today."

Beau shrugged again. "I hadn't seen her in eight years. Today was a shock."

"Count yourself lucky. She sounds like high mental maintenance."

He had never thought so. Until she'd taken the money and bailed out of his life.

✳

"Will you accept a collect call from Perri Hardin?"

Through the wire, Perri could feel Angie's hesitation. By the light of a taco-touting neon sign, she squinted at her watch. Angie would be watching ER re-runs. She should have planned prudently enough to call when Angie wouldn't be the only one still up. Damn Teddy's Cougar.

Angie finally said, "I'll accept." Exhaustion crowded the line.

"I'm sorry I called collect, Mom, but I won't talk long." The draft of a passing car whipped the tail of her skirt, chilling her bare legs. Headlights illuminated the trash-strewn sidewalk and pink stucco storefront. The ER theme hummed in Angie's background.

"Why didn't you charge it to your room, Perri?"

"Motels add service charges onto long distance calls. Is everything all right?"

"Why?"

Why? "I worry, Mom. I need to know."

"I meant why can't you talk long? You must have a date."

Angie's priorities never altered. Perri felt she was the parent and Angie was the child. "No date. I'm in a phone booth." Cold and scared. "What did the doctor say?"

Angie sighed, a release of pent-up breath. "About the same. No way to put off the surgery more than a year, and that'll be pushing it. It'll take some luck to get by that long."

Stomach roiling, Perri angled the front of her body away from another approaching car. Cat calls echoed on the night. Taillights brightened as the car slowed, stopped. She lifted her eyes heavenward as the car finally pulled away. "I was hoping for a better report."

She'd been praying, bargaining with God, promising anything.

"Sorry, baby. It's the best I can do. You know, if we'd ask the government for money, the way I

said—there's no way they wouldn't come across."
Angie launched a familiar argument. "That's what
welfare's for, Perri. People like us. That's why I
vote Democratic—the only thing your sorry daddy
was ever right about."

Perri's spine iced up. The one time she'd
sought help, she'd met with nothing but scare tactics. She sought a different subject, a solution. "I
caddied today. It was easy to get hired, actually,
and not as tiring as I expected. I'm glad I spent
time working out before I left." She had run five
miles every day for months, and lifted the free
weights stored in the tool shed at the back of
Angie's weedy lot. Those rusty weights were the
only evidence left of her run-away brother. In some
ghostly way, she'd felt his support.

"You're making things hard on yourself, Perri."
The click of a lighter resounded through the
phone. Angie sucked in and released a rattling
breath. Perri cringed at the magnified, telltale
sound. They had been over the smoking issue too
often, with no resolution Angie could stick to.
"You're making things harder on me, too." Angie's
bottom line.

Perri had no counter. "The pro I carried for
today hired me for the next two rounds. I won't get
paid until the tournament's over, but he has a good
chance of winning—maybe not winning, but a
chance of placing near the top for big money." The
customary caddie fee she'd been paid today, plus
what she'd get for the next two days, would barely
cover rent, food and her share of the gas needed to
get the vintage Cougar to Miami. Pete Jacoby had
to win or she'd be broke. "He's nice. We got along
great."

"If he's nice, you know what he's after. Just
play your cards right, Perri."

"All he's after is winning, Mom. He'll play better if he has confidence in his caddie—if we get

along." Through today's grueling round she had cast her mind on a distant plane, making each decision as though life depended on it. "If he wins, I'll send my cut home on Monday. Use it to pay for today's test. It's best if you keep current."

"I hope it's enough."

God, it had to be. "Everything depends on who I get to work for. They have to be winners. So think positive thoughts for me."

A taut pause, then, "I planned to watch television today, to see if I could spot you, but the test ran too long. Since you're in California, you should take advantage of camera exposure." Angie's voice altered to a husky timbre. "That's how Lana Turner got discovered, —not playing golf, Lord knows, but sipping a soda. You never know who's watching."

Perri had heard the story repeatedly as she and Angie watched movies deep into the night, while death lurked demon-like within the crevices of a rickety house on a dark, tree-laden street.

"I need to go, Mom. This is costing money. I wanted to hear how—"

"Did you see Beau today?"

Her heart raced. "He's here."

"Did you talk to him?"

"More or less." The day reeled unwelcomed through her mind. "I have to go."

"I thought you'd be staying with him."

Angie never relented. Perri looked down the thoroughfare to the past-its-prime motel where the majority of the caddies had congregated for the Open.

"Did you tell him, Perri? If you'd tell him, our troubles—"

"No!" she said too harshly, then added, "You know I can't, and you know why." Vulnerability. They would become an open target. "We've been over it—"

"You are so damned stubborn. One of these days, I'm going to—"

"No, you aren't, Mom." Perri calmed her tone, even as Angie's threat rubbed lime into her nerve endings. "This is going to work if I stay healthy and get the right jobs. You have to trust me, and be patient."

"I'm not getting any younger, baby." Her mother sounded anything but patient. "I want to kick up my heels in the time I have left."

Perri considered easing the phone into its cradle, cutting off the lament, the accusation. The plea? She could hang up. She could run away. Still, she could never outdistance the guilt. "I know Mom. I have to get to bed, get some rest, so I can pull Pete Jacoby through tomorrow. I'll send money on Monday."

Silence. Another click of the lighter.

Perri rested her forehead against the cool metal of the phone box. The ragged, dangling directory banged against her crotch. "Give Chelsea a good night kiss."

"She's sleeping." Angie blew out smoke. "You know she turns in early."

"Kiss her anyway, and tell her it's from me." Perri replaced the phone with a trembling hand. Winning meant everything.

✳

In the late afternoon gloom, Braden slouched in his wife's favorite chintz club chair, staring at the phone beside their bed. As he willed it to ring, despite his reluctance to disturb the sleep Winonna had finally slipped into, his mind filed over a day he'd spent hoping against the inevitable. Earlier Winonna's pain had finally become unbearable, for each of them. While pacing the hall at Louisville General in the wing donated by the St. Cyr family, he had missed Beau's daily call. Once home, when he played Beau's message, a hitch in his tone, a touch of uncustomary sullenness, left Braden anxious, not sure his grandson would call back. He could try reaching Beau at the hotel now, or on his cellular, but....

Straightening, he rested his elbows on the chair arms and steepled his fingers. His early-evening toddy was overdue, and Winonna was not up to participating in their shared ritual. An era, forty years of living with the threat of death, was drawing to a close. Braden sensed it in that seldom-wrong part of his rational.

He rolled his shoulders, massaged his nape, raking his mind in search of sweet memories to soothe death's sting. The face of his son, Braden Jr.—the first Beau—then the face of his daughter Ginger edged to the forefront of his pondering, tangling with the troublesome aftermath of Beau's voice. The phone's quiet buzz pierced his ruminating. Without hesitance he shoved out of the chair, left the room quickly and loped along the corridor at an arthritic gate. Leaving Winonna alone placed Beau first again, but she would understand. She always understood. Beau was all they had left.

Braden sank into his desk chair, seized the phone and answered expectantly. "Hello."

"That you, Mr. St. Cyr?"

Weighty disappointment settled onto him. "Braden St. Cyr. Who's this?"

"You don't know me, but—"

"Then why are you calling?" Damn solicitors. Across the way, in the antique armoire bar, Glenlevitt beckoned. A silver ice bucket sweated. Light prisms danced on crystal in the frail sun slanting through the shutters. Agitated, Braden pointed out, "It's after business hours."

"Did you watch the tournament?"

"What tournament?" What was this interloper selling?

"Have I got the right St. Cyr? You are Beau's grandfather?"

Apprehension moved in. "How did you get this number?" His darting mind aligned Beau's disgruntled tone with this stranger, finding no feasible match. "Who are you?"

"Let's say, I'm friendly to the cause. Provided the cause hasn't changed."

"Young man—" Down the hall, Winonna coughed. "Get to the point. My wife is ill."

"Sorry to hear it. You probably didn't see today's round then."

No. Winonna's Patent Ductus Arteriosus, no respecter of persons or plans, had forbidden him to watch, left no time to program the VCR. After Beau's initial good showing, Braden had anticipated today. Beau's red hair, passed down from Winonna, and his maternal great-grandfather's Cajun-olive skin, made him easy to spot. The first televised glimpse of Beau always woke that skittish butterfly in Braden's stomach. Anytime the camera covered a player other than Beau, Braden grew anxious, restless to the point of annoyance. Not watching today made him feel like a party to Beau's missing the cut.

"You there, Mr. St. Cyr?"

The voice jolted him back. "Either tell me your name and purpose or I'll end this."

"I think I'll call back, sir, when you're in a more receptive frame of mind."

Only a sense of fear kept Braden from hanging up. Country-western music thrummed in the background, along with a deep, but hollow, clank he associated with colliding pool balls. He tried to imagine the caller's face, hating his cock-sure manner. "What do you want?"

A laugh slid through the wires. "Beau said you were a real hard ass. I guess he'd know."

Braden doubted Beau had used that term to describe him. Silence ticked over the line.

"Did you watch on Friday, Mr. St. Cyr?"

"I didn't, for what it's worth."

"Too bad. If you had, you wouldn't be wondering what this is all about."

"For your information, I'm not wondering."

The caller's laugh suggested disbelief. "Suit yourself," sounded like a verbal shrug. "But if I were you, I'd make a point of watching the Miami round, to see what your little boy is up to. I doubt you'll like it, since you hated it before."

Braden's nape tingled. His heartbeat accelerated. "If you have something to tell me—"

"Not this time, but I'll call back. I can help you, Mr. St. Cyr. Be thinking about that."

The phone went silent in Braden's ear. He replaced it on the cradle, crossed to the bar, dropped an ice cube in a glass, poured scotch to the tops of his fingers gripping the glass. At the window, he opened the cherry-wood shutters and surveyed the rolling meadow. His prize Arabians grazed tranquilly while a thunderhead gathered around the dwindling sun.

That voice. Non distinctive, no regional inflection to cue where the caller might hail from. His innuendoes held more goading than threat— harassment for harassment's sake.

Sipping scotch, he stared past the putting green he'd built for Beau when he was twelve. In the grape arbor, wind whipped Winonna's two-seater swing against vine-laden posts. He'd seen discontent in Beau's eyes his last trip home. Restlessness. But from what?

⁂

Braden St. Cyr seemed like an okay old man, not a cocky sonovabitch the way he'd figured. A little snooty, yeah, but when you're born with a silver spoon jammed up your ass you can afford to be

31

a snob. On the other hand, he'd never figured Beau for a snob, just obsessed with winning, no matter what it took. He guessed Braden Sr. had enough blue blood for the two of them. If the old man caught any leftover news highlights of the tournament—but hell, the tawny little bitch hadn't been Beau's caddie, so Braden might not notice, and she wouldn't be in Miami. But sooner or later, she'd show up on the same small screen with St. Serious, and no matter how old his granddaddy was, he wouldn't miss the way Beau looked at her. The old man'd know it was a matter of time till they'd be back in the sack, maybe remarried. Meanwhile, a prank now and then, a little pressure of not knowing what to expect next round, and the Saint's game'd start to slip. Then, it'd be time to move in for the kill, roust him off his throne. The situation called for a little time biding. A little patience.

And just wait till Braden Sr. saw what was planned for Miami.

CHAPTER FOUR

Perri floated in the dregs of sleep. The day stretched out like an unused dewy fairway, until distinct physical discomfort nudged her eyes open.

Dawn had encroached on unfamiliar surroundings. The generic room contained a second bed, disheveled and empty, an arm's reach away. A pair of jeans draping a straight-back chair, running water and a slither of light beneath a door in a far wall brought yesterday rushing back. Abruptly, the ache in her muscles took on meaning.

She teetered on the brink of an even more disturbing memory. Pushing Beau's insistent face and imposing body from her mind, she sat up as the bathroom door opened.

"Good. You're alive." Teddy's voice sounded as gravelly as Perri's throat felt. "I was about ready to have your body exhumed." She raised a glass tumbler of dark liquid to her mouth and sipped. "If you're riding with me, better get your ass in gear."

Teddy crossed the close confines with a business air, seized yesterday's jeans from the chair back and pulled them on beneath a sweatshirt that swathed a Harvard University logo across her ample chest. Frowning, she watched Perri's attempt to ease off the bed and stand. "Maybe you'd rather run me out to the course, bring the car back and sleep in, since Jacoby's tee time's not till—twelve fifty, you said?" She hiked a shaggy brow.

Unconvinced the Cougar had an extra trip in it, Perri announced, "I'll go with you. I need to brush my teeth. I'll braid my hair in the car."

"Give me another minute." As Teddy brushed past her, Perri caught a whiff of Calvin Kline's

33

Eternity, she thought. The girl went back into the bathroom. "Come in. There's room."

Perri hobbled on bruised feet and leaned against the doorjamb in time to see Teddy pull the electric plug on a heating wand and remove it from a glass of bubbling water. Jars of instant coffee and powdered creamer, a few packets of sugar littered the scarred counter. Perri's stomach lurched, then settled into a rumble as Teddy stirred a heaping spoon of sparkling crystals into the hot water. "Cream and sugar?"

Perri shook her head, wrapping her waist with her arms.

"You look like hell, Princess Leia." Teddy eyed the Star Wars insignia on the T-shirt front as she wrapped a limp wash cloth around the steaming glass and handed it to her.

"I'm a little stiff." Perri checked her appearance in the mirror, running a hand through her tousled mane. Eyes framed by bruised circles stared back. She looked away, sipping gingerly. "I'll limber up. Coffee helps, thanks." She found a smile as hard to come by as last night's sleep. "I should have packed a supply of horse liniment."

"I'm a road veteran." Teddy wound the cord around the heating wand and stowed it behind the jars. "I've got Ben Gay in the duffel. Want me to dig it out?"

The smell of Ben Gay could destroy what little trust she had managed to instill in Pete Jacoby yesterday. "Maybe I'll take a minute for a hot shower to get the kinks out." She reached for the faucet with one hand, massaging her sore ribs with the other, then stripped off the T-shirt, stepped beneath the rush of hot water and held her face up to the stream. Tears of loneliness clogged her throat choking away dread of the day, leaving physical misery in its wake.

✳

Stopped at a traffic light, Teddy kept her Reebok-shod foot gently massaging the gas pedal as she watched Perri perform a braiding ritual on wet hair. "Perri Rae Hardin, huh?" A mischievous smile backed up a speculative tone. "What kind of name is Perri Rae? Were you named after some country-western singer?"

Perri's hands kept up the ritual by rote. "My mother devoured novels to keep her sanity. That's how she found the name. Only it was the masculine version. When I turned out to be a girl, Mom gave the name to me, with modification." She easily recalled the often-repeated story of how Angie had hoped for a boy to ease the turmoil in the Hardin household.

Sheba chugged through the green light to the tune of a bleating horn. Eyes on the mirror, Teddy flashed a graceful three-finger gesture out the open window. "What was threatening her sanity?"

What indeed? "An interracial marriage to an alcoholic husband, she claimed. She divorced him, but she's still reading." Angie's back room, where Perri slept when home, bulged with dog-eared books. Across the hall, Chelsea's room fared worse. Perri had taken it on herself to seal those in cartons.

Teddy urged Sheba onto the interstate. "And the lush is your father?"

"That subject fueled an ongoing debate." Thundering voices echoed in her mind. Dishes shattered against a wall; doors slammed. Her smile felt as heavy as Pete Jacoby's golf bag. "My mother was pregnant with my older brother by another man when Lee married her. They'd been married for years when I was born, but because of my mother's past transgressions, I was always suspect in his mind, even though I've got Lee Hardin stamped all over me." High cheekbones, delicate stature, caramel skin color.

Taking her eyes off the interstate, Teddy watched Perri secure the thick braid with a pink felt-covered rubber band, then work a matching scrunchie up the braid and snug it against her head with a final air. "How long did it take your hair to get that long?"

Perri studied the driver next to them, the question echoing in her mind. She had been fifteen when Braden decided Beau's relationship with her had become too serious. Beau had been banished to an English prep school for two years, no visits home. In her sixteenth year, when she should have been falling in and out of childish love, she kept to herself, growing breasts and hair, entertaining childlike visions of Beau climbing like Rapunzel's lover to dwell even deeper in her soul, once Braden saw fit to lift the exile. "About two years," she said finally.

No amount of hurt or disappointment could steal the memory of Beau's reaction once he saw her transformation from boyish pixie to virgin femme fatale. That more impressionable Beau had eventually undergone his own transformation.

A radio blaring from a passing car invaded the silence. "A man likes to run his hands through long hair, huh?" Teddy glanced at Perri, then away quickly.

"That's been my experience." And brush it. And braid it. And press his face into the pillowed mass as the last tremors of making love shuddered from his body.

✳

That day and the next, only the ropes kept Beau—at loose ends, apparently—at bay while Perri migrated the course with Pete and his pairings. Beau's presence proved a heavier cross to bear than the bag that would have brought a less desperate woman to her knees. Beau, however, did an enviable job of treating her like a nonentity, other than questioning every club she offered Pete during the thirty-six-holes. But the deep timbre of his voice as he coached Pete, his mannerisms, even his distinctive, memory-jogging smell—Kouros and perspiration seeping into fine lisle cotton—did nothing to ease her agitation.

On Sunday, the final day of the Open, Perri's hope waned when Pete's ball found the rough as though pulled there on a string, and he took two extra shots to return to the fairway. Though she tried to ignore his ongoing blame on "that sumbitchin' kikuya grass" while his play worsened, her nerves ran taut as newly strung barbed wire. When not enough holes remained to rally—never mind win—hope of seeing any prize money died. At the eighteenth hole she pulled a four iron out of the bag.

"No way," Beau mumbled from outside the rope, only three feet away. "The ball will run too much. He needs loft. Give him his five iron."

"Since you failed to make the cut, butt out." Perri jutted her chin and planted her feet, extending the club to Pete who was now too stressed to grin at the on-going argument. She jabbed Pete lightly with the rubber club grip. "Here, Mr. Jacoby. Play your own game, not the Saint's. Shave the ball past the third palm on the right."

When Pete mis-fired the four iron, she kissed even the caddy-tip she had hoped for goodbye. She'd get paid the customary day-fee, and Pete would look the other way when he saw her standing in the pick-a-caddie line in Miami next week. As Pete fired his final putt past the hole, seized the errant ball and stomped off the green with Beau in his wake, Perri did her bookkeeping. Inside the coveralls, her arms pebbled with goose bumps. She was in trouble.

Later, from her perch on a gallery-trampled knoll behind the eighteenth green, Perri brushed and re-braided her hair, watching the Riviera Club president pass on the perpetual silver trophy and award the $180,000 check. Even as David Duvall made his "It-feels-good-to-win-thank-you-very-much" speech, an army of volunteers skittered around behind the scenes, expediently ripping away tournament window dressing. The disassembly stirred childhood memories of seeing a visiting circus being torn down. Now, as then, lonely disillusionment crept in, and an even greater heaviness settled on her achy shoulders and laden mind. Heaving her body up, she stuffed her brush into a baggy pocket and headed for the dressing area to turn in the coveralls.

"Hey, Perri. Wait up."

She turned, eyes seeking out the owner of the vaguely familiar voice.

Wearing his signature arch smile, his sleek, dark good looks exaggerated by white coveralls, Mark Zamora, wove his way through the dispersing crowd. "I thought that was you, babe. I spotted you across the course. Recognized the Pocahontas braid." He tugged on the thick plait resting in the middle of her back and somehow turned the gesture into a hug.

"Hello, Mark." Relieved to see a friendly face, she tiptoed to kiss his stubbled cheek.

"Last I heard, you were on the girls' tour. I caught your act a couple of times on ESPN. Looked like you were holding your own. What happened?"

Her mind stole to a jagged scar on her inside right ankle. She shrugged, admitting, "Too tough for me, I guess," which won her a sardonic, conspiratorial grin. "How have you been?"

He quirked a thick jet brow. "Since St. Serious fired me, you mean?"

Time had engraved the incident on Perri's mind. She had argued with Beau that Mark knew his game, that Beau needed him and shouldn't change caddies in the middle of a tour. Beau argued back, "Nobody is indispensable." Once Mark was replaced, Beau began winning, earning Nike dollars, points that would propel him onto the PGA tour. His tenacity and focus had instilled even more admiration in Perri.

"He wanted to win, Mark."

"Yeah, and I was in the way."

"You survived."

"Only because I cleaned up my act. I was full of crap back then. Sex, drugs and rock and roll mix with golf about like oil goes with water. He had a right to fire me."

Perri searched his craggy-handsome face for any trace of insincerity, but detected only humility. Tilting his head, he studied her. His black, slicked-back hair and the tiny diamond stud in his earlobe caught the last glint of sun slipping into the Pacific.

"What happened with you two, anyway, babe? You were thick as bugs on a bumper."

Until Beau had relegated her to the dispensable category, too. "Lives have a way of taking different paths."

"Like you wanting to play your own game, maybe? And him wanting to play the field?" He jabbed the barb deeper. "He hasn't left many rows unplowed, I guess you know."

Her nerve endings collided, grating like pottery shards. She kept silent.

Beyond Mark's shoulder, Beau watched her liaison from the upper club terrace. Hands on hips, chin thrust forward, he struck that familiar stance that both angered her and wrung her heart. He glared with the intensity of a man who'd caught his traitorous lover red-handed. But reality, and Teddy's gossip about an on-going rift between Beau and Mark, assured Perri that Beau's rancor had nothing to do with her, other than the fact this reunion involved his adversary. She tore her gaze away from Beau and glanced around the swirling crowd. "I'd better turn in these coveralls and find Teddy Ridgely. She's giving me a ride back to the motel."

"So you're at No Name Corral with the rest of us outlaws? Wanta go get a beer?"

He glanced over his shoulder to where her focus kept straying. The two men exchanged distant, rival gazes, prompting her to rivet her visual, if not mental, attention on Mark.

He grinned knowingly. "There's a spot down on the Santa Monica Pier where we can rub elbows with the players. You up for it?"

The last place from which she wanted to make her nightly call to Angie was a bar filled with cele- brating and lamenting players. Angie's envy of what she would deem Perri's good fortune would be counter-productive to the mission at hand. "Not really."

Mark shifted his body to block her view of the clubhouse. "I doubt the Saint will be there. He'll probably be in his suite playing golf games on his laptop, or giving Pete a putting lesson in the hall." He gauged her reaction. "I swear he'll keep coach- ing Jacoby till the guy beats his butt and moves him right out of the top money spot."

Mark hadn't lost his caustic sense of humor, and unless he had a vivid imagination, someone was feeding him inside information about Beau's habits. He was a born a teacher. Through the years he had passed on to her his expensive golf lessons, his love of teaching helping her qualify for the tour. She forged back into the debate. "Beau gets more pleasure from teaching than playing."

"Yeah, well, I think he's trying to clone himself through Jacoby."

She conceded with a laugh. "I'll take a rain check on the beer. I'm beat." Weariness and dis-

appointment had seeped in like fog in a swamp.
Cold. Damp and murky. "Sorry."

He studied her while the homebound crowd
surged around them. "You going to Miami?"

"That's the agenda." Although Pete's performance had weakened the plan.

"You can have your rain check there."

"I'll pencil you in." She smiled.

"Deal. How about giving me a ride to the motel?
I'm thumbing."

She allowed herself one more look at the terrace. Beau leaned against the rail, his back to the
course now, talking with a California-blonde who
gracefully balanced a crowded cocktail tray. The
girl's tanned face glowed like polished pennies.

"Meet me at the buses," Perri decided. "We'll
check with Teddy."

Mark could help push Sheba if she delivered on
this morning's mutinous threat.

✳

Damn that David Duvall. Beau stuck the key
in the ignition of a rented Porsche, then rested his
chin on the wheel. How the hell had Duvall swept
the Open, trouncing Pete on the way? Pete needed
the win, needed to put money in the bank to shore
up his confidence. In an egotistic fit, Beau had
tried coaching him right into starring in the winner's ceremony. But having to argue with Perri
about every club out of the bag had done little for
Pete's game, and nothing for Beau's attitude. Her
being right in most cases, something he'd admit on
his deathbed, had pissed him to no end, left him
with a giant mean-on.

He started the car, massaged the gas peddle
gently, listening to the engine throb, then shoved
the gearshift into reverse and backed out of a prime
players' parking spot. He blamed Perri's angelic
face and biker's moll attitude for the bitter bile
lodged at the back of his throat. He hardly recog-

nized her anymore. Even her walk was different. Strident. Assertive. Of course, he'd never seen her struggle under the weight of a golf bag. He'd like to attribute her change to the challenge of caddying, but his mind settled on her new hardness.

He slowed the car at the club exit, then pulled onto the blacktop, driver's window down. The cool kiss of sea air did nothing to eliminate his rancorous musing. Perri was muscled now, rail thin, her eyes topaz wellsprings of wariness. Maybe females couldn't do a man's job without changing from a soft, pliable, trusting girl to a full-fledged, calculating woman.

Determinedly, he dialed his cellular. Four rings. "Braden St. Cyr. Leave a message."

Beau balanced the phone between jaw and shoulder, and shifted gears. "I had a minute, Granddad, so I thought I'd let you tell me where Pete screwed up today." Braden's version of Beau's screw up last Friday lay fresh as rainwater in his mind. "I'll call back. Kiss Nonna for me." He clicked off, wondering how Braden had missed seeing Perri on TV Friday or during Pete's heavy coverage yesterday. Why hadn't the caca hit the fan yet? The fact that Braden's shrewd eye had missed her proved Perri had changed. But surely he had spotted her today.

He dialed again. Three rings, then a sultry voice. "It's Stephanie. If that's you, Beau, darling, I'm sorry I missed you. I'll hold my breath till you call back. You hear?"

Let her turn blue; he lacked the stomach to call back. She hated the tour, yet wanted a report every night, like Braden. Beau had wearied of living his life through phone reports, always being alone. Time for a meeting of the minds. She wasn't open to touring with him, but either she had to start watching the tournaments on TV or be home when he called.

When had calling become duty rather than pleasure? He kicked it around, not liking the answer. She had agreed to meet him for the Masters. They'd hash it out then, if he could keep her out of the shops long enough for a discussion. He gunned the sports car, liking the response.

He was in a piss poor state of mind, all right, but couldn't lose the image of Perri and Mark Zamora's reunion. She was pretty free with hugs and kisses, and she'd laughed with Mark, which she hadn't done with him once in the past three days. Mark was trash, but good-looking trash, if you liked gangster types. Who the hell knew what Perri liked these days?

A few hundred yards ahead, a car had stalled. The listing heap with a corrugated trunk and frayed vinyl roof had barely cleared the blacktop. Beau geared the Porsche down. Etched against the horizon, a double set of shoulders hunched beneath the hood, two female rear-ends dangerously protruding into the road. His inclination to stop tangled with his urge to bolt when the smaller of the two women snaked from beneath the hood, straightened and turned. Curly brown hair gleamed against the ruby-trimmed sunset. His foot, independent of his protesting brain, jammed the brake; the Porsche ground to a stop just short of a mangled bumper. In the cargo area, his clubs rattled, shifted, then banged into his seat back.

Perri hugged her waist, giving him a pang of familiarity, as she leaned against one of four wadded fenders. She shot him a here-comes-a-party-crasher look. Her body posture denying his existence, Teddy slithered beneath the wheel, one foot on the ground as if she lacked full commitment. The back end of the Cougar gave an almost imperceptible wiggle, then froze.

Beau cut the engine and opened the door as a dark, sturdy image emerged stealth-like out of a distant clump of trees, toward the cars. Recognizing the figure was like a slug in the solar plexus. Streetwise Mark Zamora had taken to the woods when the car broke down, knowing a passing motorist would stop for two stranded women. Judging by her defiant posture, Perri had sanctioned the plan. Neither she, nor Zamora, had counted on Beau being the pigeon.

He got out of the car. As he approached, he studied the swell of breasts beneath her cropped T-shirt, the bare waist, shapely legs exposed by the same short denim skirt wrapping slender hips. Her hair pulled back from her face with barrettes made her look like an upper-crust schoolgirl. A walking contradiction, this beautiful and wily woman he'd loved so long, then hated so suddenly he still couldn't sort through the consequent emotions. Bitterness tightened his chest and turned to defeat in his mind. He wanted her. He could no longer deny it to himself.

"Hey, Beau Jangles." Mark stepped high through tall grass, scrambled up an incline to lean on the car hood. "You should be in Miami. The jet need a wash job or something?"

Beau singled Perri out. "What's the problem here?"

With a dismissive expression, she snapped and unsnapped the hinge of a quarter-sized hoop in her ear. Her other hand clasped the face of whatever hung from the chain around her neck. Abruptly she pivoted. Placing her back to him, she removed the sweater tied around her waist and jerked it down over her head, as though a blizzard bore in on them. When she faced him again, the sweater obscured the object hanging on the chain.

From inside the Cougar, Teddy announced, "Friggin' water pump gave up the ghost."

As Mark rounded the hood toward Perri, she moved to the open car door, settling against the

44

side of Teddy's ragged seat. Beau questioned whether he liked or hated the dance.

Beau sought Perri's eyes, somehow managing to hold a gaze that turned to hot tar in the twilight. "I'll call Triple A, tell them to bring a water pump, if you're sure that's what it is."

"You're all white meat, Beau Jangles. Guess we'll see you at the Classic, then." Mark tipped an imaginary cocktail Beau's way. "Here's hoping you play better. Wouldn't want to see you dethroned."

Like hell he wouldn't. "Triple A won't come unless I wait here. That's the way they work, Zamora. But with no wheels, why would you need to know?"

Mark spared his crooked grin, one that had pushed Beau over the edge years ago. "Got your ass in an uproar, huh, Beau? I guess you're really hacked over your protégé losing, too."

Beau turned his back, grasping Perri's arm. "Come with me." She shrugged him off, but he regrasped, fingers tightening. "I want to talk to you." He indicated the Porsche.

Her chin shot up, but she ceased struggling. "I'd rather wait here with Teddy."

His scalp tightened like lockjaw. "She and Mark can tell golf lies. We have to talk." About why she was living like a pauper, when she'd been a half-millionairess eight years ago.

Without waiting for agreement, he drew her away from the car and nudged her before him toward the Porsche. She consented with a grudging air, head high, her trim butt swaying from side to side. He deposited her into the passenger seat and rounded the hood. Even in gathering darkness, through the heavy, tinted windshield, he felt her venomous glare.

When he got in beside her, she recoiled, as though he'd brought a foul odor into the close quarters. He fished for his Triple A card, then reached for the phone in lieu of his craving to reach for her. Lips curled disdainfully, she watched and listened to him make arrangements.

He stashed the phone and turned toward her, drawing one leg into the seat. "What happened to your Triple A membership?"

"None of us seems to have a phone handy."

He pushed the issue. "But you still have your membership. Right?"

One brow quirked. "Is that the big emergency you wanted to talk about?"

The hairs on his spine stood erect. Not a good time to bring up the money. "I bought a membership for you when you began driving Lee's pickup truck. I told you never to let it expire. A woman should never be on the road without one."

Her look questioned his sanity. "That was over a decade ago. I haven't put stock in anything you told me for at least that long. I don't have a car, either, so file me in the same category as Mark, you judgmental bastard." Her hand went to the door handle.

"I'm in the dark here, Perri." She looked at him, her mouth a fraction softer, eyes curious. She touched the object beneath her sweater. For an instant he saw a glimmer of former guilelessness, an easing of defenses, allowing him to ask, "Why are you living like this?"

"Like what?" Her perfect mouth reinstated a hard line.

"Hanging with Zamora and Teddy. Caddying your butt off when you could be playing the LPGA." When she was on tour, he watched when he could. She'd had the moves at first, before her game deteriorated. The next thing he knew she was caddying for Amy Alcott, then Michelle Grand. She'd dropped out of sight for a while, then shown up here. "What gives?"

"What's wrong with Mark and Teddy?" Challenge dripped from her colorless lips.

"They're gypsies."

She folded her arms, staring straight ahead. He could hear her anger-laden breathing. "I'm researching my thesis, based on how the other half of the hallowed PGA tour lives."

Damned if he understood. She had obtained everything she wanted when she left him. He hadn't lifted a finger to stop the annulment or the settlement. Why the hostility? And why was she living this way? She'd always respected quality, even when she couldn't afford it. In the year they'd toured together, she had adapted to first class like a desert to rain. When had her values changed? And why? Surely she hadn't gone through the money. Looking at the crumpled back of the Cougar, he broached another subject. "Are you planning to go to Miami?"

"That's the next event."

He gave her clothing the once over, meaningfully. "Maybe it'll be warmer there."

"As if you cared," she murmured so softly he wasn't sure he'd heard right.

"How are you getting there?"

She feigned incredulous surprise. "With Teddy of course."

"In that junker? There's no way in hell you'll make it."

"Give it a rest, Beau." She tossed her hair back over her shoulder, her delicate chin jutting. "We don't all fly our own jets."

But she could have. "You can ride with me. I'll get you there in time for the Pro-Am."

She laughed, a throaty, angular, mirthless sound.

"Why shouldn't you? The plane flies half empty, anyway. Maybe you and Pete could make

47

up for your dumping him today." He offered a
hard-to-come-by smile.

"I can't leave Teddy."

"Why the hell not?"

"We made a deal, a kind of partnership. Some
people honor those."

If she was one of those people now, she'd
changed more than he realized. He heard himself
say, "She can come, too. There's room."

She shook her head, eyes grim, mouth stubborn.

"Sell the damn car—give it away. It's a death
trap for women traveling two thousand miles
alone." He groped for affective reasoning. "Even if
you make it before the Classic's over—which you
won't—you'll be too tired to caddie."

"Why do you care?" Her voice was too quiet, a
question, not a debate.

"All this doesn't add up, Perri." He read her
thoughts in the dark, mere vibes on the rarefied air,
concluding, "You won't be alone. Is that it?"

"He offered to ride with us and help pay. Teddy
agreed. It's her car."

Beau's skin crawled as new road-movie scenes
materialized in his mind, but damned if Mark
would fly with him, too.

The tow truck pulled alongside, radio blaring
rap music. The driver hesitated for a minute, then
gunned the motor and steered the wrecker in front
of the Cougar and lowered the tow bar. Apparently,
vintage Mercury Cougar water pumps weren't in
Texaco's inventory.

Wordlessly, Perri opened her door. Beau tried
to read her expression in the overhead light, trying
to tell himself he saw hesitation, regret. Anything
but rejection.

Her stiff back as she walked away indicated his
first inclination had been right.

Picturing the trip she planned, all that could happen, stung like acid in a gangrenous wound. He wished to hell he didn't care, just as she'd accused him. But she had been his, and in an asinine sense always would be. He'd once gloried in the right to take care of her.

Old habits were hard to break.

✳

In the empty motel room, Perri inched back a flimsy drape and watched the Porsche pull out of the parking lot. The taillights brightened at the exit, then dimmed as the back end of the car dropped, picking up speed and merging with traffic.

Beau had practically thrown a body block when she'd tried to climb into the truck cab with Teddy and Mark. He had insisted on bringing her to the motel, but hadn't spoken to her en route, other than a grudging, "Have a nice trip," when she got out of the Porsche. He'd sat with headlights blazing while she rummaged in the backpack for her key and let herself in. His concern that she get inside the room safely had allowed a traitorous warmth to sneak through her.

Beau's concern for her welfare—no matter his arrogant attitude—stirred memories of his taking care of her, sometimes lording it over her, but always with wisdom, and her interest at heart. She'd always thought her dependence on him was one of the reasons he'd left her. He was tired of the responsibility. But old habits must be as hard for him to break as for her.

She hated the way the gentleness in his amber eyes touched some core in her soul when he'd offered to take her to Miami. The sharp angles of his features had softened, and reluctantly, she'd let herself remember she had loved this stranger. Until he destroyed that love.

Come with me. His resonant voice echoed in her mind, stroking her need with the fine, soft touch of coercion. That tone evoked images of raindrops on parched skin, a banquet for the hungry, and promises for a woman who had stopped believing. For some reason known only to Beau, he wanted her to open her veins again and bleed for him, the way she once had. Bleed with love he would never return. That era was behind her.

Dragging her body from the bed, she made her way to the shower, peeled off her clothing and slipped beneath a torrent of water, willing it to wash away images of what might have been.

CHAPTER FIVE

When the phone rang, Braden's heart jumped with a sure-fire sixth sense.

"Hi, Granddad." The deep, melodic voice filled the wire. "I'm at Santa Monica Air Park. Is this a good time to talk?"

"Sure, son." Braden slipped into the smooth solace of his desk chair. "Sorry I missed you." His stomach cramped, burned, signifying the last thing he needed: an ulcer attack. No rest for the wicked. "Dinner's late tonight. What's on your mind?"

"If you spotted Pete's problem today, maybe we could straighten it out before the Doral."

"Pete may be a friend, Beau, but he's still competition."

An ancient clock labored endlessly in a quiet corner before Beau spoke. "How's Nonna?"

"Your grandmother had a bad day."

"Too bad to watch the Classic? She likes Pete. She usually suffers through it."

Winonna, who had never met Pete, watched faithfully for his infrequent television coverage. She naively believed he and Beau sensed her spiritual presence.

"I had to take her to the hospital," Braden said, then rushed, "but the doctors got her settled down, so I brought her home." No reason Beau should worry, too, beyond the sense of apprehension Braden knew he lived with. "She's napping now. Silky's holding dinner for us."

Beau took a long breath. "I'll call her when we get in the air."

"She'd like that." He thought of the mystery caller two days before. The voice remained in his ear, yet some unidentified dread of his own kept

Braden from sharing the puzzle. He stepped onto more familiar ground. "Too many missed cuts, and the media will be saying you're in a slump. It's hard to play well, when the whole world is waiting to see if you'll lose."

"You were watching. Maybe you'd like to arm-chair quarterback my piss-poor play."

Was that genuine confusion or rare defiance? Braden hadn't seen that round either, the one the cryptic caller indicated he shouldn't miss. "Most likely your head wasn't in the game."

Beau granted his mellow all-is-forgiven laugh. "Maybe you're psychic."

Not psychic, but capable of remembering what being thirty entailed, how many paths a young man's mind could travel away from the goal. "So what's the problem?"

"I'm not sure. I've been having equipment problems."

Braden pictured Beau's contemplative expression, the familiar way his eyes—Winonna's eyes—darkened to mahogany when something troubled him.

"That's nonsense. You can have the latest equipment, custom fitted."

"It's not the fit." A long silence ensued. Then, "Clubs have been disappearing from my bag. I may have to make some changes." Another pause. "Send Cal home, maybe."

Sweat broke out above Braden's lip, but his mouth felt as dry as his empty scotch glass. "Cal is more than a caddie, Beau."

"He can't spend his life indentured because you sent Cal. Jr. to med school."

Braden let the barb slide. "I don't like the idea of you sending him home."

His caustic laugh had the ring of afterthought. "My days of needing a nanny are over."

Braden craved to see Beau's handsome, weather-browned face, read his eyes. He decided the hard, insolent tone stemmed from concern for his game, for Cal's feelings, for going against Braden's wishes. "You think he's not taking care of your equipment, I gather."

"It looks that way, but—"

The clock ticked. A horse whinnied. Wind rattled the aged windows. "But what?"

"I've had other problems, things Cal's not involved in."

"Let's hear it." His mind aligned the statement with the call he'd gotten, but trying to add two and two, he got zero. He should tell Beau about the call, ask him what the hell it meant. Thinking of the Doral in Miami, how Beau needed to be in stable mental form, he hedged. "You need to spend more time practicing your own game, son, instead of Pete's. Remember, you're playing for two, so you have to win twice as much." In order to reap the once-dead dream.

"Maybe you're right."

The concession brought Braden little comfort.

"I see Pete at the Hertz counter. The pilot's got the engines running, so how about checking to see if Nonna's awake."

Braden felt as if Beau had slipped over a precipice. "Are you all right, son? Whatever's troubling you, you could detour by here and forego the pro-am. We'll work it out."

A voice rumbled in Beau's background. His hand over the mouthpiece muffled the sound for a moment. "I could, but I'll go on to Miami, maybe get in some extra practice, as you suggested. You're right, Granddad. I need to get my priorities in order and refocus on winning." A short pause. "Goodnight. Kiss Nonna. Tell her I'll call."

Braden held on to the silent phone, pressing it against his chest, staring out the window. Liquid diamonds slid down the leaded panes, backlit by yellow twilight. In the pasture, the horses huddled together, heads lowered, robbed of their tranquility by the cold spring rain. Beau's parting comment about refocusing nagged. Insolence had played no part in the remark, only determined resignation.

Beau had never been a little boy, as the stranger on the phone had facetiously labeled him. Solemnity had shrouded his life. His father's early death, his mother's easy acquiescence to giving him up had deepened the sober characteristic. Braden's desire to have him live out Beau Jr.'s thwarted legend had stolen Beau's childhood. Normally Braden avoided delving deeply into the part he had played in the loss, but tonight proved an exception.

Beau had not only inherited Winonna's features, but also her gentleness, her engaging optimism, before his marriage ended so abruptly. So cruelly. From Braden, he had inherited the ability to focus, a trait Braden practiced like religion when it came to protecting his own, seeing to it those he loved reached their goals. Especially when those goals mirrored his own.

Normally, his best club was his concentration. He had been distracted from their quest only once. Braden had eliminated that problem the way he determined best. After the Hardin girl left, for a while Beau picked up gallery groupies because he needed confirmation. Now he appeared settled in with Stephanie, a woman from his own cultural background. Whatever distraction he now faced could and would be handled to achieve the goal... as soon as Braden got to the heart of the dilemma.

※

A week later, bone-weary, rife with resentful excitement, Perri watched Beau accept the Doral-Ryder Open's perpetual trophy. He granted the crowd a solemn, St. Serious smile as he lofted the burdensome memorial cup with one powerful hand. Before Perri could finish her rancorous thought that Beau St. Cyr was the last person on earth who needed $324,000—but if she'd been caddying for him, ten percent of it would be hers— Beau declined the check, donating it to the Heart Association on behalf of his grandmother.

Cheers erupted. Some—not all—of Perri's envy and anger died. Turning her back, she melded into the dispersing crowd as Beau drew a hovering, beaming, practically genuflecting Cal close for a picture to grace the Miami Herald's Monday morning sports page.

Sticky and wilted, Perri stood in front of the golf shop for a designated rendezvous with Frizzy Collins. Finally she saw him approaching with what she hoped was a check in hand.

"Sorry." He sounded breathless. "Beau was buying champagne for the field to celebrate his hole-in-one, but first we had to wait for those candy-monger kids to get their goodies."

A rod shot up Perri's spine. According to Cal, Beau credited his bad play at the Nissan Open last week to her sudden appearance, a malady from which he had evidently recovered. She struggled not to reach for the check, nor ogle the amount. "What happened to his putter today?"

Frizzy grinned. "Speculation is Cal was using it to catch carp in that lake out on nine and dropped it. I swear, if Beau doesn't cut that old man loose..." He shrugged. "He would've never won putting with his one iron, if he hadn't started with such a big lead. I could've caught him if I'd had nine more holes to play." He kept grinning, waiting for her comment.

"Them that's got, gets," she murmured, her intended smile miscarrying.

He handed her the check. "Well, third's not so bad."

Heart racing like hummingbird wings, she folded the $15,850.00 check into the pocket of her khaki shorts. "Thank you."

He remarked amiably, "We almost whipped Blue Monster," applying the tour's adopted term for the Doral Course. "Beau was right about you, sugar. You're a great caddie."

"He told you that?"

"Beau does know diddly about caddies. He's had his share, said you were with him for a year on the Nike. That's why I asked for you."

Perri considered his disclosure. After three days and nights on the road, she had checked with the caddie master on Thursday and been told to report to Frizzy that afternoon. Assuming Mark had put in a word for her, hiding her shock at being requested, she had said nothing to her boss of four days. Now she realized Frizzy had obviously assumed she was Beau's caddie for that year on the Nike. Obviously, Beau had let him. She vacillated between being grateful or furious with Beau for meddling in her life.

Frizzy continued his testimonial. "He said you know golf like some women know pouting. He didn't steer me wrong."

"He told you I pout?"

"Well, maybe not you—but women in general," he fishtailed, still grinning. "I'd a probably won the friggin' tournament, except my conscience was killing me for four days, 'cause that bag's so heavy." He fished in his pocket, coming up with a crisp hundred-dollar bill. "Here. Get yourself a steak. Put some meat on. Maybe we'll hook up in Orlando."

Maybe fell far short of a promise.

Rather than ask if he was unsure of entering, or from begging for commitment, she forced a smile. "Thanks. Have a safe trip." With a hundred dollars, she could eat healthy for weeks.

She coerced a clerk in the golf shop into selling a stamp, borrowed an envelope, slipped the check and a note inside and addressed the envelope to Angie. Knowing caddies were barred from the shop, she glanced around surreptitiously as she handed back the envelope, hoping her street clothes were enough disguise. She aimed at an assured air, even if it clashed with borrowing envelopes, buying one stamp at a time, and asking favors of strangers.

Sheba flashed like a neon sign on her mind. All week, the car had awaited antiquated parts in a renegade shop Mark had found. If Beau invited her to fly with him again, she doubted she'd be brave or foolish enough to refuse. But her superb job of avoiding him the last four days had nixed the possibility of invitation. God and Sheba willing, she'd make it to Orlando.

※

Behind Beau's seat, Pete's soft snores mingled with the muted roar of jet engines. Across the aisle, a jiggling foot crossed over a bony knee, Cal thumbed through *Golf Digest*. The past six months had done nothing to alleviate his fear of flying, nor his craving for Silky's waist-killer food. Beau suspected he missed her rotund, ebony body as much. In his own mind he smelled peach muffins, and felt the bear hugs she gave him every morning he was home.

Cal's fingers, gnarled as Pebble Beach pines, stroked the magazine cover. He raised his voice over the engines. "I like this here picture." The cover featured Beau in full swing, body tensed, face contorted. Bold type read, "How Winners Keep Winning."

His wrist pained just from looking at the photographed swing. "Hang the cover in your school locker," he teased. "Between Tina Turner and Gladys Knight. I'll be in good company."

Cal's lips pulled into a grin. "'Minds me of when you was a kid, knockin' youself out to hit the ball longer." Rheumy eyes focused on the past. "Don't nobody take the club back as far as you, or hit it longer, and nowhere near as straight."

"It's a damned good thing, since I sometimes have to putt with my one iron."

"You blamin' me for that, and you got a right."

Beau stilled himself against Cal's defeated tone. "It's not a question of blame. Something's going on, Cal, and we've got to get to the bottom of it." Cal nodded, so encouraged, Beau leapt ahead. "You've got to watch those clubs every minute."

The magazine rattled in Cal's hand. Beau hated his hurt feelings, and the way his age was showing, but this had to be solved. "No suspicious characters came around today?"

"None. I swear."

"What about Zamora? I saw him talking to you when we made the turn to the back side"

"What you sayin', Beau?" Cal had an infant's trust and a centenarian's memory.

"Could Mark have swiped the putter?"

"His pro weren't even in the runnin'. Why would he do that?"

So Cal had dismissed the run-in with Mark on the Nike Tour, overlooking the possibility Mark could still be pissed. "You don't think he did, apparently."

Cal shook his head, looking satisfied, as if he'd taught Beau one more lesson.

"Then what, Cal? Who slashed my tires last week? Who stole my Titleist balls out of the locker, and bent my seven iron on Friday?" With the list growing too long to ignore, he was getting jumpy, lying awake nights anticipating where the deranged bastard would strike next.

Cal measured him, as if reading past his eyes, then took a dog-eared Old Testament out of his pocket, donned wire rims, settled back, murmuring, "I don't know, boy, but I'll study on it."

Beau gazed out the window, his view ending with the wing, getting lost in mucus-like clouds. Cal's snores mingled with Pete's. In the cockpit the radio kept up a staccato report, a world link. The static grated, exposing edginess centered on broken and missing equipment. He couldn't get a handle on it, just as he couldn't dismiss the coincidence of his ex-wife and the mystery showing up simultaneously. The last four days Perri had proven equally as elusive as the vandal. How else could they not have crossed paths in the close confines of a golf tournament? He'd intended to offer Perri a ride to Orlando, but her avoidance had altered the script. The hell with it. He could carry a grudge, too. But what the hell was her gripe?

✳

At close of play three days into the Bay Hill Invitational, barefoot and stripped of as much clothing as protocol would allow, Perri wiggled her toes in the St. Augustine grass, studying the scoreboard outside the main clubhouse. Her eyes straggled down the list as she ticked off numbers in her mind. Frizzy Collins occupied ninth place.

She had cursed the Cougar for breaking down in Kissimmee, delaying arrival, marring chances of Frizzy hiring her again, but now she realized it hadn't mattered. Stuart Appleby's caddie had suffered an allergic reaction to a bee sting on Thursday—probably around the same time Perri stood on the sweltering blacktop, fanning Sheba's radiator. Appleby had hired her at dawn yesterday. Now she gazed with satisfaction on his third place standing.

If Beau, whose name blazed in the top position, found the same bee as Appleby's caddie, she'd have a chance at a percentage of the $288,000 first place purse. Beau was allergic to bees. Or so he'd told her when he was fifteen, that time they'd gone fishing on Rolling River. Beau had dodged bees all day, and she had caught the most fish.

An eerie sensation crawling on the back of her neck drew her eyes away from the scoreboard. Across the lawn, Beau stared at her over the heads of her score-seeking peers, his amber eyes intent, hands splayed on slender hips. She jerked her gaze away, checking her watch pointedly, but before she could retrieve her backpack from the ground, slip it on, and step back into her Doc Martin's, he was close enough for her to feel his body heat. So close she could smell him. Coppertone, Kourous and sweat this time, an odor that should repulse her. Instead, it tugged a familiar ache, invading her groin, settling between her own sweaty thighs. Chin elevated, she made herself meet those eyes. "You're playing well."

His broad shoulders moved in a gesture barely short of a shrug, drawing her eyes to a copper bracelet on his right wrist. Memory flashed back to the childhood riding mishap he'd told her about, the resulting mildly arthritic condition. Had it gotten worse? She folded her arms across her chest, the area his gaze had drifted to, shielding the locket-bulge beneath her T-shirt.

"All playing well amounts to is having a level swing arc," he said.

"And where would you be without your trusty one iron these days?"

Those gold-flecked, auburn-lashed eyes narrowed, pinning her. "I don't intend to find out, in case you want to pass the word along."

"To whom?" And what did the accusatory tone mean?

"Never mind." His gaze took in her shorts and the mashed and mangled, big-brimmed Panama hat dangling from a leather cord around her wrist. "I saw you in my gallery this afternoon."

Damn. After she'd hidden all afternoon behind the giant fan in the cutoffs and thongs.

"Seems you'd be so tired after caddying all morning, you'd go to the motel and lay by the pool." Eyes that had always been able to read her, drilled into her gaze. "Or whatever you girls—and Mark—do."

She avoided that comment like a detested relative. "I'm surprised you spotted me with that posse of groupies on your tail. Cal needs to carry a filing cabinet to store all those phone numbers they pass you."

His easy, sexy grin slid into place. "I'll get old and start hitting short drives one of these days, and the rest of them will desert me for Tiger."

"With your luck, the groupies will get older, too." She stared past his shoulder.

Adroitly, he shifted into her view. "Never mind them. Why were you there?"

She groped for an answer that would satisfy them both. "I wanted to see if I could pick up some pointers to help Stuart Appleby tomorrow. Guess he'll have to buy a one iron."

His left temple pulsed. "What happened to you and Frizz? He said you were great."

She shrugged, prepared to choke before giving a true answer. "I prayed for a winner. Looks like it's working out."

"So far," he admitted. "How's Stu treating you?"

"Much better than some people I've associated with."

"What's that supposed to mean?"

Was the arrogant bastard squelching a smile? "What it means." Looking at her watch, she retrieved the sunglasses perched on her head and covered her eyes. "I have to meet Teddy."

He caught her hand, examining the watch, making her uncomfortably aware of its scarred face, ragged leather band, and missing diamond, but she was even more aware of the current shooting up her arm, into her chest. Her heart slammed against her ribcage.

"This can't be the same Picard I bought you for graduation." When he cocked his head, his hair took on the color of wet rust in the waning March sunlight.

"Why not?" She wrested her hand away. It darted to her upper chest, pressing the warmth of the gold locket against her skin. "It still keeps time."

Any smile he'd been toying with died. His abruptly cool gaze settled on her vintage Vuitton backpack, then moved to the garnet friendship ring on her right hand, before their eyes locked. "I figured you'd get rid of everything I ever gave you."

The irony of his words drove an ache deep into her soul. His assumption was not possible, not even worthy of consideration. "Why would I? I'm too practical for that."

Brackets formed around a sensuous mouth still etched deeply in her memory. "I recall."

Sensing his withdrawal, she suddenly felt chilled, barren, and disgusted with herself.

"Good luck tomorrow," she begrudged as she pivoted and made her way through the crowd.

She was almost glad Stuart Appleby was in third place, not second. Otherwise he and Beau would be paired on Sunday. Just possibly, she was incapable of withstanding five hours of the ambiguous sensations nesting in her head and body.

She stood in line a half-hour to place a free long distance call from the MCI courtesy phone. During her call home last night, Angie monopolized the conversation with reports of loneliness, flu, accelerated heartbeats and boredom. Any hope this call might be more supportive got quashed when

Angie's recorded voice invited her to leave a message.

Perri created one born of frustration and disappointment. "Mom, it's me. Did you watch today? My pro's in third place. He could win. Keep your fingers crossed for a fat envelope in the mail." She paused, entertaining visions of where Angie might be at 5:30 on Saturday afternoon. "I'll call back when I can. Hi, to Chelsea." Afterthought rushed in, "And hello to Larry. I'm looking forward to meeting him." An exaggerated lie.

Aware of others waiting to make their gratis calls, she hung up, shifted the backpack on her shoulder and turned—smack into Beau's chest.

His strong hands shot out to grip her forearms, saving her from tumbling backward.

"Are you following me?"

"Maybe." He drew her aside.

She shrugged off his touch. "Why, for God's sake?"

"I have to keep an eye on what you're up to. "

The gently harassing smile was familiar, but his serious tone piqued her curiosity.

"Were you talking to Angie?" He torqued a brow. "How is she?"

She glared, stalling, trying to recall anything she might have said—

"Who's Chelsea? Who's Larry?"

She bristled. "Friends of my mother's. Why are you following me?"

Surprising her, he ripped off the dark glasses she wore, peering into her eyes, interrogation style. "What kind of friends?"

"None of your business." She reached for her glasses. He held them over her head. "Damn you, you arrogant ass!"

"That has a familiar ring." He relinquished a smile warm enough to melt buttons, giving her long

63

braid a gentle jerk, a gesture retrieved from their past.

People were staring. She went for the glasses again, but he easily blocked her attempt with a forearm while slipping them into her shirt pocket. The backs of his fingers brushed her breast, searing her skin through the worn fabric. She stood rigid, dredging up stone-still denial.

The erotic shock rushing through her seemed to reach his eyes.

"What happened to us, Perri?"

"You tell me, Beau." How had she failed him enough to drive him away? How and when had he stopped loving her without her knowing?

Beyond his shoulder, a girl approached with an on-a-mission stride, intent in her eyes. A hand reached out, long fingers with bright red manicured nails, grasping his forearm, intruding on the moment. With an automatic, vaguely reluctant smile, he turned to sign his name on a naked shoulder, taking time to banter, to laugh at the girl's vow to never bathe again. His course-side manner allotted Perri time and reason to slip inside her protective shell.

As the girl walked away, hips and hair swinging, Beau turned back to Perri, voice matter-of-fact now, eyes shrouded. "Teddy tells me Sheba's history."

So he had known all along why she hadn't connected with Frizzy. She shrugged, but his reminder of Sheba's demise and the residual problems made her shoulders rock heavy. "She was an endangered species, I guess."

"Fly to the Sawgrass tourney with me tomorrow." It sounded rehearsed. "We'll talk."

"No, thank you." She intended to leave it at that, but her sucker side added, "I'm not going." Not with Sheba gone. Not in view of last night's bothersome call home, and Angie not answering minutes ago.

His eyes quickened with unidentifiable emotion. "Are you quitting?"

"I'm skipping the Sawgrass Tournament."

"Why? Because of Sheba?" Intense scrutiny moved back into his eyes. Getting no answer, he offered, "I'll take you. Teddy, too, if that makes you happy." He screwed up his mouth appealingly in mock distaste and grinned. "It's a big, mostly empty plane."

"What about Mark?"

He quirked a brow. "Is this a test?"

The elitist bastard had mastered holding grudges. "Take whoever you want, Beau." She slung the backpack onto her back, slammed both arms through the straps, fished her sunglasses from her pocket and plopped them on. "I won't be going."

*

Hope flickered in the back of Beau's mind as he watched her stalk away, the heavy, sun-streaked braid bouncing against her hard little back, making him feel all liquid in his gut. The ugly Jesus sandals that showed her sexy toes flopped rhythmically, drawing attention to ankles as small and curved as axe handles, and as sturdy looking. She was as beautiful and bull-headed as ever, but if she still wore his watch and ring, and carried the bag he'd bought her, she couldn't detest him as much as she indicated.

God, he missed her. But, he was still mad as hell she'd abandoned him. The feelings pushed each other around, vying for top billing. He might never know what he'd done to drive her away, but judging from that more-tender-than-tough look her eyes harbored, he stood a chance of winning her back.

Dar Tomlinson

But after what she'd done—what she might be doing now—why in hell would he try?

CHAPTER SIX

Angie was not in the small crowd waiting at the gate when Perri deplaned in Louisville Monday afternoon. Instead, Chelsea, dressed in too-short jeans and an oversized plaid shirt, stood at the back edge of the greeters. Her pretty, but wise-beyond-her-seven-year-old's face wore an anxious expression. She waved tentatively, as if to say, "I didn't forget you."

Perri waved back, stepping up her pace as much as possible without ramming into the couple shuffling ahead of her. She stopped a few feet short of Chelsea and lowered her heavy carry-on duffel and backpack, then sank to her knees. Chelsea walked into her open arms, tears streaming from her eyes onto freckled cheeks. She smelled of baby powder and cheap perfume.

"Hi, Mommy," she breathed against Perri's neck. "I'm glad you're home. I missed you."

"Why are you crying, sweetheart?" Perri whispered in her ear.

She drew back, swiping her wet cheeks. "I was afraid."

Chelsea's shame of fear wrung Perri's heart. "Of what, angel?" She stroked her back, smoothed her hair. In sunlight seeping through a grimy concourse window, Chelsea's thick waves shone like the garnet stone in Perri's ring.

"Afraid you wouldn't get off the plane." She glanced around and over her shoulder. Petitioning eyes, rimmed with cream-tipped auburn lashes sought Perri's again. "Afraid I couldn't find Mimi again by myself."

Perri tabled that for the moment. Standing, she drew Chelsea from the traffic flow. "Honey, I told you last night I'd be here."

Chelsea nodded, running a tiny fist beneath one eye, subduing a stubborn tear. "Mimi said you might not."

With difficulty, Perri resisted the impulse to ask why the child's grandmother had told her something so scary, or risked turning her loose in an airport alone. Infuriated, she realized Chelsea wouldn't know the answer. She smiled. "Nothing could have kept me from walking off that plane except missing it in Miami." No chance of that. She still had body kinks from spending most of Sunday night in a leather and steel airport chair. "I'm here, Chelsea, and we're going to have fun. Right, sweetie?"

"Right, Mommy." For the first time, she smiled, a close-lipped gesture too solemn for a seven-year-old. She reached for the duffel, but Perri quickly offered the backpack, fitting Chelsea's tiny arms through the straps, settling it on her back with a hug.

"Where's Mimi?" Perri ventured, feigning indifference.

"With Larry. She said they'll meet us under the hanging horse after you get your bags." Chelsea's lighter tone evidenced her love for the hanging horse.

She had carried all her bags on board, but since the hallowed horse's pasture was in the baggage claim area, she steered Chelsea in that direction, a hand resting on her fragile shoulder.

Perri gave in to agitated curiosity. "Did you find my gate all by yourself, honey?"

Chelsea peered upward. "Larry showed me, and how to get back, too, but I—"

Perri watched her daughter mentally lapse, reliving her scare, then recover with child-like resilience. "He's nice. I like him lots better than Rusty or Jake."

Oh, God. Chelsea was too young to be keeping a list of Angie's lovers. Perri had first-hand knowledge of a child being taken from its mother for witnessing moral breeches of less significance. Maybe Larry was the man Angie swore she sought for the duration. But then what kind of man was he? One who could be trusted to revere and safeguard a child's innocence? Could Angie be trusted to guard Chelsea from, or to even recognize, the disturbing potentials racing through Perri's mind? Inwardly, she shuddered, guilt nudging her.

They waited for Angie and Larry beneath sculptress Elizabeth Berrian's *Pegasus*. For reasons unknown to Perri, the horse captivated Chelsea. Did the airborne, wire-winged sculpture represent flight fantasy to her little girl—freedom from the weighty concerns of her life. Today *Pegasus* aroused Perri's own familiar fantasy of a horse for Chelsea, of keeping it in the ragged pasture behind Angie's house. But gradually, she returned to reality, remembering Angie's tiny Yorkies and how easily they could be crushed. Even if Perri came up with the money for a horse and feed, Angie would never take that chance with Sugar and Pepper.

Chelsea jiggled Perri's arm. "Here they come. That's Larry holding Mimi's hand."

For an instant Perri hoped her shock didn't show; the next instant she didn't care. If Larry were half Angie's age, even as old as Perri herself, she would be even more stunned. As they drew near, Angie waving lackadaisically, Perri noted that Larry's features were feminine fine. His canine-brown hair, worn with a pompadour and Elvis sideburns, looked dyed to match his gentle eyes. His muscular build and macho strut contrasted any feminine features. Perri felt the weight of Chelsea's all-seeing eyes, as he released Angie and strode up to them.

"Hi. I'm Larry." He offered his hand and a roguish grin.

Eventually Perri slipped her hand into his. "I'm Perri."

"I would have recognized you from TV." The handshake didn't trespass a moment past proper. He ruffled Chelsea's hair, his grin for her only now. "Even if you weren't hanging out with the princess here, I'd know it was you."

Chelsea latched onto his hand, then Perri's, shooting her an isn't-he-nice glance. Beyond his shoulder, Perri caught Angie's eyes, her pretty face rife with guilt-laced defiance.

※

When Perri emerged from the shower later that evening, wearing a threadbare cotton, knee-length gown left over from Chelsea's birth, Angie was perched on the foot of the single bed. Sugar and Pepper cuddled in sleep on the raveled throw rug at her feet. She sipped iced-tea. Her newly scrubbed face wore an expression that said, let's get this settled.

Perri lingered before a cloudy vanity mirror, toweling her hair.

"Are you planning to let her sleep with you every night?" Angie tilted her brass-blond head backward toward Chelsea, curled on the bed, snoring softly.

"If she wants." Perri kept her voice low, meeting Angie's mirrored gaze. "Shouldn't I?"

Angie took a cigarette from its pack and fired it with a Bic lighter.

"You're afraid she'll want to sleep with you once I'm gone. Right, Mom?" Most nights the other half of Angie's pink-satin-and-lace-covered waterbed would be taken.

Angie released a puff of smoke and waved a hand through it. Nothing more.

Perri offered, "I'll tell her not to ask, that your sleep would be disturbed."

"How long are you staying?"

Perri took a wide-tooth comb from the dresser and began combing her hair. "I need to be in New Orleans by next Thursday. I'm taking the bus, so I'll have to leave after we've seen the doctor." She calculated travel time. "I'll probably be leaving by–"

"Larry wants me to go to New Mexico with him to look for a job. You'll have to stay here with Chelsea."

Avoiding the nagging questions of why Angie refused to understand the problem at hand, whether she wanted to help, whether she actually loved her or Chelsea, she asked politely, "What kind of work does he do?"

"Anything he wants." A trace of devilment spiked Angie's smile. "He raced stock cars till he burned his leg. He worked as a stable hand at some of the horse farms around here for a while. Lately he's been in construction." As though recanting, she said, "He does roofing. New Mexico's economy is booming, and he's a free spirit."

She drew deeply from the cigarette, releasing a smoke stream Perri yearned to somehow trap before it drifted to her sleeping child. She crossed to the window, eased it up on its rotting sash, and propped it open with a tack hammer kept handy for that purpose. Then she sat on the bed, opposite Angie and leaned back against the iron footboard.

"Mom, I have to go to New Orleans. I can't afford to miss. We've been over this."

Angie dumped barrettes and rubber bands from a bowl on the nightstand and used it for an ashtray. "Apparently you thought you could afford to miss the TCP this week."

"All the more reason I can't miss again." She leaned to rummage in her backpack sitting on the floor, coming up with a check for nine percent of Stuart Appleby's $162,000 second place win in Orlando. The other one-percent had gone to his former bee-stung caddie. She handed the check to Angie. "See what I mean? If I can keep this up, we'll be in the black and on our way to financing the next surgery."

Angie eyed the check, full lips tightening, then stuffed it into the pocket of her clingy robe. "State-run hospitals never turn anybody away from surgery because of no money, Perri."

Her nape crawled. "I've told you a hundred times why I won't ask for help. And the doctors we need don't operate on credit, Mom. You can skip the trip to New Mexico."

Angie shrugged. "I'll leave her with your daddy. He's been pestering me to see her."

Bile filled Perri's throat. Her father had remarried recently, but hadn't stopped drinking. Though she hadn't met Nedra, rumor was that drinking was her common bond to Lee Hardin.

"How long would you be gone?" Perri phrased the question as if the issue of Angie's going was undecided. It wasn't. She read that in her mother's heavy-lashed cobalt eyes.

Another shrug. "As long as it takes."

"This is not a good idea, Mom." She reached to pull the sheet around Chelsea. "I'd like you not to go so Chelsea can stay with you so I can get back to work. The way we agreed."

Standing, Angie ground out the cigarette in the bowl, which she left on the nightstand. Sugar and Pepper scrambled up, rearing onto her shins, whining not to be left. "I'm going," she declared, scooping the Yorkies into her arms. "Even if I have to take Chelsea with me."

Perri's face and hands iced up, as though her blood had pooled at her feet. "That wouldn't be good for either of you. Be reasonable."

At the door, Angie turned, her plump, yet well-proportioned body poised at an angle that would have driven Larry wild, had he not, finally, reluctantly left. "You think Larry's too young for me, don't you?"

"His age has nothing to do with my not wanting you to go."

"If you'd make an effort to get your husband back, our money problems would be over, and who I sleep with wouldn't—"

"Mom, please." Her hushed tone pleading, she rolled her eyes toward Chelsea.

"I deserve some fun, Perri, and I'm going." The hard line of her mouth softened somewhat when she glanced at Chelsea. "You decide what happens to our little princess."

※

Chelsea's breath warmed Perri's breasts as she lay in bed cradling her, listening to the Raintrees rustle in the summer breeze outside the window. Across the room, a TV droned, casting eerie blue light on a room that hadn't felt like hers since she'd gone on tour with Beau. There had been too many hotel rooms, unfamiliar beds, meals eaten on the run. While Beau proclaimed the traveling hell, Perri found tour life glamorous, enlightening, a different perspective from her mundane life as Lee and Angie's last bothersome mouth to feed.

Her outlook had changed once she was on her own and Chelsea became a factor. For a while Perri had taken her on the LPGA, dragging a teen-aged dropout along to baby-sit during play. But without Beau's adventurous flare, his smile, his arms to negate the loneliness of unfamiliar beds, she'd grown weary, concluding the lifestyle too strenuous for a five-year-old.

Recalling that realization cancelled any brief idea she'd had of leaving tomorrow for Sawgrass after all, and taking Chelsea with her.

Her mind segued back to the child in her arms, the wounded part of her own soul she couldn't heal, no matter how much she wanted to or tried. Again she wondered if she'd done the right thing for Chelsea, hiding her from Beau. Maybe she'd be better off with him, provided he even wanted her. At least there'd be no question of her getting the care she needed and growing up with advantages Perri would never be able to give her. But a child needed her mother more, the ultimate advantage. Yet, Chelsea didn't really have her mother.

Perri crammed that guilt to the back of her mind, knowing it would surface again in full armor. She tried to tell herself Angie loved Chelsea, cared about her welfare, that she was bored, nothing else. But the choices she had given tonight were not choices at all. Enough had happened to the princess, already. Taking a chance on further damage was not an option.

✻

Chelsea's short, slender legs dangled, swinging, over the side of a leather and steel examining table, her dress unbuttoned to the waist, folding around her hips. Sucking with dedication on a Tootsie Pop, the veteran patient's prize, she smiled assurance at Perri, then did a perfect mimic of Perri's concerned frown. Perri forced a quick smile.

When Doctor Price pressed his stethoscope to Chelsea's chest, she veered off and giggled, impish eyes chastising the doctor.

"Cold?" Dr. Price murmured automatically, wearing his own frown. Then, "Take a deep breath. Good. Another." He shifted the metal piece again. "Good." He pulled the stethoscope from his ears. "How was your week, Chelsea?"

Perri quashed her urge to interpret when Chelsea answered without hesitation. "Good, but I had the flu. I threw up on Mimi's rug."

Doctor Price laughed, his hand resting loosely on Chelsea's shoulder. "Let's step into my office, shall we, ladies, and talk."

Chelsea nodded, working her little arms into the dress. Perri helped her down from the table. "I'd rather she waited for me in the reception area." She pulled a book from her backpack. "She has reading to do, don't you, honey?"

Chelsea took the book. "I'm missing school." She turned on the heel of her white-patent Mary Janes, heading for the door, acquainted with the office layout.

Perri caught Dr. Price's consternation as he raised the phone, pushed a single button and instructed, "Keep an eye on Chelsea Hardin while I talk to her mother. Would you, please?"

As Perri settled into the chair in front of his desk, his gray eyes pinned her. "What are you trying to keep from her, Perri?"

"That depends on what you have to tell me."

He smiled, shaking his head. "All mothers must be cloned from she-bears."

Not all mothers. "I want Chelsea to think of herself as nearly like the other children as possible. I try to avoid her hearing anything she might not understand." She crossed her legs and stared at the toe of her sandal, waiting, heart racing.

His nod held no real agreement. "There's been no drastic change." He opened the file before him, eyes scanning the top page. "Normally, children with Chelsea's history can wait until around age ten for a second surgery." He browsed the file again. "The cardiac catheter test she had in... October...eliminated that luxury."

"Luxury?"

"Choice, then. The way I interpret it—and Dr. Chod does, too, by the way—we're looking at eight to nine months for the aortic valvotomy. A year, tops."

Perri nodded, looking away. Her gaze got lost in the intricate boughs of a blue spruce hovering outside the utilitarian window until she found words to express her resentment. "I've been reading about aortic valve stenosis again. In most of the case histories, the heart surgery performed in infancy was sufficient." She looked at Dr. Price in time to see him frown, then they fell silent until he took up the gauntlet.

"That was what we hoped, and the surgery works in roughly ninety percent of cases. But over the years the treated valve has deteriorated. Chelsea needs an artificial heart valve now. Nothing can change that."

Perri lapsed into memory of lonely hours in a surgical waiting room. The certainty of going through that again made her stomach churn.

Dr. Price began anew. "I see no reason to hide the inevitable surgery from her. It's a good idea to be open, to explain something needs fixing again, that she'll be in the hospital for a few days, but you'll be right there with her. Generally, children have little fear of death, but your attitude is crucial." His lined face softened. "Medicine has come a long way, even in seven years. Chelsea's life is in no danger at this time, but this procedure could give her a normal life. You should look forward to it, not dread it."

A soft, sardonic laugh escaped. Her hand darted to her mouth, eyes stinging, blurring.

"You told me an artificial valve won't grow as she grows. That's not what I call a normal life."

He steepled his fingers beneath his chin, elbows resting on the leather chair arms, then rocked back. "She'll adjust to it now much better than she would have as an infant, but there will be a third surgery. Most likely when she's in her teens, when she's reached full growth."

Oh, God. At near forty, she'd be too old to lug golf bags...more years of leaving Chelsea with Angie .... "Damn it," she breathed.

His mouth pulled down at the corners. "I see you're still worried about money."

"Not compared to my fear of surgery, but, yes, money's a big problem." Along with a myriad of others. "I'll barely have the bills from the catheter test paid by then, but I'll be starting clean, at least." She shrugged. "Leaving her in order to make the money I need...is hard."

Dr. Price rifled in a desk drawer before pulling out a packet of papers. "I'm aware you have no insurance, and I know there's a problem with asking Chelsea's father for help."

Yet it could be the answer, except for one underlying fear. "How do you know?"

He granted a wry smile. "From your mother. She disagrees, of course." He pushed the packet toward her. "This is an application for assistance from Children's Medical Services. Use me as a recommendation and you'll get the help you need. You won't have to go back on tour." His gaze sought and held hers as he nudged the packet invitingly over the edge of the desk.

Her mind ran over the one time she'd called Children's Aid anonymously. After hearing Perri's sketchy story, the caseworker warned that if Perri lacked means to care for Chelsea, she should be placed in foster care. Perri never called back. Now, she took the packet, opened it and filed through the disclaimers to the application form. Her eyes raced along the questions and blank lines until she found the obstacle she knew would be there: Father's Name.

Dar Tomlinson

She stacked the pages, braced them on her
crossed knees, and tapped their edges with a finger. Finally, she placed them on the desk. "This is
not an option. I'll find another way."

"You still don't want to name her father."

Angie had told him far too much. "It's more
complicated than that." So much more. "I won't
lie, and I can't name him."

"Because—you do know? Your mother indicated—"

A shiver of memory crawled along her spine.
Beau had been so gentle, so thorough. "I can't risk
naming him. Other people are involved."

"Ask for help, Perri, and stay home with your
daughter. You'll both be better off."

✳

Perri parked Angie's Toyota convertible on a
deserted gravel lane fronting High Meadow Farm.
Chelsea curled in the seat, head resting on Perri's
thigh. In the dash light, her thick-lashed brown
eyes fluttered open, then shut, as she drifted back
to sleep.

A breeze soughing in the maple trees provided
background for the drone of locusts and an occasional whinny in the distance. Gathering darkness
barely allowed Perri to make out the barn across
the blue-grass pasture, but memory painted a clear
picture of the big white house sitting crown-like in
the middle of a lush green lawn. Verandas encir-
cled the two-story structure, the upstairs railings
laced with sturdy ironwork, and enormous
columns framed the front portico.

Her gaze settled on the downstairs wing, the
suite of rooms added for Beau when he came to live
at High Meadow. In her mind she smelled honey-
suckle vines twining wildly beneath the open window on her wedding night, and lay in Beau's arms
watching fireflies dance, listened to soft, rhythmic
breathing that stirred her hair, revived her hunger.
She had awakened alone, being greeted by sunlight

at the window and Braden standing at the foot of the disheveled bed. She had scrambled for the monogrammed linen sheet, drawing it over her nakedness.

Braden's smile hinged on apology. "When you're dressed, I want to talk to you." He turned away before she could question, then turned back. "In my study."

Minutes later she occupied a stiff-backed Chippendale chair in the study, agitation coiling in the pit of her stomach. Fighting back nausea, she clutched her clammy hands together. Only half attributing the malady to nerves, she tried ignoring it as her eyes surveyed the room. She concentrated on searching out the details related by Beau through the years.

The antique grandfather clock proclaimed the half-hour, its chimes cushioned by brocaded draperies and Persian carpets, musty with age. The carved, chest-size humidor next to the camelback sofa boasted a padlock that had challenged thirteen-year-old Beau when he'd pilfered the Churchills and Coronas inside and shared them with her. Crystal glasses and liquor decanters in a bulky armoire near the window caught the morning sun slicing through dark-wood shutters. Hallowed quality Beau had unwittingly described.

A movement drew her eyes to Braden seated behind the mammoth desk with a brown leather ledger open before him. Curious and confused, she searched his face for some semblance of Beau, some clue to the moment. Like his grandson, he stood tall and lean, but where Beau's features were defined in sharp angles, the lines and planes of Braden's face blurred as if created in wax, then left in the sun to soften. On a nearby table, a photographic shrine of Beau's father, also nicknamed Beau, depicted the same, effeminate features. Beau had inherited his striking, physical appeal

from Winonna. Or, maybe, from the mother he
scarcely knew and never spoke of, a woman Perri
had never seen and whose name she didn't even
know.

She gripped the chair arms to still her trembling, wondering why Beau was absent, yet not
wanting his grandfather to sense her quandary.
Braden's craggy gray brows knitted as he pinned
her in what passed for aggrieved scrutiny.

"I won't waste your time, Ms. Hardin, since I
promised Beau this would be over by the time he
returned."

Ms. Hardin? Her hand crept to the locket Beau
had given her the day before. She worked it back
and forth on the gold chain. "Where is he?" She
spoke around a constriction in her throat, fear and
confusion rushing to the surface. Braden had
never hidden his disapproval of her, connected in
some way to her father. But like many things in
Beau's life, she had tried denying Braden as a factor. "If we're going to talk, I'd rather Beau be—"

He held up a golf-callused palm. "That's what
he wants to avoid, I'm sad to say. So, I'll be brief.
He asked me tell you he wants out of the marriage."

She stared, emotions tangled. Shock. Doubt.
Panic. "Where's Beau? If it's true, let him tell me."

"He went to the club to practice his one iron.
He asked me to tell you he realizes he made a mistake and wants an annulment." He ripped something from the ledger, then held it in his immacu-
lately manicured fingers.

Perri's heart pounded her chest wall, last
night's lovemaking replaying vividly on her jumbled
mind. "A consummated marriage can't be
annulled."

"It can if both parties consent." He spoke gently, holding out the narrow, elongated piece of
paper in his hand. "Beau instructed me to give
you this." When she didn't reach out, didn't move,

he said, "It's a check for half a million dollars." For the first time, his eyes lost their condescending tolerance. "It's not as much as you'd have reaped had Beau not realized his mistake, but it's generous of him, I'd say." His mouth ran taut, then slackened. She watched him take a deep breath as though wrestling some inner struggle. "Of course, this is only in exchange for your promise—in writing—that you won't try to contact Beau in the future."

She refused to imagine life without Beau. "I want to talk to him. He wouldn't do this."

Braden sighed heavily. "I hoped not to have to hurt you more than necessary, but it's as simple as Beau tiring of you over the past year, hoping a marriage ceremony might counteract that, but realizing too late he's made an even bigger mistake. So you see, Ms. Hardin—"

Her scalp tightened. Anger and bile from her churning stomach congealed in her throat. Again, her hand sought the locket, fingers closing around it this time. "Mrs. St. Cyr."

"For the moment." He smiled gently, eyes drawn to her throat pulse where the locket hung. "You're wrong about Beau not doing this. Winonna and I have spoiled him, I'm afraid. He's used to having what he wants, and he's found someone else. Someone more suited to his upbringing, who'll prove more beneficial to his career."

She would've laughed at the absurdity of Beau finding someone else, if she weren't so scared, so stunned. Braden's cloud-gray eyes measured her, but instead of clueing him to her turmoil, she declared, "No woman on earth is more suited to Beau's career than I am." Then seizing onto solid argument, she demanded, "Where?"

"Excuse me?"

"Where did he find someone else? In the men's locker room? We haven't been apart for the last year." Not exactly true. Beau had played one tournament without her when she'd gone home to visit, and he'd gone on that guys-only fishing trip, but other than that...."Beau and I have loved one another since we were children." She feigned bravado. "I can't be bought off or chased away, no matter how much you dislike me."

His eyes turned to slate. Color leached from his face. He failed to deny her claim of his dislike, but still she sensed no enjoyment in his demeanor. Folding her arms below her waist, she cradled her abdomen, her ears straining for Beau's staccato footsteps on the wooden foyer floor. Deafening silence, broken only by the rhythmic tick of the old clock, settled around them. Finally, he lifted the corner of his desk pad and withdrew a small envelope, his mouth taut as a crossbow. He removed the contents and leaned forward, offering it to her. "I lied about Beau being at the club. This was delivered before he left this morning."

She held the ecru-hued sheet in trembling hands, her mind rejecting what her eyes read.

> *Beau, Darling, I know the relationship was hard to break, but I'm so happy you've chosen me. I'm waiting for you. –Christi*

A crack of lightning slashed through her, leaving her stunned, disbelieving, unable to comprehend. She read the note again. Christi? There had to be a mistake. A cruel joke. Beau wouldn't do this to her. She teetered on the brink of crumpling the phony note, throwing it back at Braden, but the name echoed in her mind. Was Christi the one who had poured herself all over Beau at the winner's party in...Tucson? Her mind raced, calculating dates and events. The fishing trip had come on the heels of the party. Now the trip seemed a sudden, out of character, happening.

No. She was hallucinating. That girl lacked the class to use the antique note stationery Perri held in her hand. But some girl possessed that class. The note was real. And whoever had written it was ecstatic with Beau's decision to trash a ten-year-old relationship and a one-day marriage for someone of his own kind. A tear brimmed, slipped over, then trailed down her cheek and splashed onto her breast.

Braden stared, grim faced.

Another tear fell, then another. I never knew Beau. Not for one moment.

Grasping the note, Perri staggered from the chair, sparing Braden a hateful glance before she whirled and crossed the room. By the time she reached the door, perspiration soaked her brow and a wave of nausea swamped her so completely that her hand flew to her clamped mouth, furiously forcing back bile. She pressed her forehead against the warm wood as inside her a battle raged. Behind her, she sensed Braden waiting. A detested vision of him holding the bribe money reverberated against the chambers of her mind as reality screamed at her, voicing her lack of choice.

I can't take the money. I can't refuse it. Cold slick fear blanketing her skin quickly turned to rage.

Gulping air, she turned and walked back to the desk slowly. Chin jutted, eyes daring, she jerked the check from Braden's extended hand. He thrust a legal-sized, typed sheet before her. His hand trembled when he offered a gold pen from a marble desk set. She signed where he pointed out a red X. Quickly, he produced a second document. Her eyes ran down the blurry page before she seized the document from the desk, ripped it and flung the fragments at him.

He flinched, mouth grave. "Give me the note, Ms. Hardin." He held out his hand.

She stuffed it in a pocket. "Go to hell, Mr. St. Cyr. And take St. Serious with you."

Chelsea stirred against Perri's thigh, murmuring something indistinguishable, almost but not quite drawing Perri back to the present. Absently, she brushed damp hair off Chelsea's forehead, drifting back again. Once she'd agreed to go on tour, Beau's and her relationship had taken on added dimension, had become a sexual romp, but beyond the playfulness, she had felt he cared. Looking back, she could pinpoint when Chelsea had been conceived, one especially tender, soul joining night in Atlanta.

Her mind filed further back, unable to recall a time before that day at High Meadow when she hadn't loved Beau in some fashion. Her mother had encouraged her while her father warned she wasn't Beau's equal, that he wanted one thing only—sex with a black girl. If he got it, he'd drop her. Though she'd tried disbelieving, Lee's crude claim had kept her from having sex with Beau until she agreed to go on tour with him. Their wedding night in his childhood bed, a year later, had been so sweetly intense that she had felt it was their first real time together. She knew now that the intensity had been Beau's appeasement for the night being their last.

If she hadn't been so naive, so prideful, knowing what she'd always known about Winonna's illness, Beau's father's and aunt's death, she would have demanded a full million. But she could think of nothing in her moment of shock other than the baby she secretly carried being Beau's consummate bequest to her. A perfect atonement for whatever had gone wrong in their union, the last gift from the man whom she detested with all the love she possessed.

When Chelsea was born so wounded, Perri, alone and scared, suffered the unbidden thought

that maybe she had made the wrong decision, that
maybe she should have listened to Angie's urgings
to abort after Chelsea's amniocentesis. But after
surgery, watching the three-day-old, screw-faced,
clinch-fisted, tawny creature's life and death tangle, all doubt disappeared. The nurses supported
the hours spent cradling Chelsea against her
breasts, an attempt to heal her with worship,
rather than depending on God and man. Years of
lying awake in the night, listening intently for
Chelsea's breathing, followed, Perri's own heart
lurching with fear at the thought her child still
might die.

A chill ran over her now as she remembered all
the times she crept to the bedside to kiss Chelsea's
incredibly soft cheek, marveling at her existence.
Many nights she grieved, yearning to share the
agony and glory with Beau, until gradually, her
pain had dissipated into bitterness.

Acknowledging tonight's emotions were more
cryptic, she started the car and stole away quietly
without turning on the headlights.

CHAPTER SEVEN

Goddammit. The old man had shown up to coach Golden Boy to victory and the bimbo wasn't there to stage her coming-out party. Great timing. Maybe she wasn't tough enough for caddie duty, after all. Maybe she'd blown Dodge, and he'd lost his leverage.

Walking on the balls of his feet, he crossed the club storage area. Rubber soles whined against the concrete surface, an intrusion on the sound of rain rivering from the roof onto the tarmac outside. His gaze shifted over the cache of golf bags lined up in alphabetical order, his heart doing a jerky dance, petitioning the gods to delay play a little longer, guarantee his mission.

Why the hell couldn't Beau's name be Appleby? He hurried down the bag line, his mind ticking off names. Simpson. Stuart. Sutton. St. Cyr! He reached for the bag and found it covered with a hood, held in place by a small but sturdy luggage lock.

Dumb sonvabitch caddie probably stuck this mother lock on here and hightailed it to eat chitlins and watermelon. Well, up his. The lock he couldn't pick had yet to be invented.

Pretend it's Perri, the little bitch. If you hit your target and stroke it just right, she'll—

In less than a minute, the lock sprung open. Another minute and he had the hood off, driver out of the bag, shaft snapped over his knee like dry kindling, the wrecked club reinserted, a note snagged on sharp steel, hood back on, lock engaged, and the storage area empty of resentful humanity again.

✳

Braden looked at his grandson across a dinner table in Antoine's restaurant. Beau, looking like a scrubbed adolescent in his Sunday-school best, luxurious red hair a little curly from his shower, worked on a rack of rare lamb. Braden's gaze fell on Beau's long, slender fingers, proficient enough to be surgeon's hands.

"What do you think happened on number eleven? You seemed to go into a fog."

Beau looked up, but his eyes focused in the middle distance, a muscle working his taut jaw. "No big mystery. I hit the tee ball way the hell off the toe, and it squirted right."

"That's one shot out of four more that were as bad. You looked as if you didn't know where you were." Or as if he wanted to be anywhere but doing battle with a golf course.

"Granddad, I'm leading the tournament." Beau's brown eyes locked his, in the shimmering light.

"A lead is only as good as the next day's round, son. So think about that when your head hits the pillow tonight, instead of resting on your laurels."

Beau's left thumb and forefinger circled the copper bracelet he wore on his right wrist. His silence rested on a background of jazz filtering in from the Quarter until at last he said, "Thanks. I probably needed that. You wouldn't want me to get cocky."

The mildly sardonic tone didn't bother Braden as long as the amiable smile remained.

※

Sleepless, Beau tossed and turned in the too-hard hotel bed until the wee hours of morning. Braden had sealed his fate with his advice. His only solace came from knowing he had an afternoon rather than morning tee time.

Braden was right about today's round being a kind of out-of-body experience. Damned if Beau

knew how he was still leading. He hadn't been able
to keep his eyes off the gallery all day. Catching a
glimpse of a woman on number eleven who looked
like Perri had jarred mightily, even though he knew
Perri was way the hell gone, and that every petite
woman with muscular legs and caramel cream skin
wasn't her. Even reasoning that if she were there
she'd be caddying instead of gallerying him hadn't
helped. He had played for eight years after she'd
left him and given her no thought—yeah, right. Yet
she'd made an appearance for three tournaments,
then taken a hiatus, and he was screwed. She'd
skipped Sawgrass last week, and now for some goddamned reason he was unprivileged to know, she
was skipping New Orleans, too.

Or maybe the whole thing had been a whim,
and she wasn't coming back.

Whatever. Tomorrow, he'd get his head on
straight. Tonight he had to get some sleep or he'd
be living proof of Braden's a-lead-is-only-as-good-
as-the-next-round theory. He flipped over, pounded the pillow and scrunched his eyes shut.
Nothing. Drawing himself up in the bed, he braced
against the headboard, his inner demons slapping
each other's backs, celebrating victory. He could
no more get Braden's warning out of his mind than
he could Perri's absence.

Tonight, Braden's expectations, his never being
satisfied, had left Beau feeling used up, old beyond
his thirty years, as though he were dead and hollow on the inside. Yet he reasoned his granddad
had been through a lot, was still going through a
lot. Nevertheless, he always put Beau's career first,
wanted the best for him and tried to cushion his
blows. Beau's victories and defeats were Braden's.
Beau owed him everything.

His thoughts drifted back to that day at High
Meadow when he had returned from practicing at
the club. Having taken the brunt of Beau's biggest

blow to date, Braden met him at the door, pasty-faced, clouded with concern.

"What's wrong?" Beau urged. "Is it Nonna? Did she—"

"No, son. It's Perri. She's gone."

Something icy ran down Beau's spine. "Gone where? What the hell's going on?"

"Come in the study, so Nonna won't hear, and I'll tell you."

Beau left the rumpled bed, slipped on a hotel robe and wandered onto the terrace, still sifting through the dregs of memory of that day at High Meadow. A lacy-edged moon migrated through heavy clouds as Florida humidity turned the walled terrace to a sauna. The weather forecast had called for a risk of rain again tomorrow. If it rained hard and long enough, the tournament would be over, and he would be the winner without firing another shot. He preferred to play it out, rather than "win by default," Braden's term for that kind of victory.

Once a rainy day on tour had meant extra hours in bed with Perri. A lifetime ago.

Reluctantly, his mind came back to her, searching for a time when he hadn't loved her in some way. She had grown on him, invading his adolescent complacency like a rose pushing through a fence. Through the years, the need to harvest her pliant sweetness had consumed him. But she'd have none of it. She swam naked with him in muddy creeks, lay with him on the sunny banks, but guarded her virginity like a gem.

Frustrated, he'd break up with her. Once he'd been gone for two lonely, regretful years, only to return with his hope and anticipation mixed up with ominous dread. Had another suitor been more convincing in his absence? She had always been there waiting. Untouched.

Once they began college, ASU for him, community college for her, their dates on his trips home

always ended in wrestling matches pitting his persuasive powers against her resistance. He would
return to school so horny and lovesick he couldn't
break par for days. Braden faulted his inferior play
to "fucking the Hardin girl" and turned a deaf ear
to Beau's ironic assurance that bedding Perri was
not the problem.

Finally, hopelessly in love, obsessed to know
her beyond the borders she sustained, with
Braden's warnings and disapproval shoved to the
back of his mind, he persuaded her to tour with
him, a kind of elopement. In a sterile hotel room he
slowly and lovingly unwrapped the fiery topaz
jewel, bringing to fruition what he had come to consider their fated love. Except for the glory they had
missed, he was glad she had held out.

He had never hurt as much as when Perri left.
Not when his father died. Not when his mother
kissed him goodbye outside of court, confirming
she didn't love him enough to continue fighting.
Never had his life represented more of a lie than
when he sat at Braden's dining room table that
night after Perri left, surrounded by club and community elite, toasting the future.

When he'd climbed into bed so wholly heartsick
he'd imagined a cavity in his heart bigger than
Winonna's, he admitted Braden had been right all
along.   Perri had been smart enough to employ
whatever means needed to hook him, her goal a
lifestyle of wealth and prestige guaranteed. But
like his mother, Perri couldn't fathom a lifetime
with him, and like a lender discounting a note in
favor of immediate pay off, she had asked for the
money Braden was happy to give, making each of
them winners. In his drunken state, Beau wallowed in loss for what he promised himself would
be the last time. In determining to prove his worthiness the only way he knew how, winning, he had
unwittingly taken up a life worthy of a gypsy.

To this day, none of it made sense. Perri had cared nothing about money. And why five hundred thousand dollars, when she knew he wanted to give her the world for the rest of her life? What the hell happened between kissing her awake that morning, whispering goodbye, then walking back in the front door and finding his world shattered?

Tonight, alone in yet another hotel room, sleepless in another unfamiliar bed, he realized he could never win enough to fill the hole in his or Braden's hearts. Admitting how empty his life had become in the last eight years, he vowed to change it. Come hell or high water.

✳

On Sunday, Perri and Chelsea cuddled on Angie's lumpy sofa watching the last round of the New Orleans Classic on TV. A tray of peanut butter sandwiches and a pitcher of lemonade filled the coffee table. While Sugar snored beneath the table, Pepper curled in Chelsea's lap. Chelsea watched with an innate love for, and sophisticated knowledge of, the sport.

Perri studied a camera close-up of Beau as though he were a stranger. When he turned his head, her gaze locked on the back of his neck. Broad. Smooth. A plane of cured brown leather. A shiver of memory oozed through her, then nestled with disturbing persistence in that cavern between her thighs. She watched the tournament in silence, trying not to grip Chelsea's little shoulder too tightly with the other. Beau was playing like a rookie. Anger for caring, and for the resentment rearing its head every time the camera covered another twosome, descended on her like locusts in the trees outside the hot little house. Eventually, anxiety pushed other emotions aside. She settled into tender concern, into silently rooting for him in her jumbled mind.

Chelsea jiggled her arm. "Mommy?"

"What sweetie?" She looked down, rocked as always by Chelsea's resemblance to Beau.

"Mimi says you've been on a trip with my Daddy." Her hand crept to scratch behind Pepper's ear.

Perri's spine turned rock rigid. Her hand rummaging in the popcorn bowl as slowly as an arthritic old woman's, contrasted a mind racing like a rat in a cage. She paced herself, moving her arm to circle Chelsea's waist, squeezing a little. "When did she say that?"

"When me an' her an' Larry watched golf."

She grasped straws, tamping down guilt for wanting to sidetrack Chelsea. "I'll bet Larry's fun to watch with."

Chelsea turned her wise-old-woman eyes upward. "You're on the same trip as these guys that play golf, right Mommy? We saw you when we watched."

"Was that fun? Seeing me on television?" She rattled on, her throat warming, tightening. This had to be discussed, but not now. When? Not now. "Does Mimi like it?"

Chelsea's Beau mouth tightened. "Is that my daddy?" Not moving her eyes from Perri's, she cocked her little head toward a screen filled with Beau St. Cyr bending over a putt. "He's the one that gives candy to little kids. Right?"

The laugh Perri mustered emerged shakily. The suspect sound peaked Sugar's ears. "Why would you think that, Chels?"

She grabbed a handful of long red hair, drawing it around to her face, eyes crossing in concentration. "Look." She nodded at the television and shrugged.

Perri feigned consideration. "His hair is a lot darker than yours, honey." Hers were a color so nearly the shade of Beau's when they'd met.

"Do you know who he is?"

"His name is Beau St. Cyr." Words she had senselessly hoped never to say to Chelsea.

Chelsea grinned. "I know that. I meant do you know which guy is my daddy?"

Jarred, she tousled Chelsea's hair, striving for nonchalance. "Sure I do." Her mind darted onto a decision. "We'll talk about that as soon as you're old enough to understand."

✳

Beau had smelled trouble on the number one tee. He was too aware of the gallery's respectful silence and the distant clinking of glasses on a clubhouse terrace directly behind them.

Once David Frost, the other half of his twosome, had hit his shot, Beau strode briskly down the fairway behind the flight of David's ball, Cal trailing behind. Just beyond the ropes, close enough for Beau to feel his anxiety, Braden hobbled along on his arthritic knee, toting his folding seat. Beau figured God provided that prime spot for Braden to gallery. Close enough for Beau to feel him breathing down his neck. Living every shot.

Cal caught up with him. "You mad at me, Beau?"

"Keep your voice down." He cut his eyes toward Braden, then focused on the green he somehow had to one putt in order to save bogey and prevent Braden from having a stroke.

"Yep. You's mad, all right. Mad 'bout not havin' no driver, I reckon."

The field had hit practice balls before being interrupted by the shower that delayed play. Cal had quickly stored Beau's clubs, and they had waited out the rain in the locker room. Because television coverage would have been skewed, they'd had no opportunity to warm up again. The broken driver had been discovered when Cal unveiled the bag on the way to the first tee. Knowing he'd have to use his three wood every time he needed a driver had pissed Beau off royally. But mad at Cal, the man who'd held him and sung spirituals the day Beau Jr. had been buried, then practically raised him after that? Could he be mad at the old, black he-nanny who always tried to ease the pain of his relationship with his mother? Not in this lifetime.

"No way I'm mad at you. You did what you thought would work, pal. Don't worry about it." He racked his brain for an assurance. "The course plays short. We'll never miss Big Bertha." Except on the ass-kicking tenth hole.

They had found a note scrawled in a nearly illegible hand, left pinioned on the jagged shaft of the broken driver: You and the babe are dead meat, St. Serious.

The warning—whatever the hell it meant—had turned his stomach and continued vibrating in his head. Cal believed the lock was enough, but they'd made a mistake in believing themselves targets of a few agitating pranks when they were dealing with a sick son of a bitch.

Beau's doubt of winning evolved to serious concern on hole seven, a three-par. He laid the ball four feet short of the pin, but while hunkered butt-to-calves to eye the putt, the little voice in his head said, "Lag up. Don't chance trying to make that tricky mother." In his tortured mind, his cinched birdie winged away, his confidence in tow. He took a couple of practice strokes to stall, then struck the ball for real and kept his head down, listening for a clunk in the bottom of the cup that never came. He looked up in time to see Braden's chin drop level with the pulse in his throat. Then, his disappointment all but palpable, he got busy adjusting his Panama hat, as though he didn't want to be identified with Beau.

Beau couldn't see Braden's eyes, but he didn't need to. Whatever they held was already engraved on his conscience. He tapped the fickle ball into the hole and handed the putter to Cal amidst a smattering of applause.

A distant gallery roared. He'd been caught and was about to be mauled by the Tiger.

When Beau reported to the score tent, they handed him Braden's note. He pocketed it. After signing a score attesting he had come in tied for piss-poor third, he smiled into the TV camera, informing the world how it felt to lose a tournament he'd controlled for three days prior. Then he took time to hand out candy and sign autographs for the throng of kids waiting outside. Finally, he made it to the bar.

Pete, who had missed the cut and moved into a cheap motel to await a ride on the jet, greeted him. "Tough day in the trenches, huh, Beau?"

"It ranks right up there with root canals and migraines."

Pete shoved a still-sweating Coors toward him and signaled for another. "Why'd you suddenly give up hitting your driver? You're long, but—"

"How did you know that?" He hadn't seen Pete in the gallery, and he'd given Cal strict instructions to say nothing to anyone about the enigma.

Pete shrugged. "I watched you from the clubhouse. Gary McCord and Bobby Clampet were feeding the network info from the tee boxes. Peter Kostis announced your three wood or one iron every time you took them out of the bag. What's the story?"

Beau shrugged, taking a long drink. "I decided I was getting too dependent on Bertha."

Pete laughed. "Great timing."

"Yeah. Timing is my forte." From his pocket, Beau took Braden's note scrawled in flawless half printing-half writing style on the back of a tournament program, turned his back to Pete and read.

*Beau, when I called home, Silky told me
Winonna is feeling poorly. I decided not to
wait for you to play the back nine.*
                                    Love, Granddad.

Once Beau would have rushed to the phone,
concerned for Nonna. Today, he ordered another
Coors, knowing truth lay in Braden's unwillingness
to accept or associate with a loser.

❋

A new canvas bag lay open on Perri's bed.
Chelsea's clothing, destined for the bag, tumbled in
the dryer as Larry's four-by-four pulled into the
drive. Irritably, Perri glanced at her watch. She
had planned to be gone before Angie returned, hoping to avoid either her chastisement or elation. Not
wanting to overly excite Chelsea ahead of time,
she'd made preparations in secret. All for naught.

When the sagging screen door whined opened,
Chelsea, Sugar and Pepper leaped from the bed
and raced in that direction. Perri stepped into the
hallway in time for the reunion. Stunned, she
watched Angie bypass the yelping Yorkies, sink to
her knees and embrace Chelsea. Over Chelsea's
shoulder, Perri's eyes locked with her mother's.

"How's my princess?" Angie crooned into
Chelsea's ear. "Did you miss Mimi?"

Chelsea's arms tightened, her head bobbing
against Angie's neck. Then she pulled back, straining upward to Larry, who stood a step away. He
picked her up with one arm, swung her around,
laughing, lowered her to the floor, and brought his
other arm from behind his back. Face glowing,
Chelsea seized the pristine-white velvet Pegasus
from Larry's hand.

"What do you say, Chels?" Perri issued an
obligatory prompt from the doorway.

"Thank you." She lowered a face gone rosy to
nuzzle her prize.

Only then did Angie gather Sugar and Pepper into her arms, bestowing a greeting similar to what Chelsea had given Pegasus. "Mimi's other babies." She laughed delightedly, taking and returning eager kisses. "Did they drive you crazy, honey?"

Amid visions of the empty bag on the bed, guilt embraced Perri like a lost lover. Through new perspective, she realized Chelsea's grandmother loved her, but taking care of her was a stressful responsibility, a strain. Perri shook her head, answering, "They were fine."

Holding the Yorkies in one arm, Angie lowered a hand to the floor in an effort to rise, but fast as a cowboy on Saturday night, Larry moved in, drew her upright and kept an arm loosely circling her padded waist.

Perri asked the customary question. "Did you have fun?"

With his rogue smile, Larry gave Angie's waist a couple of quick jiggles, his Spaniel eyes shining. "I found a job right off. That gave us license to have fun."

"That's great." Or was it? "I'm glad you're home. I barely have time to catch the four o'clock bus." Out of distrust, she'd been about to sentence her daughter to gypsy hell. She headed back for the bedroom. "I'll finish up."

Larry's voice followed her. "Yeah, we timed it close, but we made it. Huh, Angie?"

Spine erect, nape crawling, Perri turned back in time to see his guileless smile.

"I'll get your mom's bag out of the truck, then run you to the bus station."

She dealt him a harried smile, eyes meeting Angie's as she spoke. "Chelsea, sweetheart, would you help Larry? I want to talk to Mimi."

"Sure, Mommy." Still hugging the horse, she latched onto his ready hand, seeming to relinquish any gloom connected to Perri's leaving.

In the bedroom, Perri closed the door, glancing again at her watch. She crossed to the bed, zipped the bag, then stuffed it into the crowded cavern behind the bed's flimsy dust ruffle.

"New bag?"

"Yes. But I decided not to take anything I didn't bring."

"That's my practical daughter."

Perri zipped the duffel, then her backpack, and set them on the floor. Busy work.

"Chelsea looks good, honey." Angie peered at her reflection in the cloudy vanity mirror, fluffing her brass curls. "I hope you remembered to give her the medicine."

She sank onto the edge of the bed. "Mom, I wouldn't forget anything that important."

Angie turned, smiling. "Sometimes I do. It's possible, even for you." Her blue eyes measured Perri before she sat beside her, continuing to smile. "You're still mad at me, I see. Don't be, honey. I made it back with time to spare."

"I'm not mad about the trip." Anymore.

Angie's smile got bigger and more cajoling. "But you're mad. Wanta tell me why?"

Lacking the luxury of time-consuming strategy, Perri plunged in. "When Chelsea and I watched the tournament together, she said you told her that's where I've been."

Angie looked blank, smile waning. "You didn't want her to know?"

"Did you tell her I was on a trip with her father?"

"She doesn't lie, so probably." The smile kicked back into high gear.

"She asked me if I knew which one of the golfers was her father."

Angie's laugh fell into the escaped fugitive category. "She did? How sad."

98

"For God's sake." Her frustration broke free. "I don't want her to think she's a bastard."

Angie cocked an over-tweezed brow. "What do you want her to think?"

"Are you trying to force this issue?"

A cerise nail toyed with a snag on the spread. "If you mean the issue of getting help from Beau... probably." Then she surprised Perri. "You know if you'd picked your lover—"

"Husband."

"—better, you wouldn't have this problem. You knew about Beau's daddy—and his grandmother. And didn't he have an aunt—" She regrouped. "Honey, the whole town knew about that family's tragedy. You could have saved yourself some grief."

"You pushed me at Beau from the minute I told you I knew him. You started pushing me toward his bed when I began to grow breasts." Her mind raced backward. Angie had been elated when Perri joined Beau on tour. When she'd called to tell her they were getting married, Angie insisted on coming to the pitiful little wedding, playing the part of proud mother-in-law. "You were all for the marriage," Perri reminded. On the other hand, steadfast in his objection, Lee had gotten drunk.

"Marriage, yes. I didn't push you into getting pregnant, if you'll recall."

"Surely you aren't still saying I should have aborted."

Her eyes swam within smudged blue pencil lines. "That's not fair. I love Chelsea."

Perri sucked in breath, her hand stealing to the locket lying against the front of her sundress, warming her breasts. "Then what are you saying?"

Angie shrugged her meaty shoulders. "That you should stay home. Not because I don't want to keep her," she rushed. "But because this is a critical time in her life."

By rote, Perri voiced the thoughts that played through her mind every time her head found a pillow, every morning when her eyes opened. "She's not going to die. She's going to have that surgery, and she'll be fine." Until it's time to do it again.

"I know." Angie patted, then squeezed Perri's hand. "Tell Beau, Perri. He deserves to know he has a child, that she's sick and needs him. No matter what he did to you."

"To Chelsea. I don't care what he did to me. A woman can't make a man love her, Mom, especially after he's taken all she has to give." She scrambled out of the memory once again. "I don't care anymore."

"Then tell him about her and ask for his help. By law, he has to give it."

"You know I can't." Dragging her hand from Angie's, she paced the tiny room, paced back. Bracing against the window, she watched Chelsea and the Yorkies maul the toy Pegasus while Larry puttered at the rear of the slick, shiny four-by-four. "I can't tell, and I can't ask for children's aid because I'd have to name Beau as the father. He'd take her away from me—" She snapped her fingers, digging a little deeper into her resolve. "—the moment he found out."

"Beau wouldn't do that, Perri. He's not made that way."

"Braden is." She addressed the rusty screen and the scraggly-ugly pine tree beyond. "He'd take Chelsea just as he took Beau from his mother."

The bed springs sighed as Angie rose. Her bare feet padded on the linoleum floor. She touched Perri's arm. "Maybe he did the right thing, Perri. Maybe Beau's mother didn't deserve him. Braden's no saint—just ask Lee Hardin—but he must of had a reason for what he did."

Perri stiffened. "Braden doesn't need a reason. He takes what he wants. He'd want any part of

Beau because he worships him. He always despised me."

"Because of your daddy, honey."

"What about Daddy?" Rumblings she'd heard were always behind closed doors. Through the years Braden had become a vague sinister figure to her on the one hand, a looming reality on the other. Could it be as simple as racial prejudice? "What happened between them?"

Angie sighed, unfamiliarly. "Oh...it was a long time ago. Something Lee did and Braden got blamed for. Something he thought I did. He was wrong about that, though." Her tone left no room for discussion on the latter disclosure.

Perri continued to watch out the window, ghostly voices echoing in her head. Braden had orchestrated Lee's being fired. The firing had brought Lee and Angie's divorce to a head when she refused to leave Anchorage, even though she'd ended up in Louisville. Perri had always felt that in some twisted way, Lee blamed Braden for the divorce. "Something happened at Owl Creek, you mean?"

"Sure, at Owl Creek. Where else would they rub elbows?" Angie regained her gruff exterior. "But it's water under the bridge."

Through the years, some distant, shadowy notion had repeatedly occurred, a question of whether or not that "water under the bridge" had washed out Perri's marriage. That if not for Braden— But, no. She had seen the note, and Braden had actually seemed sympathetic, as though he'd held off showing it to her, but had no choice.

"There's bad blood there," Angie was saying, "And probably will be till one of them dies, but it has nothing to do with you or Chelsea. I'm saying Braden taking Beau had something to do with Beau's mother."

Perri turned. She'd been over that in her mind so many times, but she had nothing to go on. Wounded, Beau had refused to discuss the custody battle, saying only that he owed Braden everything. "We don't know that. Maybe Beau's father didn't provide for her when he died."

"Beau provided for you. He didn't know you were pregnant, and he can't help what happened with Chelsea, but if he knew, he would."

Perri shrugged it off, half wanting to believe, yet wholly knowing Beau was not the issue. "Maybe his mother loved him and was good for him. Maybe she was trying to take care of him the best way she knew how. The only way she could."

"Like you."

Their gazes locked. In the kitchen, the refrigerator hummed, rattling a threat to mutiny, and then miraculously kicked in. Chelsea's melodious laugh and Pepper's ear-piercing bark floated on the late afternoon.

"I have to do this my way, Mom. I need your help. Can I count on you?"

A furrow formed between Angie's brows. "For whatever it's worth, you're cheating Beau. Don't play God. Tell him, or you may suffer the consequence."

"I can't take that chance, no matter how much I want to."

"You're playing with fire, Perri."

"Will you help me?"

She nodded, her mouth begrudging, "For now, honey. That's all I can promise."

CHAPTER EIGHT

Satisfied the motel room was empty, Beau slipped inside and quietly closed the door. Across the cramped space, from behind a door left ajar, came sounds of a shower running. He crossed the room, sank onto an unmade bed and propped against the headboard, listening, visualizing the bathroom scene. His gaze inventoried the room, outlining the task at hand.

Pipes rattled and water stilled in unison with the ringing of the phone beside the bed. He let it ring. Once. Twice. Again. The pulse in his throat knocked out a savage rhythm.

The bathroom door opened. A slightly crouching figure backed out, dragging an oversized duffel. Creamy cheeks peeked from beneath a towel held half-closed. A hardy foot-shove on the duffel, and a reel toward the ringing phone, left Beau unsure which he enjoyed more: the face wearing a startled, pissed-off expression, seeing his locket dangling into lush cleavage, or a glimpse of spirally dark-honey hair where the towel gapped in a V formation.

"Hi." He managed not to laugh at her tug-the-towel action. "Looks like your hands are tied. Want me to get the phone?"

Wordlessly, gaze drilling him, Perri crossed to within inches of where he lounged, so close he felt the vapor from her wet body. His gaze raked down her length, settling on a small scar on her inner right ankle. New. He lifted his eyes to inquire, but she turned her back and snatched the phone. Her greeting could have cracked crystal.

Beau easily heard every over-wrought word coming through the wire. "It's Teddy. When I got to the course, Appleby's caddie flagged me down. Said he saw Beau lurking around the motel office. I bet he's looking for you."

"Why would he be?" Cool as the underside of a satin pillow.

"Yeah, right. Maybe he's only slumming." Perri held the phone away from her ear, dodging Teddy's boisterous laugh.

"Thanks. I'll keep my guard up." She clamped the phone onto its cradle, regripped the towel, and pivoted with the languid grace of a prima donna. While turned away, she had managed to stow his locket beneath the towel. "You scared the hell out of me, Beau."

Her breath came in short jabs that made him ask, "Why?"

She looked hesitant, then resigned. "Someone tried to break in here last night."

Concern shot to the forefront, the note left on his golf bag flashing on his mind like a new steel blade. Had the term bitch referred to Perri, not to Stephanie as he'd assumed? He managed a shrug. "It wasn't me. Must've been Mark."

Her mouth hardened, her gaze darting to the locked door. "How did you get in?"

He smiled. "The maid."

"Well, crap." She eyed the phone, nostrils flaring, revenge cooking. "I'll stop that."

She was never prettier than when incensed. "Give the poor woman a break. I told her we were married, we had a fight, and I'd been looking for you for two weeks."

No reason Perri should know he still carried a picture in his wallet of the two of them on the Louisville courthouse steps, taken on their wedding day, or that he'd used the photo to persuade the motherly maid to unlock the door.

"Damn you, Beau." Her beautiful mouth went sullen. "How did you know I was here?"

"I asked Mark. He keeps up with you."

He attempted to drill her with his stare, but got snared by eyes swimming in gold prisms of light, still a little sleep swollen. Red rimmed. That telltale sign assured him her time-saving ritual of lathering her hair and face with shampoo, sometimes getting it into her eyes, hadn't changed. Against her burnished-bronze skin and water-darkened hair, her eyes seemed more golden and her perfect teeth white as fresh milk. The blood rushed low in his body. The idea she might be battling a similar sensation occurred to him, when she turned away, not so gracefully this time, and not in time to keep him from latching onto her hand. She stiffened, the air crackling like stoked fire.

"Where'd you get that scar?" He brought his eyes up to probe hers. "Looks nasty."

Her gaze shifted to a far wall. "I stumbled on a sprinkler while I was on tour. Surgery left my ankle too weak to torque my swing. That's why I'm here, and not on the women's tour."

"And it's not too weak for carrying the bag?"

"I'm fine. As long as I don't torque," she added grudgingly.

"Sounds like fate set you up, Periwinkle." He got off the bed, his hand moving up to rest lightly in the crook of her arm, not holding, only touching. When she didn't skid backward, he fished the locket out from beneath the towel, knowing she'd worked like hell for weeks to keep him from seeing it. Turning it over in his hand, turning it back, he traced her engraved initials with his thumbnail. "Is my picture still in here?"

She tugged the chunk of gold from his hand, her laugh circumcising his hope. "Let go. I have to get dressed."

Giving her wet tangled hair a gentle tug, he forced a tease into his tone. "Why the modesty? I've seen everything you're trying to hide." He raked his gaze downward, then jerked it up again, grinning. "Inside out, backwards and upside down. I even had a license to look."

"You paid dearly to forego that privilege." She cocked a sable brow.

He determined not to rise to her bait. Not with today's golf yet to be played. "I'd like to debate that, but I'd miss my tee time." Was that relief flickering across her gaze?

"And since I don't have a tee time yet—"

"Relax. I've got one for you."

Easing onto the edge of the bed, she flattened her palm where the towel gapped at her crotch. "Are you match-making again, Beau?"

"Moi?" He shrugged, smiling, since he'd heard more challenge than lack of gratitude.

A brow torqued.

"You've got a tee time with me, if you'll have me."

"Where's Cal?"

He understood her quick frown. She had always loved the old man. "Probably in bed with Silky by now, making up for lost time." He hoped his smile came off with more assurance than he felt. "I put him on the plane for High Meadow this morning."

The frown deepened to a furrow between her brows. "Why?"

"He's not feeling a hundred percent. Too many Camels." And he sure as hell wasn't up to fending off the demented prankster. "The Masters is the premier event. I need maximum caddie support." He sank onto the bed, leaning on an elbow, willing his mission to take priority over the smell of soap and shampoo, silky skin, the caddie's tan marking her forearms, and the warmth of her familiar body. Her clean, shiny face showcased understated, yet exotic, beauty to the hilt. "I need you, Perri. I want you to caddie the Masters for me."

And every other tournament he would ever play, but he'd broach that subject later.

This time her laugh wasn't so caustic. "Are you out of your mind?" She swiped hair away from her cheek, her eyes measuring. "We coached Pete right into losing the Nissan Open."

"That won't happen with me and the Masters."

"Why not?"

He kicked off his loafers, sat up Indian-fashion on the bed, sensing he was gaining ground. "I won't argue club choice with you, just for the sake of argument."

A hesitant smile tugged the corners of her mouth. "So at Riviera you argued just for the sake of it, and Pete was the victim?"

"I was pissed." He shrugged, matching her smile.

The frown furrow edged back. "And suddenly you're not?"

"Not as much." He moved in for the kill. "Let's go to breakfast and talk about this." Or curl up on this bed and abolish all their ghosts, forgive, forget, and love the past away.

She shifted on the bed, her hand fluttering over his locket, then returning to shield her crotch. "Teddy brought me a bagel from the coffee shop." He waited, not knowing if her reply meant no to breakfast or no to the whole proposition. Finally she ventured, "Why me, Beau?"

"You know my game."

"Mark knows your game, and as of an hour ago, he hadn't been hired."

He waited a beat, imagining what the vandal had planned for today. He had a hunch that hiring Mark Zamora would kill any chance of winning the Masters. But the devious, sick, sabotaging bastard—he actually hoped it wasn't Mark—would have a challenge today, since the clubs were locked in the rented Ferrari. He only hoped the subver-

107

sion stopped with equipment, that the note left in
his golf bag was more bluff than threat.

Perri interrupted his ruminating. "Hire Mark.
It's time you two called a truce."

He had a different truce in mind, and only a
prayer of defusing the ticking bomb, somehow convincing her to work with him. "You know my temperament, the way I think." Though she'd never
caddied for him, she'd been there for every shot,
nodding or shaking her head as he reached for a
club. "We made a hell of a team."

A reflective look flickered across her face, one
he couldn't decipher. "That's not how our track
record reads."

He managed a shrug. "Screw that. It's spilled
milk." Or cream. Like her slender throat and the
silky suggestion of breasts above the clutched
towel. "I want to hire you, Periwinkle." He scrambled for his cockiest grin, knowing he treaded on
thin ice. "I didn't play so hot in the pro-am or yesterday, but I'm planning on winning this
sumbitchin tournament." He had to, in order to
advance toward his new goal. "You can be in on it."

Her gaze penetrated, then shifted across the
room, her mouth tightening.

"Yes or no?"

She rose wordlessly, gathered a stack of clothing from a chair, went into the bathroom and half
closed the door.

Crossing to the dingy window, he willed himself
to let her set the pace. Staring at the clubs in the
Ferrari, he found breathing difficult. He heard
deodorant being sprayed, clothing sliding over skin
as tan as a fawn's, clean as a baby's soul. He imagined he heard a bra hooking, and, in his mind's eye
saw her bend from the waist to adjust her breasts
into the cups, the way he'd watched her do in reality hundreds of glorified times. Distinctly, he heard

a zipper slide, then a snap engage and thought of hidden honey-colored hair.

She came out wearing the same short denim skirt and a sawed off T-shirt baring her middle. With a big, wide-toothed comb, she worked on the ends of damp, tangled hair. Widening his stance as if getting ready to hit a long shot, he shored up his will not to beg.

She stopped a few feet away, lowering the comb. "Why am I even considering saying yes to you?"

He drew a breath. "Because I'm a lucky bastard."

"You're a bastard, all right."

He intercepted the barb, smiling tolerantly, catching her hand, snagging her stern gaze.

"I'll give it a try, Beau. The Masters only, for now."

"That's all I ask." Her hand eased away. In the next room, a toilet flushed and then a shower came on. Outside somewhere, laughter pealed. "I'll wait and take you to the course." He could braid her hair. For damn sure, he remembered how. Stephanie could take a cab from the airport. Provided she showed up.

"No." Her voice went flat, as if she'd read his thoughts. "I'll meet you on the range."

Looking down at her, he attempted to plumb the depths of her soul with his eyes, craving to read all her secrets, her reasons, her regrets for leaving him, if any existed. Slowly, he slid his hand beneath her hair and rested it at the base of her neck, then drew her to him, ribcage to ribcage. He walked her backward, pinned her against the door and leaned into her.

She struggled, hands pushing at his chest. Finished denying himself, he took her mouth with fierce possession, tasting, savoring, drinking deep and long. She went rigid. Squirmed. He drank deeper, his hand behind her head, holding her, mastering her, his tongue pushing past the barrier of her denial. The moment she gave, the instant the fight went out of her, he released her.

Her eyes chastised as she raised the backs of her fingers to lips he had bruised. "Nice going. That proves you're stronger than I am."

He nodded. "At least that hasn't changed."

"What else does it prove?"

A hell of a lot. "I wanted to know if you taste the same."

She folded her arms across her breasts, drawing his eyes. She no longer wore the locket. Her eyes glossed over, as flat as her voice. "Do I?"

"Damn right."

She touched her mouth again and he suffered a gush of guilt, among other more ambiguous feelings.

"The privilege of mauling me wasn't included when I agreed to—"

"Right. If you've changed your mind—" His heart raced like a downhill, runaway putt.

She shook her head. "I'll be there."

"Fine."

As he opened the door, rocked by the blast of humidity-drenched Georgia heat, her voice came from behind him. "Practice your one iron, Beau. It's always a winner."

❋

As the cab Perri shared with Mark pulled out of the motel parking lot, she felt his stare and turned to meet his dark, piercing gaze.

He faked a menacing smile. "I'll bet that was the golden boy's Ferrari parked where Sheba would have been if the gods had been kinder."

"If you mean Beau, you're right."

Mark gave her a dangerous, squinty-eyed look that made her knees a little wobbly, even though she told herself he was harmlessly acting out his crush on her. "He must have had a lull in the sex marathon. Did he get what he came after?"

"None of your business." Her heart broke into a tarantella rhythm. If she didn't handle this right, his suspicions would be all over the course by the end of the round. "Actually, he made an offer I couldn't refuse."

"That's what all the satisfied customers say."

"He hired me for the tournament."

His eyes clouded. "So you've rejoined the hierarchy."

"I suggested he hire you, but—"

"He'd rather brag about having you under him than me."

She let the entendre slide. "He doesn't brag. There isn't a boastful bone in his body."

Mark lit a cigarette and rolled down the window. Stifling magnolia-scented air rushed into the cab. A hot wind whipped the ends of her rooster's cock hair style. She dreaded the Masters regulation coveralls she'd soon be donning.

In his street-smart-tough fashion, Mark conceded, "Yeah, I've noticed St. Serious sometimes rents a black Ferrari instead of red. He's got understated class, all right."

Perri laughed. "You like him. You play tough, but you can't hide it."

Squinting, he took a drag from the cigarette, admitting, "He's got guts." He settled against the plastic-draped seat back, elaborating, "I like how when everyone else lays up, playing safe, he goes for the green, come hell or high water. Like he's on some kind of crusade."

"He is," she murmured. "It's his life's mission." Beau's need to win, to achieve worthiness, was visceral, unchanged through the years. The need hinged on his mother, his father, and most of all, on Braden.

"Yeah, maybe." Eyeing her, measuring her, he failed to smile. "And you know what they say about them that's got always getting more. Now he's got you back."

"One tournament doesn't make a contract. We're taking a test."

With a laugh more harsh than amiable, he leaned toward the front seat to entertain the driver with golf tales. As she gazed out the window, the voices droned on the outer edge of her mind, and she put her head back, closing her eyes, Beau's face swimming in the space behind her lids. She felt a stab of nostalgia and closeness. His sweet persistence, his soul-stirring kiss and the insanity of what she had agreed to, packed her consciousness like flowers pressed in a Bible.

When she had exited the bathroom and found him there, she felt strange, disconnected from reality. Her mind had darted through a dozen reasons why, concluding he was about to offer her money to get out of his life again. His bid to have her caddie rocked her with surprise. His claim of remembering them as a hell of a team provoked bitter recall that his failure to take precautions, and her blind love and trust in him, had conceived a defective child.

Today's probing, searing kiss left her confused about his intent, but convinced she still loved him. Not in that blind, sacrificial, worshipful way as before, but in resolved surrender.

But behind today's proposition, she sensed some driving force, and a thread of anger or resentment toward her for making him feel guilty. She detected it in his body language, his depthless gaze, his dominant hands and possessive mouth. If she dropped her guard—if she trusted him—somehow, someway, he would hurt her again. The hurt would penetrate a wound not yet scarred over, perhaps leveling irreparable damage

For Chelsea's sake, and hers, she reaffirmed her vow not to chance being hurt again.

✳

When Perri arrived on the practice range a small crowd of children occupied the bleachers behind Beau's tee. Their expressions adoring and anticipatory, they watched raptly as he flailed ball after ball to the nether regions. Battling painful thoughts of her own guileless daughter, she checked her tank watch. He'd have to cut practice short in order to pass out pre-round Tootsie Roll Pops.

As she made her way across the grassy area, the coveralls rubbed her inner-thighs and rested heavy on her shoulders. May sun broiled down white and merciless enough to bleach the flowering azaleas and towering pines. The top of her head burned from the heat, but she'd left off her cap to get some air, gathering her heavy hair into the biggest banana clip available.

Beau stopped hitting the infamous one iron and greeted her in that old familiar way: a slow smile, eyes fixed on her as she approached. His warm-sherry gaze settled on the top of her head. "Is that thing gonna default in my back swing?"

Still miffed by his kiss, disturbed by its effect, she mumbled, "Play golf, Beau. I'll handle the aesthetics." She rummaged through the golf bag and extracted his driver. "Hit this. I picked up a glitch in your tee shot when I watched you on TV last week."

He leaned on the iron he'd been hitting, wrists crossed at the top of the shaft, a copper bracelet catching the sun. "You watched me last week? I thought you were taking a break."

"I watched the tournament. Your swing was so bad you stood out."

A muscle ticked in his jaw. A shiver of trepidation ran down her spine, but she held her ground,

113

chin jutted, eyes fixed on his. Finally he grinned and set up to the ball she had placed on the tee. When he swung the long, big-headed club, a ridge of back muscles danced beneath his Tommy Bahama shirt. Aching, she dragged her gaze away to follow the trail of the ball.

"There." She stretched to grab his arms and hold them steady at the top of his swing. "Right there. You're breaking down. Is your wrist hurting?"

He pulled out of her grasp. "My wrist is fine."

"Hit another one. I think I know what's happening." A hundred to one, his wrist was the culprit, but she had once credited him with inventing the term, "suffer in silence."

She related her theory, then balanced another ball on a tee. He squared up to it, mouth tight, and hit drive after drive, as perfect as she'd ever seen.

In the five minutes he took to pass out candy, Perri swallowed around the knot in her throat a thousand times. She struggled not to think of Chelsea and Beau in one breath, not to consider what telling him, accepting the help she now knew—from his gentleness with these children— he'd give. As they made their way to the number one tee, she pushed back the notion. Having Braden know would risk too much.

They walked in silence, Perri lugging the bag the cache of distributed candy had done nothing to lighten. Beau strode silently at her side, his heels seeming to strike white-hot sparks as they hit the pavement. She sensed his tensile alertness and followed his gaze to the horde of mulling media between them and the tee box. Understanding his sudden rigidity, she experienced a curious sort of closeness again, reluctant protectiveness.

"I guess you know you're paired with Pete."

"That's good."

"We aren't going to help him try to beat you." He shot her a glance, and she added, "Are we?"

"No way. It's every man for himself." He grinned. "Even Pete."

His steps faltered, and she shifted the bag to the ground. As the press approached, he dug in a side pocket of the bag, extracted a ball and a new glove. He shoved the ball into his pocket and pulled the glove onto his hand, forming a fist, flexing. Her mind went back to Nike Tour days, to his ritual of storing the last ball he used each day in the glove he'd worn, planning to use them to start the next day's round. A good luck ritual. Apparently Beau no longer relied on Nike Tour rituals.

A mini-cam whined as an amiable sportscaster she recognized from last night's news thrust a mike in Beau's face and needled him about yesterday's bad play.

Smiling, Beau unwrapped a stick of Dentine and eased it into his mouth. "The first day is when we can relax and have a little fun before we have to buckle down and make the cut."

He might as well have spoken Swahili. The mike inched closer. "You didn't get your nickname relaxing and having fun. You were struggling. What seemed to be the problem?"

Perri refrained from asking if the man could break seventy.

"Focus." Beau shrugged. "I had some things on my mind. All that's been cleared up."

The journalist took up what had become media obsession: Could Tiger Woods be beaten?

On the tee, Pete watched and waited. Beau waved. "Tiger's the man to beat, all right. But considering the winning streak I'm on, he's probably thinking the same thing about me."

"What do you plan to do about Woods the next two days, provided you make the cut?"

The cameraman leaned forward, aiming the camera at Beau's soft brown eyes.

Perri's nape crawled. "Beau St. Cyr played in the Masters before Tiger Woods had a driver's license."

She felt Beau's surprise, then caught his validating grin. An alien surge of pride coupled with a bolt of confidence moved through Perri. She glared at the journalist, arms folded, stance wide under the weight of the bag. "We're up, Beau." She gave his back pocket a single tug.

"My partner has spoken." He awarded her a quick, conspiratorial smile. "Thank you, gentlemen. See you in the press tent."

On the tee, Beau and Pete shook hands, then slapped backs. "Whatcha usin'?" Pete drawled, tossing his ball in the air, catching it, showing the label to Beau. "I've got Maxfli 2s."

"Titleist 4s. What else?"

"You need a little variety in your life. You know that, Beau Jangles?"

"I like consistency."

As Beau ambled to the tee amid brief, impulsive applause, Perri quietly rummaged in the bag for extra balls to initial. Whap. Her gaze followed a streak of white slashing the metallic-blue sky. Having found no balls, she shouldered the bag and trailed after his perfect drive. While they waited wordlessly for Pete to hit his second shot, she searched the bag again. Nothing. She thought of the hoard of balls on the range, illegal, off limits.

"What are you looking for?" he whispered into a burdensome quiet broken only by an arrogant bird in a nearby live oak. How could the multitude lining the fairway be so silent?

"Candy. My throat's dry." Her heart accelerated a beat with the lie.

He smiled. "Mine, too."

As he strode to his drive, her hand darted ser-
pent-like through the candy pocket, sweat seeping
into her hairline. Where the hell did Cal store the
balls? She caught up to Beau, extracting his one
iron like a sword from a sheath and passed it to
him, meeting his gaze head on.

His brow furrowed. "You okay, hon?"

"Fine." She plopped the bag down, slithered
Carmex onto her suddenly parched lips and stared
at the distant green, attempting to shut out the
threat of water on the left. Her fear had to be
ungrounded. Somewhere in its many pockets the
bag secreted enough Titleist 4s to play out the
round. Stop playing games, God. I need money,
Beau needs to win. Where are the balls?"

As he took his stance, her hand stole to the one
pocket she hadn't checked, the long, slender,
empty umbrella pocket. Perfect for a few sleeves of
balls. Her fingertips seized the zipper pull and
worked it south. Beau's back swing froze. With a
long, level stare, he lowered his arms slowly, one
auburn brow cocked. "Light, will you, firefly? Till I
can hit the ball?"

Heat shot through her body. "Sorry. I'd fade
the ball right of the pin. No sense in flirting with
that pond."

He did just that, beautifully and skillfully, body
arched in a heart-tugging, pelvic-tickling perfect
follow through. She ripped her gaze away and
breathed a little easier. Five holes later, the ball
she'd accepted as being the only one they possessed took a bad bounce and rolled into a brook
alongside the fairway. "Damn," Beau commented,
mouth grim, eyes narrowed.

Her heart rose to her throat. "I'll bet you can
hit it out of there and save taking a penalty drop. I
walked the course yesterday after I arrived. That
brook's not very deep."

"In your dreams, Periwinkle." He grinned. But like a little boy taking a dare, he did just that, laying up in perfect position to secure his par.

While they waited out Pete's shot, she rifled in the bag again, and in the deep dark cavern her hand clamped around something rough as hemp, yet supple as a tobacco pouch, and wrapping a solid, round object. Heart pounding, vision blurred, she withdrew a glove so weathered and discolored it could have survived the Nike era. Inside was—please, God—a Titleist! The ball was old and scarred, but her mind registered nothing other than the stamped-on number 4.

When Beau's ball went in the water for real on number nine, she waited until they reached the drop area beside the lake to hand him the scavenged battle-weary ball. Avoiding his eyes, she rattled and shoved clubs around in the bag, looking for the four iron.

"What's this?" He held the ball in his open palm, eyeing it as if it had rolled through squirrel dung, and then looked at her with the same skepticism.

"Where's your four iron?"

He hesitated, looking culpable. "I left it in the car trunk."

"Why, for God's sake? You need it here." Her voice screeched a little.

"What's this?" He held the suspect ball practically under her nose. "I can't hit this. Give me a new ball."

"Hit it. It'll bring you good luck." Her gaze skewered his. "Like in the old days."

"I don't need good luck. I need a ball that hasn't been buried for eight years."

He bent as if to search the bag. Across the fairway, Pete waited and watched, swinging his arms with no club in his hands. Perri insinuated her hip between Beau and the bag.

118

"You need your four iron to go with that vintage Titleist 4. Why'd you take it out?"

"To lighten the bag for you, okay? So don't waste any time looking for the extra wedge either." He looked away, then back. "Or my two iron either." His tanned cheeks took on a rosy glow. "Give me a damn ball, Perri, before they call the five minute time limit on us."

"We have no more balls." She kept her voice low, unable to look at him, impacted by the fact he'd handicapped himself for her. "You'll have to hit that, Beau. Hit it very carefully."

"What the hell do you mean, no more? What did you—"

"Me? I never touched this friggin' bag until an hour ago. If you've got a problem with no balls, whip out your handy cellular and call Cal. Ask him."

A multi-faceted expression played about his face. Panic. Knowing. Resolve. "Calm down." He held the ball at arms length, dropped it gently and watched it roll dangerously close to the water. "Give me my five iron, and wish this mother onto the green." His eyes, hard mahogany now, sought hers. "We'll discuss blame later."

No more words passed between them. Like an automaton, she handed him clubs and he executed robot-like, precision shots that extracted verbal awe from the stampeding gallery. Yet discovering the balls missing had rattled him. While she credited the loss to Cal's age, his forgetfulness, and eagerness to get home to Silky, the brackets around Beau's exquisite mouth deepened, his full lips pulling across his teeth. The target of his ire she was unsure of, but the absurdity of blaming her rankled, washing out the respect he'd gained by eliminating clubs.

On the green, he squatted to study the hole, thighs bulging inside his pant legs. She looked away, denying want and need as she worked at cleaning the ball with a dampened towel.

When she handed him the ball he aligned it to the hole and stood aside, his putter swinging gently like the pendulum on the antique clock in Braden's study eight years ago.

"Six inches outside left, Beau. Uphill till that swell in front of the pin, then it'll run like a sailor to a wh—"

His head jerked up. She swallowed the simile he had taught her when golf was still a game, when their love was as fresh and unmarred as her virgin thighs.

"In your nightmares." He stepped over the ball and stroked it. It crept to the swell and over, then streaked into the hole with a clunk. He gave her a grin. "But in my dreams."

As they neared the clubhouse, approaching the turn onto the back nine, she ventured, "Want me to get more balls from your locker?" Or from the Ferrari, parked in the VIP lot? From hook or crook or from the pro shop with her last five twenty dollars?

He looked at her as though she'd sprouted horns and a tail. She had asked an asinine question. Once a pro left the clubhouse he played with the balls in his bag. Same brand and number. The rule didn't get bent, even for golden boys like Beau St. Cyr. She cursed herself for the equally asinine guilt churning her stomach, then left the fairway to stroll the rough, far enough out to spy anything the caddies, chipmunks or squirrels might've missed.

"You'll step on a snake. Get back over here." He used his known-you-since-you-wore-braces tone. "What the hell are you doing?"

"Looking for balls. What else?" Stung by his abrasive frustration, she vowed he could go to hell and take his incessant, insatiable desire to win with him. "You just figure out how to hold onto the one you've got."

"You know even if you find one I can't hit anything that didn't come out of my bag."

When had he become so pious? He'd had no trouble deceiving her. "So we'll cheat."

His laugh contained less humor than gears stripping. "Well unless you find a Titleist 4, leave the son of a bitch in there for the next poor bastard who's been sabotaged."

"That's a little harsh," she hissed. "I doubt Cal set out to sabotage—"

He held up an open palm, his eyes a little wild. Continuing her forage, she decided to punish him with silence.

Pete strolled up beside her, careful to stay in the fairway. "Whatcha doin' in there?" "Cleaning my shoes on the grass. I stepped in some mud."

"They don't allow mud at the Masters." He grinned flippantly "You looking for balls? Used ones don't bring much around here, if selling em's what you have in mind."

She searched for another excuse, anything other than the truth. Beau didn't need the pressure of Pete worrying about him. "It's shadier over here under the trees." In her side vision, Beau veered to the right as if to give her and Pete privacy. She tried changing the subject. "You're playing good. Keep it up, and you've got the cut cinched."

"Thanks. If I make it, you want to go to the party tonight?" She felt his close scrutiny, but sensed only casualness. "Big doings at the clubhouse to kick off the next two days' play."

Her spine tingled, memory rushing back to her days at Owl Creek. "Caddies aren't allowed to attend those parties." Nor the hired help, like Lee Hardin. She could still feel his bitterness, hear his scorn, recall Angie's longing.

"If I make the cut, they'll welcome anyone I bring as my guest."

She weighed that, wondering why he'd chosen her.

"What do you say? Wanta go?"

She kicked grass. "Thank you for asking, Pete, but I don't date married men." Or hang out with disloyal husbands. Normally.

He guffawed. "What's this date crap? I hate partying alone, and I'll bet you're tired of watching ESPN and reading *Ebony*. We might as well sample some of these rich bastards' Dom Perignon." He flashed a cajoling smile. "Anyway, I've got Paula's blessing. When I make a cut, she wouldn't care if I took the real Halle Berry long's the check's in the mail."

Perri bent to scoop a ball from the tall grass, examined it and tossed it aside.

Pete hiked a brow. "You're pretty choosy about your balls, aren't you?"

Glancing at Beau's broad back ahead of them, she murmured, "That one had a cut in it."

Pete's gaze trailed hers, then returned to her face. "Beau can't take you to the party. Stephanie's in town. She's a party animal, and she's not into sharing her man."

Stephanie. Perri made a quick, wild search of the gallery, looking for someone who fit Teddy's description of Ms. Current Favorite who drank mint juleps wearing sandals with gold rings around her toes. If she was attending the Masters, where the hell was she? Beau needed support. A lot more support than Perri wanted to risk giving. "Call me at caddie heaven, tonight. I'll see how I feel after the round."

On the ominous twelfth hole the ball dilemma came to a head. For lack of the sacrificed four iron, Beau squared up to the ball with his five wood. A zealous fan snapped a camera during his back-

swing. With the grace of a gull after a fish, the ball
dived into water just short of the famed Hogan's
Bridge. The gallery's stunned moan hung a perfect
backdrop for the splash and residual water circles.
Perri and Beau stood staring.

"I've got it," she breathed, to herself more than
to him.

"No, I've had it. It's gone." His voice barely carried above a cheer on a distant green.

Her heart quailed; then she hardened it. She
began walking, gaze glued to the path of entry. As
she stalked, she rolled the sleeves on the coveralls,
then freed her hair and shoved the banana clip into
a bag pocket that should have been crammed with
Titleist 4s.

"Perri!" Beau called from behind her.

She sped to a lope, the bag's cumbersome
weight preventing a full run. On the creek bank,
she dropped the bag, kicked off her Nikes, and bent
to roll up her pants legs. Beau caught up as she
stripped off her socks. He grasped her arm,
whirling her around. She shoved him off, fighting
not to lose sight of the last row of ripples forming
far out in the water "Let it go, Perri."

She found breathing abnormally difficult. "I
know exactly where it is." She needed that ball,
needed what his win could do for her, but not nearly as much as he needed to win.

"That creek is full of balls. You'll never find
mine. It's over."

She wrestled free and jumped flat-footed into
waist-high water.

"Jesus, baby." He moaned a resurrected
endearment. "At least take off those damned coveralls. You'll be wet the rest of the day."

She took a step forward, mud oozing between
her scrunched up toes.

"They're too heavy. They'll pull you under." He raised his voice as she edged away. "Get rid of the coveralls, Perri." An order.

Behind him, a cameraman raced up the fairway, camera jostling on his shoulder. He skidded in behind Beau, so close she could hear his strident breath. He steadied the red blinking light on the two of them. Outside the ropes, the crowd milled and thrummed in speculation.

She took a bead on her target, risked a glance at Beau over her shoulder, waded forward gulping humid, magnolia-flavored air, and slipped beneath the cool, dark water.

CHAPTER NINE

In Beau's mind, eternity passed before Perri emerged clutching an armload of balls against her breasts. She cleared hair out of her mouth and eyes with her free hand, then swam with one arm, kicking vigorously until she was near enough to the bank to toss out her catch. Before he could say thanks, or offer his hand, she ducked beneath the water again.

Cursing under his breath, aware of the camera grinding away, he searched the cache of balls like a Hoover on the prowl, eyes straining for the yellowed Titleist 4.

Pete strolled up. "Why don't you just drop one? Or have you lost your fucking mind?"

Beau shot him a look he hoped could seal an acid tank. He peered anxiously at the creek, eyes straining, imagining a form below the swirling water's surface. A breeze kicked up, stirring the collar of his shirt, ruffling the hair at the back of his neck. That's it. I'm going in after her.

Perri's head bobbed and the gallery applauded on cue. They had no way of knowing the reason behind her mission, but had adopted the spirit of the hunt. She swam purposely, tossed her new yield onto shore and climbed out. Without taking a moment to breathe, she scrambled on hands and knees and joined Beau's search.

"Christ, Beau," Pete grumbled from overhead. "Time's racing. Hit another one."

"How about some help?" Beau kept his eyes on the pile, voice low. Pete sank to his haunches and began raking an obligatory finger through the pile, mumbling obscenities.

"If it's not in here, I'll go back," Perri panted.

Liking that, the cameraman stooped and duck-walked closer.

"No time." Beau ground out a hoarse whisper. His hands and Perri's worked like maggots on road kill. "If it's not in here we're screwed."

She awarded him a look of disgust. "Shut up and look, Beau. It's in here."

Pete and the cameraman shared a laugh.

A pair of wingtips appeared in Beau's downcast vision. He kept his eyes on his task.

"You have less than a minute, Mr. St. Cyr," the official warned.

"Thank you, sir."

"We have watches and we can tell time, you—" Before the classification could clear Perri's lips, she yipped with delight, her wet hand seizing a muddy ball, then thrusting it toward the official's shins. Beau grabbed her wrist before mud marked the khaki pants. She looked up, eyes full of sun prisms, lashes clumped with creek water. "Here it is," she announced triumphantly. "You can turn off the stop watch."

They stood. She wiped the ball on her coveralls and held it out to the man in the wrinkled blazer.

"Unless that's the same ball . . . " He ventured in a molasses drawl before Perri's look castrated his warning.

Leisurely, she turned the errant ball to the new marking she had apparently applied while Beau played golf, thinking he had a bag full of balls and the world by the testicles.

Allowing a full breath, Beau willed himself not to touch her, not to jerk her into his arms and vow his eternal love and gratitude. Instead he searched the official's face until he saw concession. When Pete and Perri stepped aside, he took his penalty drop, accepted a sand wedge from Perri and eyed the pin, some seventy yards away. The little voice in his head kicked in, reminding him he'd promised Perri he was going to win this tournament.

"The green rolls left to right, Beau." Her voice was hushed, still rattly from the water.

Their gazes locked. "You think so, huh, partner?"

"I know so." She didn't smile.

The ball landed on the verdant surface, rested like God on Sunday, then began a slow trek toward the hole. The gallery packing the bleachers sucked in breath. Then a unified moan evolved to an ear-shattering cheer as the hallowed yellow ball trickled into the cup.

"Son of a friggin' bitch," Pete said.

Beau slapped Pete's back. "Your lesson for the day. Never underestimate a woman." He waited for Perri to look at him; she hoisted the bag and trudged toward his miracle par.

From the fifteenth fairway, while Pete searched for his own ball in a dogwood forest, Beau focused on the green, wrestling the inner voice's badgering. Never before had he realized how many water hazards came into play at Augusta National. He needed to reach the green in two, then two putt for a birdie. Hell, maybe he'd one putt and guarantee making the cut here and now. But, the voice warned that with only one ball in inventory he couldn't chance going for the green. He had to play safe and settle for par. His gut writhed. His wrist throbbed. Braden's face swam just back of his briefly closed eyes.

"Go for it."

For an instant he thought the voice in his head had spoken aloud. He opened his eyes.

"I've seen you hit shots like this a million times, Beau." Her eyes glittered. A smile trembled on pretty lips still a little blue from the cold water.

"I can't risk it, with just one ball."

He had to get to the bottom of this sick puzzle. First clubs. Now balls. Someone had it in for him, big time. And after the attempted break-in at Perri's room last night, her welfare had to be considered. The crazy bastard might even be watching them now. Probably not, though, since Zamora was on another hole.

He jerked his mind back to the issue at hand. Focus. Just focus on the game. "I have to lay up. Makes me want to puke, but . . . ." He shrugged and smiled, his gaze latching onto hers and holding like a magnet to steel.

"If you miss, I'll dive for it." Her smile came slower than grass growing; probably still pissed over his earlier bad temper. "But try to hit it closer to the bank. Okay?"

"Got it." Praying, he took the club back and down, and laid the ball in for a sure birdie.

"Child's play," she quipped on a raspy breath.

He handed back the club. "Easy for you to say."

Eyes grave again, she shouldered the bag, giving off rhythmic squishy sounds as they walked side by side up the fairway.

He broke down, asking the nagging question. "Why didn't you take off the coveralls?"

"I had my reasons." Her burden aborted her attempt at a shrug.

She stepped out in front of him a bit, as if to distance his query. When she turned to the side slightly, rummaging in the bag for only God knew what, wet fabric clung to the mound of her breast. Imagination let him envision a dusky circle around a pert nipple. Or was it imagination? He experienced much the same sensation as when he'd come home that summer and she had aged from fifteen to sixteen—with breasts.

His gaze drifted south. Like a wet sheet, the coveralls wrapped her firm little rear, outlining the pronounced curve on her cheeks into the backs of

her thighs. Imagination didn't apply. Focus, fool,
on the game, on the shot coming up.

He risked a glance at his crotch. That birdie
would be damn hard to come by now that he'd have
to putt around Woody, a condition growing ever
more chronic in Perri's presence.

✳

In the hushed atmosphere of the legendary
Eisenhower Cabin, Beau lounged in an upholstered
Chippendale chair, watching the television crew fill
the room with a bristle of cables and light poles. In
a twin chair beside him, her dried coveralls emitting a fishy odor, Perri worked at arranging her hair
into a quick, loose braid. He could feel her body
manipulations, but since the braid ritual had
always been a favorite of his and Woody's, he did-
n't chance watching. Instead, he surveyed his hallowed surroundings, picturing the golfers, as legendary as the room, who had gone before him, the
ones who would come after, some not yet born.

But the crap was about to hit the fan. He'd bet
that Braden was glued to the television at High
Meadow. Braden and Nonna. Silky and Cal. The
kitchen help and the stable hands, out in the barn.
The whole world was about to know Beau St. Cyr.
had made this year's Masters' cut, how he'd made
it, and who he'd be forever indebted to. Most likely, Braden had phone in hand, Beau's cellular
number already dialed, except for the last number,
which he'd punch the instant the television cameras faded off him and Perri, and to a final Footjoy
commercial.

He heard a snap and turned to see Perri drape
the braid over one shoulder, down over one breast,
the big tortoiseshell clip holding the loose ends in
place. The tip of her nose boasted new freckles. In
the lights from the television lamps, her skin
glowed like warm caramel, reminding him of morn-
ings when he had wakened to bright sunlight in

129

alien hotel rooms that seemed like home simply because Perri lay in his arms. She was classic, his annulled wife, and as he watched her, he felt a jumble of emotions: tenderness and resentment, lust and confusion, anger and longing. In view of the task they were about to share, he tried to focus on today's events.

She had always been a scrapper, a hustler. He'd seen that in the way she progressed from never holding a golf club to starring on the Owl Creek team, then being the only girl on her high school golf team. She was scrapping on the tour now, hustling high paying jobs for whatever the hell reasons. But apart from that mystery, he liked the way she'd gone to bat for him with the media, how she'd stood up to the PGA official. Loyalty, his mind chanted. She rated top marks when it came to unswerving devotion to the cause. Despite their years apart, the bonds they'd shared were as strong as ever. He told himself to dwell on that, rather than the way today's loyalty contrasted with her past desertion.

She turned to face him suddenly, face warming, color deepening, as though she'd felt him mentally stripping her, viewing her motives, her intent, her soul.

"Nervous?" He kept his voice low, rolling his eyes toward the cameras and the sports anchor in a crisp blue blazer and white pleated trousers who was about to interview them.

She nodded, teeth catching her lip for a moment. Nothing else. Just enough to revive every protective feeling he'd ever had for her. For one stolen instant, he covered her hand with his where it gripped the chair arm, for across the room, sequestered with spouses and hangers-on, Stephanie watched, her greedy-bird eyes alert. Suspicious, as she had every right to be.

"Ready?" Peter Kostis moved into a chair across from Beau and Perri, crossed his legs, aligned the creases in his pristine pants and settled back. A media veteran. Feeling Perri go taut, Beau shifted in his chair until he made a whisper of contact, his shoulder to hers. She ran supple.

"Ready," they chorused.

"Remember to talk to the red camera eye, not to me or each other." Peter signaled the cameraman. "Good afternoon. I'm Peter Kostis," he said needlessly. "I was lucky to catch Beau St. Cyr and his caddie after a memorable round where he rallied from being buried in the pack and made the cut with room to spare."

His gaze speared Beau's as he launched into a spiel lauding Tiger Woods, second-guessing Beau's chance of winning with Tiger in the field. Perri tensed again, shifting in her seat. She crossed her legs and swung a muddy Nike. But discovering he couldn't rile Beau, Kostis drifted back to the reason they'd been invited to the Eisenhower Cabin.

"You had some trouble with balls out there today, Beau."

Beau could afford to laugh now. "I'd say."

"What happened?" Peter looked at Perri, then back to Beau, mouth twitching.

Beau exchanged a long, loaded look with Perri. "We're not sure. We're working on it." He damn sure didn't need all of golf-loving America speculating on the cause or the culprit.

"Well, thanks to..." Kostis fumbled, coming up with the name from the cue screen. "...Perri, all's well that ends well."

"She saved my butt." Forgetting instruction, Beau looked directly into her eyes.

Her voice soft and melodious, she said, "I found the ball. Beau did the rest."

Across the room, Stephanie sank onto a window ledge, hands braced on either side, and crossed her ankles. The gold rings holding her sandals on gleamed in the sunlight. Her little red Chanel bag banged her sharp hip. She caught his eye and glared. Stephanie was nobody's fool. She knew his and Perri's history, knew he'd never gotten over the breakup. She'd bought into believing she could change his mind. She hadn't succeeded, yet she didn't deserve to be hurt. Confusion, guilt, and something close to desperation swirled in his head.

"I have to ask this question," Peter announced.

Beau nodded, knowing, wondering about, and imagining the outcome.

Peter and the camera shifted to Perri. "Why did you go in the water in those coveralls?" He wrinkled his nose in an upper crust, comical rebuke, then went for drama. "They're so heavy, and so big, they could have filled with water and drowned you."

Silence fell. Perri looked at Beau, disregarding the camera, rejecting protocol. Consumed with his own curiosity, he made a deferring gesture with his hand. He aimed his grin at her, not the red eye. If she didn't care about the script, neither did he.

"Golf balls weren't all we were short of." She returned his smile before eventually facing the camera. "In fact, we had more balls than underwear."

Peter sat silent, one brow cocked. A half smile formed as his gaze bounced between them. "Pardon?"

She gave a slight tug on the front of the coveralls. "I'm naked under here."

Laughter rolled over the room, warm as sunrise over Rae's Creek.

Kostis turned his full attention to the camera. "There you have it, golf fans. Mystery solved." He turned back to Beau and extended a hand. "Good luck tomorrow."

Beau shook the proffered hand. "Thanks. I'll need it." I plan to whip Tiger royally.

Kostis grinned. "If your old caddie comes back, pretend you don't recognize him."

Before Beau could utter a word in Cal's behalf, Kostis signaled and the red eye turned black, dismissing the interviewees. Stephanie bolted upright, broke ranks and moved toward Beau. Perri shot out of her chair. Beau reached for her, but she eased away. He couldn't very well hang on, not while a room filled with people watched his fiancée's approach. He could do or say none of the things he wanted to do or say. "Wait, Perri. I'll introduce you to Stephanie."

"No thanks, St. Serious," she whispered, smiling as though still on camera. Gracefully, coveralls swishing, Nikes plopping, she brushed past him and out the door.

He swore in his mind, hunger ripping his body, settling in his loins. The next place he wanted her loyalty and devotion was beneath him in bed. Screw the past and the consequences.

✳

Perri Harden. Braden snapped off the TV. So that's it. Beau's erratic play, his occasional vagueness, the reason he sent Cal home against my wishes. He pitched the remote onto the cocktail table. Winonna's frail body jerked with the reverberating clatter. Curiosity nestled in her eyes as she resettled wordlessly into the petit-point chair.

Memory of his recent trip to New Orleans penetrated the shock of what he'd just viewed. Suddenly the focus of Beau's distant, preoccupied stare, the way he had vacillated between surliness one minute, indifference the next, no longer presented a mystery.

Christ! Thanks to her high color and show-off antics, Lee Hardin's strident, greedy daughter had usurped Beau's limelight on the course. Then in a nationally televised interview, she'd repeated the faux pas with a delicate beauty and saucy sexiness Braden was not too old to recognize. The little brown minx had held Beau captive since adolescence when she had developed her mother's sass and curves and Hardin's good looks and phony affability. Braden's bribe had bought Beau a reprieve, but now she was back. How far had the reunion gone? Had she and Beau exchanged stories? Instead of Beau sleeping with the enemy, was the enemy now Braden? His blood ran cold as a crypt.

Shoving off the sofa, he headed for the armoire that held the liquor.

"Ready for your toddy?" He forced a lilt into his voice, glancing back at Winonna. Sun filtering through the slanted shutters turned her graying auburn hair to pink taffy, a pleasant contrast to the yellow cast of her skin. With a dubious look, she glanced at the grandfather clock in the corner, and he coaxed, "It's a little early, but we'll celebrate Beau making the cut." He poured her scotch tall and light, the way she liked it, then splashed three fingers of amber in a chilled glass for himself, disinclined to dilute it with ice.

Thus far, Winonna's reaction to the TV spectacle had been, "Look, Braden. Isn't that the little Hardin girl that Beau married?" As if his gaze hadn't been riveted to the screen.

Winonna had sat tense, her shoulders round until Perri surfaced, swam, dragged her soggy self from the creek and helped Beau claw through the stack of muddy balls on the ground. When the one they sought surfaced, Winonna whispered trance-like, "She's found it. I declare!"

During the interview, Winonna had sat mute, attuned to his agitation, Braden suspected.

Beau was right about Perri saving his ass. But any fool could see his aim was to get that celebrated ass into her bed—if he hadn't already—and in the long run, that would undo him. Beau needed a woman. Braden had enough life left in him to know that, but not Perri Hardin.

As he handed Winonna her cocktail, she spoke wistfully, her head back at the Augusta circus. "She's still such a pretty little thing." Tilting her head upward, she smiled coyly. "Don't you think so, Granddaddy?"

"Too coarse for my taste," he grudged into his scotch.

He watched her mull that over in her mind, sipping gingerly on the single cocktail she'd have before her glass of wine at dinner. "Yes, well...." Typically softening her disagreement.

"She's a gold-digging strumpet."

Winonna's aged-lioness eyes turned wistful. "It seems a shame that she and Beau..." She shook her head, gazing at a limp, liver-spotted hand. "A real shame."

His memory reeled backward. He had secured Winonna's promise to never discuss the annulment with Beau by telling her he hurt too badly, that she'd only damage him more by saying the wrong things, that she'd end up offering him sympathy rather than solution. Evidently her sentiments hadn't altered with time.

He made his way back to the liquor cabinet, wanting more scotch, settling for ice. Leaning a shoulder against the window frame, he stared out at the putting green. A child's laughter, a mother's grief, a younger woman's sobs, a young man's disbelief echoed in his head.

"I wonder where Stephanie is," Winonna said absently, swirling her drink, readjusting the linen cocktail napkin that kept the chill from her gnarled hand. "She called, don't you know, to say she was on her way to Augusta, and she hoped to have a date for me when she returned to Nashville." To

Braden's vacant stare, she added, "A wedding date, Granddaddy. It seems she and Beau can't agree on one that fits both their schedules." She smiled to herself, entertaining some hidden image Braden wasn't privileged to. "What's the world coming to, I wonder, when children can't find the time to get married?"

Nor the need. Why buy the cow when you're getting milk through the fence? And as for Stephanie, Braden hoped the hell she was back at Beau's hotel preparing to greet the warrior as he deserved, eager to reap the spoils of his victory instead of going to battle alongside him. He hoped she bowed to his male rights, rather than extrapolating some new-age female philosophy on him of how he couldn't have triumphed without her.

Saved his butt be damned. National TV was no place for a golf icon like Beau St. Cyr to admit as much. He voiced his foremost thought. "I wonder how long she's been there?"

"Who dear?" Winonna's eyes fogged.

"Perri." He tried to hide his impatience. "How long has this been going on?"

"Caddying, you mean?"

He felt like the lonely captain of a sinking yacht. "I'll send one of the yard boys over to Lee Hardin's nursery to see if he can pick up anything on what she's doing there." Other than invading Beau's life, dislodging it from its axis. "Or Silky can accidentally bump into Angie at the market. She'll talk."

But first he'd talk to Cal, find out how premeditated Cal's leaving Beau and showing up at High Meadow had been. He had to find out how much Beau knew and how he planned to use the information. Damn.

The ringing phone, a conduit that locked his gaze to Winonna's, pierced the quiet.

"That's Beau." Her tone carried a familiar sense of marvel. "I want to talk to him, too."

Braden knew Beau wasn't the caller. Not only the sixth sense barbing his spine and setting his heart to race, but rationality told him he'd be the last one Beau would want to talk to after the interview. Still he strode to the phone, seized it and answered with a swell of hope.

"I thought you might be wanting to hear from me."

He had heard the voice only once before, yet had no problem with recognition. Something almost sinister quickened his head and chest. "Why would I?"

The mirthless laugh emerged. "What did you think of today's little show? Surprised?"

Braden avoided Winonna's eager gaze. "Damned surprised." More laughter. Braden's neck glowed like smoldering coals.

"Ready to do some business, sir?"

Again, his mind groped for a clue. Regional inflection, speech characteristic. He heard nothing other than politeness uncommon to a harasser. He'd never been so aware of his wife's presence, her innocent trust in him to take care of them and theirs. "What kind of business do you have in mind?"

A brief silence ensued, broken by voices in the background and muffled by a hand over the mouthpiece, Braden thought. The caller came back on the line. "How about if I do a better job of getting rid of her than you did?"

Panic seized him. No other word in Webster's thick, hallowed book fit the feeling. "What are you basing that on, if I may ask?"

"'Scuse me?"

"I believe you used the term, `better than I did.'"

Laugher again, sounding genuine now. "The old lady must be listening."

Braden's spine stiffened. He risked a glance at Winonna, who, apparently having decided the caller was not Beau, gazed into the distance, for-lorn.

"And she doesn't know about all that happened back then, huh? Figures. Looks like you've woven yourself a tangled web, Mr. St. Cyr."

Braden could think of nothing more distinct or devious to say than, "Did you understand my question?"

"You mean like how'd I know you ran a sting on the lovers? I made an analytical guess, I guess." He chuckled softly. "But don't you worry, sir. Beau doesn't know what hit him."

Braden thought he heard the snap of a cigarette lighter, an intake of breath, then a release. He imagined smoke swirling in the close quarters of a sequestered, graffiti-etched phone shell.

"And your secret's safe with me, Mr. St. Cyr." Another deep, sucking sound. "For now. If that's what you're worried about."

"I'm not worried." The lie reverberated in his head, like a hard-driven putt rattling in a metal cup. Bile torched his ulcerated stomach.

"Then I'm wasting my nickel. Maybe I should be talking to Beau."

Heart hammering his ears, Braden willed himself to silence.

"Or talking to your ex-granddaughter-in-law, maybe, and let her break the news to him. Nothing bonds two people like a little shared victimization. Ever notice that?"

"No, don't." He swallowed, hoping the man hadn't heard the croak wrapping the protest. "That wouldn't be the best way to handle this."

Winonna stirred and then rose stodgily from the sofa. Braden's hand squeezed the phone, but she shuffled off in the other direction before turning to whisper, "If Beau does call, I'll talk to him in my room."

He released pent-up breath. "I can talk. Where's this leading? Do you want money?"

"No way. I'm prepared to do you a favor, gratis."

"What kind of favor?"

"Get rid of her, like I said."

"How?"

"I'll make her look like a bimbo. She'll make so many mistakes, he'll have to fire her."

"That won't work." Beau had protected her from the start. He'd find excuses, reasons for her ineptitude. Or for challenge, play so well she couldn't screw him up. Besides that, Perri Hardin knew golf as well or better than Beau. "You'll have to think of something else."

"You leave that to me."

"I don't want any harm to come to her. Bodily harm, I mean."

"Somehow I didn't think you would, sir."

He almost felt like thanking the sinister bastard. "As long as that's understood."

"I'll get right on it. Tonight, in fact. I'll call you later. Or maybe I won't have to. Just keep watching television."

"What are you getting out of this?"

Another click of a lighter, a drawn and released breath. Finally, "Satisfaction."

What had Beau ever done to cause this? Then he realized it didn't matter. Whatever the end this bastard had planned, he, Braden, had given him the means to accomplish it. An ominous buzz filled his ear. His first thought was to call Beau. He shuffled through notes on the burl-wood desk, looking for the hotel number in Augusta. Too soon. He wouldn't have reached the hotel. Automatically, his finger punched out Beau's cell number, then quickly pushed the disconnect button.

Let it go for now, he told himself. Don't expose your hand when you don't know which cards the girl holds. If she and Beau have compared stories, if Beau knows, let him come to you. By then, if the caller can be trusted—the irony of that curdled his stomach—reticence may have been the best wager. Suddenly the adage, suffer in silence, took on new meaning.

＊

So the original friggin' plan to sabotage Beau's game had ricocheted into total backfire. Might as well call a spade a shovel. After the CBS interview, anybody who cared a flying fig about golf knew Beau St. Cyr had played today's round with one ball. He'd made the cut with the one goddamned ball that had somehow been overlooked during that last rapid-fire bag search that Cal Johnson's senility had allowed. With Beau taking responsibility for his clubs, keeping them locked in his car, opportunity to pilfer wouldn't happen again. Not unless getting next to the new and improved version of Esther Williams proved easier than her cool-shit actions indicated. Time to give the bitch a few inches, all right, just enough to make her squirm. But unless he missed his guess, the little bit it took to make her squirm would be more than enough to turn St. Serious wrong side out.

But the old man didn't want anybody hurt. Just fucked up. Royally.

The old bastard had qualms, which was kind of touching, considering the way he'd screwed Golden Boy and Bitch Beautiful in the past. But like all control freaks, Granddad wanted his way. He wanted her out of there, wanted his pretty boy puppet back, dangling on the right string. But now Gramps was playing in a new foursome, and he had to hole out, or forfeit. It was fucking time an underling got a St. Cyr on the ropes, even if it was only the old man.

For now.

ℛ

CHAPTER TEN

In the lobby of the hallowed Augusta Country Club, Perri hung up the phone. Hinging on Angie's news, wariness settled into the back of her mind. Larry wanted her to move to New Mexico with him. Fresh memory of Chelsea's bubbly laugh echoed in Perri's ears, giving her strength to push out of her cushiony chair. Angie's warning would never materialize.

She replaced a pearl earring and glanced at her wrist, finding nothing but a white demarcation line in her tan. But she didn't need a watch to assure her she was late for the auspicious Masters' Leaders Party. She breathed deeply, went back into the hall and headed in the direction of humming voices and clinking glasses.

She stood in the arched doorway for a prolonged, uncomfortable moment. In the center of the staid room, Tiger Woods held court, his beautiful almond eyes attentive, smile wide, filled with even more guileless glee than normal. Greg Norman and entourage visited quietly, while nearby, Arnie and Winnie Palmer chatted with Jack and Barbara Nicklaus. Rustling silk and linen settled on Perri's ears, along with spicy and flowery aromas of costly perfume wafting toward her. Red-coated waiters circulated through the crush, brandishing drink-laden silver trays above celebrated heads.

She patted sweaty palms against her dress. God! What was she doing here?

Her stomach knotted when she caught Pete's wave. He stood with Beau and a tall, sleek, dark-haired woman whom Perri had prayed a migraine would incapacitate for the night.

So this was Stephanie. Strange discomfort and immense dislike rose like mercury in a thermometer. Stephanie was the embodiment of the girl who had written the note Braden had shown Perri that spiteful day, eight years ago. But Stephanie wasn't that girl. Chelsea's father intended to marry this woman. Her mind formed, then rapidly rejected, images of Beau and Stephanie together in more erotic situations than this staunchy command performance. When she had known him, he'd been mildly anti-social, adhering to protocol to please Braden and Winonna, and to further his career. She had fit his philosophy perfectly, preferring to spend her evenings in bed with him rather than dressed to the nines, saying and doing all the right things.

Yesterday's era, a lifetime ago.

She sucked in an invisible stomach. Shoulders back, head erect, she threaded her way through the arena of past and present show-ponies, stopping to greet Frizzy Collins, meet the woman on his arm, and entertain his comical comments on the day's round.

When finally she drew near, Pete cupped her elbow and steered her in close. His face shone cleanly, sprinkled with fresh freckles. A whiff of smoke clinging to his navy blazer surprised her. He never smoked on the course, protecting his camera image. Soon, he would be handing out candy, perfecting that image, competing with Beau in a new arena. Banish that thought. Pete was Beau's friend and protégé, no concern of hers once the Masters was over.

"Hi." Pete smacked an air kiss next to her temple. Beau shot him a surprised glance before leveling a scowl on her.

"Hi. Sorry I'm late."

"You have trouble getting here?"

"My motel is five minutes away. I had to make a phone call that couldn't wait."

Beau's auburn brows torqued. His eyes clouded, as if he recalled a time when he'd had privileged knowledge of such calls, most of which had gone to him.

Pete motioned with a glass of clear liquid, a lime, and rattling ice cubes. "No problem. We plunged right in." He cocked his head, eyeing Beau, with a wry smile. "Well not all of us. St. Serious is nursing a Shirley Temple."

"Roy Rogers," Beau murmured.

Sipping bubbles from a slender, long-stemmed glass, Stephanie laughed low in her throat.

In Perri's peripheral vision, Beau's hand stole behind Stephanie's back, leaving Perri to wonder where his touch settled and to hate herself for caring.

"Good evening, Beau." Perri kept her eyes off his, and off his companion, focusing on the lapels of his elegant wheat-silk jacket. "Seems we just parted."

"A shower and a few phone calls ago. This is Stephanie Kane. Steph, this is—"

"The caddie who saved your ass." Stephanie spared Perri a spiteful glance, resentment of the intrusion almost palpable, before focusing violet eyes back on Beau.

His boyish smile fell short of maximum potential. "I believe I said butt—actually, I know I did. I saw the rerun on CNN."

"But you were thinking ass."

Pete laughed, holding his glass aloft, signaling a waiter and pointing to Perri.

With a long-suffering look, Stephanie extended a hand that engulfed Perri's, her lengthy nails the shade of an old bruise, her smile resembling a mechanical shark's. "How do you do?"

"Wonderfully, thank you." Perri dropped the hand the moment the cold fingers uncoiled, but not before scrutinizing a diamond solitaire whose cost would pay for Chelsea's impending surgery. "As for saving Beau's anatomy, I want him to win as badly as he wants to. I didn't do anything he wouldn't have done for me, had the situation been reversed."

Even though Beau quipped, "Count on it," she doubted the validity of her statement, based on history. Nevertheless, she'd obtained the desired result, even if she wasn't sure why she wanted it. Jealousy raged in Stephanie's eyes, the kind capable of making one woman want to plunge a dagger into another. Stephanie didn't write the note. Credit for breaking her heart belonged to Beau, and by being here, seeing him with this woman, she trifled with allowing him to hurt her again.

She jumped skittishly when Beau gently clasped her wrist, thrust a champagne flute into her hand, then clinked his glass to hers. "To tomorrow's round, partner."

Perri sipped wordlessly.

Pete's cheer for Beau's toast plummeted into taut, lingering silence. "Wanta meet some people, Perri? You didn't get all dolled up for nothing, I'll bet. And since you're a TV celebrity now . . . ."

Two sets of eyes bored into her as he steered her away. Determined not to glance back, not to let her intimidation show, she decided that in their elegance, Beau and Stephanie Kane resembled unmatched but perfectly suited bookends. Braden must be ecstatic.

※

Beau made small talk with Stephanie and Nick Faldo, unable to keep his eyes off Perri. Neither could he shake gripping regret as he watched Pete's hand stray to her bare upper arm when he introduced her to a group. If he'd known what Pete was up to—not that he knew now—he would've skipped the party. Even had Pete told him he'd invited her, the idea of Perri accepting wouldn't have warranted a second thought. She knew Pete was married. Or didn't she? Hell if he was privy to what she knew these days, what went on in her head. For damned sure she deserved to be here as much or more than he did.

He made an effort to rejoin the conversation, then slacked off, letting Nick and Stephanie rehash Perri's swim in Rae's Creek. Against Nick's clipped English accent, Stephanie's drawl reminded Beau of sorghum molasses overflowing Nonna's pewter syrup pitcher. If he'd known Perri was coming, he wouldn't have brought Stephanie. But, since attending this party was her primary reason for being in Augusta, he had about as much chance of not bringing her as making an eagle on number thirteen tomorrow. As soon as the Town and Country photographer worked his way to her and she charmed him into promising not to cut her picture from next month's addition, they could leave. Yeah, and then what? Bed? Feeling as he did about Perri, sex was not in the cards, an enigma escalating by the minute.

His mind and gaze settled back on Perri. He'd always been attracted to her tomboyish demeanor, her no-frills way of dressing, and minimalist make-up, but how in hell had she managed to look this beautiful out of that duffel she'd dragged out of the bathroom? Even from here, her mouth looked like pink peppermint, soft and full and sweet. No Carmex tonight. Helplessly, he ran his tongue over his own lips. A black, body-skimming dress, showing a lot of bronze leg and the swell of breasts, was the only window dressing her body needed. In fact, the dress resembled one she'd hauled around to wear to Nike command performances; after closer scrutiny, he knew they were one and the same. His thoughts grew ambiguous, other than the increasing certainty she'd spent the money. Being on tour was no half-million heiress's lark.

He recognized her grandmother's pearl choker she'd had since her sixteenth birthday. She wore them paired with his locket, which hung beneath the neck of the dress. Was she taunting him with that trinket? For damn sure, she didn't want him to see whose picture replaced his. She was cagey enough to risk wearing it tonight, since he was tied up tight as a vise, no chance of getting his hands on the locket. Or her.

Giving in to agitation, he helped himself to a flute of champagne from a scurrying waiter's tray. He took a gulp big enough to bring a patronizing smile from Stephanie. After failing at paying attention to the conversation droning in his ear, he surrendered his gaze across the room again. The low light gave Perri a shine that reminded him of antique copper coins. A flush played along her cheekbones, and her hair hanging loose and curly glittered like honey in sunshine. No nylons. Earlier he'd seen the small scar on her ankle again. From this distance, in the tall sandal heels her feet gleamed below her ankles as if bathed by a white-hot strobe light. He used to drive her wild by nibbling her toes. Would they still taste like generic hotel soap or more like mud and creek water tonight? Did she still dot perfume on her ankles and at the backs of her knees? Did she still prefer Lauren? Predictably his crotch tightened. He longed to take her to bed, thank her properly for today's sacrifice, and then hold her through the night, wake up with her, and begin all over again the life he had once thought they'd share forever.

Suddenly, she turned as though aware of his thoughts. The long measuring look she gave him, before turning back to Pete, sent an ache to the center of his chest. Abrupt silence jolting him, he tore his gaze away from Perri to find Stephanie and Nick staring at him.

"Beau, for God's sake." Stephanie's lush mouth tightened. A mutinous crease formed between artfully made up eyes. "Her swim is over. At least until tomorrow."

Nick laughed, an embarrassed edge shoving in. "Well, after all, she was naked under those regulation whites. I'm sure every man in the room is remembering that right now."

Hating the comment, Beau reluctantly acknowledged its validity. He didn't know why Perri had come on tour, setting herself up to vulnerability. He didn't care. She belonged to him, always had. No legal papers filed away in some cold steel cabinet could change that. Once this tournament was over, he would take care of her, make things easier for her, and maybe get the answers he needed as to where they'd gone wrong. Somehow. Some way.

When Pete headed for the men's room, Beau made a feeble apology to Stephanie and her celebrity find and followed. He approached Pete, eyes meeting in the mirror above the urinals.

"You want to explain what the hell you had in mind bringing Perri here?" He lifted his voice above the sound of trickling water.

Pete grinned, zipping his fly. "Is she stealing your limelight, Beau Jangles?"

"Piss on that." Beau zipped his own fly. With emphasis. "You're married and you've got my ex-wife out on a date. What's the idea?"

"Get outta here." Pete moved to the sinks, humoring. "What is it with you Kentucks? She said the same thing—not the ex-wife bit, but about this being a date."

Beau joined him at the sink, bracing one hip against the marble counter, arms crossed, head cocked. If she'd called it a date, did that mean she wanted it to be?

"I didn't want to come alone, okay, Beau?" Pete lathered up as if he'd been shoveling manure. "How many of these leader shindigs am I eligible to attend?" His eyes petitioned in the mirror. "How many does she get to go to—now that the two of you are history, I mean? I'm sure she saw her share back in the Nike days."

"I'd have brought her, except Stephanie—"

"Oh. So you and Perri have made up."

"She's caddying her rear off for me. We're not enemies."

"Glad to hear it." He reached for a kelly-green linen hand towel. "But Stephanie is here, and judging from what I saw during their little get acquainted session, if you had brought Perri and Steph got wind of it— She does know the story?"

"She knows."

"No offense, Beau, but Steph's claws could shred metal. Don't let her get to Perri."

Beau's hairline tingled. His neck warmed. "Don't change the subject."

He laughed. "Don't get your dander up. It's bad for your putting. She cabbed it here, and she'll be going back to Motel Six the same way." He eyed Beau, amusement gone. "Do you think you've cornered the market on show-ponies, St. Cyr?"

"She's my wife, Pete."

Before he completed the thought that his false declaration sure as hell sounded lame, Pete countered, "Even you can't have your cake and eat it, too."

"Thanks for the reminder."

"Would you rather I brought her, or someone else did?"

"No one else would have."

"And you don't think she has a right to be here?"

Beau let the needling slide in favor of getting his point across. Time was dwindling. "Don't let her take a cab back." When Pete stared dumbly, he reiterated, "Take her back to her room and wait there—in the car—until she's inside her room and the door's locked."

"What gives?" He looked stupefied, but hooked.

"She had a problem last night. Some jerk tried to get into her room."

Pete's brow creased. His hands jammed into his pockets. "Who?"

Beau had settled on Mark, but that didn't figure. Mark wouldn't have to exert the effort of breaking in a door since Perri was nibbling out of his hand. A gentle knock would gain him entry. But he sure as hell could have written the note containing the veiled threat that Beau deemed was aimed at Perri. On the other hand, maybe the attempted break-in and the note were coincidental. He shrugged. "Who knows. Probably some drunk, but Perri's jumpy."

"Probably some broad after Teddy."

Beau shrugged again, an attempt to dismiss that gut clinching implication. "Whatever. Have we got our signals straight?"

Pete saluted. "It's not a date, but you want me to treat her like it is."

"Something like that." Beau relinquished a grin. "Now get the hell back out there. She's all by herself in a den of rattlers."

✳

"Down there." Perri motioned Pete toward the parking lot. "Past the video store."

Slowing the car, he signaled to change lanes, grudging, "Motel Six. I've seen a few of these in my illustrious career." Following her hand gesture, he guided the car past registration.

She gestured again. "Number twenty-three. One from the end."

Pete swung into an empty space. "You really are five minutes from the club."

"I told you there was no need to bring me back."

"Saint's orders. No problem." He cut the motor and half turned in the seat.

Perri's gaze registered the dim light filtering from the window. Teddy had a cavalier attitude toward privacy. Even last night's attempted break-in hadn't ruffled her. "Augusta National isn't exactly in the best neighborhood, I guess. Maybe it was in Bobby Jones' day, but not anymore." She smoothed her skirt. "Beau has an early tee time tomorrow, so being this close to the course lets me sleep five more minutes."

Pete's hand snaked along her seat back. "Well don't look for him until the fat lady finishes singing. According to St. Serious, Stephanie's got a gluttonous libido."

He slanted her a measuring glance. She stiffened voluntarily. Even though traffic blurred the words, they stung like a frozen lash. Noticing, he suddenly looked penitent.

"Sorry. Maybe you don't want to hear that. I forget you and Beau were a twosome."

So Beau had told him about their shared past. But how much? What? About the marriage? The bribe? "I forget, too." She reached for the door handle, relieved he'd made no effort to get out. "Well....I have to be bright eyed tomorrow, especially if I can't count on Beau's peak performance. I enjoyed the party."

"Sorry I left you alone so long at dinner, but with my kid having the flu, I had to make that call." His smile struck her as youthful and contrite. "I kind of rushed you out of there after dinner, but Paula's gonna let me know the verdict on Austin. Pisses her if I miss a call."

Perri slipped her purse strap over a shoulder and cracked the door, flooding the car with light.

"When they're so young and sick, it can be scary."
She got out and closed the door, stooping at the
open window. "Maybe our fairways will cross
tomorrow." She walked away, spike heels loud
against the concrete. When she glanced back he
was lighting a cigarette, watching her over the red
glow of the dash lighter. At the door she slipped
the key into the lock. The door swung open without a twist of the knob, surprising her. Only then
did the car motor fire, sounding like Angie's old
electric sewing machine. She waved. Pete was not
in the Ferrari category, but if Beau kept coaching
him, and got his way, prosperity couldn't be far off.

She slipped inside the room, expecting to find
Teddy and her caddie friends sitting cross legged
on the beds, smoking, drinking beer, reliving their
rounds, hole by hole, preserving the ritual Perri
had accepted. The room lay eerily empty. Back
pressed against the door, hands on the knob, she
fought down unidentified dread, telling herself she
was wrong, she couldn't smell a presence. Yet
there were so many places to hide. The closet
alcove. The bathroom. Her gaze roamed the dim
room. Nothing seemed amiss, other than signs of
dressing for the party, and Teddy's casual house-
keeping. Gradually the dripping shower registered
on her mind, an almost familiar, reassuring sound.
No one was hiding in the room. Teddy had simply
gone out without pulling the door closed or listening for the lock to snap into place.

Then she saw it. The wall-mounted swivel light
above the nightstand illuminated evidence of invasion. Her pillow had been pulled from beneath the
spread and bunched against the mock-wood headboard. A sinister crimson stain glowed against
dingy white cotton.

Heart knocking like an out-of-sync engine, she
moved gingerly in the close space, toward the bed,
then froze. Outside, footsteps and voices

approached. She retraced her steps and fell
against the door, seized and finally engaged the
dangling chain. The threat filed past the window,
laughter echoing back. A car rumbled by, ghetto
blaster screaming obscenities, vibrating the room,
shattering the night calm. Her eyes riveted to the
bed. The pillow. The stain. No matter who had
been here—no matter the motive—they had gone.
However sick their calling card turned out to be, no
physical harm threatened. She crossed the room,
sank warily onto the side of the bed, and leaned to
examine the pillow, testing the stain with a shaky
finger.

Lipstick. Hers. Teddy wore only Chapstick. A
set of lips had been haphazardly drawn to form an
open mouth. A brown phallic symbol pointed at
the mouth, three tear-shaped drips trailing below.
Her uncapped lipstick and fawn eye-pencil lay discarded on the nightstand. Hesitantly, she touched
a darker spot of pillowslip in the center of the mis-
shapen mouth. Wet. Sticky. Starting to crust and
blend into the cheap muslin. She lifted the pillow,
and sniffed, then gagged, throat convulsing, eyes
stinging.

She flung the pillow against the wall. It slid
down and landed in a heap. Smeared and gaping,
the red mouth sneered. The phone beckoned, nagging her to tell someone. She craved to hear a
laugh, a calming voice assuring her this was a
harmless joke—a vulgar prank. Hope soared,
raced through her, a demented, selfish groping at
the possibility of Teddy being the target, until her
gaze rested on her green duffel on the end of the
bed. Her Doc Martins peeked from beneath the
faded chenille spread. Teddy's bed lay bare of any
identifying items.

Heart lurching, Perri reached for the phone,
jerked her hand back. She had no one to call. She

had no one but herself. Shivers ran up her spine when she looked at the duffel again.

Grabbing her purse, she propelled her body across the room and out the door, slamming it so hard it jarred the frame and rattled the window. She stood for a moment, staring across the parking lot, up a set of iron stairs, and along the second story walkway.

Which door had she seen him enter that afternoon after they'd shared a beer by the pool, laughing about her Rae's Creek adventure? Gaze clamped on the third door from the end, she stalked across the lot in the near darkness. Her heels tapped a jerky rhythm on steel steps.

"Mark!" Breath tangling in her throat, chest heaving, she waited, suspended. In the wake of silence from within, she banged, rattling the rusty knob. "Mark, if you're in there—"

Abruptly, the door gaped. A caddie known as Divot glared at her, one hand holding the door, the other scratching his privates through his jockeys.

"Where's Mark?" Folding her arms across her breasts, she strained to get a look around him into the dark room. "I want to talk to him."

"He ain't here, I'm pullin' an early nighter. A single. Last I seen him, he was at that bar across the street." Divot's shaved head nodded toward flashing neon identifying the Putt Around. "There's a bunch of 'em over there," he called after her. "Big table in the back."

Mentally fending off wolf whistles and catcalls, she stood inside the door of the nearly empty bar. She let her eyes adjust to the light while Willie Nelson's plaintive, mellow voice vowed, "You Were Always On My Mind." The big table in the back sat empty. Gripped with disbelief, she watched a couple slow dancing in a corner next to the jukebox. As she started in their direction, they turned, enabling the woman to see her. She couldn't read Teddy's face, but her body language portrayed surprise. She stopped dancing. Mark's arms fell away from her as if she'd burst into flames. The two of them met Perri at the empty table.

"Hey." Mark pulled out a chair, angling it toward her. "The Masters mermaid is here."

"Hey." Teddy reached for cigarettes atop the table. Movements jerky, she fired up, dropped the lighter in the pocket of a—skirt?—and exhaled to the side. Perri caught a whiff of spicy-sweet perfume. Teddy grinned. "Thought you were partying. They run out of caviar?"

Mark sat down and inched the chair toward Perri with the toe of a cowboy boot. He picked up a bottle of near beer; circles on the wooden table had formed a dull sheen.

"Wanta beer? Or whatever's politically correct after champagne?" The dim light played up his slick, hard-planed looks, eyes that glinted as he lit a cigarette. He started to offer the pack to her, then pocketed it, giving her measure in the murky light. "What the hell's wrong? The big wigs swear you to silence when in the company of golf course swine?"

Teddy laughed as she sat down and swiveled her legs beneath the table, bringing her upper body uncustomarily close to Mark's. She reached for an ashtray and tapped the end of her cigarette. "Take a load off, Perr." She nudged the chair a bit more. "Tell us about the party."

"Have you been in my room?" Perri addressed Mark.

He looked at Teddy. Teddy stared up at Perri, face void. "Moi?" Mark grinned.

"Yes, you." Aware that silence—except for Willie—had descended, conscious of straining ears, she tried lowering her voice, but anxiety and anger beat out propriety. "Were you in there? The door was unlocked."

"I went by for Teddy. Maybe we didn't close it all the way."

"Someone pilfered my things."

Teddy stiffened. Her unusually painted mouth formed an O. She breathed, "Shit."

"What things?" Mark arched a thick, jet brow, smile waning.

The scene reeled across her mind. The stains. Discarded lipstick and eye pencil the intruder had to pilfer the duffel to find, since she kept the bath vanity cleared for Teddy, who before tonight disdained cosmetics. "Never mind what." If the culprit was Mark, he already knew. Having traveled with her, he was familiar with the duffel, and he often commented on the ugly Doc Martins, so he knew her bed from Teddy's. And now, recovering from shock—or only now settling into it—she knew her bed had been specifically selected to foul.

"Were you in there, Mark?" Her voice pitched upward an octave

He caught her arm and eased her onto the chair. "Calm down. Tell me what happened."

She glared. "I think you know. So you tell me. What and why?"

He looked at Teddy, as though soliciting aid.

Teddy shrugged. "I told you we got hustled last night. She's jumpy. I just figured Don Juan DeMarco had the wrong room." She eyed Perri, acquiescing, "But maybe not."

"Perri—" Mark raked back his dark hair. "Why would I—" Abruptly, he stood, drawing her up. "Come on, babe. Show me what the hell you're talking about."

Teddy stood as Mark queried, "Did Jacoby bring you back? Does he know what you're bitchin' about?"

Perri shrugged off his touch. "Pete has nothing to do with this."

"I never said so. I want to know if he saw whatever the hell you're blaming on me."

"Forget it." Composure settled on her in shattered fragments, yet she felt defeated, emptied out, flattened as if she had been run over. Finding a smile as difficult to come by as complete trust, she fished in her purse for a quarter, held it out to him. "Play Willie again. Get back to where you were when I went hysterical."

Teddy retrieved the quarter from Mark's palm and forced it back into Perri's. "Let's have a beer for the road. You'll sleep better."

Perri eyed the scarred, empty dance floor. Recall of Mark and Teddy's intimacy ushered back her surprise and curiosity. The world tilted on its axis. "I have to get up early."

Teddy leaned over the table, crushing her cigarette in the ashtray. "Me, too. I'll go back with you." Her glance at Mark appeared perfunctory, now. "'Night. Catch you tomorrow."

Smiling ruefully, he shifted his gaze. "Get a grip, huh, babe? If I'd done the dastardly deed—whatever—I'd have blown Dodge instead of waiting for the fallout."

Somehow, she couldn't muster the strength to withdraw the accusation or apologize.

✳

"Holy, shit." Teddy stood over the soiled pillow, hands on hips, nose screwed up in repulsion. "This bastard is sadistic. Where'd you get the idea that Mark—" Seizing the pillow by a corner, she held it at arm's length, stalked to the door, opened it and tossed out the object of disdain. She slammed the door, dragged over a chair and wedged it beneath the knob. "Get a shower, Perr." Her authoritative demeanor returned intact. "Scrub it off. It's only some sick guy's idea of a joke." She kicked off her cheap but conspicuously new sandals. "They're a diseased bunch. Down to the last son of a bitch."

In the bath, Perri dropped the lipstick and eye pencil in the trash and slipped beneath the pelting shower. She lathered her body, rubbing hard with a flimsy wash cloth. Although the water scorched, a cold emptiness crept through her. Beau's face took precedence in her mind, weighing heavier than the repugnance of what she'd found awaiting her here.

He'd had only to look at her across the room tonight to make her feel as if some primal thing seized her in its fist, unleashing needs no man other than Beau had ever stirred. The realization frightened and intrigued her. For years she had controlled her emotions, driving them through a gauntlet of anger and resentment by staying away from him as he wanted. This past month revealed that control to be illusionary smoke and mirrors, too effortlessly shattered.

The boy she'd worshipped, her lover for a year, husband for a day, father of her child, was now a finer man than she could have imagined or wanted to admit. Denying Chelsea the privilege of knowing him grew more difficult by the day. And Perri had seen it in his eyes, felt it in his touch, heard it in the timbre of his voice; he still had feelings for her. If he had wanted her to stay away from him eight years ago, at what point since had he changed his mind?

For the first time she began to wonder how much of their breakup had been Beau, how much Braden. If not for the note Braden had shown her, she would confront Beau now. But she wasn't ready. The scars were too deep and Stephanie too much a reminder of that day, that note, that pain. Still, the sense of Braden's involvement persisted, growing to a toothache-like nagging. Confronting Beau would mean sharing Chelsea with him. She had grown used to being Chelsea's sole support, comfortable in her daughter's unconditional love.

Thoughts of giving that up, sharing her, subjecting her to the influence Braden exercised over Beau— influence she was unsure Beau could shun—gave her grave qualms.

Shutting down the thoughts and the water, she shoved back the flimsy curtain, stepped into a puddle on the pitted linoleum floor and pulled a towel off the rack. After blotting her hair, she ran the towel across her chest, down her stomach, and squeezed it between her thighs. Sinking to the edge of the tub, she rubbed her hair, her thoughts taking a different bent.

Stephanie had looked almost mean. Exacting, inflexible. Not tolerant enough to live Beau's life, fit into his plans, his goals and dreams. Not loving enough to make him happy. That realization left Perri feeling as if her heart harbored rocks. But, then, she had been tolerant. She had loved Beau. Shared and honored his goals and dreams. He had left her anyway.

She met her gaze in the steamed mirror. No tolerance tomorrow, though. No time for dreams. Now she had her own goals. Beau St. Cyr could be no more than a means to an end.

✳

In the hotel bar Stephanie ordered a brandy, then took her cigarettes and lighter from her evening bag. Her head snapped up, mid-flame, when Beau asked for decaf coffee.

"I thought you invited me in here for an after dinner drink."

"You're getting your drink. I have to play tomorrow. Bright and early. I don't have time to let a hangover wear off." He waited, hoping for understanding, encouragement, getting nothing but a narrowing of eyes. "This is how pro golfers live, Stephanie. The winners, anyway. If you're not up for it—or maybe I should say, down to it—don't sign on."

158

She waved cigarette smoke, her six-carat engagement ring gleaming in candlelight flickering in a crystal bowl. "Did anybody ever tell you you're a lot of fun, Beau?"

Small hairs rose on his spine. "You're starting to push me a little too hard, darlin'. All night you've been..." Somewhere he found a smile. "How shall I put this, Steph?"

"A bitch."

"That'll do." He stirred cream and sugar into the coffee the waitress had brought, giving Stephanie time to offer the explanation he knew was eventually coming. Getting nothing, he took a sip and invited over the cup rim, "You want to get it off your chest? The problem?"

"It really burned my ass, Beau. Every time someone congratulated you on today's play, you gave credit to that girl."

"Her name is Perri." He watched her face grow still and narrow. "If not for Perri, I'd have been finished on number twelve. You're damned right I played good after that. I had one ball, and no choice. If not for Perri, I'd have had no ball. So I owe my excellent play to her."

"Why would she let you go out there with no balls? She sounds like a loser to me."

"That's another story, one that doesn't concern you. Drop it, okay?"

She ground out the cigarette and crossed her arms over big breasts.

"What else is eating you?"

She jumped at his second invitation. "You couldn't keep your eyes off her. I expected you to leave me and go sit with her when your friend pulled his disappearing act at dinner."

"She's my ex-wife." Part of my soul. "I'm looking out for her."

"Then maybe that explains something else."

"What?" He knew, and she was right as rain.

"The fact I've been here two days and you haven't gotten around to screwing me."

"I didn't want to mess up your hair. In case you got a sudden photo op."

A moment passed in which nothing was said while everything was understood. In the wavering light her face loomed fox-sharp, her nostrils pinched.

"You know, Steph, it's sad to think we've been screwing all these months when we should have been making love."

"When did you become such a puritan?"

"Become?" He smiled, leaning forward to light the cigarette she popped into her mouth. "That's even sadder. Shows you don't know me at all."

"Is that what you did with her—Perri? Make love?"

"I've loved her since we were kids, Stephanie. I'm not going to lie to you about that."

"You bastard." Her eyes shone like amethyst. "You let me believe you hated her."

"I let me believe I was angry with her for leaving me. I was. I still am."

With a grave intake of breath, she declared, "You're definitely no puritan. You screwed half the girls in your gallery before we met—maybe afterward, too, for all I know."

True enough, except for her suspicion that he'd cheated on her. He shrugged. "That's what they wanted. Apparently that's what you want, too."

She looked away, fingers digging into her bare upper arms, the cigarette smoldering in the ashtray. He stubbed it out and placed the ashtray on a nearby table. She lifted her brandy glass, swirled the roan-brown liquid, took a long drink and then surprised the hell out of him.

"I want you to fire her." To his stunned silence she reiterated, "Fire Perri tomorrow."

"Are you out of your mind?" Especially after what she'd witnessed today.

He was about to soothe her jealousy, offer reassurances, when she said, "I mean it, Beau. I won't be humiliated like this again."

He knew she referred to being upstaged. First at the interview, then at the party. Their gazes locked in the dim, smoky room while he ran the scenario across this mind, projecting into the near and distant future: Stephanie calling the shots in his career, his basing every decision on her dictates, playing only the tournaments that appealed to her, associating with whom she deemed suitable. Jumping through her velvet-lined hoops.

"Her or me," she said finally.

In light of her ultimatum the guilt he'd been feeling from wanting out of the relationship waned. The senselessness of firing Perri paled when compared to Stephanie armchair-quarterbacking his life, especially when she chose to participate so seldom. He took a drink of coffee, waiting for the right words to germinate, unable to believe it had come to this so quickly.

"Your turn, Beau. I relinquish the tee to you." Her voice had gone smooth, as though a kinder, gentler spirit had conquered her animosity. Yet underneath he detected a slight tremor.

"We're too different, Stephanie. Unless one of us is willing to change—and I don't have that luxury right now—marriage would be a mistake."

One brow quirked, a wry smile working her mouth. "You want me to change." It was not a question. "If it involves that caddie—"

"Maybe you can't. Or you don't want to." Braden had always told him people never changed. They only revamped their strategy. "You're a beautiful woman. You want to go places and be seen. Maybe you're not cut out to be a pro's wife. That takes a special gift. I can name on one hand the women who have it. They're saints."

Her smile waned. "And where do you think I fall short of sainthood?"

He veered onto a different route. "You may as well know the plan, so you can accept or reject it." Her eyes gave him the go ahead. "The reason I won't drink with you, Steph, or stay up all night and party is simple. I want to win. I have to. I'm in a hell of a hurry to win all the majors so I can quit the tour."

One hand flew to her chest in an unrehearsed, theatrical reaction. "And do what?"

"Settle down and raise a family."

Now she looked bilious. "I don't see how you can even talk about having children considering the genetic problems in your family."

Diplomatic wording, he'd give her that. "So you'd be afraid to risk it with me."

"I never considered—" Her gaze skidded beyond his shoulder, but then he saw a light come on. "I suppose I thought . . . "

Never, before this moment. "Thought what?"

"We'd adopt." She colored slightly under his noncommittal stare. "What else, Beau?"

"Teach golf somewhere. Get off the treadmill." Saying it felt like soaring out of a deep chasm that kept threatening to close in on him.

"And give up—"

"What, besides celebrity? I've already proven I can play the game better than most."

"What's wrong with being a celebrity?"

"That's really what you want, isn't it? To be married to one? And I'll do."

"That's mean." Her eyes fogged, her chin quivering. Familiar.

"I'm not trying to be mean. Just honest, because I think it'll hurt less now than later.

You're not in love with me. You're in love with celebrity. Anyone would do."

She sat silently, her long legs crossed at the knee, swiveling the barrel chair back and forth. Her hand rummaged in the little bag beside her, but came out empty. "I can't believe you'd quit."

"Suppose I didn't? Suppose we get married, and I keep plowing through tournament after tournament until I'm fifty. Then I start plowing a different pasture. The senior tour."

"What would be wrong with that, for Christ's sake?"

"Would you travel with me?"

"You know I don't like to leave Nashville."

"Then you'd stay home and raise those kids I'm talking about. Right?"

Silence fell between them, invaded by voices less caustic than their own, by soft piano music from the corner. He watched her grope for persuasive words. After all these months he knew her and her real wants and needs. In Nashville she pursued the life of charity maven. Her name linked with his gave her status, rendering saying no to her solicitations difficult, affording her celebrity status of her own. Married to him, she'd be willing to put in an appearance at the major tournaments, commiserate by phone with some of the wives who chose to stay home and raise a family. Anything else would be beyond the call of duty or obligation. Determining to out-wait her, to let her voice the inevitable, he counted the moments, his breath threatening to give away his eagerness.

Her right hand raised to her left. She looked as if she might speak, but then her mouth closed like a fist. She worked his ring off and placed it on the table. It glittered. It mocked.

"Keep it, Steph. Sell it and use the money for a needy cause."

Without hesitation she retrieved the ring and stuffed it into her bag "How generous."

At last breath began to pass through his lungs without a hitch. "Okay," he said, stifling his relief. His gratitude. "Here's the plan. Braden's wild about you. He'll probably try to talk you out of it, maybe even try to bribe you. Take his money, put it with what you get for the ring and build a park. Donate a hospital wing. Whatever." He shrugged, smiling, his tone cajoling as he hoped for an amicable split. "I'll take the blame for the failed reconciliation."

With an incredulous look, she shouldered the bag. He heard the heavy ring clunking around inside. "Stick Braden's money up your beautiful ass, Beau. I don't need it."

She marched away. Not toward the elevator and their two-bedroom suite on the sixteenth floor, but across the lobby and through the revolving doors. She was right. Bottom line, she personally didn't need his money. In the beginning, that had been her most endearing quality, the possibility she could love him for himself.

Before reality kicked in. Before he'd gotten another taste of Perri.

✳

He awoke somewhere in the night. His glib remark about Braden's possible bribe echoed in his head like four-letter words yelled into the Grand Canyon. He tried wrestling down a sudden, glaring notion, tried ignoring the improbable odds, but he couldn't go back to sleep. Slipping back eight years, his thoughts turned to a roller coaster running down track, out of control.

℞

CHAPTER ELEVEN

A wailing siren stalled the next day's play on the seventh hole. The air-renting sound climaxed warning signs of far-off lightning and darkening skies Perri had kept an eye on since the practice range. Like magic carpets, vans arrived to provide the players shelter from the summer storm, on course or off. Justin Leonard, the other half of Beau's twosome, climbed into a van, intent on waiting out the delay at the clubhouse. His caddie made for a golf cart poorly sheltered by a stately pine. Perri shouldered Beau's bag and followed in the caddie's wake.

Beau caught hold of her arm, his touch warm and firm through the sleeve of the coveralls. "I'm waiting the storm out here." He nodded toward an empty van parked on the cart path, motor running. Glancing skyward, he speculated, "This will blow over in half an hour. No sense hauling all the way to the clubhouse and back." He tugged gently on her arm as rain splattered their feet. "Besides, talking shop with the rest of the field screws up momentum."

A typical St. Serious theory. She stood her ground. The pounding feet of the gallery heading for what little protection the pines and dogwoods would provide, echoed around them. "I'll wait with the other caddiecourse." She jerked her head toward the man in the golf cart.

"Not while I'm alive." Beau smiled. "Get your pretty little butt in the van."

He relieved her of the clubs and sought shelter, fat dollops of rain marking the flowered fabric stretched across his shoulders, spattering on the

big bag. As Perri followed reluctantly, a tournament official looked on in disapproval. Beau
stowed the clubs in the front passenger seat,
slammed the door, hoisted her into the back,
climbed aboard and slid the door closed. He fished
dry towels from behind the seat, handed her one,
and blotted his face with the other.

Settling back, she dabbed her face, aware of
how his lanky body filled the remainder of the
bench seat, of long legs, wide shoulders and muscular forearms sprinkled with golden hair. She
shivered, blaming the zealous cooling system and
wet clothing.

"Want me to turn the A/C off?" Without awaiting an answer, he leaned through the opening to
the front seat, found the button to lower the side
windows a fraction, and then shut off the engine.
He settled back into the seat, running a towel over
his wet hair, darker and wavier now. "I left the key
on, if you want your window down."

Leonard's caddie hovered under a yellow slick-
er, body curved over Leonard's clubs as the open
cart pulled away. She should be there. If Beau
wanted his clubs in the van, so be it. But her place
was in that cart with her peer.

Rain pelted their sanctuary, ran down the windows and turned the windshield to a murky shower curtain. Loosening the straps on her Nikes, she
eased them off, then tucked her legs into the seat.
She stared out the window, aware Beau had quieted with the towel and now braced his shoulder
against the obscured glass on his side, gazing out.
The dash clock clicked off each advancing minute,
loud as hammer blows, except when drowned out
by a clap of thunder.

Taking out her Carmex, she smeared her
mouth, then gripped the tube in her palm.

She stared. He stared. In opposite directions
while rain formed a shelter around them in which

their breath fogged the windows, sealing out the world. The close quarters magnified the scent of cologne, tanning lotion, wet clothing. Their breathing seemed inordinately loud.

She ran her tongue over the sweet-slick taste on her lips, and leaned her head against the window, trying to ignore his overpowering presence. Closing her eyes, she thought of last night's call to Angie, envisioning New Mexico, a place she'd never seen, never a factor in her life and Chelsea's until now. Would Angie take Chelsea with her? Could Perri let her go? Was Angie threatening her, forcing her to tell Beau about his daughter? No. She couldn't call it a threat. She had stopped thinking of Angie as the enemy and begun thinking of her as a woman with her own dreams. Her talk of New Mexico was a wish, one that might come true. Her craving was forcing Perri to expedite her own plan and reach her goal sooner.

Beau had to win this tournament. The money would strengthen her position, and the notoriety would guarantee her good carries at every event. Maybe by the end of the season . . .

With her mind rejecting those disturbing uncertainties, she reluctantly switched to a review of the scene that had greeted her last night. If the prowler wasn't Mark, then whom had she offended who'd be capable of such retaliation? Surely Mark understood she could let nothing interfere with her goal of becoming the best freelance caddie on tour, that her consistent rejections of his advances were not personal. But how could he? She'd never told him about Chelsea or her responsibility, and in light of her past with Beau, she probably came off as snobbish and money grasping. Still, the message left by the intruder had been vile and pointed, failing to fit Mark's profile. But if not Mark Zamora, then who?

Again, she rejected the thoughts swirling in her head and opened her eyes.

Just as Beau predicted, the rain slowed, then fell gently on the van roof. Her mind caught memories of a tin-roofed house where she'd lived in Virginia, before Lee got the Owl Creek job. Rainy nights and dawns beneath that roof had been wonderful. A child snuggled in a feather bed, her big brother next to her. The serenity, warmth, and security, had allowed her to believe, not to question her life, what had gone before or what would come. Sitting next to Beau now, unsupported remnants of that feeling edged into her mind.

Her musing migrated to their temporary arrangement, the fact he deemed these three days a test. He had grasped a quick, easy solution after Cal left, imposing on her because she knew his temperament, abilities and flaws on the course. Working for him permanently, she'd have the financial security she needed, but the stress of the intimate conditions negated that luxury.

Too much heaven. Too much hell. More than she could endure.

"Ain't this a hell of a life?"

She jumped, whirling around as though caught stealing.

He stared for an instant before a grin crossed his face like ripples on a creek. The smile held the simple purity of a child's. "We're holed up like prisoners, when I could be on a driving range somewhere in Scottsdale teaching kids to chip with a three wood—like Tigger does."

Though touched, she dismissed his wistful tone, uncapping the lip balm, running it over her lips. He slumped in the seat, one ankle crossed over a knee, a wrist draped there, a cleated shoe jiggling. The air reeked of his fear of losing, his anticipation of winning. Her gaze dropped from his profile to the elastic bandage cuffing the wrist of his right hand, so much darker than the left, which

168

wore the golf glove. "Are you sure a bandage is the right way to handle that injury?"

She might not have spoken. "Where would you like to be this morning, Periwinkle? If you had your wish?" He looked at her, eyes soft, mouth equable.

Her fingers sought the locket, the question floating on her mind like foam on surf. With you. You and our daughter, Beau, in a different world. A world without Braden and my fear of him. Without Christi or Stephanie or groupie galleries. No sick bastards who jimmy door locks and paint foul pictures. No grandmothers who don't want to age, gracefully or otherwise.

A world with no innocent, ravaged hearts that can't be mended.

She nodded toward the tee box with her capped head. "I'd like to be back out there. Getting this round in the bag. Getting you to the top of the leader board." She spared him a smile. "I have things to do this afternoon—such as my laundry in the bathtub."

He returned her smile. "I promise I'll play fast when the rain stops. I won't hold you up."

"Thanks." She screwed the cap off and onto the Carmex, then stuck it into her pocket.

Beau shuffled forward, searched a pocket in the bag and came up with two Tootsie Roll Pops. He held one out to her. "Chocolate. Right?"

Damn him. His memory was sharp as a serpent's tooth. With feigned indifference, she accepted the offering, discarded the wrapper, and stuck the sucker in her mouth, lips pursing around the stick. He did the same. Spellbound, she watched his jaws work in a sucking motion. When he cut his gaze toward her, she jerked hers away, stomach lurching, face flame-stitched.

He twirled his sucker within his mouth, took it out and appraised it. It loomed wet and shiny.

Reinserting it, he mumbled, "Sugar hits the spot, huh?"

"It's great. Thanks."

He twirled the candy again, his nimble fingers working the white stick. "What were you thinking about—when you were looking out the window?"

"About Leonard's caddie. About how I should be drowning with him."

"You're with me, though. So what were you really thinking about?"

She shook her head, knowing no way to tell him, too weak to lie when his eyes rested on her with concern and interest. "About some things going on at home."

"Angie antics, huh?" His empathetic smile reminded her how well he knew her, how deeply he'd understood her life before taking her into his. "Am I right?" A bead of sweat, or a laggard raindrop, glistened at his temple before trickling down a bronze cheek.

Perri lowered her window. Mist kissed her face. "Of course, Angie's antics. Does a leopard change its spots?" Remembering his own pensive posture, she invited, "What were you thinking about?"

"Home, too." He lowered his own window, then shifted his position, long legs brushing the back of the front seat. "Nonna mostly. Granddad was concerned about her when I called this morning. I think she's dying." He turned his head quickly, fiddling with the window button. In profile, his throat moved. The hair at his nape, longer than usual, had begun to curl. His left hand circled his wounded wrist, gripping. Loosening. Gripping.

She clasped her aching hands. "I'm sorry." Through the years Winonna remained a virtual stranger; a curtain had hung between them, filmy as gauze, steely as a vault wall.

He smiled, casting a mock leer on her, saved from childhood. "Are you naked under there?" His eyes bored hers as if he didn't trust letting them roam. "Don't those coveralls rub? Or chafe, maybe?"

"Rubbing. Chaffing. Roasting. I took the least of three evils. No clothes."

"You're either a glutton for punishment or a trusting soul." The words seemed to echo from off stage instead of from the man with burning eyes who sat so close she would only have to relax her body for her knee to touch his thigh.

She looked toward the sound of the other van returning. The soaked gallery had begun to emerge from the trees. "I figured you'd learned your lesson, and you'd bring extra balls today—so I wouldn't have to swim again." She pushed forward in the seat, bending to put her shoes on. The Velcro straps engaged, making soft staticky sounds on deadly quiet. Then she heard the words she'd sworn she wouldn't say. "According to Pete, since Stephanie's here, I'm lucky you showed up."

"Lucky?" The word hung in the charged air like the last persistent raindrops. Finally he asked, "Given Pete's meaning, how'd you feel about that?"

She straightened, hand going to the door handle. "Pissed." Threatened. "I want to win, Beau, and I can't do that without you." She opened the door. He reached past her and jerked it closed. Across the fairway, Justin Leonard stepped down from the van. "We're due on the tee."

"It's over with Stephanie and me, Perri."

Her head jerked around, eyes rapacious, searching for his emotions. Finding little to go on, she examined her own. Surprise tangled with disgusting glee, then with forced indifference. "You've found someone else."

He smiled, eyes quickening, one brow forming a V. "What makes you think so?"

You beguiling, phony bastard. "An educated guess. Been there, had that done to me."

"Actually, Stephanie left me. That happens a lot with me and women."

At a loss for words, conscious of the critical timing, she raised the door handle again, but his arm crossing her breasts, his hand securing the door, barred her exit. In the distance a rainbow pitched a roof over the forest, forming a glorious mockery. She sat back against the seat, releasing an exasperated breath. "Look, Beau, you can quit man-handling me. I'm not interested in your extracurricular activities."

His eyes narrowed. "You sure as hell sounded interested when you brought it up."

She met his gaze. "Idle conversation."

With one finger beneath her chin, he turned her to face him. "I don't think so. We've got a lot to talk about, Perri. We might as well bite the bullet."

Thoughts of rehashing that eight-year-old day, or what had led up to it, curdled her blood. "Not in the middle of the Masters. We're smarter than that, I hope."

His expression registered relief and triumph. "Thanks for that, partner." Still holding her chin, he dipped his head and whispered a platonic kiss on the corner of her mouth. Grinning, he licked Carmex off his lips as he released the door. "Let's go whip butt."

✳

Mildewed and fatigued from the sweltering Georgia heat, they trudged up the seventeenth fairway with Beau only a par short of shooting a solid sixty-seven.

"Getting tired, Periwinkle?"

"No way." She wiped her brow on a stiff sleeve. "I'm just looking forward to Hilton Head next week, where I can shed these coveralls."

His hand eased between her back and the bag, lifting, lightening her load a bit. Her gaze caught on his. She didn't bother to hide her gratitude.

"You're really naked under there, huh? You weren't just teasing me."

She felt the pressure of his fingertips against her buttocks. "Naked as Eve when she fed Adam the apple."

He glanced at the gallery lining the ropes, down at his crotch, then surreptitiously ahead to where Leonard approached the number eighteen tee box. "Watch it, partner. I've got another hole to play. There's more than one way to get disqualified."

She laughed, stopping to lower the clubs and rummage in the bag, her merriment giving way to frustration. She eyed the narrow, doglegged fairway, even scarier today than yesterday. "How do you feel about hitting your driver here, trying to go over the water? Seeing as how you've taken out half the irons, that might be your only choice."

"Give me my trusty one iron."

Guilt reared its head. "I'm strong, Beau. Leaving clubs out only makes it hard on you."

"No, you're doing that." He grinned nefariously. "Keep it up. It feels familiar."

He extracted the iron and took a powerful practice swing. Lowering the club, he stared down at the ball, addressing the turf. "I think we should try again, Perri."

Her heartbeat jarred her entire body before bleakness prevailed, an old, deep tidal pool of grief. For a wing-flutter of a moment she wanted to drop the bag, jerk the club from him and move into his arms, but the conditioned part of her mind stopped her. "That really scares me."

He looked up, a fine wire of tension fusing his gaze to hers. "What?"

"We never had to try, before. We would now, and it would never be the same."

"Yeah, maybe you're right." His face shuttered closed, and his gaze went blank.

She spoke past the constriction in her throat. "You're up."

His first drive split the fairway midcenter, shaming Leonard's. Amid applause, Beau hoisted the bag onto Perri's back, helped her adjust it, then marched forward, eyes riveted on his tee shot. Longing and fear vied for top slot as she focused on his easy, long-legged stride, the motion of slender hips, the determined set of broad shoulders. Try again? She knew what that entailed. Forgiveness and total memory loss. And honesty. Visions of Chelsea and Braden spun behind her closed eyes as emotional inertia pinned her feet to the ground.

"You okay?" Leonard's caddie called over his shoulder as he loped past.

Shaking off the malaise, she stepped out, remembering where she was and why.

On the fringe of the eighteenth green, she stood next to Beau, his shallow, tensile breath echoing in her ear. They watched as Leonard squatted, putter at arm's length, an eye clinched. Beau whispered into the death-like quiet shrouding the green and gallery. "What I meant earlier is, I'd like another chance—whatever the hell I did. Is that what you want to hear?"

She kept her eyes on the ball in her hand, rubbing briskly with a wet towel.

"Lighten up," he breathed. "You're rubbing the numbers off. They'll disqualify me."

Eyes averted, she handed him the ball, looping the towel back through a bag ring.

Leonard left his putt short and marked it. Beau stepped to his own marker, placed the cleaned ball in its place, stroked it, while Perri's heart hammered. The ball veered off the cup leaving a final knee-jerking chance for par. He marked, picked up the ball, stepped aside, whispering. "How about it?"

"It's downhill a fraction, a ball outside the hole. Breaking left to right."

"Screw the putt. How about the second chance, Perri?"

Their gazes clashed as the echo of Leonard's ball dropping into the cup melded with gallery applause. Beau crouched behind his ball, drawing her down with him in pretense of studying the putt.

"Well?" His voice fell softly on her ear. Coaxing, yet expectant, too conclusive.

"You haven't suffered enough to deserve another chance." She pulled away from his hand on her knee and stood, warning in a whisper, "If you miss this mother, I'll kill you."

"How the hell do you know how much I've suffered?"

"Putt the damn ball." She strode off the green to the sound of the ball swirling in the cup.

He insisted she accompany him to the score tent, challenging another PGA tradition. Waiting for their turn to make today's play official, she tallied the numbers on his score card once again, heart clubbing. Hope ran rampant. Beside her, Beau shifted in his chair, unwrapping and re-wrapping the bandage, his profile grave. He'd secured an excellent position for starting the last day's round. The Masters could be his if he maintained the composure he'd shown today—kept up the skillful play. Yet, she saw no joy in his beautiful lion eyes.

Tenderness rippled her heart, allowing her to place Beau and Chelsea in the same frame within her jumbled mind. How had their lives been shattered? Braden's face and a feminine one she could only imagine whirled like a kaleidoscope. Beau's motivation for restoring their union puzzled her even more. Or were his words would-be pillow talk? Did he want to conquer her again to prove he could, like winning another tournament?

"You're too damned quiet." He reached for the Carmex lying on the table beside the score card and smeared balm over his full lips. "You're thinking again. What about?"

"A hot bath. Getting some baby powder on all these raw spots."

His hearty laugh drew a frown from the reigning official, equaling the scowl she'd been dealt earlier for following Beau into the van. "I've missed you, Perri," he said huskily, subduing his laugh. He tucked the balm into her breast pocket, his warm fingers lingering while a smile lingered on his mouth. "The time we spent on tour was the best time of my life."

Until when? When had Christi become a factor? And how many before Christi, while she worshipped him, trusted him enough to get pregnant? She'd always been afraid to love him, afraid the fairytale would disintegrate, the prince would desert the alien princess. And as she'd feared, when she'd let her guard down, he had. "At what point did you change your mind?"

His smile died, eyes clouding. His fingers circled his wrist. "When you left me, and I realized what a fool I'd been."

She moved the chair back on the grassy surface and stood. His hand darted out, but she dodged his touch, turning her head quickly to hide her stinging eyes. "I have to go."

"Sit down. I'll take you when I'm finished here."

"I'm working for you, Beau. Nothing more." She focused her gaze on the center pole of the tent, up high where a permanent rusty patch marred pristine white canvas. "Dole out your favors and fantasies where you'll be rewarded."

❋

Body tense, muscles and wrists aching, Beau pounded range balls in the gathering twilight while Pete watched, arms crossed, head cocked. Beau realized he'd retreated into a white fugue of thought when Pete jeered, "Give it a rest. You're making me tired."

"I'm trying to knock the cover off the friggin' balls, Peter."

"What the hell have you got to be pissed about? You're tied for the lead. Some of us are out of it and headed for Hilton Head with our tail between our legs."

"Right." Beau wiped his face on his sleeve, then peeled off a sweat-soaked glove, nodding toward the spectator bleachers. "Teddy's been over there giving me the evil eye for an hour. I'd better check it out."

"Maybe she heard Stephanie gave you the ax, and she's got the hots for you." Pete fished a club from his bag, used it to drag a ball to the edge of the huge divot Beau had plowed in the turf, and stepped up to it. "Hope you've got a pocket full of condoms."

Beau shot him a quelling stare and left him there. As he approached, Teddy gave him a lop-sided, begrudging grin that sent an ambiguous message. A trace of past-its-prime lipstick clung to one corner of her mouth. Mascara coated her sparse lashes, and her growing-out crew cut looked as though the curling iron had defaulted. A change was in the wind with Teddy, and for some reason, he felt a sense of relief.

"How's it going, Theodora?"

"Hey, Beau. You played like a demon today. Think you can keep it up?"

"Are you wishing me luck?"

She shrugged. "Perri could use a notch on her belt." She fished a cigarette from her jeans pocket. "I don't guess she told you what happened last night." She fired the lighter and took a long draw, then turned the Bic end over end in her fingers.

His gaze bolted to Pete, then back to her. Hackles of unknown origin moved along his spine. "We didn't talk about last night. Is there something I should know?"

Teddy shrugged, looking uncomfortable. "Maybe. Maybe not. She's pretty spooked, but if you put the screws in her, she'll probably tell you."

Considering the way she'd exited the score tent, he found that unlikely. "You told me. What gives?" From behind him came the solid whapping sound of driver striking ball. "Does it have anything to do with Pete?"

Teddy shrugged again. "Who the hell knows. But probably not, since he was occupied at the party." She squinted through the aftermath of another long draw. "Somebody broke into our room—or got in somehow."

A red mist of rage gathered at some unknown horizon and rolled inward, making it difficult to speak. "The same guy as two nights ago?"

"You know about that, huh?" When he nodded, she repeated, "Who knows. Two locks and a chair under the knob stopped him then. This time he made it in. Maybe we left the door unlocked. We haven't figured out that part."

"You know for sure it's a man?"

She looked pained. Her nose wrinkled, and the corners of her mouth turned down. "Yeah. He left his calling card."

"What does that mean?"

She exhaled a plume of smoke and told him.

The tale disgusted him. What kind of sadistic fiend were they dealing with? Gutter pictures in lipstick? Semen on a pillow? He would welcome sabotaged equipment anytime over Perri being terrorized. Teddy's conviction, like his, that she'd been singled out and rendered a victim rather than a random choice of a sick-minded prankster, upped the ante considerably.

Anger evolved to determination.   "Thanks for leveling with me. I'll look into it."

⁂

"What the hell are you saying, Beau?" Confusion—mock or real—washed over Mark Zamora's chiseled face like waves on a shore at low tide. He placed his bottle of near beer on the ringed lip of a pool table in the Putt Around. Bracing his pool stick against the wooden floor, he leaned on it as if he'd been kicked in the solar plexus. "You think I broke into Perri's room? Get a grip. I'm not the one who had her out wining and dining her. Maybe your buddy Jacoby didn't get the payoff he wanted."

The timing for that theory wasn't right. "Never mind Pete. Let's hear your story."

Mark took a swig of beer and shook his head. "You get the prize for holding a grudge. You know that, Saint?"

"This has nothing to do with that."

A crooked grin bared straight, white teeth in his dark face. "So enlighten me. How did my number come up?"

"You were wild about her when we were on tour, Zamora. Why would you have changed your mind?" Malice curled into a barbed knot in his stomach. "For all I know, maybe she's been with you the last eight years."

Mark's grin turned to a sneer. "I've been on this tour the last six of those years. Have you noticed her tagging around with me?" He lit a cigarette and blew smoke at the ceiling. "You're pissing me off, Beau. Big time."

He was either innocent or a meritorious actor. Beau waited. He wanted to be wrong, and   some inner sense that wouldn't quell came too close to being jealousy.

"Use your head," Mark said at last. "If I've got the hots for her, why would I treat her like crap? That's more your style than mine."

The use of present tense didn't escape notice. "Is that what Perri told you? That I mistreated her?" Was that a clue to her statement today that he didn't deserve a second chance?

"She's told me zilch. But she's told Teddy enough that we put the rest together." His dark eyes took on a benevolence Beau had once relied on, would like to rely on now, but couldn't. "Get off my case, huh, Beau? Maybe I could have done something like this back when the three of us were together, but not now. I'm sober, and she's too fine to mess with. You screwed up with her, buddy. Don't blame me."

"I guess you can prove where you were last night."

"Right here, dammit." Mark hammered the end of the pool stick on the floor.

"All night?"

He looked contemplative, then reiterated without conviction, "For the most part, yeah. Some of us who didn't go to the ball got together and raised a little redneck hell." A light seemed to go on behind the dark eyes. "Teddy was here. Ask her."

"I'll check you out. Count on it."

Mark eyed him, head cocked. "You really ought to get off my case, St. Cyr."

"You really ought to give me a reason, Zamora."

The look in Mark's eyes haunted him, but not enough to renege on his suspicions.

As he made his way to the Ferrari parked at the curb, a siren's wail rent the night, raising the hairs on his neck. His gaze stole to the motel across the street, to Perri's door. Light filtered through tightly drawn curtains. He leaned against the car fender, fighting the urge to cross the busy street, pound on the door, kick it open if he had to, and convince her she belonged with him. Then today's parting words, "Dole out your favors and fantasies where you'll be rewarded," echoed in his head. Favors and fantasies?

Crossing the street in the Ferrari, he framed a plan, sheer grit enabling him to pass up Perri's door. Once inside the rental office, he arranged for a private security guard to be stationed unobtrusively across from room twenty-three. No male was to enter the room before being checked out and judged harmless. Zamora's name topped the otherwise anonymous list.

As he pulled out of the parking lot, he let Teddy's account run through his mind again, examining it, searching for a name and a face other than Mark's. From memory, he reread the note that had been left in his golf bag, searching for a clue. He gave the motel one last look in his rearview mirror before turning the corner. Was Perri scared? Was that the reason for her pensiveness in the van this morning? Anxiety and guilt tightened his gut.

One more day. He had to finish the Masters before giving his full attention to ending this game of charades. Whoever the grudging bastard was, by centering on Perri, he'd tapped Beau's most vulnerable spot. But if Mark was guilty, maybe tonight's discussion would curtail more activity. If not, Beau had to hope Mark's feelings for Perri would lead him to watch out for her. Unless it was Zamora, and he was sicker than Beau hated to think he might be.

ℛ

CHAPTER TWELVE

Few words, other than strategy, passed between Perri and Beau during the Master's final round. Once they walked off the green amid thunderous applause, he didn't suggest she accompany him anywhere, which led her to assume he'd taken her at her word in the score tent yesterday. As cameras flashed and media clamored, they exchanged a perfunctory handshake.

"Thanks, Perri." Keeping his voice low, his back to the camera, he positioned his body to gain a moment's privacy. "You did an awesome job. I'm not sure I could have won otherwise." His manner seemed grave, his mouth void of smile muscles.

She met his solemn gaze. "You were destined to win, Beau. From the cradle." Even if it fails to make you happy. He was rich and famous, at the apex of his looks and skill. Yet none of these attributes had attained whatever kept that cloud of yearning in his eyes.

She stretched to kiss his cheek, low on his rigid jaw line. A camera clicked near her ear, a flash momentarily blinding her. She stepped back, murmuring, "Congratulations."

Abruptly aware of the throng of waiting children, a sense of urgency moved in. "You go on. I'll hand out the candy, and then I'll guard your bag with my life. You can pick it up later."

"I've arranged with security to take the clubs." He glanced over his shoulder, nodding to an alert, lurking blue uniform. Security. From some depth she could neither fathom nor understand, his mouth formed a smile his eyes didn't portray. "Once the junior masses are fed, turn the bag over to him."

"Don't you trust me, Beau?"

A muscle bunched along his jaw. "I'm not sure what's going on with you and Zamora. I can't take a chance."

She knew at that moment she hated him, even as her maniacal love for him raged somewhere within the same sensation. "Asshole," she whispered. Then reason moved in, allowing her to wonder desperately who had vandalized his equipment, and if that person and the intruder were connected. "Beau—"

He waited, his body emitting the sense of immediate interest and distant obligation.

He didn't trust her, just as she'd never trust him again. Nothing remained to be said.

Pivoting, she rummaged in the bag for Tootsie Roll Pops. When she turned back, she glimpsed his auburn head and broad shoulders above a sea of bodies ushering him toward the score tent.

Now as Sunday evening closed in, she sat cross-legged on her bed, wearing a towel, wet hair streaming down her back. She watched yet another rerun of Beau being presented the coveted green jacket, signifying his Masters win. The actual award ceremony had taken place while she'd shared a hot, windblown cab ride back to the motel with Teddy, Mark, and Divot.

She'd felt mentally wrung out, physically exhausted, disinclined to share a half-liter of cheap, hot champagne Mark produced from his gear and passed among his three peers while the driver pretended not to notice. Her mind had lingered at Augusta National.

Shaking off her malaise, she pointed the remote control at the screen. She snapped off Beau's image, reached for the phone and dialed. Larry answered. "It's Perri. Can I speak—"

"Hey, Perri!" Excitement bordered on homage. "We watched. You did great. Congratulations."

With spread fingers she combed hair back from her face to her crown. "I only carried the bag. Anyone can do that."

Undaunted, he quipped, "Easy for you to say," and then, "That Beau can play, huh? Amazing. He shot the props right out from under Tiger. You gonna caddie for him again?"

"Could I speak to Chelsea?"

"Sure, honey." Muffled, Chelsea's name filled the wire. Perri envisioned Larry yelling over his shoulder before coming back in a more intimate tone. "I'll get Angie. She's watering the weeds." He chuckled good-naturedly. "She'll want to talk, too."

She heard the phone being laid down. A dog barked. The front screen squeaked. Twice. Then finally, "Hi, Mommy. I was helping Mimi. I saw you on TV." Innocent glee filled her revered voice—glee and an edge of breathlessness that nagged Perri's instincts. "That guy with my hair won, didn't he? I'm glad. He's my favorite. Mine and Mimi's."

"Yes, he won." And because he had, because Perri had been part of it, she had felt compelled to call Chelsea, to hear her voice, to somehow share. Now the celebration took on a painful, hollow tinge. "How are you, sweetheart? You sound...tired."

"I'm good, Mommy. I had macaroni and cheese, and now me'n Larry and Mimi are going for frozen yogurt 'cause Mimi's on a diet."

A lonely weight gathered in Perri's chest, and spread outward to her limbs. Her fingers ached to touch, to savor her child. "Sounds good. Chocolate, I hope."

"Are you on a diet? 'Cause you looked skinny on TV. Mimi and Larry both said so."

"I get a lot of exercise." She looked at the sweat-drenched Nikes sitting inside the door, eye-marking them for a shower of their own before she allowed herself to sleep tonight. "You're sure you're okay, honey?"

A pause ensued in which Perri heard a Yorkie whine, heard the phone being shuffled, and Chelsea's murmured comfort. In her mind her daughter swooped to pick up and hold the interloper close to her bony little chest, burying her tiny chin in coarse short hair, nurturing, being nurtured in return. Loving and being loved. If not for Chelsea's surroundings, the hell of leaving her could be so much worse, she suddenly realized. "Chels?"

"Sorry, Mommy. Pepper wants to say hello."

"Honey, I don't have— Hi, Pepper. Kiss Chelsea for me, okay?" She spoke loud enough for Chelsea to hear. Then, louder, "Chelsea? Talk to me, sweetie."

"Okay. You made him happy. He's smiling." She giggled. "He's kissing me."

Even knowing that Yorkies were notorious kissers, the coincidence left Perri trying to swallow the broadening in her throat. "I have to go. You're going to the doctor tomorrow, right?" No answer. "Tell Mimi, I'll call tomorrow night."

"She's right here. She wants to talk to you."

Perri cringed, not wanting to hear Angie verbalize all the unanswerable questions worrying her own mind. "Not tonight, sweet—"

"Hi, Perri. You did good, honey. We were proud of you."

"Thanks, Mom. It was Beau, not me." A replay of all the shots, the skill, his finesse, raced through her mind. "I'll be sending the check . . . tomorrow, I hope."

"I'll watch for it, but, honey, you need to give yourself some credit. The camera mike picked up some of your and Beau's discussions. He wasn't an island out there, you know."

"Thanks, Mom." She waited, knowing what would come next, preparing her answer.

"You're getting along so good, I guess you've told him what we talked about when you were here." She paused, getting no response. "About Chelsea."

"We aren't getting along that well."

"Oh, Perri." Her how-dumb-are-you tone. "I can just tell by the way he looks at you—"

"It isn't Beau I'm afraid of. You know that." Although the thought had occurred to her in the last two days that maybe she should be. Beau's candy ritual, his patience and tenderness toward the children had shown her a new facet to his makeup. She now feared that learning he had a daughter seven years after the fact would not be accepted benevolently. "You have to let me work this out, Mom. I got myself into it, not you."

"Chelsea knows."

"Jesus! I told you not to tell her."

"I didn't. She knows in her heart, or she wants a daddy so bad she's adopting Beau."

Regret and anger reared. "I find that hard to believe. Are you sure you didn't plant so many innuendoes she formed that conclusion?"

"Of course I didn't." Angie's lowered voice indicated Chelsea's nearness. "She told Larry that her mommy was working for her daddy now."

"Then correct her." Perri groped for reasons. "She'll go out and tell someone Beau's her father. It's a small town, Mom. The word will get back to Braden."

"So you want me to lie to her."

Do I? There'd been too many lies of omission. "She shouldn't watch the tournaments."

Angie's hushed laugh fell short of genuine. "I'll let you tell her that."

"Put her back on."

"Perri, surely you aren't—"

"I want to say goodnight."

Angie's muffled words filled the background as the phone changed hands.

"Night, Mommy. Sleep tight. Don't let the bed-bugs bite."

Perri's gaze circled the room. A chill played across her naked shoulders. "I miss you, Chels. I love you."

"Bye, Mommy."

"Wait!" A salty, hot tear ran into the corner of her mouth. "Do you love me?"

She drew an exasperated breath. "Sure I do. Bye, Mommy."

Perri replaced the phone and turned the television back on. She lay back and closed her eyes, listening again to Beau's CNN interview. Curling into a fetal position, she entered a zone deep inside herself, a silent, numb, safe place from which she wasn't sure she wanted to emerge.

✳

Beau dialed the High Meadow number as he pulled out of the Augusta National gate. Braden answered on the second ring. "High Meadow. Braden St. Cyr." Formal as always, but the tone assured Beau that Braden knew whom to expect.

"Hi, Granddad. Sorry, I couldn't get to you sooner." He jammed a smile into his voice.

"Congratulations, son." The voice lacked the buoyancy a major tournament win warranted. Beau waited for more, getting only, "One down, three to go."

Last year he had won the PGA and the British Open, leaving the Masters and the American Open on the table. Braden's disappointment and his own guilt had not let him forget. "What's wrong with your wrist, son?" Even though he'd been there when Beau had the riding accident, arranged treatment, paid the bills, the old man's impregnable denial was intact.

"The copper bracelet wasn't doing the job."

"The press will pick up on that, Beau. They'll start riding you about an injury. Once you admit one..." He drifted off, having painted the scenario Beau knew only too well.

He wondered if his grandfather was born with a granite heart or if a transformation had taken place over years of disappointment and fear of loss and failure. "I'd rather they ride me about an injury than about losing the Masters. I thought the bandage would help."

He opted for a different subject. "That eye doctor—Doctor Brazzleton—called." The latest golf guru to hit the scene. Braden had read his promo and hired him. "He's meeting me in Hilton Head to explain his putting theory. What makes you think I need help with my putting?"

"Can't hurt. What have you got to lose by giving his method a try? You did miss that short one on fourteen yesterday."

"Christ, Granddad. I just won the Masters." Screw the short one I missed yesterday.

After a taut silence, Braden broke the three-day standoff. "I see that girl's back."

Beau felt he had vomited up a lead knot and could suddenly breathe. "You mean Perri."

"I don't like this, Beau. It's bad enough that you've got her caddying for you—"

"She's a damn good caddie. The best I've ever had. Over the years I taught her everything I learned, so she knows my game as if it were her own." He paused, then charged on, happy as a reprieved thief to be airing his convictions. "Perri fits me like a new golf glove."

"Then why did she leave you?" The jibe contained more reminder than assertion.

"On the golf course. Perri's good for my game."

"She's bad for your image—for your golf etiquette."

He caught a glimpse of his own smile in the rearview mirror as he checked the lane behind him. He had expected this. "How do you figure?"

"She had no business in the score tent yesterday."

"She'd just helped me tie for the lead. She had every right to be in there."

"You know that's not how it's done."

Maybe not. But pros took their wives and children to the score tent for celebration or consolation. They were a team. Beau envied them that. He had wanted Perri with him yesterday even though she'd felt out of place, even though his broaching what remained a taboo subject had spoiled it. He'd missed her like hell today, feeling like an alien during all the festivities. He voiced a conclusive thought. "Maybe it's time some of the old rules changed."

Beau heard ice rattle in a glass. He could imagine Braden taking a quick drink of dark scotch, almost hear him swallow. "You're getting a bad attitude, son."

You're damned right. Winning a tournament and getting no credit had a way of producing that result. "I guess I'm tired." Damn tired.

"That girl was never good for you, and I see that hasn't changed."

"I'd say that's between Perri and me."

Braden reacted as though he hadn't heard. "I'm seeing far too much of her. She's stealing your thunder, son. Pro golf is marketing as well as playing. You've got to build an image. She's black, and she's not—"

"You're going to be seeing a lot more of her." If tonight's mission proved successful. He glanced at the clock, switched to a lane with less traffic and stepped down on the gas.

"Why, for God's sake?"

Because I love her. Because I'm only whole in her presence. Because somehow I hurt her, and I want to make amends. "I'm going to hire her. We're going to work together." If she'd have him, now that she could have anyone on tour. "No disrespect, sir, but you'll have to get used to it." Eternal silence hung heavy as death's hand. "Are you there, Granddad? How's Nonna? Did she watch today?"

Braden released breath as if he'd been punctured. "She's getting weaker. Cal and Silky and I watched in her room with her."

Beau examined and failed to dismiss the sad connotation of the picture Braden painted. He imagined his grandmother propped on a rack of lacy pillows, wearing a pink satin robe, her hair curled and poofed by Silky, as though Beau and his gallery could see her and she wanted to make him proud. "Where is she now? Should I talk to her?"

"She fell asleep during the CNN interview. I've recorded it all, though. We'll watch it together... sometime. She has an appointment tomorrow with the chief cardiologist." After a moment, Braden added, "I dread that, for damn sure."

Beau waited out the silence. Rarely did Braden express emotion so blatantly, which gave Beau a portentous pang. "Could be good news. Things aren't always as they seem, Granddad."

"I'll hold you to that statement, Beau."

A dial tone blared. Nothing like guilt to keep a would-be legend hell-bent for leather.

℞

CHAPTER THIRTEEN

As she had promised Teddy, Perri showed up at the Putt Around for the celebration being held in her honor. She shared the big round table in the back, sitting between Teddy and Divot, surrounded by other caddies, including Mark, and some she didn't know. The television in the bar blared Masters reruns. Colliding pool balls echoed from the back of the room. Footsteps rasped on the small dance floor, and boisterous voices attempted to drown out competition, but she felt chilled by a cold wind of emptiness.

As though sensing her melancholy, Mark leaned around Teddy and flashed Perri a roguish, seductive grin. "Drink up. You've earned it."

Beau's suspicion about Zamora, and his parting shot today, reverberated in her head. "I'm only having this one. I'm trying to make it last."

He tilted his chair onto its back legs to get a better angle behind Teddy's back. "Our bus doesn't leave till late afternoon," he reminded. "A few raw eggs and some hair of the dog will get rid of any hangover by cab time."

So he wanted her to get drunk. She entertained images of Chelsea licking a yogurt cone with Angie and Larry at the Anchorage TCBY. In her mind, Perri wet a paper napkin with her tongue and blotted chocolate dribbles from Chelsea's chin. If teleporting were a reality, choosing between that party and this one would present no dilemma. But, she took an obligatory sip from the beer mug, making an effort to tune into the conversation around the table.

Mark shoved back his chair and crossed to the jukebox. He jiggled coins in his pockets, stretching the fabric of his shorts across his slender rear. Weight on his heels, he swayed absently to a Vince Gill ballad while his gaze ran down the printed selection inside the machine. Decisively he deposited coins, punched a series of buttons, and moved on to the bar where he ordered another near beer and traded golf stories with the man on the end stool. When the ballad ended and a country rock song began, he materialized between Teddy's and her chair, O'Douls in hand. Perri's hope died when his hand clapped her shoulder instead of Teddy's.

"I know why you're moping, and he's not worth it. Let's dance."

"I'm tired. I'd rather talk to everyone." She kept her eyes on her drink.

"This is not multiple choice." He tugged with one hand, dragging out her chair with the other, as effortlessly as if it were empty. Around the table, several heads snapped in their direction, cued either by the electrified air or Mark's resonant voice and non-refutable insistence. "Loosen up, babe. You showed up, so let's party."

She peered up into his sable gaze. His normally confident smile now harbored an uncertainty that stirred her guilt for accusing him last night when she had nothing to go on other than his feeling for her. Her resolve weakened.

One dance. She wouldn't have to touch him. Then she'd finish her beer and go.

She swiveled in the chair, but Teddy's hand gripped her knee, fingers piercing hard flesh. "I wouldn't, Perr. You'd be better off dancing with the devil."

Abruptly conscious of the possibility of Teddy's jealousy, Perri looked into her eyes, prepared to reassure her. But Teddy's eyes focused beyond Perri's shoulder, a lopsided grin in place. As if tethered to a yanked string, Perri swiveled in the chair in the wake of Teddy's gaze. Hands on hips, Beau stood in the open doorway wearing the coveted green jacket. The last throes of twilight framed his body in pink and gray hues, highlighting the auburn hair, erasing any ambiguity toward his identity. Unmoving, he stared around the room, letting his eyes adjust to the light. Or searching. She couldn't see his lauded amber eyes, but she felt their frisson when they passed to her. His glance was barely a flicker, but she reeled from its impact.

"You coming?" Mark's tone held new determination now that he'd spotted Beau.

"Are you nuts, Mark?" Teddy shot over her shoulder. She looked at Perri, her grin growing as she continued berating Mark from the corner of her mouth. "Didn't you see Pretty Woman? Richard Gere has come to take Julia Roberts away from all this."

Mark's hand eased from Perri's shoulder. He slipped back into his chair, sinking low on his spine, draining the O'Douls. Perri's heart tapped a grateful beat when he raised his hand as if asking to recite. "Over here, Saint," he called, piercing the quiet that had settled on a crowd suddenly rife with recognition.

Beau crossed the crowded room toward the greeting. As he approached the table, Mark kicked out a spare chair. "We started without you, but join the celebration."

Graciously, Beau accepted congratulations from the caddies around the table as the convivial air ebbed into hushed reverence. He lowered his long body into the chair, listing to one side, thumbs hooked in the waist of his khakis, an ankle crossing over a knee. A sockless foot jiggled an Italian loafer. His eyes swept Mark with a glacier gaze before settling a narrow-eyed stare on Perri. Her blood heated with irritation. At last he smiled. "Party on."

"Well sure thing, Beau Jangles." Teddy sighted Beau down the barrel of her Bud bottle. "But how can we get down in the company of a living legend? In the presence of a Saint?"

"Get off my case, Theodora." Beau grinned, managing to make the expression both combative and imploring.

Mark chuckled mirthlessly, as though hearing a worn-out joke.

Beau signaled for a waitress who approached the table with a smile as wide as a fairway and much more inviting. "Got any champagne?" When she laughed in raspy, good-natured mockery, he hiked a brow, granting a conspiratorial smile. "Wine, then?"

"Not wine you would drink." Kohl-rimmed eyes on Beau, she cocked a hip. One hand rested there while the other held a crowded tray. "How 'bout a pitcher of Margs?"

The crowd around the table stirred like kids who'd been offered ice cream.

"Make it two." He cast his gaze, less flinty now, on Perri, motioning with his head. "I'm sure you know the famous Perri Hardin. She just won the Masters."

The girl granted Perri a tolerant smile. "Not in this lifetime, honey." She swished away.

Sensing opportunity, bar patrons began sidling up to the table. Beau scrawled his signature on five flimsy cocktail napkins and the naked shoulder of a brunette in cheek-revealing cutoffs. Then while Perri watched, ears straining, he engaged Divot in conversation, rehashing his round, hole by hole, until the Margaritas and a tray of frosty glasses arrived.

Beau rose and circled the table, distributing and filling glasses with frothy liquid. He sat down and lifted his glass head high. "To Perri. The smallest, prettiest, best caddie in the PGA."

Applause and Teddy's "Damn straight" rode the smoke-fouled air. Gradually, the remaining bar clientele joined in the tribute. Everyone drank but Perri.

She smiled. "Female soldiers comprise fourteen percent of the American army. Why is everyone so amazed a women can caddie?"

Across the table, a caddie piped, "We're not amazed you can carry the bag. We're amazed you can think." The comment drew a group laugh.

Beau countered, "I'm not. She's a regular Einstein in the trenches." He rifled inside the green jacket, then leaned to pass Perri what could only be a check. Between the paper and his fingers, he sandwiched a small wrapped package. Lifting his glass again, he toasted her. "To you, partner. Let's make this the first of four major wins."

Neither could she drink to that. His proposal carried too high a price. Feelings played a paramount role in her life. Anger, fear, even joy and anticipation—most of all, faithless love—could weaken her, make her his pawn again. She ran her finger around the salty glass rim, gaze fastened there until she glanced at the check. A shock of anger raced through her and plowed her hairline. Her hands shook as she folded the oblong paper in thirds, creasing it with her nail. She crammed it into her pocket and shoved the wrapped package toward Beau with the base of her glass. The contents sloshed onto the scarred table.

"The check is more than enough." The package lay there, beautifully wrapped in gossamer tissue, tied with a yellow bow, her favorite color. Silence fell on the table, except for ice rattling in the glasses and margaritas being gulped. She blanched under embarrassed stares.

"Are you nuts?" Teddy nudged her roughly. "Open it. It might be the key to a Rolls."

"Or a jet," Mark quipped. "Hope it'll haul at least—" He counted off around the table. "At least ten."

Perri shot him a stifling look. In her corner vision, Beau retrieved the package. Wishing to be any place else on earth, she watched him untie the ribbon, peel off the paper. He opened a white box and took out a delicate gold bracelet. Reaching past Mark and Teddy, he grasped Perri's wrist and worked it over her left hand. Her right hand flew to the bracelet, but he held on, his gently pugnacious touch preventing her from taking it off. Her heart jolted when Mark shoved back his chair and stood. She released the bracelet as though it was hot as hell's hinges.

Abruptly, a little unsteadily, Teddy rose, too, drawn upward by Mark. Glancing over her shoulder, she followed him to the dance floor. The other caddies drifted toward the pool table and shuffleboard area. All but Divot. He refilled his glass, begrudging, "Thanks for the Margs, Saint. I gotta see a man about a dog." He headed for the neon men's room sign, glass in hand.

Chin tilted, Perri stared at Beau across the now empty table.

His sultry gaze ran down her body, returned to her face. "You look beautiful."

"Save your flattery for the waitress."

His eyes narrowed for a breath before he gave her a slow, intimate smile.

"That jacket doesn't belong here." Her tone indicated he'd committed a more severe sin.

"Neither do you. Let's get out of here."

Dread and need warred within. "Why? The party's here." She glanced at Mark and Teddy dancing, at the game area where her peers had migrated. "Your caveman tactics put a damper on the festivities, however." She folded her arms over her breasts, which had suddenly warmed from his gaze. "Either stop manhandling me, or I'm going to whip you, St. Cyr."

"Childhood habit." He laughed, eyes crinkling, the lines forming around his mouth more pleasant than she'd seen lately. He shrugged. "But you've got to admit it works. You're wearing the little token of my gratitude." His gaze lifted from her wrist and fastened to the locket around her neck, unspoken words screaming in the noisy surroundings.

Her hand darted there before she could curtail the motion, fingers grasping into a fist.

Signaling the waitress, he pointed to the pitchers of melting margaritas, stuck up two fingers, then stood and tossed a hundred-dollar bill onto the table. He held his hand out to her. "Let's go. I want to talk to you."

Should she tell him to go to hell or cut him some slack? His earlier words echoed. We have a lot to talk about. We might as well bite the bullet. Had they used their last reprieve? Despite her dread and seething bitterness she wasn't sure she could express in a rational manner, his invitation drew her like a lodestone. She stood wordlessly and preceded him outside.

※

Beau slid behind the wheel of the Ferrari, hooked his achy wrist over the steering wheel and watched rain splatter on the windshield. Overly aware of Perri's presence, he passed her a glance, unable to squelch a smile. "Asshole, huh?"

"At the moment, definitely." She stared out the side window, but her words were clear.

"At the moment?" Grim silence. "Hey." He jiggled her shoulder. "At the moment?"

She measured him, while in the flash of the Putt Around's neon sign, her face went from garish pink, to green, to blue. "You're the only asshole who can pull a real Jekyll and Hyde."

This was interesting. "Such as?" He turned sideways in the seat, drawing one leg up. His hand stole down to massage the gear knob, the safest grasp at the moment.

"Such as trying to buy champagne for that crowd. Including them in your celebration."

"You're wrong there. I tried to improve on your party. I haven't had time to celebrate."

She folded her arms, a sign she was settling in and didn't intend to dash across that god-awful busy street the moment the rain let up. "It's lonely at the top, huh, Saint?"

"It damn sure is, but let's talk about how I slipped from host of the year to asshole."

She dug the check out of her pocket, unfolded it and held it out. Were her hands trembling? What the hell? He'd made the check out for fifteen percent of his winnings and given her another five-percent tip. Was she trying to corner Wall Street? Her new love for money was rampaging. He looked at her in invitation, prepared not to like what he'd hear.

"This is made to cash." Sounding breathless, she jabbed the check closer to his face.

His nod brought an emphatic, "Why?"

"You go first."

"Because of Braden. Right, Beau? Because you don't want him to know about me."

So that was it. "Where the hell's your head, Perri? Do you think he doesn't watch television? That the reporters don't call him after every tournament and get his reaction to every little detail? That's the stuff *People* thrives on. The crap the tabloids are made of." He drew a breath, pacing himself. The subject lacked merit, but they were talking, and he had no desire to close the flood-gates. "Making the check to cash works for me, so why do you care? The numbers look the same once you put them in your bankbook."

When she fell silent, as though regrouping, his mind skidded around. Sometimes he'd catch her looking at him—like when he'd shown up tonight—in a way that made him think she might love him again, until he remembered how she'd left him. No prior complaints. No explanation. Nothing. She'd left him for money.

From a fog, he heard himself confess, "I made the check to cash because I don't know what you're into—what you need money for. My mind's playing all kinds of tricks. For all I know you may not want to leave a paper trail. So you can cash it if it suits your needs better."

"Goddamn you, Beau." She flared so quickly, so violently he jumped, striking his knee on the steering wheel. She glared, chest heaving. "There's nothing between Mark and me if that's what you're insinuating, you distrustful bastard. As if you had a right to question me. "

The incongruity of her exotic beauty and ability to swear like a preacher still appealed to him. Although his meaning had been far from her interpretation, relief sluiced through him like blood through his veins. He believed her. He told her as much.

"Then don't accuse me of that again."

He didn't bother to defend himself. "I get this feeling you're in trouble, baby, and it has to do with money." When she offered nothing, he ventured, "The half million is gone, isn't it?"

For an instant, she looked scared as a trapped fox; in the next she appeared closed like a fist. In the same instant he sensed she was torn, troubled. His mind ran over the math he'd been juggling since seeing the dilapidated backpack and worn-out Doc Martins. The black dress she'd worn to the party had solidified her financial state in his mind.

When he divided half a million by eight, her lifestyle, her urgency for money, didn't equate. "That was a small fortune, Perri."

"Everything is relative." She spoke so softly he barely heard above the rain.

"Does it have anything to do with Angie? Or Lee?" Maybe he'd screwed up again and someone else had sued him. He thought of her brother, his wild habits and scrapes, his eventual disappearance. "Chip?" No reply. "I'm out of guesses. You tell me."

She shook her head.

"But I'm right. The money's gone." Her silence answered his question. "Okay, then. You'll tell me when you're ready."

"You have no right to know, Beau. It's my life and you gave up any privilege to it a long time ago. For the last few days our paths tangled again. But that's over and—"

"No." He turned her in the seat, a little too roughly, considering her warning in the bar. But he had to stop her before she put the kiss of death on his plan. "I know I've got no right, but logic and protocol don't always match."

She tucked her legs beneath her, wrapped her chest with her arms and hooked her chin into the hollow of one shoulder. The thick braid trailed down her front. He clicked the cooling system down a notch, although he doubted cold air was what she attempted to ward off.

"Look, Perri, whatever's going on—or went on— you're not in it alone. At least you don't have to be. When you're ready tell me. If I can help, I will."

He sensed war raging inside her compact body, within her pretty head. He rubbed a finger along the burl-wood center console, knowing she was on the verge and could jump either way. His heart raced with the possibility of getting the answers he craved.

"Are you compiling an inventory of discarded women in case the groupies dry up?"

Discarded women? "What the hell does that mean?"

"Figure it out." Her hand grasped the door handle. "I'm expecting a call. Thanks for the check."

He locked the doors, the mechanical action echoing like gunfire in a canyon. Did locking her in qualify as manhandling? "It's raining. I'll drive you over there." Quickly, he started the car. When he rammed the transmission lever in reverse, she settled against the plush leather seat.

As he waited out traffic, seeking a chance to dart across the street into the motel parking lot, he mulled over the term "discarded." A parade of women ran through his mind headlined by his mother, his Aunt Ginger whom he'd secretly slotted to take his mother's place, Perri, the three fiancées before Stephanie. None of them remained in his life, but they, not he, were guilty of abandonment. And now Nonna would lengthen the list. He felt it in that corner of his mind where he steeled himself against loss. What kind of fool would lure Perri back, knowing she wouldn't stay? Even as he faced hopeless reality, he schemed to execute the plan.

He drove past the security guard's car without glancing that way. Had Perri noticed the same car and guy had been there two nights in a row? Had that alone frightened her? He swung the Ferrari into an empty slot and shoved the gear into park. "I need to come in for a second."

She looked skeptical.

He shrugged, shutting off the engine and the lights. "All those margs I guess."

Finally she said, "Sure," opened her door and got out.

He lagged behind as she approached the room. Right on cue, the guard got out of his Chevy. Beau motioned him back and held his breath, hoping his recognition of the man as a guard identified himself as the employer. As the door to Perri's room swung inward, the guard made a thumb and finger circle, leaning his rangy body against the car door, legs crossed at the ankles. He fished a cigarette from his shirt pocket, lit it and smoked in the rain.

Beau slipped inside and headed straight for the bathroom. He waited a timely interval, flushed and washed his hands, avoiding his eyes in the mirror. When he went back into the room, Perri sat curled in an ugly club chair with frayed arms, shoes on the floor, bare feet tucked.

"Feel better?" she asked.

Her got-your-number smile was tolerant enough to be encouraging. He wondered if she shared his feeling of being on an emotional roller-coaster.

"Much better, thanks." He pulled a straight-back chair close to hers and straddled it backwards. The odor of dried, adrenaline-induced sweat settled onto his awareness. He ran his finger around the collar of the golf shirt he hadn't had time to change, smiling an apology. "I should have asked to borrow the shower, too."

"I'm not that generous."

"I can be very persuasive."

"I remember." She made an issue of examining nails that could use a manicure.

Shrugging out of his jacket, he tossed it on the bed, studying her from the corner of his eye. She looked out of place in this stark, dingy room, an alien passing through, desiring to connect with nothing. He couldn't believe she wanted to be on tour anymore than he did. He'd sensed it in the distant look harbored in her eyes, seen the look dissipate only when she concentrated deeply on club selection and how best to employ the one they agreed on. If he could win the rest of the majors this year, they could each go on to a real life. More than a gypsy existence, and goals that could never satisfy him, no matter how often they were reached.

He ventured into his mission. "Since we bombed at discussing our past and the personal side of our future, how about we talk some business?"

Her brow knitted, umber eyes going murky in the dim light from the bedside lamp. In a predictable move that he'd noted coincided with mental discomfort, her hand went to the locket. She worked it gently back and forth on the chain. "What kind of business?"

"I thought the test went great, Perri." He smiled, hoping to clear the air, even though a lot of questions remained unanswered. "You passed with me, anyway. Did I? With you?"

She held her silence. He imagined reels turning in her mind, running backward, then forward, as she graded his every move over the past three days. Why the hell did her answer matter so much? But it did. He'd crossed that bridge and burned it behind him.

Eventually she said, "You were great. Once we got past the swim, that is." He thought her lips twitched, but in the screwy light he couldn't be sure.

"Then let's make it permanent."

Her answer surprised him. "Braden would never stand for that." Her tone could only be called sardonic. "He'd take you off the tour before he'd see us together."

"He'd see me in my grave before he'd let me quit the tour. And forget about how he'd react to us working together. He knows. I told him tonight."

"Told him what?"

"That we'd be working together from now on."

"Damn it. You had no right to tell him that without talking to me."

The little hellion. "I told him I was going to try to hire you. How's that? Can I hire you, Perri?" Can we be partners? Get to the bottom of this? Forgive and forget? He kept a gruff tone for protection. If she said no, it would hurt like hell. But if he didn't let her know how much he wanted her, it could hurt less if she refused. "For whatever reason, you've decided to be the world's richest caddie, and I'm in a position to aid the cause. I'm offering you fifteen percent of my winnings, plus perks. I'm on a hot streak. You might as well hitch to my star."

Rain pecked the window. A faucet dripped in the bathroom. He waited, one heel rising off the floor in a repeated, jerky rhythm that he knew, yet suddenly couldn't seem to care, exposed his eagerness.

Sounding as though she pulled herself from a deep mire of thought, she announced, "Nicki Stricker is skipping Hilton Head. Steve asked me to carry for him at Harbor Town."

"What did you tell him?"

"That I'd call him tonight."

He laughed, relieved and encouraged. "You were waiting for me to ask you. "Call Steve. Tell him you've been hired. Permanently"

"I want twenty percent."

What the hell is she into? "You're worth it."

She leaned forward in the chair and solemnly offered a handshake. In the pale light, the bracelet gleamed against her caramel skin.

He shook her hand and held on. "There's more."

A tawny brow torqued. She eased out of his grip. "Like what?"

"The perks."

She shrugged. "You'll buy me a hotdog and a coke between rounds."

"I'll spring for that, but I want you to travel with me, too."

"Why?" She tensed, mouth grim.

"So I'll know for sure you'll be there when it's time to tee off. Can't have you missing red-eyes or waiting while the bus driver changes a flat." He smiled, hoping to get one in return.

No way. "Can Teddy go on the plane, too? I wouldn't feel right about...."

They had come full circle. "No problem." Before she could present an addendum, he bluffed, "Not Mark, though. If you insist on Mark, that blows the deal."

She bristled visibly, but he didn't sense being the target of her ire. "Not Mark."

"There's more."

After a moment she said, "Tee it up, Beau."

"I want you to stay where I stay."

A brow quirked. "You know it's not kosher for caddies to stay with their pros. There's always been a class distinction—"

"I'm not Jewish, so kosher is no problem."

"No one would believe we're not sleeping together."

He hoped to hell they'd be right.

She shifted in the chair, folding her legs the opposite way, pulled the braid around and tugged it, meeting his eyes. "I'm not sleeping with you, Beau. Let's get that straight. Too much has happened—"

"Who asked you, Periwinkle?" He found a miraculous grin with which to chastise her, making damn sure his tone didn't divulge his exasperation. He wanted to make a new start, but battling over sex reverted to their post puberty days. "Considering what happened here two nights ago, I want you in my hotel so I can keep an eye on you."

She frowned, clearly irritated. "How did you know about what happened?"

205

"It's a small tour."

She rose suddenly and paced to the bed, sinking down. Palms at her sides, making indentations in the mattress, she stared at her bare feet. "Nothing's happened since. It was some sicko with a crush." She looked up. "I'll be fine staying with Teddy."

No sense telling her the guard had probably deferred another incident. "And the sicko?"

"What do you mean?"

"I think it's another caddie. So he'll be staying where Teddy stays. He's the same guy who's been harassing me, and he's decided to have some fun with you. It'll be harder for him if we stick together." He left the chair and sat on the bed opposite her, their knees almost touching. "Now that the Masters is over, I'll find out who the bastard is and what kind of game he's playing. But until I do—"

"You mean he's traveling with the tour?" He hated the fear in her eyes.

"Think about it. I had equipment problems at three different tournaments. I doubt he pulled that off by chain letter. Somebody who obviously knows our connection decided to kill two birds with one stone. He's got a hell of a hard on for you or a mean on for me." He managed a shrug. "Safety in numbers is how we'll play this. So you go with me, and stay where I stay till we beat him at his game. Agreed?"

"I hate leaving Teddy alone."

"He doesn't want Teddy, honey. He wants you—or wants you to think he does."

She nodded, meeting his eyes, giving her agreement, granting compliance.

"Okay." He could barely keep from high fiving her. He gazed around the room until he spotted the green duffel, rose and hoisted it onto the bed. "You finish packing. I'll call the hotel for an extra room. I'll either get one on my floor or have them move me

to yours. We'll sleep late tomorrow. We deserve it."
This was more like it, taking care of her again.
"We'll take off around noon, and get to Harbor
Town in time for a practice round."

"Not tonight."

He turned from the phone, choking back an
argument.

"I want to explain the new arrangement to
Teddy."

He forced a smile. "Fair enough." Based on the
unrest he saw in her eyes, the way her body jerked
every time voices could be heard outside, he
reneged on an earlier decision. "Don't be scared.
I've got a guard outside. He was there last night,
too."

Her eyes brightened, then swam. She turned
her face away, murmuring, "Thank you."

His heart felt like it had been ripped. Whatever
had come between them, at this moment she was
twelve years old, raking a sand trap at Owl Creek,
sneaking covetous looks at the junior golfers playing by. He was fourteen, knowing as surely as only
an adolescent boy could, that he loved her and
always would. He felt no different tonight. At the
door, he said, "I can't pick both you and Teddy up
tomorrow. The car isn't big enough."

She traced a jagged pattern in the soiled carpet
with her toes. "I've gotten good at hailing cabs."

"Be at Combs—the private terminal—by noon,
okay? I'll have lunch brought on board." He
smiled, throat tight. "I'll get champagne this time.
We'll celebrate. Again."

"You'll spoil me." After an eternity, she added,
"Again."

He hoped to hell to spoil her to the point she'd
stay this time. "I'll take that chance."

He leaned in. She didn't skitter backwards. He
kissed her on the corner of the mouth as he'd done
yesterday in the van, this time testing the tiny

opening with the edge of his tongue. Pliable. He took her in his arms and pressed his mouth to the top of her head. A lifetime later, her arms circled his waist . . . loosely. "Partners?" he whispered.

She nodded, her cheek moving against his chest. "We'll try, Beau."

And this time, by the grace of God, short of outside interference, they'd make it.

CHAPTER FOURTEEN

Following Winonna's Monday morning appointment, Braden took her to her favorite luncheon spot. In subdued lighting, surrounded by droning voices of stylish patrons, she nibbled salad, then pushed stewed trout around her plate, anywhere short of into her lap. Rather than ride herd on her silent pretense of eating, Braden drifted into his thoughts.

He'd been unable to rid his mind of his conversation with Beau. He couldn't cease thinking he'd lost him, as surely as he'd lost Beau's father at Beau's age, and for the same reason. A reason that galled him. A woman. Only the names differed. The foreboding sense of loss fit tidily into guilt-laden memories of his son. Beau Jr.'s heart had healed in his teens, then the hole had reappeared, killing him at age thirty. For years, the possibility he had contributed to his son's death by interfering in his marriage had provided Braden an endless supply of tormenting nightmares. Yet he'd done the same to Beau. Endeavoring to cram down the nagging thought, he signaled the waiter and ordered a scotch, only to have his retrospect drift into a different vein.

Considering yesterday's nationally televised kiss, odds that Beau and Perri hadn't compared stories were not in his favor. The change he sensed in Beau reminded him again of his son's rebellion, and recast his reflection into a downward spiral of rusted, jagged culpability. He examined the issue of the Hardin girl and what he'd seen in her eyes, a naked look even the damned media couldn't muck up. She loved Beau. She would never have left him without a fight, without confronting him, if not for Braden's ace in the hole. The note.

In a fit of drunken camaraderie, Nonna's Cajun grandfather had once assured him anything worth fighting for was worth fighting dirty for. As a young man, Braden had embraced the romantic theory, but had long since begun to question. He took a healthy pull of scotch and signaled for a second drink.

His eyes lifted to Winonna. Sorrowfully, secretly he watched her attempts to breathe. According to what he'd learned today about her condition, Beau's trip home would come soon enough. Much too soon.

After their son's death, and then their daughter's, trying to avoid more hurt, he and Winonna had all but stopped participating in life, except for the partnership they formed around Beau, an unspoken goal of seeing their thwarted hopes and dreams fulfilled in Beau. In Braden's dream Beau would replace his dead father, surpassing all he had never lived to accomplish. Today Beau was well on his way to fulfilling that dream.

Winonna dreamed of a wife for Beau, a woman to replace her own dead daughter. But Lee Hardin's mulatto offspring had not been the right one. Barring a miracle, Winonna would die with her own dream unrealized. Lately, however, since Perri's reappearance, he'd gotten the sense Perri would suit Winonna. He wished it were as simple for him.

A rustle from Winonna's side of the table drew his eyes. Relieved, he noted she was eating the crème brulé he had persuaded her to order.

"Taste good?" He stirred cream into his coffee, placing his napkin over a scarcely touched éclair. Getting no reply, he prompted, "Winonna?"

She looked up as though recalling she was not alone. The shaded candle in the center of the table cast a warm glow onto hollow cheeks, camouflaging an ever-increasing pallor. But Braden had ceased to pretend, vowing instead to find pleasure in the time left to them. He concentrated now on the airy, spun silk quality of her beauty, overlooking the ravages of age and illness. "What were you thinking about?"

She sipped water. "About the child I saw with Angie Hardin."

Her wistful tone and off-the-wall reply left him dumbstruck. "When?" She had been nowhere without him for weeks. Was she hallucinating, due to the lack of oxygen to her brain, as the doctor had predicted? "Where did you see them?"

She smiled like an ingenue taking a quiz. "I forgot you weren't there."

"Where was I?" He joined the game.

But it was no game.

"At the Institute, while you went for the car, Angie came into the lobby...while I was waiting for you." She pushed the crystal custard bowl away. One hand migrated to the diamond brooch on her lapel, which temporarily held the grotesque tubes of an oxygen tank on the floor beside her chair. The other hand fidgeted at her chest. "She had a child with her—a little girl."

"Did you talk to her?"

"The little thing seemed shy." Winonna tugged the tubes into position, holding the end plugs between the thumb and forefinger of each hand, the way a person paused before putting on glasses. "Except for her high color, she reminded me of Ginger...when Ginger was that age."

She hadn't spoken of Ginger in years, as though their daughter had never existed. She'd taken down all her pictures, had Silky pack them away in an attic trunk. "What age?"

Her hands lowered to her lap, still holding the tubes. Once-vibrant golden eyes focused in space, calculating. "Oh . . . I'm not certain." She looked to him for support. "School age, don't you think? What would that be? Six, I suppose."

His throat constricted while an eerie sense nudged him, the sensation of a cold, awakening wind at his back. "I didn't see the child, Winonna."

She smiled, contrite. "I keep forgetting. She looked just the way I remember Ginger."

"How's that, honey? How did she remind you?"

"Why, the red hair." She spoke as though he were daft. "Surely you must have noticed."

He took a long pull from the watery scotch and rephrased his original question. "Did you talk to Angie? Why was she there?" In that building filled with nothing but heart doctors.

"I only spoke with her for a moment. I think she's still angry, Granddad. Even after all these years." Her eyes clouded all the more. "Either she's angry, or she was in a terrible hurry."

He waited, suspecting her first assumption was correct, but giving in to roiling curiosity. In the silence, Winonna ducked her chin to her chest and unobtrusively as possible, inserted the breathing tubes into her nose, murmuring a hushed apology to humanity in general.

Finally, he voiced his raging question. "Did Angie say who the child was? Her name?"

"I thought she was a grandchild at first, but then she's so young—Angie, I mean."

And still beautiful, he'd wager. Vibrant. Alive. Come hither eyes and smile.

Winonna worked at setting the nosepieces, then lowered her hands with finality. "She said she was babysitting."

Braden's breath snagged, rendering him as debilitated as his wife. "For whom?"

She frowned. "Why I don't know. I didn't think—I had no time to ask. But now, I can't stop thinking of Ginger." Her voice quavered. When she lifted the glass, water sloshed, wetting her gnarled fingers. "I haven't thought of her in such a long time." She gave him a despairing look, eyes haunted and haunting. "I really wish I'd never seen that child."

Braden understood. If his hated suspicions were true, he wished it even more.

✳

The cab pulled past the private terminal and stopped before a metal gate separating the parking lot from the tarmac. Perri peered at a needle-nosed white jet, not a hundred yards away, engines running. A scripted High Meadow Farm logo beneath the cockpit window provided identity. Beau and Pete, along with a man in uniform, stood near the tail, stuffing luggage in a gaping hole in the jet's side. The driver's arm extended out the window, forefinger jabbing a nipple-size red button. It buzzed loudly. The gate began a slow, lumbering slide.

With an expectant look, Beau turned and strode in the direction of the car as it pulled through and forward. He opened the back passenger door before the driver had finished parking, pushing his aviator glasses to the top of his head, revealing welcoming, but inquisitive, eyes. He peered into the car, checking all seats, a satisfied expression lighting his face. She noted he had neglected to shave. Khaki shorts, a black Armani T-shirt, and scuffed docksiders, sans socks, didn't discount his officious, possessory air, however.

His legs proved as long and muscled as she remembered.

"Good morning." Fitting her sunglasses over her eyes, she gathered her backpack, the morning paper, and what remained of a Styrofoam cup of coffee. She sat on the edge of the seat, balancing it all on her knees, while Beau blocked the door.

Behind him, Pete continued to arrange bags in the cargo area.

Finally, Beau reached in and extracted her, waving the driver to the trunk for her bag. "Where's Teddy?" Definitely no remorse in the question.

"She decided she'd rather stick with Mark."

He flashed a Cheshire cat grin. "Oh, yeah?"

"Yeah," she echoed in the face of his glee. "Disappointed?"

"Crushed." He walked her toward the plane steps, hand placed at the back of her waist.

Perri watched the pilot stow her duffel as Pete worked with the golf bags. Rearranging clubs? He took one out, examined it. His bag and Beau's were similar. From this distance she couldn't be sure where the club ended up. Beau's voice reclaimed her attention.

"How do you feel about her shunning us, Periwinkle?"

She gave in to his contagious smile, forming an opinion at last. "Amused."

He waited for her to precede him onto the plane. "A definite change in the wind. Maybe now that Mark's got his hands full with that, he'll leave you the hell alone."

From halfway up the steps, she shot him a quelling look. But she silently shared his theory, even while questioning its validity. Despite her bravado, Teddy was vulnerable. Perri hoped she wouldn't regret her decision, that Mark would recognize her susceptibility.

Inside the plane, Beau offered her a choice of seats. Noting a *Wall Street Journal*, two Tootsie Roll Pops—one chocolate, one grape—and an Ace Bandage on a bulkhead seat, she eased into the seat opposite and buckled up. Pete clomped up the steps and took the spot behind Beau, emitting a heady odor of cigarettes and acrid Georgia sweat.

"Hey, Perri." He mopped his freckled face with his forearm, then ran that over his thigh. "Where's your buddy, Theodora?"

"She took the bus." She improvised a smile. "Thanks for doing my job out there."

His glance flitted to the back of Beau's seat, then to her, eyes vague.

"I saw you with the clubs. Thanks for taking care of Beau's for me."

"No problem." He engaged his belt, reclined his seat, and closed his eyes.

Perri stared out the window at the gooey tarmac until the pilot came on board, eased past them in the narrow aisle, and claimed his cockpit seat opposite the co-pilot. "Ready, sir?" he called backward, twisting knobs, flipping levers, adjusting his headphones, eyeing Beau in the rearview mirror.

Beau's eyes sought hers across the aisle. "Ready, partner?"

She nodded, unsure of her readiness or exactly what it entailed, but committed. For now.

"Wheels up," Beau called above the engine noise.

The plane taxied forward, radio crackling. Beau passed the chocolate Tootsie Roll Pop across the aisle. "Here, baby," he murmured, gaze sultry, mouth twitching at the corners. "Bite this bullet till the champagne cools." He rolled his eyes in Pete's direction, voice barely audible. "Give Peter time to doze off, so we can celebrate in private."

With an undeniable ripple sluicing through her, she took the candy and unwrapped it, her gaze fastened on his right wrist. A strap that looked like a long Band-Aid held what resembled a flat, round, dime-sized battery positioned at his wrist bone. She stuck the sucker in her mouth, then took it out, compelled to ask, "What's that? On your arm?"

215

Face solemn, he touched his forefinger to the round protrusion beneath the rubbery strip. "Bio magnetic therapy. The latest."

Had the injury progressed this far? "What is it?" The plane picked up speed, engine revolutions increasing, fuselage vibrating. A sense of foreboding moved through her. "What does it do?"

He shrugged. "Probably nothing, but it's supposed to provide a magnetic force that allows changes in the tissues and increases the blood flow."

The jet lifted, soared, graceful as a fawn clearing quicksand.

She put the sucker in her mouth and twirled it, pacing herself, fighting a prevalent dread. "Increase it for what?"

As if hiding the device might stave her interrogation, he began wrapping his wrist with the elastic bandage. "To speed recovery," he grudged around the sucker clamped in his teeth.

"How bad is it hurting you, buddy?"

His head jerked up, around, reminding her she hadn't called him that...in years. Her eyes burned. Her throat constricted. Did she see or imagine her emotions mirrored in his gaze?

"Not much," he said guardedly. "Don't worry about it. Okay?"

She had to worry. So much in each of their lives depended on his being able to play. To win. "Maybe the Ace Bandage on top of the magnet is overkill."

Eyes narrowing, he hooked the grippers into place. "I'll take care of it."

He stared at the bulkhead for a moment, an ankle crossed over a knee, foot jangling, striking a familiar, heart-tugging pose. Perri watched his calf muscle flex, unflex, flex, remembering how strong his legs had been, how he'd favored making love standing, considering any shower stall an erotic playground. She watched, drowning in memory.

Eventually he peered around the seat back, drawn, she supposed, by the sound of Pete's soft snores, then looked at her, his face sober. "Ready for that champagne, partner?"

In view of the news about his wrist, the celebration palled. "Bottoms up, Mr. Masters."

✻

Perri rolled onto her stomach, pulling the pillow over her head. The phone rang on, as if the mechanism were broken, or hung, assigned to eternity in hell. She counted twenty rings.

Emerging from the pillow, she checked the lighted hotel clock. Three in the morning. The twenty-minute interval calls had started almost the moment she'd walked into the room, increased to ten minutes apart, then five, and gone on for five hours. Not unlike labor pains.

What were they working up to? What could she expect at the point of delivery? She sat up, reaching to take the receiver off the hook. Her hand froze.

What had changed since the last call, when she had almost given in? Had she ceased to be a mother whose child suffered from a fickle, vindictive disease? Could she suddenly afford to take a phone off the hook and slip into blissful, uninterrupted sleep? After the first few calls, she had called home to give Angie a calling code. That had caused her to fire questions for which Perri had no answers. She had an eerie notion the caller was capitalizing on her plight. Yet outside her family, no one knew she had a child, certainly not an ailing one.

Getting out of bed, she drew the hotel robe onto her naked body. As she stood in the dark bathroom splashing water on her face, the ringing began again, amplified by the bath extension. She turned on the shower, stripped off the robe and

stood beneath the pelting water. The phone rang
on, too near, too shrill to be camouflaged. Her back
to the water flow, head beneath, hands clamped on
her ears, her thoughts drifted backward.

When she'd followed the bellman into the stark
but opulent room earlier that afternoon, she'd been
overcome by staggering waves of homesickness for
Angie's tacky little Louisville house, even for the
dingy motel rooms she'd shared with Teddy. Most
of all, she ached with loneliness for Chelsea. So
severe was her need, it left her feeling ill.

A solicitous bellman adjusted the cooling system and drapes, pointing out her ground-floor
proximity to the ocean, and bowed his way out of
the room. Finally alone, she curled on the bed,
grieving until Beau knocked on the door, collecting
her for the scheduled afternoon practice round
with Pete. Lethargy persisted through the afternoon, making her sluggish and heavy, club decisions and strategy hard to come by, harder to artic-
ulate.

At dinner in a beach café where they could eat
in their sweaty golf clothes, she sat uncommunica-
tive, aware, but too morose to apologize. Tension
lay palpable between Beau and her. Yet she could-
n't pin her malady on him, other than his eight-
year-old antics, and she endeavored not to go
there, not to dwell on what could never be changed.

Following dinner, Pete stopped at the hotel bar.
After picking up a *Wall Street Journal* in the gift
shop, Beau saw her to her door, waiting until she
was inside, locks engaged. The phone had begun
ringing moments later.

Perri shut off the shower and pulled back the
curtain to blessed quiet, filled with one conclusion.
She was physically ill, clammy and cold, all but her
forehead, which blazed.

She crept back to bed and burrowed into the
covers. When the ringing had failed to resume ten

minutes later, she formed a second conclusion. The caller was on the circuit with them, as Beau had surmised, and whether caddie, pro or groupie, had an early practice time, like Beau, and had called it a night. Grateful for unorthodox blessings, she drifted into sleep.

❋

Only a few local club members and a lone cameraman made up their entourage for that afternoon's tense, mostly silent practice round that she somehow had to get through. Before tomorrow's round, she had to shake off the scourge invading her body.

She knew her malady had become evident when they trudged onto the sixteenth tee and Beau fixed her in his gaze, venturing, "Are you pissed? More than usual, I mean?"

Even though every muscle ached, and her stomach churned, she couldn't help smiling. The question reminded her of how they'd once shared her PMS days, of his good-natured, cavalier approach back then to her recurring bitchiness. "No. Why? Should I be?"

"You didn't eat this morning, and you've been quiet as a cat all day."

He'd had breakfast brought to her room and joined her there, no doubt planning on their inevitable hashing out past issues. She'd spent the time in the bathroom, sipping coffee and fighting back nausea, barely making their tee time.

"Are you having second thoughts about the job?" He voiced that tentatively, as if testing the water.

How much should she tell him? "I didn't sleep well last night."

He accepted the driver she pulled from the bag, the naked relief in his eyes assuring her his poker expertise hadn't improved. "Something wrong with the room?"

Dar Tomlinson

She recognized his I-can-fix-it tone. Waiting for
an answer, he took half-assed practice swings, taut
shoulder muscles working beneath the fine white
shirt, forearms flexing. Her eyes riveted on the bat-
tery-under-a Band-Aid contraption strapped to his
wrist. In view of that, she decided to go easy on
him. "The room was okay, but why do I have to settle for the Taj Mahal? Wasn't Buckingham Palace
available?"

With a complacent grin, he hit the ball, which
faded to the right. He placed a second ball on the
tee and swung. Another fade. He eyed the ball's
landing and then the camera cranking away.
Handing back the driver, he rummaged in a bag
pocket, coming up with an elastic bandage, then
watched closely as she struggled to lift and position
the bag. As they walked, the cameraman on their
tail, Beau wrapped his wrist, hiding his desperate
Bio Magnetic theory.

"Did that outfit come out of that duffel you haul
around?" He kept his voice low.

The way his eyes had repeatedly stolen to her
bare arms and middle in the cropped tank top, and
to her legs exposed by the mid-thigh shorts hadn't
escaped notice. "It doesn't take up much room."

"About as much as a pair of pantyhose, I'd
wager."

"No big sacrifice. I don't wear pantyhose."

When their gazes connected, she imagined an
audible click. "You don't, huh?"

Years of playing this groin-tickling, nipple-
hardening game made it recognizable. "What's
wrong with what I'm wearing? We're only practicing."

He shrugged acquiescently. "Nothing. I like it."
They moved up the fairway in silence broken only
by the raucous sound of a party cruiser on Port
Royal Sound until he seemed to remember, "Why

didn't you sleep? Maybe they served you real coffee at dinner."

She decided to level, since he was convinced the harassment going on involved him. "Our friend kept me on the phone all night. Or until three this morning. It felt like all night."

He came to a halt. She kept walking, and he caught up. "You talked to him?"

"Not after the first time." Answering his quizzical look, she said, "I answered the first time, right after I came in. All I got was breathing and music—a television, I think—like a sitcom theme. After that, I let it ring." And ring, and ring, and ring.

"Why didn't you call me?" His gaze drilled her, making the back of her neck singe.

"Over the last eight years, I got used to not calling you, Beau—used to taking care of myself." And our daughter.

"Whose fault is that?"

His face swam a little when she attempted to level him with a denouncing stare. Stopping, she swung the bag down, thankful they'd reached his first errant shot.

He speculated, "I think I'll try my one iron here. The three wasn't enough yesterday."

She rummaged in the bag. "It's not here."

"Sure it is." His brow corrugated as he shuffled clubs, then looked at her, eyes narrowing. "Where the hell is it? It was here when we practiced yesterday."

Her mind skidded into reverse, hole by hole. "How do you know? You didn't use it."

His tanned hand gave the clubs another quick once over. "Son of a bitch." His mouth went hard, eyes glinting like melting resin. "These clubs haven't been out of my sight."

"Where do you keep your extra clubs? The ones you stored to make the bag lighter?"

"In the plane, the cargo area. But I'd never take the one iron out." He regarded her as if she'd incriminated him. "Hell, I can putt with it, if push comes to shove."

Or if someone stole his putter again, right from under his nose. "Pete took the one out."

"Why the hell would he do that?" He looked troubled. "And when?"

She told him what she'd seen when she arrived at the airport yesterday, what she hadn't been positive she was seeing. Until now.

The sweaty curls peeking from beneath his cap glowed like claret in the sun when he shook his head, but his eyes showed agreement. "The only place it could be is in the plane."

"Why would Pete take a club out of your bag?" Reasonably sure she knew, she wondered if he had a clue.

With a critical squint, he weighed her question. "Not intentionally, that's for sure." His eyes adopted resolve. "No harm done. I'll drive out to the airport when we're finished and get it—make sure I have it for tomorrow."

Tamping down her suspicions, she reasoned Pete couldn't have taken the club out intentionally, especially since he and Beau had practiced together yesterday. Yet, Beau had played that entire round without knowing the club was missing; the same thing could have happened today. Then tomorrow in the pro-am, when Beau's performance counted, suppose the wind came up, or it rained, and he needed more distance—distance the one iron could guarantee. She shuddered, trying to rid her mind of every wistful expression she'd witnessed on Pete's face when he watched Beau make shots Pete wouldn't live long enough to master... every triumphant smile when Beau had gone into the rough, or the water. Pete's voice came back to her, chiding Beau's frantic search for his only ball that day at the Masters. In Beau's quest to be liked for reasons other than clubs and clothing he passed on, free lessons and jet rides, the last thing he would ever want to believe would be Pete's envy and disloyalty.

Neither did she want to believe it, no matter how much the notion persisted.

When she handed Beau his three iron, their hands brushed. His head snapped up. She danced backward, but not before he seized her arm and clapped his palm to her forehead.

"You're on fire," he accused.

"Don't flatter yourself." She tried turning his discovery into a lame joke.

Grasping her chin, he lifted it to examine her eyes. "Hell, you're sick."

She shrugged. "I've got some kind of bug." Clandestinely, she rolled her eyes, reminding him of the presence of the cameraman, who, sensing a scoop, was recording every move, every word. "Hit the ball, so we can go."

Without further delay, Beau addressed the ball, aligned his shoulders and swung, executing perfect delivery onto the center of the green. The sparse gallery murmured appreciation.

"Amazing what a little concentration will do." She reached for the bag.

"No way." He pushed her hand away, and moved the bag out of her reach.

She attempted to wrestle it from his grip. Clubs rattled, louder than normal on the humid, breeze-less morning. He held on. She ground out, "Turn loose and start walking. I'll catch up."

His determination faltered. "You're sure? I can get someone else to carry it."

Mouth clamped, arms folded, she fastened her gaze on the green. After an eternity, he slowly released the bag and stepped out, protesting with body language. Just beyond the ropes, the small gallery fell into step. Perri mopped her brow and shouldered the bag. She attempted to stay out of communication range as much as possible. At the seventeenth green, she raked a sand trap while Beau putted. When she finished raking and began to climb out of the steep bunker, he was there, offering a hand. The other held the bag in place on his shoulder.

She panicked. "You can't carry that," she warned, voice low, teeth clinched. She took advantage of the cameraman's location, halfway to the next tee box. "Put it down, for Christ sake. We've only got one more hole to go. Read the rulebook. They'll disqualify you."

"Get your little butt in gear and come on. I'm carrying it." He started walking.

She ran around him, walking backward, sending a plea with eyes that barely focused. His free arm circled her shoulders to turn and tow her, forcing her to match his long stride. Shrugging as much as his burden would allow, he countered, "So they disqualify me. We'll spend a week on the beach pouting and evening out our tans."

She tried to balk. He kept walking, forcing her to march or be dragged. "Damn you, Beau. I can't afford a vacation. I told you—" She felt suddenly bleached with frustration. "You don't seem to get it that I'm in this for the money."

His laugh frayed her nerve endings. "That fever's got you delirious. Relax. I'll take care of it. We've got to get the hell off this course and get you in bed."

The statement contained no double entendre, she assured herself. Shrugging out of his grasp, too weak and exhausted to keep up, she followed in his wake, feeling naked and aimless but grudgingly grateful without the weight of the bag.

Once he'd hit three practice shots off the eighteenth tee, hating them all, the battle began again.

Had the gallery now watching them wrestle over the bag suddenly grown? And where had that second photojournalist shouldering a cannon-sized camera come from?

Quickly assessing her odds, Perri warned, "If you get disqualified, shove it. I quit."

He gave her a humoring smile, rankling her more. "Settle down, Periwinkle." Giving the bag a final, undefeatable tug, he swung it onto his shoulder.

Was it really that light? So effortless for him? She cursed being female, cursed her roiling stomach, achy muscles and joints. Visions of stalking away, off the course and up the cart path to the clubhouse, flared behind her feverish eyes.

Only Braden's imagined satisfaction stopped her.

As they approached his shortest drive, Beau's tone turned empathetic. "You need to study the rule book a little more, I guess. You know what people say."

She shot him what she hoped was a hard, punishing look. "What?"

"A little knowledge is a dangerous thing."

Her scalp tightened. "I know the book well enough to know that if you carry your own clubs you're disqualified. Why are we even playing out this charade? We're done for."

"We're practicing. Like the rest of the field, the Tiger included. Any one of them can jerk this tournament out from under me if I don't have my partner—" He gave her the renowned closed-mouth St. Serious grin. "—the world's best caddie, come Thursday."

Damn. Her already swollen throat welled up. She swiped a hot, stinging tear from the corner of her eye, jerking her head away, denying him of the pleasure of her sappy weakness.

"They can't disqualify me for carrying my own bag on practice day, Perri," he consoled. "Lighten up, baby. We're almost out of here. We'll get you some chicken soup."

"Asshole." She turned back to face him, smiling. Even her lips ached. "You could have quoted me that rule three holes back."

He raised his brows, eyes incredulous. "What? And miss the tantrum? No way."

At the end of the round, Perri slunk into the ladies room to throw up, while Beau surrendered to autographs and the interview she knew would wreak hell's fury, once Braden saw it on ESPN. God! How would she shake this before tomorrow?

In the midst of praying to the toilet, it occurred to her that Beau no longer appeared to be living life according to his grandfather's dictates. Somehow, in her feverish delirium, the realization seemed significant, but she knew better than to discount Braden's power over Beau.

℞

CHAPTER FIFTEEN

On his way to the hotel fitness center, Beau stopped by Perri's room. He let himself in with the key he'd wangled from her earlier and crossed quietly to the bed. In the hushed twilight, her breathing floated on a ragged plane, alarming, and, yet, reassuring in its rhythm. The spread and blankets had been thrown back. Beneath the sheet, she slept with her arms crossing her chest, knees drawn against her stomach, chin tucked onto her shoulder. Was she guarding her body or her heart? Even though she acted marine-tough, her vulnerability sometimes left him feeling helpless. Like now.

As if sensing a presence, she moaned and stirred, feet churning the sheet, exposing a shoulder, the curve of a breast as bare as one of Gauguin's Tahitian women. Restlessly she turned onto her opposite side and resumed the fetal position. She moaned again, her breath evening out for an instant, then gradually accelerating. He refrained from touching her until his will broke, then he allowed only the backs of his fingers against her brow. Warm. But not burning. She'd be fine once the fever totally broke.

Drawing the sheet over her, he tucked it beneath her chin and sank warily onto the edge of the bed. He eased off his loafers, watching her sleep in the gathering darkness, considering lying down beside her, holding her, healing her. Instead he watched and remembered.

God, she had been so sweet, so shy, and so damn tight when she'd finally said yes to what had driven them wild over the years. His hands went clammy with the memory of entering her, making her wholly his at last. Even though he hurt her, she had clung to him, arching her hips, urging him to love them into oneness.

And one they had been, for that year, in their own invincible world.

Then suddenly, seemingly without reason, she'd left. Not the tour, but him. And he couldn't lose the dread she'd do it again, with the least provocation. With the other losses, he had been forewarned. Perri had revealed nothing. He didn't ever want to hurt that bad again.

Quiet as a dream, he stood, stepped into his shoes and left the room.

※

A television droning behind Pete's door tipped Beau that he wasn't napping. Beau rapped on the door. After a second knock, the door swung open. Pete stood with a towel draped around his soft middle, soapsuds ringing his wrists.

"Hey." He stepped back. "I was doing some laundry and listening to Seinfeld reruns."

Beau followed him through the cramped room to the bath, noting the one double bed and a back-of-the-hotel view that denied water being anywhere near. He stood in the bathroom door watching Pete wring out jockey shorts and socks, place them on the counter and run a basin of fresh water. Pete took a swig of beer from the bottle on the counter, meeting Beau's mirrored gaze. "Gotta get the soap out or they itch me. Bet you wouldn't know about that, huh, Saint?"

He took another drink, staring down the bottle length. "Bet the fairies have already picked up your shitty shorts, scrubbed 'em and whisked 'em back to you." Grinning perversely, he raked the soggy stack off the counter and into the clean water with the butt of the bottle. "Or do you just toss your laundry out and get new stuff?" Torpidly, he swirled the clothing around in the basin, then

228

released the plug. Eyeing Beau's running shorts, tank and Nikes, he spoke above the sound of gurgling water. "You been to the gym?"

Beau nodded, settling a haunch onto the counter, arms folded.

"You look like Goddamned Schwarzenegger now. Ever heard of moderation?" Pete eyed him skeptically. "Besides, lifting weights is probably hurting more than helping that sick wrist."

That theory had a familiar ring. "I don't work out for vanity, Pete. You know that."

"So you tell me." He wrung out a pair of shorts and spread his handiwork across the shower rod. He flung the last sock haphazardly over the rod, then dried off the sink area with a wad of Kleenex. "Wanta beer? I've got a couple in the ice bucket."

Beau stood and followed him back into the room. "No, thanks. After the pro-am drawing, I have to take a drive. I thought you might want to come along."

"Where's Perri?"

"Under the weather."

"Like how far under?"

"Some kind of bug. She's sleeping it off. You want to come with me?"

"I can't. A ride where?"

"To the airport to get that club you left in the cargo section."

Pete gave him a pop-eyed gape, mouth slack. "What club?"

"My one iron. It's not in my bag, but it was when I loaded the clubs yesterday." He scrutinized the freckled face for clues, anything to substantiate or deny what Perri had intimated. Her hinted-at theory didn't jive since Beau believed the club pilferer and her stalker to be one and the same. Believing Pete guilty of the first offense was difficult; deeming him culpable in the second was impossible. "So where else can the iron be?"

229

"I hope you're right, but what the hell does all this have to do with me?"

Beau related Perri's version of the missing club while Pete opened a fresh beer, hands working by rote, eyes focused on Beau's mouth so intently he might have been lip reading.

"I'll bet she's right," he said finally with a sheepish grin. "I was checking your grips, seeing how much wear you had compared to mine. That's how the iron got left out, I'd say, but funny you only discovered it this afternoon." His grin had a chiding edge. "Shows you don't need it as much as you've got yourself psyched up to think."

Beau shrugged, unable to detect anything suspect in the tone or demeanor. "No harm done. You're playing in the pro-am tomorrow, I guess."

Pete's lips curled in disgust before he pulled a fresh but wrinkled polo over his head. "Yeah. I'm really looking forward to spending five fuckin' hours with another fat millionaire whose best wood is his pencil. How about you?"

"Most of those guys are nice enough." Beau smiled. "Once they get over being scared."

"You are a saint, aren't you?" Eventually Pete grinned. "I meant are you planning to play without Perri, since you two seem to be joined at the groin these days?"

His tone left little doubt of disapproval. Or was it envy? "We'll see."

❋

Returning from the airport, one iron in tow, Beau stopped to check on Perri again. When he let himself into the room, his first sense was of cold, saturating dampness, thick as a swamp. Then he sensed movement. Wispy and silent. Invasive. In the dark, his eyes sought the sheer drapes covering the glass slider that opened out to the beach. The curtain danced and tangled in the ocean breeze, sucked tight, then billowed like a wind-blown sail again.

Beau surmised Perri's fever must have been over the top for her to choose this remedy.

He thought of last night's phone calls she'd mentioned, her apprehension in Augusta, the security guard he'd hired. What was there about Hilton Head that made her feel safe enough to open the door to the cold spring night? Could it be his presence in the hotel? But he hadn't been in the hotel for the last four hours, and if he had, he'd have been at the other end of the hall. He credited her abrupt bravery and folly to the fever.

In darkness, by memory, he made his way across the room to close and lock the door. He unhooked a metal bar attached to the inside frame, lowered it and slipped it into a groove that acted as an extra lock. Even if the door could be jimmied, which Perri's irrationality had made unnecessary, it couldn't be opened now.

Her breathing had quieted. He bent over the bed and placed his hand to her forehead. Icy, like the room; the fever had broken. Now she quaked, as if with a chill. She stirred and tried to sit up. He sat on the side of the bed and eased her back down, whispering, "It's me."

"Mmm hmm." She pulled covers, held them in each hand and wrapped her chest. A sweaty-bed-clothes and soured-body smell rose up.

"The fever's gone. How do you feel now, baby?"

"I'm so cold."

No joke. "Why'd you leave the door open? This time of year, it gets cold at night."

He felt, rather than saw, her eyes open. "Hmm?"

After smoothing her hair back from her face he let the backs of his fingers steal down the side of her throat, connecting with the fine chain that held the locket. "I closed the door. You'll be warm in a minute." He felt her nod. "That's not your best bet, Perri, leaving the door open. I'd feel better thinking you're more careful than that."

She bolted upright, swayed against him, then pushed back to peer at him in the darkness. The covers rustled down around her waist. "I didn't leave the door open." Her fingertips squeezed his forearms, her voice croaky. "I locked it and pulled the blackout drapes."

The way they'd been when he'd stopped in earlier. On the heels of realization, nauseating spurts of adrenaline coursed through his veins. "You didn't get up later and—"

"No!" Her body went rigid, but she eased her vise grip on his arms. Eyes adjusted to the darkness now, he saw her lower her face into her palms. Her rigorous shiver had nothing to do with the flu. "Oh, God. He was in here. He could have— Oh, god."

He damned sure could have, while Beau was out chasing a wandering one iron.

After making a quick check of the bathroom, the closet, he returned to the bed. Pulling her hands down, he held her face between his palms, imagining he could see her eyes, read in them the panic he heard in her voice. "You didn't see anybody, or hear anything?"

She shook her head so hard the locket banged against her naked chest. "I'm scared." Her ragged whisper sent fingers of ice down his spine. When he took her in his arms, molding her against him, burying his face in her soured, tangled hair, she gave no protest. Chest to chest, their hearts hammered, as though each was bent on pummeling life from the other.

Footsteps passed the hall door, voices rising, falling. The electric clock on the bedside table purred. Her breath slowed from a race to a canter. As if waking from a deep dream, she pushed back from him. In the darkness, he felt her withdraw with regret-filled determination.

She lay down, snuggling into the covers. "You can go. I'm sorry I acted like such a baby."

"That was acting?" His voice projected a smile he didn't feel.

She pulled the sheet over her head. "I'm fine, now. Please go, Beau."

"In your dreams, Periwinkle."

Standing, he stripped his shirt over his head and stepped out of his shoes. He shed his pants and jockeys in one quick, unified motion, leaving them crumpled on the floor.

No questions had been answered about her leaving all those years ago, nothing had been solved. Blame had not been established, rejected or accepted. No reasons had been given, or excuses made. There'd been no threats or promises. He knew no more than he'd known in Braden's study eight years ago. In his lifetime, Beau could never recall caring less about knowing so little.

When he pulled back the cover, she skittered sideways like a Frisbee gone aground. "What are you doing?"

Her startled gasp hung on the stillness. In the amber light from the clock, her body gleamed against white linens. She made a dive for the sheet, but he held on, taking his fill.

"I'm not doing this, Beau. Do you hear me?"

The self-proclaimed baby was suddenly a shrew.

He got into bed and drew her into his arms. She tried to knee him, but his butt shot backwards, thwarting her. Laughing, he forced her knee down with his, then plunged a thigh between hers. His head swam, but he held onto his wits, reminding himself—

"Christ, I'm sick. Are you out of your mind, you mercenary bastard?"

233

"Shh . . . ." He kissed the top of her head, envisioning getting her into the shower in the morning, reacquainting himself with an old familiar pleasure. "I'm going to heal you, if you'll shut the hell up and be still." Making love had once been the cure to end all maladies, emotional and physical. Gently, he rooted his leg until it fit snugly between the warm folds of her most intimate flesh. Familiarity rushed his head and groin like a torrid storm. Her breasts melded against his chest, the locket cool and hard between their bodies. When morning came, he'd get a look at whose picture was in there.

"You can't do this, Beau." Her assertiveness was paling. "You'll catch what I have."

"Not if you don't kiss me. So restrain yourself. Okay, Periwinkle?"

Her cold, clammy body shook with soft laughter; like a chagrined child, she pressed her face against the hollow of his shoulder, suppressing mirth. Withdrawing his leg, he moved her onto her back and stared down at her in the darkness, arguing with himself. She was his, and he wanted her, so much that his hands shook. Still, she was sick.

With all the self-control he possessed, he turned her onto her side, her back to his front, and pillowed her head on his outstretched arm. Fitting her petite body into the undulations of his, he looped an arm over her waist, his hand inching up to cup a firm, cold breast. She stiffened. Her hand darted up to push his away, before she went slack, the avenging hand closing over his, holding on.

After what seemed an eternity, she murmured, "You're manhandling me, again." The faint-hearted admonition in her voice told him she was drifting back to sleep. Having no legitimate argument, he kept quiet, willing his erection into resentful self-denial.

Somewhere in the dark night, he whispered against her ear. "I love you, Perri."

Her body contorted, as if in agony. Again her feet thrashed, as though running in place, hellbent on escape. Beneath his chin her head rolled from side to side. She murmured protest, inarticulate except for the word, "No."

"Yeah, I do." Freed at last, the words cast him back to an innocent, less vulnerable time. He waited. She put up no physical struggle, no murmured or shouted protest, a positive sign.

"I love you," he whispered for good measure.

And I always will, unless you screw up worse, and what could be worse than leaving me?

✳

Scotch in hand, nearly catatonic with disbelief, Braden watched Beau's latest ESPN interview. He stood with his golf bag thrown over his shoulder, grinning into the camera eye. Whiskey-colored eyes danced in his classic, tanned face with more animation than Braden had seen in a long while.

With his own shit-eating grin, ESPN's Chris Kearney commented, "That bag looks a little light on clubs, Beau."

Beau set the bag down and passed his hand over the tops of the clubs in question. "Well, my caddie is the runt of the litter, if you haven't noticed."

Braden's stomach kicked like a frigid mare coming into heat.

Kearney kept grinning. Beau had played right into his hand. "Rumor has it, she's your wife. Any truth to that?"

"Perri Hardin's my ex-wife."

The drink in Braden's hand sloshed onto the Persian carpet. He took off his shoe and blotted the spot with his socked foot as the sports journalist laughed outright. Braden's neck burned beneath his stiff collar.

"So that's why you're carrying your own clubs? She's still making you toe the mark?"

Beau gave the idiot his best-natured laugh. "Actually, she's got the flu. She took a turn for the worse while we were on the course, so I'm helping out."

The flu, my ass. She wanted to put Beau through a few hoops, to keep in practice. Braden lunged for the remote control, but not quickly enough.

"Rumor also has it that you're injured. Any truth to that?"

Braden's eyes darted to the ace bandage on Beau's right wrist, the one that looped the bag strap. The bandage, right there in camera range, might as well be a neon signing flashing "kick me while I'm down." Braden willed Beau to deny the injury, to make something up. A wart. A bug bite. A scratch from that little alley cat.

Beau looked at his wrist as if reminded of the injury. "It's a childhood injury. Flares up now and then." He shrugged, eyes and mouth soft, serene. "It's fine."

"You were fading the ball to the right out there, especially off the tee. Any relation to the bad wrist?"

"Guess I'll have to open my stance a little and line up to the left, won't I?" He shifted the bag and aimed a broad shoulder at the camera, announcing the interview had ended with, "Have a nice evening."

The camera picked up Kearney's surprise. "Well, good luck tomor—"

Braden squeezed the red button on the control and slammed it onto the coffee table. He seized the cellular, stalked to the liquor cabinet and poured liberally. Before he could make his intended call, the phone rang.

"Braden St. Cyr." Not a damn chance of the caller being Beau, and only one other person had the cellular number. "Is that you?" Whoever this guy was, he had impeccable timing.

"So, how'd you like the interview? Did you know Golden Boy is injured?"

"All I know is you haven't done me a damn bit of good."

"Patience, sir. Rome wasn't built in a day." He snapped his lighter and exhaled.

The fool's originality with words matched his success record. While Braden had the vindictive bastard, he'd try to ease his own mind a bit. "How are they getting along? Beau and that girl?" Their cavorting, tussling like horny puppies, as though Beau's brain had suddenly dropped to his crotch, rendering him unable to keep his hands and eyes off her, painted the question moot.

"I'd call it a strained truce. Apparently they've decided to let sleeping dogs lie." He laughed, a sound growing too familiar. "Pun intended."

Braden got lost considering the possible miracle of Beau and Perri's failure to compare stories. He pictured the note in his mind, wishing he'd forced her to give it back that day. Without proof of his deception, he could deny it. The thought of losing Beau now because of bad execution back then galled. But maybe they had talked, and the truce they'd formed was not strained, just volatile. Maybe they were biding their time, letting him suffer. He tried to read behind the lines of Beau's failure to call. He could draw only one conclusion. Again, Beau had chosen Perri over his family. Braden had to think of the bottom line, switch tactics. Winonna didn't have long, and she couldn't take another loss. Beau had to be drawn back into the fold. "I want to terminate our agreement."

Gut-curdling laughter filled the wire, then silence.

"You've done me no good. I'll mail a cashier's check, if you'll tell me where to send it."

"Keep your money in your pocket, Mr. St. Cyr. You can't buy everything. I'll be the one to say when the agreement's terminated." He hung up.

Later, lying beside Nonna in bed, mesmerized by the hushed sound of her shallow breathing, taking in the lavender scent of her talcum, the sheets, the air they breathed, Braden let the time since yesterday's doctor's appointment run through his mind.

In Cal's battered truck, he drove to where Angie Hardin lived. In a slouch hat, he'd hunched behind the wheel pretending to doze, watching, waiting. Nothing. His luck, if it could be so called, proved better at Lee Hardin's nursery. A red-haired child—one resembling his dead daughter as much as Winonna claimed—played about piles of bark chips and bleached tarps, building a sandcastle from a mountain of peat moss at the back of the lot.

Petite like the Hardin girl, she had Beau's grace, his economy of movement, his rust-red hair, and mix of Cajun-olive and tawny mulatto skin. Suddenly all the pieces fit. Perri's rage at being offered money could have been more real than he'd thought that day. Her sudden change of heart could have hinged on knowing she was pregnant. Beau had agreed not to pursue her because he didn't know. Otherwise, no utterable lie could have kept him away from his child. This child—if Braden's perception could be believed.

Anger burned like a hot iron behind his all-seeing eyes. He hated Perri for depriving him and Winonna of a natural heir all these years, despised her for leaving someone this precious and defenseless in the company of a no-good picayune like Lee Hardin.

As clearly and cleanly as a line drawn in a sand bunker, he knew what must be done. This was

Beau's child, born of the St. Cyr bloodline, from what the distance revealed. But no court of law would take his word for it. The heritage must be proven. After that, the battle must be waged and won.

Motivated by his wife's fragile breath in his ear, he cast out memory of tears and pleas from a different mother. If Perri deserved this child, she would be with her now. Beau's mother had left him, too, and she had never gotten him back. Now, sordid history would repeat itself.

✳

Shit. The old bastard was getting the shakes. Not only over what the two of them had been up to, but over what he'd done before. Probably thought that dirty prank was gonna come back and bite him in the ass, and judging from the way his dupes behaved on the course, he's probably right. Seems like they were getting down to the pillow talk stage. Almost made him feel sorry for the old man. He guessed that proved Fitzgerald was wrong. The rich weren't really so different from the peons. Shoving the whole thing in the tanks was not that easy, though, cause he kind of liked it. Hell, he'd get off on it, watching her squirm and watching Saint play macho man. She'd better watch her mouth, though, get off her high horse. She was like him, not one of them. She was born with street smarts Beau couldn't buy, but she and Beau were playing the who-done-it game. Once they got their heads together....

The old man didn't want her hurt, and hurting her would be a shame, but there was lots at stake here. A bad rap—even legit—could get him thrown off the tour fast as a cockroach on casters. And he'd come too far by the white-knuckle route to risk that. Not many handouts on that road, no gimmes like the Saint'd had all his life. But considering the liability, and the way they were guarding those sonvabitchin' clubs like they were hauling a kilo in the bag, maybe it was time for the fat lady to sing, then to get her off stage with a bang.

Goddamn pun intended.

CHAPTER SIXTEEN

Perri woke to dawn oozing through a crack in the draperies. She drifted back into sleep fog, then surfaced again with a mental jolt. Lying in Beau's arms, the night rushed back to her. Every sore muscle, nerve, and sinew felt like frayed wire, sparking, burning. A familiar, instinctive longing woke and uncoiled in her like a snake in her belly. Her emotions ran from desire, thrill, panic. She heard a low whimper, and appalled, realized it came from her.

Beau stirred and opened his eyes. She found herself staring into a tender, beautiful gaze.

"Well, good morning." His voice was deep with leftover sleep and smooth as kidskin. He rose on one elbow, and cupping her chin, peered into her eyes. "Looks like you've passed your crisis." He lay back, drawing her into his arms, lapsing into silence, eyes shrouded.

He was aroused. She sensed it in his breathing, as quick and labored as hers, in the perspiration dampening his chest, seeping onto her breasts. Most of all in the throbbing swell pressed against her stomach, creating a delicious hunger within her as well.

She worked her hands between them and pushed back, quickly and adroitly dragged a pillow between them, wrapping her arms around it. "Crisis is in the eye of the beholder."

He rose on his elbow again, then tugged gently at the pillow, his eyes resembling a hungry cat's. Finally, he smiled with impunity. "You frigid wench." Like an agile predator awakening, he stretched his limbs, lean and hard with muscle. Uncoiling from the bed, he gave her the pleasure of gazing on broad shoulders tapering to narrow hips and tight buttocks as he unhurriedly gathered his clothing and walked naked to the bathroom, his erection pointing the way through the semi-darkness. Wracked with indecision, and apprehension, she listened to the commode flush and water run briefly at the sink.

"I'm borrowing your toothbrush," he called through the open door.

The gall of the fool. Now he'd catch the bug for sure and cost her a day's pay.

She lay like petrified rock, lips clamped against retort. When he came out of the bathroom—dressed she hoped, since she declined to look—he crossed back to the bed and bestowed a perfunctory kiss on her cheek. She willed her eyes to remain closed, her arms to hug the pillow. Not to reach for him.

He lingered. She felt his indecision, her heart racing like a hunted deer. When the ringing phone pierced the quiet, her eyes shot open, heart knocking for a different reason.

His gaze locking hers, Beau answered, "Who is this?" Silence, too lengthy for Perri. "Answer me, you coward."

She flinched, when after another shorter silence, he slammed the phone on the hook.

"Did you get any of those last—" It rang again. Mouth grim, movements purposeful, Beau lifted the receiver, pressed the disconnect button and placed the phone on the nightstand.

Perri lunged, triggering her weakness and a swimmy head. She replaced the receiver with a bang. He reached. She clamped her hand tightly on the hard plastic conduit between her and her daughter. "I have to answer when it rings." Even if it meant listening to the breathing on the other end, imagining the thoughts, the intent.

"Why in hell would you want to? You know who it is. Why humor the bastard?"

His fingers worked hers, but she held on, attempting a severe warning with her eyes. "I don't know who it is. That's why I have to answer."

Eyes as fixed as a stone idol's, he demanded. "Who the hell's so important to you?"

Oh, God, Beau. She grasped at words. "It's a thing I have, a fetish." She sat up against a bank of pillows, drawing up the sheet, hugging it to her, feeling the new sharpness in her ribs. She switched tactics. "Just because you're paying the bill...."

He held up a staying palm, murmuring, "Get some more sleep. I'll be back."

A promise or a threat?

The moment the door closed, she rose on her elbows, staring at the flat, polished slab of wood, not quite believing what had gone on last night or what had not happened this morning. Her head lolled back between her shoulders, eyes closed. Agony stabbed her for letting him go.

Before he returned last night, she had lain feverish and lonely, imagining going home, collecting Chelsea and escaping to some hidden place, taking a chance on the ailing heart, believing in her delirium that her love could heal her daughter. Later when Beau had held her, doing for her what she imagined doing for Chelsea, she was torn, tempted to whisper the words, "Would you hold our daughter this way? Could you heal her?"

When they had woken, for an unguarded moment she'd caught the glint of defiled love in his eyes, like shards from a stained-glass window. Inside her head now, his voice echoed. "I love you, Perri." The vow resounded like the waves outside, and she felt compelled to rush into the hall and call him back. She lay frozen, gripping the pillow until once more the cold, constricting anger that had sustained her for the last three months restored itself.

If he loved her now, why had he stopped so suddenly that day eight years ago?

✳

Two hours later, while she was brushing her teeth, he appeared in the bathroom door, braced against the jamb, arms crossed over his chest as though content to watch. His hair, still wet from the shower, gleamed beneath the ceiling light, and his skin glowed healthily. He looked like Chelsea all scrubbed up for school. She rinsed her mouth and then the toothbrush, flicked it on the side of the sink and stowed it. Eyes locking with his in the mirror, she tied the robe more tightly around her middle. "I want my key back."

He snapped his fingers. "Damn. I left it in my room."

Rolling her eyes, she brushed past him, the smell of shampoo filling her nostrils.

"What are you doing up, Perri?"

Making myself less vulnerable. "I have to eat something. I'm kind of weak."

She rummaged through a stack of folded clothing, selecting a pair of modest length shorts and a sleeveless T-shirt. With her back to him, she slipped panties on beneath the robe. Under his fixed scrutiny, getting a bra on would be trickier.

His voice came from behind. "I'll order you breakfast, but you're not working today."

She wheeled around. His eyes held the unyielding edge of a sniper poised with a rifle. But his voice was soft. "I need you for tomorrow, when it counts. I want you to rest today."

Damnit! She felt like she'd been caressed, just as she was ready to issue another I-need-money speech.

As if he'd read her mind, he added, "I'll split whatever I win with you, after I pay my caddie. How's that?"

Beneath his macho strut lay a gentle and persuasive manner, one she'd once worshipped. She put the clothing back into the stack. "More than generous."

"Keep the chain lock on the door. I'll be late getting back. I don't tee till noon, and then I'm working with Brazzleton, Granddad's putting guru." He measured her reaction.

"I'll be fine."

"We'll have dinner, if you aren't worshipping the commode again by then."

She squelched a smile. "Do you have any clean khakis?"

"Sure. Why?"

"Either that shirt"—wild tropical flowers that turned his skin to pale milk chocolate, his hair to russet velvet. "—has to go, or those white pants do. The shirt is showing through."

He laughed, pulling his room key out of his pants pocket. "Bossy little bitch. And here I thought you were sick."

"I'm better." *You healed me.*

❋

Perri floated on her back in the warm, serene water beyond the breaking surf. The sun had gone behind a few pillowy clouds, lighting them orange and purple from behind. Day's end crowded in. Down the otherwise empty beach, a few boogie boarders shrieked and called to one another, voices hanging weightlessly above the water.

Adhering to a sudden portentous sense of being watched, she rolled over and treaded water. On shore, between her and her beachfront room, a lone figure stood tall and motionless, the position of the sun and the distance rendering him unidentifiable. Her scalp tightened, her mind forming Mark's name, his face. She hadn't thought he knew where she was, but finding her would be easy enough. And after last night...

She began a laconic stroke, hesitant to reveal her visual disadvantage or her apprehension, abandoning the easy pace when she determined the man wore swim trunks. She swam harder, unwilling to be caught beyond the breakers, should her visitor decide to meet her in the water. As she drew near enough for recognition, her heart slipped into calmer gear.

Beau's gaze impaled her as she walked out of the water toward him. He crouched next to the blanket she'd brought from the room, elbows propped on tanned knees, the chain of her locket laced through his fingers. Her heartbeat revved again. Had he opened the locket? Even as her mind framed an escape for her and Chelsea, it darted a thousand different directions, forming answers to the questions he would ask. At last she stood over him, looking down. Remnants of sun shone in his eyes, narrowing them, turning them to piercing chips of clear amber. The locket swayed from his fingertips, looming large as a lie.

He had opened it. She felt she'd seen it in those eyes before his gaze broke away, moved out onto the water for a heartbeat, then back? But then he smiled, and her heart skittered, with knowing the secret was safe. She wrapped her bare waist with her arms. "Hi. How'd you do?"

A slight lift of massive shoulders. "I played decent, but I didn't bring home money."

She fought back disappointment, misgivings for not being there. "Was it your wrist?"

He ran his gaze up and down her length, settling at her wrapped middle. "I couldn't keep my mind on golf. How do you feel?"

"I'm fine. I guess it was the twenty-four hour thing after all."

"So what are you doing out here?"

"I thought you'd be late."

"I thought you'd be in your room with the door locked, the way we agreed."

She only recalled him issuing an edict. Catching her hair, she twisted the water out, draped the heavy mass over one shoulder. "I'd be in the room if you were as late as you said you'd be."

He hiked a brow, still looking up at her. "Oh, so that's the game we're playing. What I don't know won't hurt me, huh?" He smiled wryly.

His amusement rankled. No such game or theory existed. What a person didn't know could hurt the most. She bent forward, swiping at the locket. He jerked it back and placed it beneath the towel where he'd found it. Her heartbeat began to calm as he abandoned his gentle harassment to nonchalantly finger the scar near her right ankle.

Her throat tightened. She stared down the beach to where the boarders were packing up, straggling back to their hotel, leaving a deafening quiet in their wake Briefly, her mind retraced all the different swings she had toyed with after the injury, the failing remedies she had sought. She wondered if her regret of losing her independence showed. His intimate touch and unspoken empathy brought her eyes back to his. Light was fading fast, the hushed evening veiling them in blue and purple shadows, wrapping them in a brief moment between day and night, when time stops and everything seems sweetly possible.

He ran his finger across the wet scar, then placed it to his mouth and sucked, eyes cast up at her. His tongue ran over perfect teeth gleaming in a tan face, then rimmed his lips. She closed her eyes, closing her mind against the portrait and the quickening between her thighs.

"Hmm...salty. Just like you, Periwinkle."

Before she could react, he karate chopped her behind each knee. She folded forward onto the blanket. With deft and sure movements, he caught her and rolled her over, pulling her arms above her head, pinning her wrists with one hand. Looking around wildly, to see who might be watching, she felt she'd been captured and tied at the stake. Except his touch was as gentle as his eyes...as his mouth when it covered hers in a kiss that thrummed through her blood like mulled wine. Warm. Sweet. Spicy. God....

But this couldn't be happening. Not with so many things still unsettled. She broke the kiss only to have his mouth move to her throat, nuzzling, nipping. Her neck arched against his mouth while her lower body curled backward in a half-hearted attempt to escape.

"Amazing how the body can separate from the mind, huh, Perri?" he tormented, lips feathering her ear.

"I hope you're having fun, because your antics are doing nothing for me."

"Yeah, right." His tongue dipped into the salty pool at her collarbone, trailed down and plunged into her cleavage.

Hips bucking like an unbroken colt's, she moaned. "Beau, for God's sake."

"Maybe," he mused. "But mostly for my and your sake." His mouth covered hers again, hot, full, working the angles and planes, dredging up the past.

She struggled in earnest now. "This is not fair." Her voice came from far away, born of memory bitter and sweet. "You do know what you're doing, don't you?"

He ran his hand up her bare ribcage, cupping a breast, lifting, brushing his lips over the mound of soft flesh he had created. "Damn right. I'm man-handling you. So whip me, if you can. But you can't. You never could. You can't outrun me, and you can't out swim me. Hell, you can't even win at arm wrestling. You're a girl, Periwinkle, so you might as well lie still and enjoy it." His head jerked up, his voice smoky with menace. "What's that I felt? A laugh? Better not risk that. When you laugh at me, it makes me horny."

The sexual romp he orchestrated rang familiar, born in puberty and nurtured through adolescence and adulthood. She'd been with no one before him and no one after, but could imagine no man more highly sexed or more skilled at the game than Beau. She didn't move. She couldn't, even though he wasn't really holding her down now. Only a leg resting lightly across her hips, one hand still holding her arms above her head, his touch light as a beloved ghost's. Only his gaze, dimmed by lust to dusty gold, held her in place, like a moth held by a straight pin to a silken trophy board. Lying motionless, she determined not to acknowledge or express her own want, or most of all, her need. She fastened her gaze to the vermilion-streaked sky, her breast lifting into his hand with every reluctantly labored breath. Beneath her, the hard mound of the locket gouged into her back, giving her voice. "I won't stand for this."

His hand moved to the other breast, stealing beneath the thin strip of her suit, a finger teasing her nipple. "Standing's my favorite, but I'll take it lying down."

She met his gaze, striving to convey, to fight him with cutting words rather than willpower. "You can't just happen by here and have your way with me, asshole. Not when there are so many things—"

"I didn't just happen by. I'm on a mission. I threw the putting guru over for this."

"We can't have sex here." Her head turned willfully, eyes testing their surroundings.

"Who'd see us? The rest of the world is in the shower." His nefarious smile was infectious. "We've been working hard. We deserve a reward."

She tried again, reaching deeper. "I've never been into sex for sex's sake."

He nipped the corner of her mouth, running a palm over a rapidly swelling nipple, soft chiding in his voice. "How well I remember."

She relinquished an achy smile. "I gave you a hard time all those years, didn't I?"

He glanced in the direction of his crotch. "What's changed?"

"You didn't suffer." Not the way she had, based on what she now knew was Lee's self-serving warning. "There were plenty of other girls standing in line to supply what I didn't."

He kissed her, a delicious hovering of lips, a whispery promise. "I didn't want the other girls. I took them because I couldn't get what I really wanted."

"We always want what we can't have." She twisted her face away.

His fingers against her cheek turned her back. "Not this time."

His hand moved from her breast to her hair, winding it around his fist, holding her face beneath his. Insistently his tongue parted her lips and slid deep between, to tease and twine with her own. A mass of sensations erupted. Old. New. Sweet and treasured. Brash and terrifying. She sank back. "Damn you, Beau."

"And you, Perri." He let go of her wrists, finger by finger, eyes sharp as bayonet points.

Freed, she felt cold, vulnerable, even more torn. She moved against him, exploring her craving, finding his body hard and taut. A quickening close to pain brought a soft sound from her throat. His heat flowed through her, a molten stream unleashed beneath her skin, thawing all the frozen places. His hands laid bare her want, no other emotion viable. Unrestrained and insistent, his mouth steeped her in the sensation of coming home. She ventured onto a plane free of score keeping, doubt, mystery or revenge, and slipped into a flawless era of their past.

His hand stole down her back to her buttocks, his fingers inside the fabric, scorching her skin, opening her soul. God, how she loved him...always had...always would. He couldn't hurt her enough to make her stop. How she wanted him now. She drifted back to waking with him this morning, to her unrequited hunger; realizing she was now being offered a feast, she surrendered to gluttony. Somewhere on the sound, a cruiser's horn rent the air, jerking her back to time and place. She froze, her body stone rigid.

They pulled apart. Beau rolled onto his back. He lay hollow bellied, shoulders broad against the blanket, chest heaving in sync with her breath. Then he braced on his elbows, head lolling back, eyes on the gloomy, darkening sky, his hair falling back in soft, deep auburn waves. He looked bone-less and inert as a Raggedy Andy doll, tossed down, discarded. He sighed, looking at her in defeated acquiescence.

Her need and desire raging, Perri thankfully closed her eyes, and felt like weeping.

✳

Beau lay there with the warm sand beneath his back and the sound of the surf in his ear. He did-n't trust himself to touch her again. Last night had been lust-filled torture, and he knew he would be fighting the same battle every night—though not from those same close confines—if he didn't hone his tactics. But with his sexual frustration grow-ing, how long before self-control broke? It wasn't only sex he wanted. He could get that anywhere. It went with the territory, just as Perri had said. He wanted sex all right, but he wanted it with her. He wanted her back.

Ultimately, he aimed to get that bag off her back and one of those little silver pins on her chest, identifying her as the wife of a pro. She belonged on the terrace with Ashleigh Sutton, looking that cool and beautiful, corralling babies as fine as Samantha, Sarah and Sadie, wearing Chanel shoes and David Yurman bangles. But first he had to get her into a negotiating-on-eternity frame of mind. Once they cleared that hurdle.... "Let's go swimming."

She lay motionless, one wrist covering her eyes.

He jostled her gently. "I mean it. Let's go swimming."

Lowering her arm, she rolled her eyes. "Swimming? Talk about euphemisms...."

He granted her a laugh, then leaned over, coaxing her with a kiss. "You're my best swim buddy, 'cause I taught you in a muddy creek." He nuzzled her ear, urging, "Let's go."

She shook her head as she sat up. Gathering her belongings with a rankled air, she drew the locket from its hiding place. With emphasis, he shoved it back beneath the towel and stripped his shirt over his head. "Butt in the water."

He pulled her to her feet, scooped her up and ran toward the surf. Even kicking, cursing and pounding his shoulders, she was about as burdensome as a pregnant gnat. He laughed, wading far out, then swimming, towing her along, dodging flailing arms while tuning a close ear to her sputtering coughs. When he reached deep water, he slowed his strokes and treaded, his hands on her waist. Eventually, her body began to move in her own treading motion.

"This is crazy." A smile captured her stern mouth. "If you wanted sex why didn't you simply point to one of those show-ponies in today's gallery?"

"I want you. Get used to it." Legs pumping double time, he eased a hand behind her head and unhooked the halter strap of her suit. It fell forward, billowed and floated between them, the midriff strap still fastened behind her back. He lifted her out of the water and directed a hoarse whisper at her breasts. "Hey, girls. Remember me?"

Perri laughed, breasts jiggling. "You're impossible."

"Right. There's probably a beach ordinance against what I want to do to you."

His declaration registered in her eyes, turning them from topaz to onyx. Assured he was gaining ground, he lifted her full, round breasts in his palms and brushed his thumbs over the nipples. A pleasure shock ricocheted through him, one her face mirrored. Still, she wasn't convinced. She paddled backwards, out of reach, vowing, "I don't want to do this."

His turn to laugh. "The hell you don't."

"I'm mad at you, Beau. I've been mad at you for eight years." He tried to ignore the thundercloud whirling in her eyes. "I don't even like you."

That gave him pause. If anyone deserved to carry a grudge, he did. But now was not a great time for debate. He swam around behind her. She revolved to face him, as though he pulled her on a string. She wasn't as mad as she would have him believe. Bent on conquest, he presented his best argument. Maybe you don't like me right now, but you love me."

She pitched onto her back and gave a well-directed, water-spraying kick. He grasped her feet, stripping her suit bottom down her legs and hooking it in his waistband in one continuous motion. Beneath the dusky blue water, cream-caramel hips, crowned by dusky-gold pubic hair, undulated with her languid stroking motion.

"You love me, Perri, and you're gonna be a lot less mad in about twenty minutes."

She cocked her head. "It never took you twenty minutes before."

With bait like that, he figured he had about thirty more seconds, tops, to donate to foreplay. "I'm older now, and wiser."

In a move that conveyed the end of the courting rite, he swam backward in the early darkness, drawing her through the chilled water toward the shallows. There he stripped off his suit, tossed it with hers into the breakers to wash ashore. Leading her, he waded to thigh-high depth, sank to his knees and took her in his arms. She was an appendage of his body. She fit those niches known only to Perri, the missing fragment of his soul. Their breaths soughed together as he slowly slid his hands down her arms, cupped and stroked her breasts, igniting a fire in him, and in her. Yet she whispered, "Beau, really, I shouldn't do this. I'm not...ready."

"Forget all that for now, Perri," he whispered back. "Make love with me."

Feeling her compliance, he pulled her tight against him and caught her buttocks in both hands, lifting her onto him, pressing his erection hard against her. Her legs circled his hips, and she clung to him like a barnacle, burying her face against his neck.

She moaned and flinched as he carefully worked part way into her, for she was tight, the water creating friction that within moments would be forgotten. He sought her mouth, kissing her softly, lingeringly, holding back, waiting, wanting to make it right for her. Then he realized she was taking care of herself, moving on him, grinding, deepening the kiss, expressing with lust what he knew went so much deeper, yet what she refused to say. He plunged, driving into her. She gave a little cry, and then their bodies found an ancient rhythm that spiraled them through the obstacle of a past that had kept them apart.

She tore her mouth away, her head tilting back, body arching, trusting, oblivious at that instant. He recognized her agony-ecstasy cries from deep, sweet dreams he'd indulged in while asleep and awake. He swayed, regained purchase and absorbed her shudders, her hushed whimpers the sweetest sound he'd ever known. The last labored gasp died into quivery quiet.

He held her until she began to move on him again, sending him rolling toward a pleasure peak, bringing him quickly to the crest he'd held back from. Set free by her caring, sanctioned by an urging mouth, he soared over the top, sailed in ultimate blackness, thrusting mightily, his own groans echoing in his ears, then he glided downward to reality. With her still astride, he sank back on his heels. In the darkness, he peered into her eyes, seeking out her satisfaction. Maybe they would never reach that soul depth of intimacy they once shared; or maybe the depth had existed only for him. But the sexual compatibility they had shared was intact, and other wrongs could be righted. Wounds could be nursed and healed.

"I love you, Perri." He kissed her, then eased out of her, wrapping her legs more tightly around him, breaking one bond, sealing another. "You know that, don't you?"

"You got what you wanted. Are you happy, Beau?" Her voice, free of chastisement, crammed with wonder, might have belonged to a child. Still, the words stung.

"Tell me you love me." His fingertips traced the planes of her face, her mouth.

"I love you. Does that make you happy?"

"Not when you say it like that." As though she'd been tried and sentenced.

In answer, her arms circled his neck, and she kissed him, slowly and sweetly.

They gathered their suits and dressed, then strolled in silence through the warm sand to the blanket. Immediately, she rummaged beneath the towel and slipped the locket over her head before pulling on a shirt and cutoffs. She braided her hair quickly and loosely, securing it with a band from her pocket.

As they folded the blanket, he ventured, "After what happened last night, I had the hotel staff move your things into a room next to mine."

Her movements faltered. "Why? So you'll have a steady bed partner?"

He grinned, heart quickening. "So you will, buddy."

Impunity-filled laughter floated on the crisp night air. "I wish it were that easy, Beau."

"We'll make it easy, Periwinkle. This tournament's not a major, and I don't tee off till noon. So we're going to have that talk if it takes all night. "Are you ready?"

"Yes." Her voice lay quiet, resigned. "I want that, too. I'm ready."

✻

In the shower, Perri discovered the bruises on her inner thighs and smiled.

Smacking of the fun and innocence they'd once shared, their sex had been good. It had been good to join, to shatter, then linger in the aftermath, pleasuring and being pleasured for the pure joy of it, drifting on the dream that they could make it right again.

For the first time in eight years, she felt alive, hopeful, ready to listen, hear, try to understand. While he'd been inside her, she had forgotten all that had gone before. She'd cared only for the way love had triumphed as they united in seeking and bringing fulfillment. A part of her had been reborn tonight. She loved him. He loved her. From there, they could start to rebuild—or perhaps only build— what she'd once believed they had.

Decisively, she turned off the shower, ran a thick, thirsty towel over her wet hair, and pulled on the hotel robe. When she walked into her bedroom, Beau stood beside the nightstand, holding the open locket in his hand, face rigid, eyes narrowed.

"Who the hell is this?"

She felt as if he'd struck her. His harsh tone and privacy invasion burned hot in her heart.

"It's..." She struggled to find words. "She's my daughter, and you have no right to open that locket." Hand extended, she crossed the room, bent on taking the locket from him before his malice contaminated the treasure inside.

He held it back, his stare unflinching.

"Give it to me." She kept her tone low and even, no longer intimidated by the threat of his seeing the picture inside. She faced a new qualm now. "You had no right to open that."

"I didn't. You left it lying here open. I think you wanted me to see."

His summation wasn't totally skewed. When she had gone into the shower, sealed in the sweet aftermath of their lovemaking, she'd been prepared to tell him about Chelsea. She reaffirmed her intention. Once his shock waned she would tell him; he would tell her what had gone wrong between them. Deceit would be behind them. "Why would I care?"

His laugh was caustic. "The way you haven't cared for the last three months, you mean?" Strategically positioning a shoulder to keep her at bay, he studied the picture in the dim bedside light, a jaw muscle ticking spastically. "Let's hear it, Perri. The whole story."

She held her hand out. Mouth grim, eyes narrowed, he placed the locket in her palm.

She studied the picture as if for the first time. Chelsea didn't resemble her nearly as much as she did Beau, but the black and white snapshot failed to reveal his vibrant hair coloring and the olive cast to her milk-chocolate skin. Only her delicate features showed. When she closed the locket and met his eyes, their unrelenting accusation strengthened her resolve.

"How old is she? Who's the father." His voice was dry as ashes, abrasive as steel wool.

"You forfeited the right to ask when you discarded me."

A spasm of disbelief raveled with knowing in his eyes, then flicked across his face, followed by something deeper, more vulnerable. An emotion she refused to give him credit for.

Her control gained ground, assuring her that her first instincts to hide Chelsea had been wise. She felt a sharp pain in her hand and realized she clutched the locket so tightly its hinges had cut into her palm. She slipped it over her head, wrapped the robe lapels over it, and held them in place. Her other arm stole up to grasp her waist.

"Why aren't you home with her, instead of gypsying around the country?"

His menacing tone stoked temporarily lapsed emotions; guilt and fear. A spurt of adrenaline coursed through her. "My working for you doesn't give you the right to pry into my private life."

He glared, but then his granite edge seemed to chip, hardness easing out with an audible release of breath. He crossed to a window overlooking the beach. Hooking his fingertips over the frame above his head, he swayed forward, staring into the darkness, back muscles pronounced. "Apparently Granddad was right." His voice sounded as if it came from a distance.

She sank to the edge of the bed, mention of Braden negating all bluster. Her mind reeled. Yet somehow she knew her focus and Beau's were the same. "Right about what?"

"He said you left me for someone else. Why the hell else does one person ever leave another?"

Sickened by his words, she held on to the carved bedpost, scarcely believing they were finally having the dreaded and craved discussion, finally talking about that cursed eight-year-old day. Her hammering heart contrasted her icy-calm demeanor.

He shifted to one shoulder against the window frame, still staring onto the dark beach, like a voyeur witnessing what had passed between them mere minutes before. His voice came heavy. "He said you mentioned California, and then you insisted I not try to find you."

Anger propelled her from the bed. "Braden is a liar." Cold, calculated and damning.

He whirled around.

Her nails dug into her palms. "He told me the same thing about you. He showed me a note you had gotten. A note proving you had someone else. That I shouldn't contact you to try to change your mind."

"You're the one who asked for money to leave. Have you forgotten that?" He glowered, spitting out the words.

Was he claiming no knowledge of the note? Only the relief of airing it all kept her from storming across the room and beating him senseless, defying his claim that she wasn't capable. "He lied, Beau. He played us against one another." She paced to the dresser, caught a glimpse of her harried reflection, whirled and paced back. "He already had the check made out when he called me into the study that day. The check, and the papers I signed. He said you wanted me to have the money in exchange for getting out of your life, so you could have the other woman."

"What the hell are you talking about?"

She stared at the garish carpet beneath her bare feet, her feelings that day materializing in the petal of an overblown purple orchid, zooming in and out of focus. "The woman better suited for your social standing and your career. Quote, unquote."

He crossed the room and jerked her up, his fingertips pinching her arms. "You're lying."

She shoved him off. "And you aren't? What about the note I read?"

"I never touched another woman from the time you agreed to tour with me." He ran his fingers through his hair, leaving it a little wild, a look that matched his eyes. "Jesus, Perri. Why would—" He clamped off the words, then began again, as if he couldn't help himself. "You were a playmate, and then a goddess, and finally my lover. I loved you. What happened? What the hell, happened?"

"I loved you, Beau. You were my protector, my knight. I saved myself for you, the only gift I could ever give you. You tell me what happened."

He returned to the window, hands gripping the side frames now, feet spread as though digging in for a golf swing. An inner voice warned her not to go to him. She waited for him to clear the slate. To explain the note. Silence lengthened. Hope plummeted.

Beau pounded a fist against the window frame. "Goddamn him! I can't believe he would do this." He fell silent, as if regrouping his thoughts. "I can't believe we let him, that we took him at his word."

She shuddered, revisited by loneliness and grief, by panic that had arrived with Chelsea. "Not hearing from you proved Braden was right."

"I tried to talk to you. You disappeared. I took that to mean he was right."

He turned around, glaring. "Not one word, Perri. Not one returned phone call. One letter. What was I supposed to think?"

A gentler voice urged her to tell all. Make a new start. "I—" His voice cut her off.

"He's old." He paced a few steps, paced back, hand in his hair again. "He's been through a lot— lost a lot of people he loved. But to do that to us— He must be a little crazy."

Spellbound, she stared at him.

"I was supposed to make up for all those losses. When I chose you over his...edicts...he thought he was losing me." Frowning, he paused in his rationalizing, then murmured, "And there's that asinine thing between him and Lee."

Fury propelled her across the room. She grabbed his arm and turned him roughly, demanding, "You're siding with him? Defending him? Forming a union against me? That's it, Beau? He's old? Never mind that he's a selfish, manipulating bastard carrying some kind of mysterious grudge. He's old, so that makes what he did to us okay?"

"Hell, no. But it makes it understandable. That's all I've got to go on right now." His gaze, haunted now, held hers. "Compared to everything else I've learned tonight, Granddad's lies and motives pale out."

Her stomach fisted. "Not for me. He took my life in his hands and twisted it. He should have given me the chance to deal with—" She had her chance now.

"I guess I have a different priority," he grudged. "One that hurts more."

"Which is?" She knew. She could read his emotions like a school primer. Except for the years Braden had stolen, she'd been reading them practically that long.

"Knowing you've been with someone else. Knowing you had the son of a bitch's kid." Some of his belligerent fervor returned, but not enough to erase the depleted life in his eyes. "Is it Zamora, Perri? Is that why you need money?" He pinned her in a hard-edged glare. "Is he stalking you because he wants you and his kid back? Christ, I can't believe this."

"Damn you." Her quavering voice angered her even more than his words. The wounded, unrequited part of her threw lye into his wound. "It's been eight years. What did you expect?"

"Eight frigging years doesn't apply. The guy must have been warming up in the wings. She's damned sure not an infant."

"And she's not a commodity. Her name is Chelsea."

"Whatever." He shrugged. "Chelsea." Eyes softening, he regarded her, as though letting the name settle on his tongue, while she allowed it to move from his lips into her heart. Then he regrouped. "I have a right to know whose kid she is, since you left me for the bastard."

Warring factions—sorrow and revenge—almost doubled her over, until her will strengthened. "Why does her father matter so much?"

"Because I had some wild-assed hope that Granddad was wrong. That leaving had nothing to do with me—you'd come back—you loved me."

She had. So much that the pain had turned her cold as dry ice, until Chelsea thawed her, allowed her to feel again, to secretly hope.

"Eight years I kidded myself that you weren't somewhere out there with someone else."

"The same eight years when you were going through groupies and debutantes like Attila the Hun while the whole world read about it in *People*."

He held up a palm, mouth rigid. "You can goddamn bet I knew it was an unrealistic dream. But I kept dreaming just the same."

A wisp of awareness allowed her to peer behind his own bluster to an emotion she hadn't yet let herself name. Tears clogged her throat, threatening to reveal her vulnerability. As much as she loved him at that moment, she distrusted his ability to stand up to Braden. "You aren't angry are you, Beau? You're hurt."

He looked away, then back, fixing her in a soft, level gaze. "Is victory sweet?"

Victory described what they had surrendered to in the water when they suspended blame and grudges to share love. "Bittersweet."

With a loud release of breath, he reached for her. She offered no resistance. He caught her face between his hands, pressing his forehead to hers, turning his head from side to side. Then he held her away, eyes seeking hers. "So you have a child, and she's not mine. That changes a lot, Perri, but it doesn't change the fact I love you."

"Are you lying about the note?" The thought had evolved to words.

"I've never lied to you. All the time we were growing up, I never told you one lie. When I went out with other girls, you knew it, and you knew why, but for some reason you waited. That made me want you even more. When you went on tour with me, I made a pledge to myself to have no one other than you. I kept my promise until you left me." The backs of his fingers lifted her chin, bringing her eyes up to his piercing gaze. "I've had a lot of sex, Perri, but you were my first love. My only love. You were the only one I wanted."

She stepped back, fearful of falling into the trap door that had opened in her mind.

He sighed loudly. "So you have nothing else to tell me?" His eyes burned with mute appeal.

She navigated through an emotional mine field. Her conscience tugged. Her mind waved a red flag. He couldn't be trusted with the precious truth involving their daughter. "I love you," she begrudged. "I've never stopped. How's that?"

His face blurred in a mask of resignation. "Who's the father? How old is Chelsea?"

She thought of a birthday party. In the picture Chelsea was.... "Five."

"And that's all you have to say?"

"Yes."

At the door, he turned. "I'm going out, but I'll have the desk post a guard in the hall."

"Don't bother."

"Look, Perri." Exasperation hung heavy and thick as moss in the South Carolina trees. "I'm trying to play golf here. I don't need to be worrying about you."

"I've taken care of myself just fine for the last eight years."

"So we've come full circle. Is that it?" His voice lay wooden, distant.

Her eyes misted, stirring gratitude for the dim lighting. "No. That's not it." At least Braden had now been exposed. "Thank you for the guard, Beau. That's very thoughtful."

She waited until he'd left, then got into his bed, hurting, quaking with a chill. At first she thought she'd had a relapse of the flu, but gradually she surrendered to the realization of the empty ache in her soul, grief eating like cancer. Defeat tangled with the senseless elation of being right about Braden's involvement in evil sordid enough to change her life.

On the beach tonight, lovingly, patiently, insistently Beau had taken them past a boundary that should have enabled them to confess, forgive and renew their love. When he entered her, brought her to completion and released his seed in her, even then he had belonged to Braden. Was she any better, withholding the truth about Chelsea? A calm, pragmatic voice surfaced, reasoning her out of her guilt. If Braden got hold of Chelsea she would grow up turned against Perri by any lie he chose to concoct.

Once Braden had been exposed, they should have commiserated in their loss, told all, banded against him, yet years of untruth had built a wall. Even knowing of Braden's treason, Beau defended him, just as he would if he wanted Chelsea. Beau would forever be Braden's puppet, be on tour, resentfully carrying out his grandfather's dream. If he would defend their enemy in the same breath with which he professed to love her, he could not be trusted to safeguard the bond between his child and her mother. She rose and went to her own bed.

Somewhere in the night, Beau pounded on the closed door between their rooms, calling her name. Jolted from sleep, she jerked on a robe and stumbled in the darkness toward the noise, heart pounding, head swimming. Opening the door a crack, she peered around it. He stood swaying, trying to focus, reeking of sweat, smoke and liquor.

"I want this door left open," he warned in a voice flaccid as a worn-out golf glove.

"Fine, Beau." She opened the door back against the wall.

Seemingly satisfied, he turned and staggered across the adjoining room and fell onto the bed fully clothed. When she was certain he slept she removed his shoes and drew the spread over him, as much as his sprawled position allowed. She lay down beside him, her hand caressing his prickly cheek until his ragged breathing turned to a hushed, melodious purr. Chilled again, aching, she looped her leg across his hips, her arm across his waist, and burrowed her head against his chest, seeking the peace of sleep.

℞

CHAPTER SEVENTEEN

She watched him go through the throes of grief, watched the same empty ache she had suffered at Braden's hands gnaw Beau's soul. While his depression was rooted in ignorance, it was nonetheless recognizable or real. He withdrew from her almost entirely in the remaining days at Hilton Head, to the extent of offering to rent a car for her and hire a guard to accompany her...wherever. She declined, but agreed not to leave the hotel alone, choosing to wait it out, believing he would accept Chelsea's existence once shock wore off. Their relationship would return to the amiable working arrangement they shared before giving in to their hunger and making love on the beach.

As though another man inhabited his body, each morning somewhere between midnight and dawn, he staggered in, turned on the television, then fell across his bed and slept fitfully until a wakeup call came through. Any short periods of time he passed in his room were spent in the shower, or staring out the window at the beach, drink in hand, shoulders rounded, head cocked in contemplation. The hours between the end of play and his newly adopted party routine, he spent on the range, pounding mounds of balls, lifting weights in the work-out trailer that followed the tour, doing further damage to an already excruciatingly painful wrist.

After the first night, she stayed in her bed, nursing a kind of sinister irony. While he grieved over a misconception, she grieved over her fear of blowing that misconception away like smoke. Constantly vacillating on whether to level with him or not to give him solace, she allowed guilt to chide her into silence, the bed her own cold, half-empty prison.

On Sunday, while the Harbor Town Links president awarded the MCI Classic trophy and a $270,000 check to Nick Price, Beau passed Perri the keys to a rented Mercedes, announcing he'd be in the bar getting drunk. "In case Granddad calls," he added with a sardonic smile that never touched his dead eyes.

"Fine." She fixed him in what she hoped was a glare ominous enough to make an impression. "Get it out of your system. Or don't. But nothing has changed—"

"A hell of a lot has changed."

"Not for me, Beau. Especially the bottom line. I'm gypsying around the country, as you so elegantly put it, for one reason only. To make money. If I can't do it with you, because you're hell-bent on tossing your game in the sewer, I'll find someone I can do it with."

His eyes quickened at last, pricking like an ice pick. "You're good at that. Finding someone you can do it with, huh, Perri?"

Only Pete hulking in the background, wearing a half smirk, half frown, kept her from slapping Beau's leering face. "Mark my words, you vindictive ass." She threw the keys at his feet. They ricocheted off his ankle, onto the hot pavement and skidded against the club house wall. "And grow up, Saint," she tossed over her shoulder as she strode away. "It's a hard-assed world out here. Especially once you color outside the lines."

"Lock the damn door. You hear?"

Without turning around, keeping her hand at hip level, she shot him a one-finger gesture, not as gracefully as Teddy could have, but pointed, nonetheless.

*

"So what's eating her, anyway?"

Beau's head jerked up from staring at the Absolut rocks in front of him. For an instant, he'd forgotten he was not alone. "It's not her. It's me. And you don't want to know."

"Sure I do. It's fun watching you progress down this path to self-destruction. She sure as hell pissed me off, claiming I was messing with your clubs." Pete eyed him, inviting comment.

When Beau kept still, he said, "So what's she bitchin' about? This time?"

Chest tight with burned-out anger rapidly dwindling to regret, Beau watched a replay in his head. "Besides me being drunk the last three nights, coming in a piss-poor fourth in the Classic, and chewing her out for letting Mark Zamora within ten yards of my clubs on the range this morning, I'm not sure."

Pete laughed. "Didn't I tell you?"

Beau made an effort to focus, then shoved the half-empty drink away. "Tell me what?"

"That a wife can settle a guy with a permanent slice on the ball. You proved that today."

Beau granted a begrudging smile, fishing in his pocket for money to pay the check.

"But since she's not your wife, maybe you can't blame her if your game's in the sewer."

"I'm not so sure." His voice emerged from the mind-fog Pete's words had leveled.

"What'd she do? Club you wrong today?"

"I'm not so sure she's not my wife." And it's damn sure time I find out.

✳

As Beau had ordered, Perri locked the door when she got back to the hotel—the one separating her room from his. Behind the closed and locked bathroom door, she called Chelsea, juggling the phone from shoulder to shoulder while she scrubbed the sweat and grime from her face with Noxzema. Then, heartsick with missing her daughter, brooding over Beau's behavior and how it threatened her finances, she got into the shower and indulged in a long, loud cry.

Twenty minutes later, her hair in a towel-turban, another tucked at her breasts, she opened the bathroom door and barreled into Beau. He stood with his hands braced against the doorframe on either side of her. Even recognizing him instantly, she fell back against the counter, breath snagged in her throat. Leftover terror set her ears afire. His contritely amused expression lacerated already chafed emotions.

"Damn you, Beau! You scared the hell out of me." Had he been hanging outside the door listening to her cry? Worse yet, eavesdropping on her conversation? She peered around him, eyes settling on the locked door between their rooms. "How did you get in here?"

Languidly, he lowered one arm, issuing her a license to pass. "They gave me a key."

Knees knocking, she sank onto the closed commode. "I thought you were getting drunk."

"Been there, done that." He gave her a placating smile. "I thought we'd do dinner and a movie... in the room—Antonio Banderas, maybe. You had the hots for him, as I remember."

She searched his eyes, his beautiful, wounded face for malicious intent, and came away with an innocent verdict. "How about Sharon Stone? We could do one of her movies for you."

"Don't use that word."

She hiked a curious brow, helplessly infected by his sudden boyish affectation.

"Don't say do okay, babe? I think I exhausted that word's limit today."

Laughter bubbled out of her torment to lie between them uncomplicated and unmarred.

※

While the movie credits and disclaimers ran down the screen, he turned to her, where she propped against his headboard in the hotel robe, the remains of a BLT on a tray beside her.

"I let you down, partner. I'll try not to do that again."

Her mind darted around and then settled on that period of which she had no concrete knowledge, other than the note, a period he had refused to acknowledge, and then eight years of painful fallout. Was he going to explain the note now? "You'll try?"

"I dumped you in the Classic. I'm sorry."

Teeth clamped on her lower lip, she bit down, disappointment silencing her.

"I'm sorry about the thing over Mark this morning, too—him getting too close. I know you're taking care of my clubs."

She nodded, beginning to taste blood on her punctured lip. "I'm doing my best, Beau."

"Maybe we're screwed as lovers, Perri." His throat moved, his eyes liquid, warm again. Beautiful. "Right now, I'd be grateful as hell just to know we're still partners and buddies."

He had opened a floodgate. Tears ran down and dripped off her chin into the absorbent terry robe. She laughed at his stricken look, suspecting he'd gotten what he wanted all along. Her helpless compliance.

"Is that a yes?" he ventured.

"Maybe." Brushing away tears, she scavenged a fry he'd left on his plate. She dipped it into a ring of leftover catsup, popped it into her mouth with phony indifference to his petition. "We'll call it probation."

Smiling, he raised the TV volume, eyes on the screen. "I'll call it a reprieve."

After the movie and a second room service delivery of ice cream, she found going back to her

270

own bed as difficult as she found talking to Chelsea each night, then severing the connection. But until the note was cleared up, until he confronted Braden, she'd never give her heart and soul, her body, mind and spirit again. She owed their daughter that and more.

CHAPTER EIGHTEEN

Braden sat at his desk still clutching rather than hanging up the phone. He feared that breaking the connection would open the gate on the barrage of emotions instigated by the private investigator's report. Damn it. He needed a scotch, but the final chime from the grandfather clock marked six in the morning, not evening. Adding to his misery, his stomach already felt like Silky had salted his eggs with lye, instead of salt.

He slid his hand off the phone, opened a desk drawer and took out a bottle of Maalox. Absorbed in the echo in his head, he loosened the bottle cap and took a sip. The sick-sweet taste gagged him. What he'd learned severed the last thread of doubt about the red-haired, caramel-skinned child.... Chelsea.

His eyes skimmed over his scribbles on the desk pad, his mind sorting facts: Chelsea Angela Hardin. Delivered to Perri Hardin seven years ago in Louisville General. Born with Patent Ductus Arteriosus. Surgery in the first hours of life. Second surgery pending.

He struggled to get his mind around it, to sort the onslaught of facts and feelings whirling like a dust devil in his head. Having copies of the medical records was illegal as hell, the investigator had reminded him, warning of the imminent consequences if the pilfering was discovered. While the coup provided Braden with familiar grief and a deeper understanding for Perri than he wanted, beyond that, the sordid fact of his great-grand-daughter's illness was virtually useless. Just as well, for now. He was unsure what to do with the knowledge other than try to swallow around the goddamned boulder it had lodged in his throat.

He shoved up from the desk, running a shaky hand through his hair. Maalox in hand, he crossed to the window overlooking the barn, the paddocks and corral, and watched the morning sun turn the meadow to pyrite. He detested the thread of pity running across the back of his mind. Pity for Chelsea, whose fate was determined too far back in Winonna's heritage to even trace. Then, like a starving mongrel puppy, Perri had sealed that destiny by taking up with Beau.

Braden sipped the sweet, chalky liquid. His gaze drifted to the corral where a new foal suckled, a gentle breeze ruffling its mane and tail. Braden relived the colt's birth two nights before, the agony the mare had endured to give life, the devotion she'd shown since then. She stood now, braced, serene, eyes cast in the distance, one with her world and her offspring. Braden tore his gaze away. Having played God twice, he was unsure he had the stomach, or inclination, to do it again.

He strode quickly back to the desk, and pulled out the Anchorage phone directory. Rifling through, he took a swig of Maalox, then ran his finger down a page and dialed the number before he could change his mind. A woman answered, her voice hoarse, sleep logged. He fought against apologizing and hanging up. But the vendetta had gone on so long he was no longer able to analyze or justify it clearly. Humiliation and anger had lost some of its sting. Reliving the incident that seemed almost petty now, failed to produce the intense hate he once thrived on. To inflict that hate on a third generation St. Cyr, one equally or more innocent than Beau, lacked appeal.

"Lee Hardin, please." His words emerged coarse, as though caked in rust.

Dar Tomlinson

He endured a pause filled with muffled voices, then, "He's in the shower. Can he call you back?"

"No." The refusal sprang forth of its own volition. "Tell him it's Braden St. Cyr. I need to talk to him." He refused to examine the word need, lest pride defeat him.

His heart hammered his ribs. Sweat seeped onto his upper lip, wet the collar of his robe. The repeated muffled sound brought images of a woman cradling a mouthpiece against her breasts. For a senseless, gauzy moment, Angie's face and ripe body swam in the murky depths of his memory. But Angie wasn't the woman censoring this call. That marriage had been sacrificed to a bottle—a side effect no doubt of what had happened twelve years ago.

"Lee said to ask what you want."

A pulse rioted in Braden's ear. His stomach kicked like a prodded stallion. Spurred by his new knowledge, his regret, and by a conscience too long ignored, he mustered determination. "I want to speak to him about a matter of mutual concern."

She didn't muffle the phone this time. Braden heard her repeat the words as though practicing a foreign language. Then he heard male laughter. Coarse. Vulgar. Amusement boasting no validity. "Tell the old son of a bitch to call my lawyer."

The words echoed through the line as if it was a dark, musty cave. Braden recognized the venom, the grudge, at the same moment he recognized the voice. Renewed humiliation reared its head like a bear disturbed from hibernation. With quiet rage, ignoring gut-wrenching disappointment, he hung up. He wanted to think of Perri, to remember how Beau had suffered when separated from his mother, his scars, but behind his wrath he saw only Hardin's bloated, vengeful face, heard his spiteful words.

Hands steady with purpose now, he flipped trough the yellow pages to Physicians and Surgeons. He ran a gnarled finger down the pages. Calvin Johnson, Jr. Family Practice. Braden wrote down the phone number and the address, assuring himself he had been willing to try another way. Time to call in a long overdue favor. A favor amounting to a DNA test.

✳

On U.S. Open Sunday, Perri unlocked the door to her Bethesda, Maryland hotel room, legs wobbly from hiking eighteen holes in intense heat and humidity. Slumping onto the bed, she reached for the phone, dialed information for Delta Airlines, then dialed again.

She was out of the shower, dressed in slacks and a T-shirt, a wet braid streaming down her back, when she heard Beau unlocking the door to his adjoining room. Her heart tripped, but she sucked up resolve. Steeling herself against facing him, she added her hairdryer and brush to the duffel on the bed, then glanced around yet another opulent hotel room she'd never see again.

As she rushed to zip the bag, Beau appeared in the common doorway. He braced a shoulder against the frame, looking exhausted, his sweaty body emitting the pungent aroma and relaxed posture of victory. His gaze took in the zipped, flight-ready bag.

"Where did you run off to while I was giving my speech?" He hiked an auburn brow and cocked his head, accentuating the cowlick in his hairline above his right eye.

She looked away, overcome with a desire to see Chelsea, to hold her.

"You didn't need me, and you had your hands full." Full of a huge silver trophy, which took two hands to lift, and a check for $465,000. In a search maneuver, she lifted the thick bedspread. A boxy platform supporting the mattress allowed nothing to hide in dusty darkness.

"I looked around and you were gone. I wanted to show you off on camera, then take you in for victory champagne."

She peered behind the bulky dresser, then opened and closed empty drawers. "Women aren't allowed in the men's locker room."

Beau dislodged from the doorway to sit on the bed beside her bag. "You're my partner. They'd bend that stodgy rule for the U.S. Open winner."

"I'd rather they bent the rule for me, and since I know that will never happen—" She pulled aside the draperies and checked the space they'd occupied.

"Perri."

Meeting his eyes for the first time since he'd entered the room proved difficult.

"What are you looking for? And why are you packed? We don't leave till morning." He gave her an effervescent grin. "We've got two majors under our belts and two to go. Get that black dress out of the bag. We're going on the town tonight to celebrate."

"I'm looking for my shoes."

"They're right there." He nodded to a pair of new, nutmeg-leather Bandolino sandals resting on a club chair. "But dig out those sexy black, high-heeled things. Okay, buddy?"

Her hands stole to her hips. "I'm looking for my Doc Martins."

"The maid's probably wearing them by now."

She stared at him. Considering the valuables he left scattered about his room, the tattered Doc Martens would be the last thing taken, no matter who the thief.

"I trashed them." He smiled. "Looks like I win the Bandolino-Doc Martins war."

"Damn you, Beau." She expelled air, folding her arms over her waist. "I told you—"

His smile fell a notch short of genuine. She supposed they shared the memory of her expansive I-don't-want-your-handouts-speech when he had returned from the hotel gift shop their first night in Bethesda with the Bandolinos in hand.

"I haven't changed my mind. I'm working for you, and we settled the perks in the beginning. Handouts weren't on the list." Every time he offered her one, she thought of all Chelsea had gone without, including a mother, as of late. Including a father. Her fingers circled the Masters' celebration bracelet on her wrist. She broke their gazes to look in the wastebasket beside the desk, in case the maid had given her a reprieve. Then she remembered how Beau had left her in the hall that morning, claiming to have forgotten the car keys. Taking no chances, he would have stuffed the shoes in his own wastebasket. They were gone.

She stared at the Bandolinos as though eyeing a bed of vipers. She jerked them up, balanced to slip them on, and secured the soft leather strap at her heel. "You get what you want, don't you?"

Gaze narrowed, he stared at her feet. "Sometimes. Enjoy, Periwinkle."

She hefted the duffel, knees almost buckling, and started for the door.

He intercepted her half way, wrested the burden from her—using his stable wrist, she noted—and dropped it to the floor. "What's going on here?"

Stepping out of his hold, she met his gaze. "I'm dropping out for a few days. I'll meet you next week for the Buick Classic."

"Why?" His hard-eyed look contained no glimmer of concession.

"Then I won't meet you if that's how you want it, but I'm taking time off, either way."

"Am I going to look around on practice day next week and find Mark missing, too?" He fixed her in a scorching stare. "Or maybe you'll be with Chelsea's father. Providing they aren't one and the same."

She seethed in silence. If she took up the debate, she'd miss her plane. "If you don't want me back, I'm sure I'll still be able to work." Her heart grew heavy, yet filled with a sense of release. Being with him every day, sleeping in the next room, watching his triumphs and losses, presented a heavy toll, left her longing at times, incensed at others.

"Screw me not wanting you back. I don't even want you to go."

Grasping the bag strap, she dragged it closer to her feet.

"Why all of a sudden?" His eyes filled with question now, bright and large as a child's.

From her pocket, she produced a cocktail napkin with a Congressional Country Club logo and placed it in his hand. "I was given this on number eighteen. It's for you."

His gaze incredulous, he crumpled the note. "Christ, Perri. How many of these have you seen since we've been together. They don't mean anything."

"I've seen one too many."

He caught her hand and drew her, half stumbling to match his long strides, into the bathroom, where he flushed the crumpled note down the commode and slammed the lid. He let go of her hand, their chests pumping in unison.

"You're running out on me." His eyes burned like autumn fire, then cooled to a wounded, guileless look.

"I'll be back, but what I have to do now comes first, Beau."

Having the last word granted no satisfaction as she left him standing among the sterile marble and mirrors, retrieved the duffel and left, the sound of the closing door deafening.

✳

The last night of her visit home, Perri curled on one end of Angie's ragged sofa, with Chelsea's head resting on her thigh. Angie occupied the other end. The blue light of the muted television played on Chelsea's sleeping face, her soft snores rivaling those of Sugar and Pepper.

"So that's the story of the new Bandolinos," Perri's mouth curved in a reticent smile. "Beau's as strong-willed as ever."

The ice cubes in Angie's tea rattled on the sultry night air as she lifted the glass to her mouth. She took a drink and twirled the sweating glass against her robed knee, smiling. "Sounds like he's finding you harder to handle this go round, honey."

"I'm trying, but he's like a little boy. How do you give a little boy a hard time?"

Angie drew her legs beneath her, burrowing in, delighted, Perri could see, to be discussing Beau civilly. "A little boy how?"

Perri considered. "Vulnerable. He's king of the tour, but beneath it all, he's frightened he can't hold that spot." She thought of his wrist, the pain, but saw no reason to reveal the trauma to Angie. "He hates traveling, hates the hotels. He sleeps with the television on every night, without the sound, almost as if he's afraid of the dark."

He had always slept like that to stave off loneliness. He'd stopped the year she'd toured with him. Now she'd lie in her bed each night and watch the eerie gray-blue light flash, tenderness building as she fought the urge to go to him, turn off the intrusion and love away the loneliness. For each of them.

And Mark had been right about Beau and his
laptop computer. While the rest of the tour partied,
celebrating victory or defeat, Beau spent evenings
in his room. He poured over the Wall Street
Journal while his room service food grew stale.
Then he passed what remained of the evening at
the laptop, not playing golf games, as Mark had
suggested, but searching genealogies, as though
looking for his errant mother, his dead father.
Those evenings enforced an admired quality for
her: his ability to operate apart from the crowd, not
needing safety in numbers. Somehow, in the small
confines of the tour, he maintained a mysterious,
aloof quality.

"I love him so much, Mom." The whisper lay on
the hot night, until a weak cross breeze from the
open windows carried it away, leaving a tremulous
pall in its wake.

"Oh, honey." Angie leaned to rest her hand on
Perri's knee. "Just tell him."

Her memory drifted back to making love in the
warm water of Port Royal Sound, feeling complete,
then barren. "He knows. But there are so
many...scars."

"You don't sound all that unhappy about being
back with him, Perri."

Which left her in a constant state of flux, drawing closer, then away. "We're not together like you
mean. I'm working for him. The agreement is, I'll
travel and stay with him, which makes it easier for
both of us."

"If you've slept with him, honey, you're together."

A twisted, torturous arrangement. "I'm not
unhappy with Beau. I just miss Chelsea."

"Now that he knows about her, tell him she's
his, and start over."

"I can't. Braden is too vindictive, and I can't
count on Beau standing up to him."

She pictured a mouse in a maze, constantly worrying the path with no end.

✳

In the Westchester Country Club men's grill, Beau wrapped his wrist in the icy towel he'd gotten from the attendant. Hugging the ailing arm to his chest, he lifted a sweaty mug of Coors with the opposite hand. He sipped, feigning rapt interest in a televised Nike tournament rerun, leaving Pete to swap golf stories with the waiter.

God, the wrist had killed him in practice today. He couldn't even shoot Braden's age.

In Perri's absence, he had agreed to join Pete and two other pros in a heavily wagered practice round. The coin toss had rendered him and Pete partners, and Beau had been as useful as a blind brain surgeon. Pete covered their butts for the first five holes. Then he'd mentally disintegrated, choking fatally as they lost hole after hole, the dollar losses getting to him. He hadn't argued when Beau insisted on covering their losses. Beau could only hope today's game wouldn't set Pete's pace when real play began on Thursday. Pete's swing was screwed. Again. He needed help, and Beau was in no shape to give it.

But the last damn thing he needed was to worry about Pete's game on top of his own.

A distantly ringing phone barely penetrated his musing until the bartender sang out his name and held the phone aloft. "You can take it over there." He nodded his balding head toward a plush chair in the corner, done up in golf-scene fabric, a phone beside it. Gut twisting, Beau shoved up, headed in that direction, beer in hand. He could plan on either Braden's or Perri's voice, and considering the mood in which she'd left on Sunday, his chances of it not being Braden sucked. Still, he kept his tone light, on that trillionth chance. "This is Beau."

"Congratulations, son, on winning the Open!"

His heart sank right through the cushy chair. "Thanks, Granddad.

"I'm a little late, but I couldn't seem to catch up with you back in Bethesda."

Beau had been lying low where his grandfather was concerned. The Open was old news. Another town, another tournament. "How'd you find me here?" Until Perri had joined the tour, he hadn't made a habit of frequenting bars after play.

"Took a chance. I wanted to make sure you're okay, since we haven't talked in a while."

Not since the night he and Perri had exchanged memoirs of their marriage. He imagined Braden chewing on the fact he'd gotten no apologetic accounting, but he had no heart for tossing around golf strategies now that he knew the old man was a traitor.

"Your grandmother is worse. I thought you should know."

"I do know. I've been talking to her doctor every day."

"Her doctor?" The words sounded as if they'd squirmed out, like a mouse from a trap.

"Yes, sir. I wanted the word straight from the horse's mouth, since that might be the only way I'll get the truth." Information that couldn't be twisted and used against him in some way. Or against Perri.

"Excuse me?" Braden gruffed.

In his mind's eye, Beau could see a cocked eyebrow, a familiar frown. He'd had one beer too many. "Never mind. I've given the doctor my itinerary as far into the schedule as I know it. If she loses more ground, he's to get word to me no matter what."

"You didn't think I'd do that?"

Braden sounded like he'd been punched in his ulcerous stomach. For the first time, Beau found it difficult to care. He sipped beer, the Nike rerun

suddenly doubly absorbing. Then wondering if
he'd had enough Coors to develop a cruel streak, he
relented. "No reason to trouble you. You've got
your hands full." Full of being a grieving, aging
man, to whom life had dealt a harsh hand, one that
would only worsen once his deeds came home to
roost.

"You sound a little strange, Beau. Are you sure
you're all right?"

"You want the truth?"

A long silence ticked by. "Yes."

"I'm skipping the pro-am tomorrow and thinking of withdrawing from the tournament." Besides
his wrist having defaulted, both events loomed
pointless without Perri.

He might have said he was converting to
Buddhism.

"Why, for God's sake?"

"My wrist is giving me fits. I shot in the nineties
today." Reluctantly he relived a few of those shots,
along with a few of Pete's. "I haven't done that
since I was ten years old. I don't want to embar-
rass you on CBS."

"You've seen a doctor, I hope."

"Several. Guess what? They're advising me to
hang it up for a while."

"For how long?"

"Don't worry, Granddad. I won't miss the
British Open. I've got a month till then."

Beau heard fresh ice dropping into a glass. He
saw the warm glow of scotch as clearly as if he were
at High Meadow, couched in the mellow richness of
the study, along with Braden.

"You know, son—" Braden took a drink,
coughed lightly. "I believe you when you say your
wrist hurts, but I'm not sure laying off is good for
your game. You can lose your touch in a month. If
you can bite the bullet till the PGA Championship
is over—let's see...." Beau waited while Braden

compiled dates in his mind. "That's a couple of
months. When winning is in the bag, you can take
off the rest of the year and heal the wrist."

It was never going to heal, but at least Braden
was generous enough to believe him about the hellaceous pain. "I have to go, Granddad. Thanks for
the pep talk."

"Beau!" The wire snapped with tension.

"I'm here."

"Maybe this tournament's not so important. If
you win, your taxes will only go up." He laughed, a
half-hearted attempt. "Why don't you skip it and
come home for a few days. We can play Owl Creek
to keep your muscles oiled."

Beau easily detected disingenuous lightness.
Braden was rattled, which caused Beau a twinge of
regret, even over the lingering resentment he'd be
unable to address as long as his grandmother lingered a step away from death. Nevertheless, he
tested the water. "I'd better not do that. I hired
Perri for better or worse, which means playing. I
can't let her down."

A pregnant pause hung heavy, along with hard
breathing and rattling ice. He waited, half-hoping
for Braden to suggest he come home anyway, bring
Perri, that the three of them play Owl Creek. He
would never hear those words in Braden's lifetime.

Finally, tone obligatory, Braden asked, "How is
she?"

"She hasn't changed, Granddad. Me neither,
where she's concerned." He stared out the window,
remembering how lonely he had felt out there
today, all his loose ends exposed. "Even though all
that water almost washed the bridge out." And still
could if they let it.

"You aren't making sense, Beau. I'm getting
concerned. Hell, I'm worried about you."

"Don't be." He finished off the Coors, held the
glass aloft. "Just take care of Nonna. Tell her to

wear pink when she watches on Thursday, so I can pick her out of the gallery."

Braden seized on that. "Would you like to talk to her? I'll get her."

No way. Nonna would see through his half-drunk sarcasm to the hurt, which would only hurt her in turn. The last thing he wanted. "I'll call tomorrow, before I tee off. I have to go, Granddad. Pete needs a ride. Thanks for calling."

Hanging up, he entertained the dread of facing another cold and empty hotel room.

✳

Hours after Angie went to bed, as Perri stood in the opened refrigerator light dipping into a pint of mint-chocolate-chip ice cream, the phone rang. Knowing rushed in on her. Pulse echoing in her ears, she snatched the phone from its wall cradle. "Hello."

The momentary silence felt interminable.

"Hi. Did I wake you?" His intimate tone reminded her of the night she'd had the flu, his warm skin searing her. Healing and agonizing.

"That's okay." She clapped the top on the ice cream and stowed it.

"I'd have called sooner—like two days ago—but I was too busy checking out your possible illicit interludes in sleazy motels." She heard apologetic coercion and imagined a cajoling smile lighting his face.

She refused the bait. "Well, you found me. Is something wrong?"

"Hell, yes. Why didn't you tell me you were going home?"

"You were too busy playing judge and jury." She eased out a kitchen chair and sat down, her legs suddenly gelatinous.

"You're right. When all you wanted was to see your little girl." She heard him release breath. "Is she there?" A moment ticked by. "Chelsea?"

"Of course. Where else would she be? Why else would I be here?"

"I thought you left because of that asinine groupie note."

In her mind, she relived the gurgle of crumpled paper being eaten by the Bethesda sewer system. "That was a coincidence."

"You were jealous as hell. Admit it."

"It reminded me of Braden's note. I hated that feeling. "

"Forget about it. Somehow it was part of his scheme. We're beyond that now."

She could still see the note vividly in her mind. Suddenly he said, "Let me talk to Chelsea."

Her chest knocked, the sensation moving into her throat, threatening to suffocate her. "She's been asleep for hours."

"It's that late, huh?" She imagined him consulting his Rolex by the television glare, or a lighted clock in another unfamiliar hotel room. "Does she sleep with you?"

Could they actually discuss Chelsea so casually? "When I visit."

"She's a lucky kid, Periwinkle."

The intimate suggestion brought a light flutter to her stomach. Knowing her voice would betray her, she said nothing.

"Are you coming back tomorrow?"

"I'm coming to Wry, if that's what you mean."

"You know what I mean."

"Maybe I don't."

He laughed softly. "I want you back. Okay? I've said it. Happy?"

"Not particularly, but it's easier than scrounging for work." Her relinquished smile colored her tone. "Especially at ten percent instead of twenty."

"Give me your flight data." His voice lightened. "I'll pick you up."

She hesitated. "No. I have an errand to run. I'll take a cab. Where are you staying?"

"Hyatt, downtown. I'll take you wherever you need to go. Delta right? When do you get in?" To her curious silence, he provided, "I found the Delta number on the night stand."

Feeling slightly invaded, she said, "Don't pick me up. I'll see you at the hotel."

She sensed disappointment, sensed him waiting for more, but offered nothing.

"Why don't you bring Chelsea back with you," he suggested softly.

This time her breath seriously snagged. Her stomach clenched, palms going clammy, wetting her grip on the phone. She couldn't imagine what it must have taken for him to say that.

"I took her with me on the LPGA for a while. The tour's no place for a child."

His pause made her wonder if he was doing chronological math. "She was younger then," he pointed out. "And the way we travel, it would be easier on you. I'd help." He gained impetus as he spoke, as if the plan were unraveling in his head. "We could hire someone while we were on the course."

We? Oh, Jesus. "That's sweet, Beau." She ached, imploding, breaking up from inside out. "But I'm afraid— Having a child underfoot would affect your game."

"We'd work it out."

"It's not a good idea."

"Well, if you change your mind...."

"I'd better go. I don't want to wake Mom."

"Are you sure you don't want me to pick you up tomorrow?"

"I'll be fine."

"What if I said I'm sorry I acted like an asshole over your leaving?"

"I'd believe you, but I'd still say no." She swallowed furiously. "Goodnight, Beau."

"Night, Periwinkle."

The phone was halfway to the wall when she heard him call her name. "Yes?"

"What if I said I love you?"

"I'd probably say I love you, too." This time she hung up.

She finished the mint chocolate chip with her eyes clenched to hold back the tears.

✳

Perri braided her hair as Larry drove her to the airport the next morning. A steady rain peppered the roof of the pickup truck, increasing the gloom she had felt since leaving Chelsea at the school door. Two days had been only enough to whet Perri's appetite, to make her reconsider Beau's suggestion she bring Chelsea on tour.

The car wipers echoed in her subconscious as she reminded herself Chelsea was happy, missing her, but normally so. Knowing she could be home in a matter of hours, if needed, made the continued separation bearable.

This visit home had interrupted another trip to New Mexico, this time to find a place to live. Angie and Larry were moving. "Don't worry," Angie had said. "Larry wants Chelsea."

Perri looked out the truck window now, giving her hair an extra hard tug, Angie's phrasing raising hackles on her back. When she had objected to Chelsea leaving her doctors, Angie argued that New Mexico had doctors. Angie's confession that she planned to apply for assistance there, naming herself as guardian, claiming the father's identity unknown, left Perri feeling sleazy. In the end Angie had granted a reprieve by agreeing to wait until Christmas break, which meant both the British Open and the PGA Player's Championship would be history.

She could leave the tour then, if Beau continued winning the way he had been. Her cut of the
Open purse had been almost seventy thousand dollars. In the past few months, she'd done well, and
since Chelsea had had no flare up, most of the
money was intact. There would soon be enough to
schedule surgery, and money to live on while
Chelsea healed. Then she would decide about
going back on tour.

Her thoughts shifted, melding into last night's
call from Beau, into numerous possibilities she was
afraid to consider. Beau loved her enough to ask
her to bring another man's child into their relationship. If she told him Chelsea was his—he'd know
if he got one look at her—would he love her enough
to marry her again, take her and Chelsea under his
protection? Or would he side with Braden and
stage a custody battle she would lose.

Was having a goal, a time frame, better or
worse? Would she be able to keep her secret for
five months? Would leaving Beau be as much hell
as it was at the moment? Or would his loyalty to
Braden kill her renewed love?

Her mind raced. For certain, his wrist was getting worse. His continuing wins were a mystery.
He had given up bio-magnetic therapy, opting for
cortisone, a time-bomb solution. He took too many
Motrin every day. How long could he last without
asking for something more potent from the different doctors he saw in each new city? Would he give
in to the pain? Drugs would affect his performance, affect his win record. Affect her plans for
Chelsea.

A hiatus was the only answer. But she could-
n't afford that, especially now that she'd agreed to
Angie's schedule. Beau would never agree to lay off
now that he had won the Masters and the Open,
and halfway to a grand slam, could smell blood.

✳

At destination, Perri rented the cheapest car available at the airport, stipulating it could be dropped at the hotel. Half an hour later she pulled into a mall parking lot, pursuing the errand that had prevented Beau meeting her plane. An errand she had meant to take care of in Louisville, but each time she tried Angie found reasons to accompany her, thwarting her privacy.

Inside the store, she surveyed the aisle markers. Small Appliances. Greeting Cards. Shampoo. Cold Remedies. Sanitary Products. She headed in that direction. The object of her search rested on a shelf near the floor, between Tampax and Trojans. She reached for a small green and white box. Quick & Simple. New! Improved! Virtually 100% Reliable.

Throat aching, she tried to find comfort in the product's name. ANSWER.

CHAPTER NINETEEN

When Perri returned Angie's call the second night of the Quad City Classic, Chelsea answered, but engaged in a serious game of Chess with Larry, had little time to talk. She had inherited Beau's competitive spirit and love for the game. Hearing the apology in Chelsea's voice, Perri's emotions tangled between gratitude and regret for Chelsea's self-reliance, healthy and normal for her daughter, but for her, the attributes were somehow painful.

While the phone was being transferred to Angie, Perri heard the door to Beau's room open and thud closed. She waited, but he didn't appear in her adjoining door. Probably because she'd tried badgering him into not working out, not abusing his wrist more. Perri strained for telling sounds. The television came on, then she heard the shower door slide open with a bang.

"Hi, Perri. How's it going?" Angie's voice held apology, too. Not for Chelsea's inattentiveness, Perri knew, but for the calamity she'd no doubt witnessed on TV that afternoon.

"Since Beau missed the cut, I thought you two might have moved on."

"Tomorrow. This is the third cut he's missed. It's beginning to get to him, and now he's facing the British Open."

"Well, give him my love, honey. Better yet, give him yours. That's what he needs."

All the love in the world couldn't heal him. Only time could. She listened to the water running in Beau's bathroom, wanting to go to him, wanting to run away. "Sorry I missed your call earlier."

"I have something to tell you."

She sank onto the bed, her legs spastic, for no reason she could name. "What?"

"Some guy's been here interviewing Chelsea. She's going to be a star."

Apprehension curling in her stomach, she listened to a tale of a stranger Angie referred to as "an interviewer researching an article on children in this...region," Angie thought.

He had gotten Chelsea's name "from...the census, maybe?" He had asked where Chelsea was born, why she lived with Angie. He had looked at Chelsea's room—her bed, her clothes, what she ate. "All kinds of things." Angie's voice held awe for the media, anything to do with fame.

The fact he had gone to see Nedra, even though Lee wasn't there, even though Nedra had no children, made Perri's heart club, but not nearly as much as knowing he had tried to talk with Larry and he refused. Her scalp tightened. "Larry not talking makes him look guilty."

"Guilty of what?" Defensiveness crept into Angie's tone.

She grasped at calm rationale, something more than her gut feeling. "Braden could be behind this. Did you think of that?"

A pause. "You're too jumpy, Perri."

"If he comes back, don't talk to him. Do you hear me?"

Hearing a noise behind her, she spun on the bed. Beau stood in the doorway, a towel around his waist. She clamped her hand over the mouthpiece, arching her brows in a question.

"Is that Chelsea? Let me talk to her." He came toward her, holding out his hand.

"It's not Chelsea." She groped for a gentler tone. "She's asleep." She stood, dragging the phone perilously near the edge of the nightstand, catching it before it fell. "I have to go," she said to

Angie. "Remember our agreement. I'll call tomorrow."

Beau's eyes sparked, brows hiked, mouth pulling into a derisive smile. "Don't hang up on my account." His voice held an edge of challenge.

Perri slapped the receiver onto the cradle, eyes drawn to the loose fold of towel at his waist. In the last sun rays seeping through the window, water beads glistened on his massive shoulders, in his hair. He smelled like shampoo and deodorant and man. She pushed her mother's advice to love him out of her mind, forcing her eyes back to his. "We were finished."

"That was Zamora. Right? That's why I couldn't talk to Chelsea."

"Damn it, Beau. Don't start. Just because you missed the cut, don't punish me."

"So talking about him is punishment."

"I'm not fighting with you. I had enough of that on the course today to last a lifetime."

He wheeled and covered the room in a few strides. She followed, mind darting, threatened by Angie's news, wanting to believe the interview was harmless, or were her fears concerning Braden materializing? If so, having agreed with Angie's timetable meant she'd never have enough money for surgery and a custody battle. Yet should she be home now, fighting Braden—if by some chance he was involved—from a closer range? Her spine iced up. Beau's mother had lost to Braden; the loss had scarred Beau, left him feeling abandoned.

She caught up to him in the bathroom. When she appeared in the door, he stripped the towel from around his hips and raised it to his hair, rubbing laconically, eyes taunting. She shamelessly took in his body, heart thudding—from the sprint, she told herself—from Angie's ambiguous news. He lowered the towel, dropped it on the marble floor. She turned her back, but the mirrored room

293

reflected multi-faceted images of a man more beautiful than any had a right to be. Aching, she pivoted toward the open door, shutting out the sight.

With fluid grace and startling quickness, he came up behind her, circled her waist with unquestionable possession and turned her back to face the mirror. One hand cupped her chin, holding her eyes straight ahead while the other moved up her body to caress her breasts, one, then the other. She closed her eyes, shutting out the image, a ripple rising in her belly, then plummeting to ache between her thighs. He turned her in his arms. His mouth moved back and forth over hers, his tongue flicking the corners until his hands came up in vise grips, imprisoning her face. His mouth abused her before turning sweet and gently invasive. He was rock hard, warm, menacing and petitioning at once. She returned his kiss as her mind whirled through an emotional tangle of reluctance, longing, need, then miraculously retrieved her harbored fear. She pushed against his chest. He released her, his eyes registering satisfaction for her hunger.

Turning her back on him, she kept her eyes up, matching her gaze to his in the mirror. "Are you torturing me, Beau? Or maybe you want an instant fix for playing badly today."

He shrugged. "You used to understand that."

She still wanted to fix it for him, if only temporarily, but too much barred the way. "I'm going to take a shower. Then let's go downstairs for dinner."

His smile stopped short of his eyes. "As in foreplay?"

"Dinner. As in I'm hungry."

"We'll get room service."

Knowing she'd be too vulnerable to reason, she turned away, refusing his offer.

✳

Candlelight flickered on Beau's face, illuminating his disbelieving eyes. Feeling a powerful tug of empathy and remorse, Perri fixed her gaze on his. He deserved to know that her thoughts of leaving the tour left her equally as miserable as what she saw in his eyes.

He lowered his fork, shoved his plate forward. His fingers gripped the table edge, then his right hand jerked back, but not before proof of the pain streaked across his face. "Look—" He exhaled audibly, gaze darting to the ceiling, then back to her. "I know I gave you a hard time on the course today." She watched that memory reflect in his eyes. "And I acted like a manhandling asshole upstairs tonight." He shrugged without verve. "My game's in trouble—"

"It's your wrist, not your game."

"—and I took it out on you, but threatening to quit is over-reacting."

Her eyes stung. Lashes lowered, she aligned an unused spoon with the knife. "It's not today. I understand that. It's something Mom told me when I called tonight."

He leaned forward. "What, for Christ's sake? Just tell me. I'll help you work it out."

"If it comes to pass . . . you'll know. But for now, it's something only I can do." She poked at her salad, sipped tasteless mineral water. Gathering courage, she waded into deeper water. "The fact I may be needed at home is only part of it. If I don't have to go home—" She took her turn at pushing her plate away. "You're injured. I don't see that changing this season unless you drop out long enough to heal, and Braden would never stand for that." While he measured her warily, she chose her words carefully. "I have to work for a winner. I so badly want it to be you. But if not, I have to find someone—"

"You think I'm washed up? You used to have enough confidence for both of us."

"You haven't won pocket change in the last three events. Money is the reason I'm here. The reason I agreed to work for you."

He sat back in his chair, one brow cocked. "Is that so? I got a different slant on the beach the other night."

She struggled with that memory, feeling as if pieces of herself had gone askew, jagged puzzle parts not quite fitting together. "I would never have left Chelsea if I didn't have to."

His gaze quickened. "You don't. We'll go get her tonight. She's part of you, and I love you, Perri. How complicated is that?"

How could a man who could love her so deeply grant his loyalty so unwisely elsewhere? Guilt for her deviousness broadened, deepened, clanging in her mind like pebbles in a bucket. If the stranger did turn out to be an investigator, continuing to hide Chelsea only invited Beau's wrath when he learned the truth. Fingertips pressing her temples, she lowered her head for a moment, then straightened, meeting his eyes. "This is no life for a child. I have a goal. Once I meet it, I'm going home to Chelsea."

"Screw the goal," he said, his voice low, intimate. "I'll write you a check after every tournament—fifteen percent of first—however the hell I finish."

Why couldn't he let her go? As he had eight years ago? She searched for words that had yet to be invented. The objective was saving her child from the St. Cyr bondage that held Beau captive.

"I'm going to win the British Open, Perri." His mouth formed a rigid line. "If it takes a miracle, I'm winning. Believe it."

"I really hope so." She caught his hand and held it between her two, fingers snaking inside the jacket to stroke his feverish wrist. "You should eat, bud. You haven't eaten all day."

He shoved the plate again. "You're blaming me for what Granddad did. Is that it?"

"I'm not blaming you."

"Then I rephrase the question. Are you holding me responsible? Punishing me?" His eyes shone like knife blades. "If you do, he wins. Are you willing to let him win by default?"

Possibly, she had a different battle to fight now. "Have you talked to him, told him you know what he did?"

"There's something I have to work on first."

"Such as winning the grand slam?" He would never make the break, and he expected her to fall in with his weakness.

"You're damn right." A jaw muscle pulsed. "I want to lay that in his lap when I confront him. That and a few other things."

Trying to ignore the mystique of that, she placed her napkin on the table. "I'll stay through the British Open." And pray Chelsea's interview was not an inquest.

He hooked his fingertips inside the gold master's bracelet she wore, caressing the tender skin of her inner wrist. Irony crammed his pensive smile. "Now I'm taking charity."

"You've treated me like royalty these last few months. I owe you that much."

His eyes darkened from gold to wet rust. "And what kind of argument do I have to come up with after that?"

"You know I love you." Though she couldn't justify the feeling beyond him fathering Chelsea, she loved him more than ever, was falling more deeply in love every day. Her mind searched for reasons she shouldn't, and as had become the pattern, seized only one. "The last thing I want is to leave you."

"Then don't. We'll work it out, Perri. But it will take both of us."

She left the restaurant with his proposal echoing in her head, then lay awake wrapped in a sense of smallness in the vast bed, feeling inadequate and futile. Her mind darted crazily, toying with a wave of fogged up scenes of Beau's mother, a woman only her imagination could picture.

For the first time, a hint of what she must have felt after battling Braden and losing—or surrendering—overshadowed Perri's empathy for Beau. Yet, other than having developed a warped sense of loyalty, had Beau suffered from being raised by Braden? When all was said and done, if Braden prevailed in the possible dilemma Perri faced now, would Chelsea suffer? Growing up, she'd have every advantage, every amenity Perri could never hope to give her. Had she instilled enough character in Chelsea for her to recognize and reject Braden's deceitful traits? When Chelsea reached womanhood, would she come back with empathy and gratitude for her sacrifice, or become indifferent to her, just as Beau had become indifferent with his mother? Had that woman surrendered her son at the onset, she could have spared him days in a witness chair, being tugged in two directions he was too young to understand. The scars he carried in his eyes today might be shallower.

Knowing the odds of defeating Braden's money, his strength, his standing with the powers that be, should she fight? Or should she surrender her daughter rather than put her through years of a hellacious court battle?

To fight Braden, Perri needed unity with Beau. Without his undivided support, she would be sacrificing Chelsea to a battle that couldn't be won

✳

Beau filled out a new-patient form at the doctor's office, checked the *Wall Street Journal*'s

Investors Wanted ads, then glanced at his watch, gauging the probability of seeing any of Pete's round today. The news he had for Pete, plus not catching part of the round—at least a beer afterward—could seriously damage the friendship.

His mind rambled from Nonna's frail voice when he had called home that morning, to airline reservations he had to make now that he'd volunteered not to take the High Meadow plane to Scotland. Then his thoughts migrated to Perri.

In spite of his request that their adjoining door remain open, it had been closed and locked when he woke that morning. A note slipped beneath advised she'd gone to the tournament, hoping to hire out for the next two days. With anger sinking into recrimination now, he decided that if his bad luck held, she would end up in a pairing with Zamora, providing a cozy reunion. If his luck miraculously changed, Pete might be in the pairing as well, allowing Beau to keep an eye on Zamora and Perri while following along. Was he turning into a sick bastard, or what? Unless he managed to put down his distrust—jealousy—their chances of making a new start were zero. Braden's sorcery had left a hell of a lot of scars.

"Mr. St. Cyr?"

He stood to follow the nurse through a doorway and down the hall to an examining room.

The doctor leaned against an instrument-lined counter studying papers on a clipboard. The room had the familiar antiseptic smell, as though bleached of all humanity. In fact, the scene reeked of déjà vu. Beau read diplomas issued to Dr. Richard Petty until the doctor looked up, frowning. Beau's heart shimmied. Dr. Petty tapped the clipboard. "Osteoarthritis that's progressed into Repetitive Stress Injury. Where'd you get that diagnosis?"

"The Internet."

Smiling, the doctor seized his wrist, held it as
though taking a pulse while observing Beau with
miss-nothing eyes. "You didn't make the cut this
weekend."

"No joke."

That got a laugh. "Any other physical complaints?"

"Insomnia." While he lusted for the beautiful
woman in the next room.

"Goes with the territory. Why not lay off play,
give the injury a rest? There's no cure."

That made the opinion of the previous four doctors unanimous. "Laying off is out of the question.
I'm facing the British Open in four days. I need a
cortisone injection."

"You've done your homework, so I don't have to
tell you, that while injections are powerful therapy,
over a period of time you run the risk of infection to
the injected area, atrophied muscles, and blind-
ness."

"I know, but I'm into something right now that
I've got to finish." Beau shifted his gaze to a window offering a view of brick wall. Muzak provided
background for a ringing phone in the hall, and the
echo of Perri's voice: The tour is no place for a child.

He met the doctor's eyes. "If you can't help me,
I'll have to look elsewhere. I need time for the medication to take effect before I play on Thursday." He
despised begging—groveling—but the drug needed
twenty-four to thirty-six hours to invade the blood
stream. Resting the wrist for a few days would
keep the Cortisone in the joint, allowing it to work.
Postponing an injection had cost him the Classic,
but he was after the big prize. "I've got a lot riding
on the British Open. I can win if you help me."

Petty grinned. "Nice speech. Maybe you should
take up politics. But I sure as hell don't want your
failure to win on my conscience."

He pushed a wall button and asked for Cortisone, Beau's remedy of choice.

✳

In the Oakwood men's grill, Pete twirled a mug of micro brew and stared at the wet rings on the wooden tabletop as if memorizing them. "I figured this was coming," he mumbled, taking a drink, then wiping his mouth with the back of a tanned hand.

"All I said was, I'm flying commercial. What was coming, for Christ's sake?"

"Perri. She knows I can't afford to go to Europe if I don't fly with you."

He managed a laugh, tabling a lecture, but somewhere, something was awry. "Surely you don't think she'd opt for commercial over private for any reason. Use your head."

"First class is not exactly steerage. You ought to try it in the back where the peons fly."

Beau held up a palm. "Save it. Okay, Pete?"

Pete played with the wet circles, then hunched forward, his body folded around a basket of Gold Fish, chin actually resting on the edge of the beer mug. "Anyway, she's got it in for me, cause we spend too much time together." He shrugged, drained the mug and held it aloft. "Typical old lady stuff. I warned you about it way back at Riviera. It's gonna cost me a bundle, cause she's pussy whipped you."

Figuratively maybe, but not literally. "She doesn't even know about the plane yet. I only decided this morning when I talked to Granddad. The distance is too great for the pilots to be able to get back if Granddad should need the plane, so I'm leaving it hangared in Louisville."

Pete began working on the second beer, eyeing the one Beau hadn't touched. "The old man never goes anywhere. Why the sudden concern?"

Irritation inched up Beau's spine. Suddenly, Pete's declaration struck him as odd. "How do you know he never goes anywhere?"

"I figured. He's a hundred years old and your grandmama is sick city. Why would they leave la-la land? I wouldn't." His lips formed a sullen line, eyes not quite meeting Beau's.

Beau shoved the beer away. Foam slopped over the rim and dripped onto the table. "You've never seen High Meadow. You don't know what the hell you're bitching."

"No, but I've watched Life Styles of the Rich and Famous, so I know how they live, Beau Jangles." He hiked the chair onto its back legs, balancing with one hand on the edge of the table, his smile cynical. "And I've been living vicariously through you for a couple of years."

Resentment pinched Pete's face, colored his tone. Up to now, Beau had considered Pete's jibes about wealth to be just that. Jibes. No bitterness involved. Now insight, too slow in coming, glommed onto him thick as the freckles on Pete's brow. Still, he didn't feel right about jerking the rug from under him on short notice. "You're welcome to ride as far as the Chicago airport with Perri and me on Monday. We're taking British Airways from there. I'll loan you the money for Europe. You can pay me back when you get this week's purse."

"I know you're up for sainthood, Beau, but I guess I'll skip it, unless the sky opens up and rains us out tomorrow." He finished off the second beer. "Which is about the only way I can guarantee being anywhere near the leader at the finish. That just might cover the fare."

Beau was wasting time. "You've got nothing to bitch about, Pete. You're playing the Classic and I didn't even make the cut. Or had you noticed?"

"I've noticed you don't give a flyin' frig about these piss-ant tournaments. Money wise."

How would Pete have coped with the ultimatum
Perri had issued last night, one that made purses
as important as trophies? At a past point in the
friendship, Beau might have asked. He might have
revealed the intricacies of his and Perri's relationship and where it actually stood now, how his
desire to win had refocused, how winning could
reshape his life, while losing could plunge it into a
downward spiral. He might even have told him
about Braden's deceit, and how not being able to
confront it until he had all the facts in order, curdled his blood.

But the time for confiding in Pete had passed.
He'd been told far too much already.

He headed for the hotel, stopping by the desk to
pick up a FedEx package. Standing at the registration counter, he eagerly rifled through the contents of the envelope postmarked Phoenix, stuffed
the legal documents back inside and headed
upstairs where he found the door between his room
and Perri's still locked.

He rammed his hand in his pocket and fingered
the key to her outside door, then pulled his hand
out empty. She had called this shot. Damned if
he'd beg her. He'd find another way.

Emptying the envelope onto the bed, he
stretched out and read with interest.

✳

Somewhere in the midst of the following night,
while he lay still but sleepless, their adjoining door
opened. Perri entered the room, her naked body
small and lithe and ghostlike in the flickering light
of the mute television. She drifted across the room,
quietly located the remote control unit and turned
off the television, then stood staring down at him in
the darkness as his heart ticked off moments that
resembled hours. Gingerly, her weight no more
than a breath, she sat on the edge of the bed and
placed the backs of her fingers against his cheek.

He felt the cold metal of his friendship ring and closed his eyes, remembering. She laced her fingers into his hair, her touch warm but tentative. He kept his eyes closed, feigning sleep, held his breath and lay waiting for more, sensing her want. Need. Indecision.

Don't reach for her. Let her come to you. It's the only way she'll ever stay.

A silently moving wisp of white in the dark, she left him, this time leaving the door ajar.

He waited the next day until they'd checked luggage, gotten boarding passes and were tucked at a corner table in a noisy concourse bar to broach the subject. She sat across from him, her hair in a straggly I'm-too-sexy-for-my-clip do, a clingy black T-shirt, a sarong skirt, and the Bandolinos they didn't talk about. Show-pony personified. This beat the hell out of solo travel.

"What happened when you came into my room last night? Why didn't you stay?"

A flush covered her face, then receded, leaving two bright spots on her tawny cheeks. She made a production of adding sugar to her coffee, then spent eternity trying to tear the foil top off a tiny cup of hazelnut-flavored cream. He took the packet, punctured it with the end of a plastic spoon, dumped it into her coffee and stirred, waiting for her to look at him.

When she did, he cocked a brow. "Should I repeat the question?"

He watched her slip back a few hours, her voice reticent. "I thought you were asleep."

"Nope, but if I had been, I'm a light sleeper. Plus I wake up horny and in a good mood."

"I remember." She sipped coffee, staring at the bustling concourse.

With a fingertip at her chin, he turned her back. "Want me to repeat the question?"

A resigned smile broke free. "At the crisis point, I came to my senses."

"Leaving me in crisis. How'd you do that—find your senses? If it works I'll try it."

Her eyes clouded. "It doesn't work for me. It's more like bullet biting. Most of the time I feel like two people in one body. Maybe I am emotionally addicted to you, but I'm fighting physical addiction."

"Our history's doing a replay, huh, Periwinkle?"

"I'm no virgin now, holding onto my bargaining power. There's a lot more at stake."

He settled against the back of the frail wooden chair, measuring her, sensing she spoke of something other than his making-love-makes-every-thing-all-right theory of years past. Years before they had been duped by Braden. Maimed for life. "Why do I feel my future's being decided and I wasn't invited to the caucus?"

"You're writing the agenda, Beau."

"Okay, propose any deal you want, and you've got a lay down. Pun intended."

She laughed, her eyes showing more pain than amusement. She sucked her plump bottom lip between her teeth. Predictably his groin kicked against the crotch of his Levis, settling into a half hard reminder, ready to spring.

Was Chelsea keeping them apart? Or guilt over Chelsea's father, whoever the hell he was? Probably so, considering the fit he'd pitched when he finally got a look at the picture in the locket. And his continued barbs about Zamora were wrecking her peace of mind. After his initial shock, Chelsea had gradually moved into his conscious-ness and taken a corner of his heart, generating the same protective instincts he held for her mother. The last thing he wanted was to blame Perri for anything resulting from Braden's deceit. Vowing yet again to ease up on the subject, he urged, "Let's work this out and get on with our lives."

Defeat and exasperation clouded her eyes before she looked away, staring at the concourse, at their gate down the way. For a nano-second he envisioned her standing and walking away. His breath evened out when she leaned forward instead, a hint of agreement sparking her eyes. The next moment she looked past him with a half frown, half smile

He swiveled in his chair. His gaze clashed with their intruder's, black and luminous in a handsome, swarthy face. Beau damned fate and timing.

"Hi, Mark." Perri's voice sounded as if it emerged from a fugue.

"Hey, Perr. How're they hangin', Saint?"

Mark's eyes, falsely boasting a priest's piety, fastened on Perri, amazing Beau that he had gotten an acknowledgement, such as it was.

"You must be on our plane." Perri's tone evened out admirably.

"British Airways." Mark examined his ticket envelope while lowering a worn duffel to the floor. "Flight four thirty-two at six-fifteen. I like night flights."

His voice and body language held a youthful verve in which a woman might find promise, Beau mused, keeping an eye on Perri's reaction, but gleaning little.

Mark shrugged, grinning. "Go to sleep, wake up, you're there. Is that your flight, too?"

Perri glanced at Beau, and he managed a nod. "That's us." Even more miraculously, he managed an invitation based on desire to observe the two of them together, negating the vow he'd made moments before. "Want some coffee?"

"Better not. It wires me." But he turned a wooden chair around and straddled it backwards; thigh muscles bulging beneath his Dockers as he planted highly polished cowboy boots on either side of the chair. "How's the wrist?" His dark eyes measured Beau in a way that made him feel culpable, as if they discussed a social disease.

"Healed. Alert the press."

Perri shuffled in her chair, cheeks coloring, mouth pinched. "Where's Teddy?"

Mark lit a cigarette, exhaled at the ceiling and dropped the Bic into his shirt pocket. "She couldn't swing it. Most of what she makes gets sent back home. She's got a single mom and a house full of little sisters, I guess. Feels strange without her, already."

Mark's easy admission of feeling Teddy's absence triggered Beau's thoughts of how he'd gotten used to having Pete along, how Pete had taken the edge off his loneliness before Perri appeared. Playing the Royal Troon course without Pete would feel strange.

Mark announced, "I've had my ticket since this year's schedule came out. Always wanted to see Troon." He dished Beau a wry smile. "No Triple A membership, but I've got frequent flyer miles, so I'm not a total waste of skin. Huh, Beau Jangles?"

"The jury's still out on that."

Mark laughed, rising, pleasing the hell out of Beau. "I need a boarding pass. I'll let you two get back to it." He grinned. "Whatever it was, it looked serious." He kept grinning, like a horny brown bear. "You're in first class, so if I don't see you till Troon, have a good one."

Beau addressed the taut silence as they watched Mark walk away. "I think you were about to tell me something."

"This is not a good time."

"Apparently it was before Zamora showed up." Christ...there I go.

She shook her head, looking away, leaving him unsure of the target of her soberness.

"What is with you and Mark, Perri? There's something. I feel it."

"He scares me, probably because you think he's stalking me."

Her answer indicated that any of her thoughts about Mark didn't include Chelsea.

"He's on the plane to Troon. I'd call that setting up for the European rendition."

As if he hadn't spoken, she said, "When I'm not being influenced by you, I admire him for the way he took charge of his life, how he lives now."

"How? Hooked on being a gypsy? Living from tournament to tournament?"

"He's in good company." She leveled a look of irony on him, then concluded, "I admire how he never judged Teddy, how he's helping her change her life."

Beau detected no emotion other than honesty. No resentment or jealousy. No regret. "Yeah, he's a regular Robin Hood. But Chelsea's not his, huh, Perri?" And whether she was or not, Beau's continued harassment left him worthy of being castrated and left in the sun to fry.

Mute appeal gathered in her eyes, ran to apathy, then died. Gracefully and without haste, she gathered her carry-on and the mangled Louie backpack. "Asshole," she breathed as if she were choking. She spent the remainder of pre-flight time at a bank of pay phones.

Beau sat alone in the bar, realigning all the reasons he deserved her tribute, until he joined her at the gate. Once they'd been fed filets and plied with Cabernet, which Perri declined, the cabin lights dimmed, the hostess closed the curtains between first class and coach and passed out blankets. Beau kicked off his shoes, punched out his reading light, lowered the seat back, and spread the blanket over his chest and lap.

308

Perri, who hadn't spoken since the coffee shop, watched silently.

"Sleepy?" he asked.

In the pale glow of the pin-light above her head, resignation softened the eyes he loved. Bronze dark when she was pissed, bright as amber when she was amused, murky as rain clouds when she was troubled. Like now. "I'm not sleepy."

"Me neither. Wanta fool around."

After a moment she smiled the old Periwinkle smile, sweet, containing no suspicion or reservation. "No, thanks."

"I liked your 'not yet' answer better."

She punched off her light, shed her sandals and spread the blanket over her lap. Beau thought of a child readying herself for bed.

"How about I just hold you? No strings attached." He raised the arm between their seats.

She lowered her seat back and drew her feet up. "I like that offer better."

Turning on her side, she curved her back against him and burrowed in, her firm little ass against his groin. She smelled like Pantene shampoo and hazelnut coffee. Beneath the blanket, her hand sought his, drawing his arm across her waist and covering it with her own, their fingers interlaced. For the first time since he'd last held her, Beau felt whole, completed.

℞

CHAPTER TWENTY

After morning practice, he'd killed two hours at the Jigger Inn down by the Old St. Andrews course, trading lies with local caddies, impressing the hell out of tourists with where he'd been, what he'd seen and done. Then he caught the train back to Troon and took up watch outside the Piersland Hotel, overlooking Royal Troon Golf Club.

He waited in the soft sun for a couple of hours, smoking, thinking, stewing, until the lovers finally came out. They preened in the sun, stretching, looking across to the club, down the street to the village. Coming up for air.

The Saint hadn't practiced. Probably nursing the wrist. Plus, he didn't need to. He'd played the friggin' course ten years ago as an amateur, given Nicklaus a run for his money, and played it every year since then. Last year, he'd aced the damned "Postage Stamp," the eighth hole, then won by a stroke. Saint had led a charmed life, all right. Never had to qualify at Q school with some red-assed sponsor breathing down his neck. He'd earned his PGA card by winning friggin' Nike tournaments. No damned wonder he'd rather screw than practice.

Tracking Saint and Bitch Beautiful was a lay down, shuffling with the crowd along the docks and into the village. Hanging back, stopping when the lovers stopped. He liked watching her walk. Brisk. Shoulders back. The cocky way she held her head. She walked the same way on the course, carrying heavy clubs, as if she had something to prove.

He'd lost interest in pilfering the clubs she lugged, becoming more interested in her little brown body, knowing that was the quickest route

to rattling the Saint. The day she'd come on tour,
Saint had gone under like a drowning man. But he
was weak. You couldn't let a woman—even one
fine as the Bitch—lead you around by the thang.
Saint had, and was, and it showed.

It showed a lot, today.

Figuring out where they'd stop next, what window they'd ogle—like kids ogling a bakery, acting
like they couldn't have any goddamned thing they
saw—spiked his brain. It made him laugh, but the
laugh left him feeling pissed off. Anybody watching
those two could tell Saint was rich, that he carried
a platinum Visa card instead of a vulgar wad of
bills. Any bulge in his Polos came from wanting to
do the Bitch again, already, even if they had just
got out of bed. The Visa guaranteed she'd get anything she pointed at, and the Saint could have her
anytime his pecker pointed. A sweet payoff, the
kind the rich took for granted.

She was too damned haughty for a black.
Treated people cool as Lady Highhat, even Saint
Beau. Like right now. Getting a wild-horse look in
her eyes, shaking that mane, planting her feet
when he tried to coax her into a shop, like none of
the stuff inside would be good enough. Like, if not
for the Saint, she'd be able to fly first class instead
of steerage, or stay in the Piersland instead of that
flea bag hotel down the road where the rest of her
kind holed up. Too cool to be caught dead getting
soused on cheap ale in the hotel's Laddie Bar, like
they'd all done last night. Acting like she'd have a
pot to pee in if the Saint wasn't around to pick up
her tab.

She knew how to play him though, giving in,
letting him lead her into a sweater shop, allowing
anyone watching her—waiting, wishing—time to
cop a smoke. And enough time to imagine boxing
up one of those scratchy, wooly mother-of-all-
sweaters and shipping it home. He got off on think-

ing about what kind of favors that would reap.
How much gratitude and tolerance? How much
more of putting up with his shit it would buy?

Yeah, money talked, okay. The Saint had
dumped her for a while and had his fling. Now he
had her back under him again—a second chance
he didn't deserve. Where was the fucking fairness
in that? Life's a Bitch, and then you die.

But no dying talk. The old man didn't want her
hurt. But he wasn't running this show.

They came out of the shop with an armload of
packages. The little cunt tucked her head against
a breeze off the Firth of Clyde, turning up the collar on a red jacket hot off the rack. Her muscled
legs scissored along the cobblestones in new boots,
the tops hitting just below her knees, leaving
enough leg to turn even the heads of the old farts
on the street. Not to mention any studs that might
be following along, watching, feeling shortchanged.

Next they entered a candy shop, staying longer
than it should take to pick out friggin' suckers for
the local brats, then coming out with more bags.
This time Bitch was smiling. She let Saint slip his
arm around her shoulders, lead her across the
street and into Highgrove House. Two o'clock. The
rich ate late and well. Probably drank champagne
with it.

He'd cool his heels in the bar across the street,
see how their day on the town turned out. Treat
himself to more second-hand living while he wondered what difference a broad like her for a partner—smart and tough and beautiful—might have
made in his life. Wondering, too, who deserved to
be punished for the raw deal he'd got? How much
and how? And how soon? He'd grown used to the
game, even without the old man playing. He might
never give it up.

From a window table in the bar, he watched as
they came out of the restaurant. Almost four

o'clock. Not much daylight left, with the fog rolling in.   No more sun, for damned sure.   Eerie. Lonesome.   Maybe he'd call them over, act surprised to run into them, spring for ales, and enjoy some close-up coveting. Let them see him grovel.

Instead he shoved up, dropped some funny money on the table, and watched from the dimness just inside the bar door.

Splitting up? Yeah. They were dividing the packages, big ones for him, little ones for her. The Saint checked his watch, eyed the gloomy skies and gave her an apologetic, this-is-cutting-my-balls-out look. Then he changed his mind about letting her go and tried to take the packages back.

She backed out of reach, slung that beat-up backpack over a shoulder, tossed her head in a way that guaranteed wrecking whatever Saint'd be doing alone. Then she did a curious thing. Caught his hand, pushed up his sleeve, lifted the sick wrist to her mouth, eyes closed.

Parasitic slut. Hot beads of sweat popped out on his upper lip. She knew how to play the Saint, okay. She'd bleed him dry. Women were born with the knack. He stepped out of the bar, but held back, pressing into a closed doorway, getting the lay of the land.

Down the street, Saint ducked into a bookstore, of all damn places.

Bitch headed in the opposite direction, back up the hill at a fast clip.

Indecision played no part in his action. He left the doorway and fell in behind her, a hundred yards back. Shuffling with the crowd, eyes on her head as if attached by a string, he followed her as she retraced her steps. His pulse speeded up when she turned in at the hotel, then idled when she stopped out front to talk to the valet. She fished in the backpack. Handing over something too small to make out, she followed the uniformed man to a

closed door that he unlocked and entered. She
waited, an arm gripping packages. The pleated
skirt rippling around her thighs hiked up in front
with her one-handed effort to button the new
leather jacket. She eyed her watch, swiped hair
back behind an ear. When the valet appeared
through the doorway, she exchanged her packages
for the set of clubs he carried.

What the hell was going on? The tournament
had ruled all clubs got stored at Troon, not at the
hotels. He doubted even the Saint could get special dispensation. Then suddenly he understood
her opting to split from Beau. As caddie, her job
was to comply with the rule before the tournament
officially started tomorrow. He watched her run
her arms through the backpack straps, centering
the pouch on her chest, then bend and shoulder
the clubs.

His pulse revved, jumped into his throat.
Without waiting, committed, he loped off the short
distance between the Piersland and the Troon clubhouse. In his mind, he reviewed how the big bag
had swung against her hip, landing with a bang.
She must be a goddamn solid bruise under those
clothes. Beau was a sadist. But maybe Beau got
off on that. Maybe he would, too.

As he neared Royal Troon, the golf club storage
shed came into view. Quickening his step, he mentally reneged on his half-assed promise to the old
man that she wouldn't get hurt.

✳

Before hailing a cab, Perri debated whether or
not to walk to Royal Troon, as she'd done the day
before for her pre-game inspection of the course.
But the high-heeled platform boots would make the
hike difficult. No time to go upstairs to change. By
the time the boxy English cab pulled away, leaving
her in front of the Troon clubhouse, darkness was
minutes away.

Fog shrouded the hulking, castle-like structure. Though only steps away, it was a murky blob on a bleak, windswept, virtually treeless landscape. A restless sea back-dropped it all. Reminded of every gothic saga she'd ever read, she shrugged off the feeling and hoisted the clubs, then she made her away around the building and down a winding path that led to an outer region of the property. Moving through the fog on yesterday's memory, she placed one boot gingerly in front of the other, footsteps echoing on the concrete path. She practically bumped into the corner of the club storage building before seeing it. A light burned dimly above a door that stood open. She looked around, eyes straining in the fog. Voices and laughter carried on the wind from the direction of the lighted putting clock she'd passed. Though the golfers had been only unrecognizable outlines in the soupy air, she'd felt comforted. Now they seemed far away.

She inched up to the door. In a heavy iron ring bolted to the stone door facing, a big padlock hung open and waiting. Fate had allowed her to arrive with the clubs before the lock was used for the night. She slipped through the gaping door and stood listening for life: straggling caddies, a conscientious caddie master, security. Nothing.

Yet she'd been assured security guarded the clubs around the clock.

She advanced into the darkening building. Across the way, light slivered beneath a closed door. She called out. No one answered. Only raspy wind rattling the one high window, and the creak of the old building. In her ears, her pulse throbbed, pounded inside her forehead. Blinking, she tried to clear a vision blurring around the edges.

Glancing over her shoulder, she failed to spot a light switch. A sudden blade of fear knifed though her. She stood frozen among the rows of golf bags.

An image flashed in her mind like quick snapshots: The note left on her pillow that night in Augusta. The phone calls on Hilton Head Island. The jimmied hotel door. There'd been no threat from the stalker since then, yet the hackles on her spine never eased.

She lowered the clubs. Boots clicking off her steps, she crossed the rough concrete floor, rapped twice on the closed door. Anticipation wound like a spiral, tighter and tighter. Even in the clammy cold, a strange heat warmed her; a slick gloss of sweat wet her face. She knocked again. Her hand grasped the rusty knob, then froze, heart rioting. No one was in there, or they would have answered. No one else was here, not a soul in the deserted, dark cave of a building.

She spun on her heel, clomped back across the barn to the clubs. Was she insane? Crazy to have taken this chance? Just because she was on foreign soil had she thought he couldn't be here, too? She'd been wrong to argue with Beau about doing this alone. Why try to convince him of her independence when she was so aware of her helplessness at this moment? She'd leave the clubs and go. Never tell him she'd been woozy with fear.

Assuming an alphabetical arrangement, she threaded her way along the last row of bags. She would never get Beau's clubs correctly filed, just close enough to be found tomorrow morning. Picking her spot, she lowered the bag from her shoulder, engrossed with wedging it into a slot with her knee.

Behind her, an explosive charge echoed like gunfire through the concrete and metal building. She dropped the clubs and whirled. The opening where the door had been was gone. Adrenaline pumped furiously through her. Her body quaked painfully. Lunging forward, she stumbled in the blackness, almost going down. The suddenly pungent smell of leather and steel almost gagged her. She felt a scream building in her throat, mounting up, as impossible to contain as an orgasm. She clamped her hand over her mouth. With every ounce of her will, she held the scream back.

Wind. Only wind. The door had blown shut and her imagination had gone wild. She stood still. Listened. Somehow she'd make her way back to the door in the dark. In moments she'd be running up the twisting path to the clubhouse. Running all the way to the hotel.

But then she saw it. A shadowy figure passed between her and the light that edged around the door at the back of the shed. Hinges creaked. The door gapped and light streaked across the floor and up a far wall. Then an arm snaked around the jam and the light went out. Silence. She stood frozen, heart slamming painfully behind her breasts. She prayed for sight in the dark. Or sound. Willed herself to wake from the nightmare. Then she heard the footsteps, squeaks on the pavement. Slow. Unsteady. Veering away. Coming back toward her.

Time passed in jerky intervals. She had to stop panicking and think, shift her survival instinct into high gear. Licking her lips, she swallowed hard against a tightness in her throat that threatened to steal her air.

He was somewhere in front of her! She felt him like weight on the frigid air. His breathing, raspy and ragged, reached into the far recesses of her mind. She smelled him. Onions. Cigarettes and beer. Her stomach clenched. She sank to the floor, wrapped her arms around her knees, shaking with cold and fear. She crouched there, time ticking by like water dripping from a leaky faucet.

Outside, she heard voices from the putting clock. A distant siren bleated, far off, but getting closer. She waited. No breathing now. Had he left? Had the voices scared him off? The siren?

Had he gone through the door in the back? She couldn't know, because he'd turned out the light. Or was he still here? Patient as a spider weaving a web. Waiting for her to break.

The siren wailed past and faded into the sound of wind and sea. Silence again. He was gone. But where? Still she crouched. Her knees ached where she'd banged them on the rough pavement. Her hands stung with cold. She'd never been so aware. Her brain checked every sound, alert to the very air around her.

Then she saw him. Her eyes had begun to adjust to the blackness. She made out the edge of his shape. Before her, a few steps to the right. He shifted his weight, the shoes squeaking. Thoughts of Chelsea dragged through her fear, anger slowly trickling into her veins. She hated him for making her cower like this. Unless she acted, she had lit-tle time left.

Let him come after me. I'll fight.

She stood. "Who are you, you bastard? What do you want?"

A grunt, then silence. If he wouldn't talk to her, was he afraid she'd recognize his voice? But if he planned to hurt her—kill her—would he care?

"I'll scream," she warned. "Security is right outside."

His laughter told her he knew better. She saw him move. She scurried backward, but not before his hand wrapped her forearm. She had to bite her tongue to keep from crying out. His hand was sweaty. Trembly. With power? Anger? Fear that matched her own? She felt something cool against her skin. Metal. Her heart knocked against her ribs. She writhed, kicking at the darkness, losing the backpack. The toe of her boot connected with flesh and bone. A shin? He swore, his voice strained as if muffled against a sleeve. She kicked again, but he held her at arm's length. She missed her target and went down, breaking his hold on her.

Wadding into a ball she rolled away from him, hoping, praying for an opening in the row of clubs. Her hands groped. Jesus, yes! She scuttled through, not knowing how deep the reprieve would be, but glad for once for her size. Bags toppled as she crawled into the deepest darkest part of the unfamiliar lair. Steel clubs scattered on the concrete floor, the commotion echoing in the cavernous building. Then quiet fell like the thud of a dead bird. She clamped her mouth to silence her breathing, while her heart tore holes in her chest. He stomped around in the dark, pushing, shoving clubs, cursing. Now rage made the voice unrecognizable.

Then she heard him running, bumping into more clubs, into racks, tripping, falling she thought. She heard the main door open, creaking on its hinges, heard it slam. She huddled there, panting, trying not to gasp too loudly. But why? He was gone, and she was no worse for wear, other than a throbbing arm where he'd grabbed her. He could have killed her. Raped her.

But for some reason only he knew, he hadn't.

Tears sprang to her eyes, rolled down her cheeks. She dropped her forehead against her knees and cried until she realized she didn't have that luxury. He might come back.

She worked her way out of the hole and stood on wobbly legs, trying to get her bearings. Straining to remember how she'd gotten to where she stood, she turned in a circle. Moonlight, pale and spun like cotton candy, seeped through the high window. The door had been to the left. Heart thudding steadily, she moved along the length of the shed slowly, hands extended, until she bumped into the wall. Hurriedly, she worked her way left to the door.

With a cry of relief she shoved, shoved again, then sagged against the unyielding barrier. Her strength formed a knot of self-will. She heard pounding, felt pain in the heels of her fisted hands. A voice from somewhere deep inside warned her to be quiet, that he'd come back. Another part of her wanted freedom more than safety. She cried out, pounded, then waited. Pounding again, she called to anyone who'd listen. Waited.

The lock rattled against the galvanized steel door.

The voice that called her name catapulted her into reality.

She sprang back as the door swung open. Through the fog, the amber glow of a security lamp outlined the unmistakable.

He had returned to silence her. Oh, God! If only she had believed Beau's warning.

She backed up as Mark came toward her, the padlock dangling from a finger. Another nightmare engulfed her, one in which she was underwater, an anchor holding her down. She backed. He came closer, his form silhouetted in an eerie orange light from behind, his face masked by darkness. Somewhere inside her a dam of adrenaline burst, gushed and churned. Her breath came rapid and shallow, one notch short of hyperventilation. Her knees would give out. She'd tumble to the floor and he'd be on her. There'd be nothing or no one to stop him this time.

One question fought through her hysteria. Why? Why was he doing this?

She backed against something—a table—a bench—and he was there, seizing her wrist. He glared at her in the dark. She trembled under his grip, gasping.

Miracle of miracles, he let go.

"Perr, it's me. Mark. I won't hurt you." He reached to touch her hair, then jerked back his hand when she flinched. "I know you're scared. Don't cry. It's okay now."

Was she crying? Panic seeped out of her like air from a balloon that had been popped by the timbre of his voice, his smell, his stocky bulk framed by the light.

In no way did he match the man who'd been in the barn earlier.

Her gaze ran down his body. He wore rubber-soled shoes. Caddie shoes. Her mind whirled again, coming up blank. Then it seized on the possibility Mark and the stalker worked together, taking turns with her. Had Mark drawn the guy-in-the-white-hat role tonight?

"What happened? Where's Beau, for Christ sake?" He held the lock aloft. "How'd you get shut up in here?"

"How'd you know I was here?" As she spoke, she pivoted, backing toward the door.

"I saw you go by the putting clock. Some pros were having a contest. I was shagging balls." He followed her out onto the lawn. "When I heard the shed door slam I thought I'd see you come back by. I didn't, so I came looking for you."

Wet air shrouded her like a cold blanket. She trembled, still, insides jerking from the cold, the aftermath of shock. From not quite believing him. "How did you get the lock off?"

"It wasn't locked." She heard puzzlement, feigned or real, in his voice. "Some joker strolled by and hooked it through the loop. But he wasn't sadistic enough to close it. He wanted to harass whoever was inside."

She decided to play the game—if there was one—to feel Mark out by omitting the grisly stalker. "Probably. I couldn't find the lights. I panicked."

His laugh sounded strained. "Well, you're a girl. What else?"

The hairs on the back of her neck saluted his arrogance. She pulled the jacket closer around her, hunching her shoulders, willing the quaking to subside.

His hand came to rest on her forearm, covering the ache, the inevitable bruise, making her wonder if he somehow knew it was there. "Come on. We'll notify security, then I'll take you for a drink."

She shook her head. "I have to get back. Beau will wonder where I am."

When he paused, her heart hammered. She envisioned him dragging her back into the building, rankled by the mention of Beau's name.

His voice an acquiescent shrug, he offered, "We'll call him to come get you."

She failed at trying to push that scene from her mind. "I—"

"What? What the hell's wrong with you, Perr?"

"I lost my backpack. I have to go back in."

"Tell me where. I'll get it."

"I'm not sure. I guess I set it down somewhere. I have to have it."

"I'll look for the lights. You wait here till I find them." Gentle concern. The same qualities she'd heard when he talked about Teddy in the Chicago airport two days ago.

When the lights came on, she entered the building and stood just inside the door, looking around, replaying the scene in her mind. Mark began righting bags wordlessly, then walked directly to where the scuffle had taken place, causing an eerie sensation along her spine. He spied her backpack, replaced the spilled items and returned it to her. Outside, he closed the door, hooked the lock through the hinge and shoved it closed with finality. "Let's go."

She tightened the drawstring on the backpack and draped it over a shoulder. "How did you know where my bag would be?"

Through the darkness, his stare burned her. "I was here earlier today. I knew where Beau's clubs should be—where you would have put them." He cocked his dark head, haloed by the amber mercury-vapor light. "Am I taking a test, here, Perr?"

She shook her head. "I'm just...undone. Thanks, Mark. For coming to look for me."

He released a loud breath, looking uncompensated. "Let's go. I'll talk to security later."

He didn't touch her as they picked their way up the twisty path, past the now deserted putting clock. But he took her arm when they crossed the street fronting the clubhouse. He led her along the deserted strip mall where she had shopped with Beau earlier, through a doorway opening off the sidewalk, and into the dark and boisterous Laddie Bar.

CHAPTER TWENTY-ONE

Beau spotted Perri in the back corner of the bar, facing Mark in a narrow booth. They watched him cross the crowded room, working his way between tables. His mind, frazzled from not knowing her whereabouts for the last two hours, raced. When he'd returned to the room from looking for her, voice mail had rocketed his imagination into overload.

Beau, I'm with Mark in the Laddie Bar at the Scottish Landing Hotel.

When he reached the table, Mark leveled those onyx, benevolent-priest's eyes on him. "I know you're pissed, Beau, but it's not what you think."

Well, at least one of them knew what he was thinking. He felt as if these two were a step ahead of him in time, that he was joining the cast of a play already in progress, and he'd missed his cue. He folded his arms and looked at Perri, seeking a clue.

Looking dazed, she sipped what looked like water, eyes fixed ahead.

"I'd offer to leave," Mark said. "But it's my hotel. You're the one who's slumming." He took a drink from a thick coffee mug and settled back against the wooden booth, drawing one leg up, resting his forearm on his knee. After he glanced at Perri, his eyes met Beau's again. "You let her wander around at night, so you deserve what you get. She spent half an hour with me, get over it."

Fury turned his hands to fists, but he kept them hidden, arms still crossed. "What I can't get over is why she'd want to. You do remember she's my wife. Right, Zamora?"

Mark gave a raspy chuckle that moved his muscular shoulders. "You wish she was."

"Cut the testosterone rodeo, you two." Perri's voice was hushed, but she gave them a visual blast capable of curbing a riot.

In slow motion, she placed the tankard on the table and worked her way out of the booth, moving close enough to Beau to almost ease his misery. But something was out of kilter. Her hair was wild, clothing rumpled, her eyes hollow and dull. His arm went voluntarily around her shoulders. When she raised her head to meet his eyes, hers went from dull to wet. Glistening.

She frowned as if a molar ached. "Could we please just go?"

"Not until I know where the hell you've been and what's going on here."

Glaring, she shrugged out of his half embrace, slung the backpack into position and wove her way through the crowd toward the door. Heads turned to watch. To covet.

"You're batting a thousand, Saint." Mark's grin contained no amusement. He made a move as if to rise. "Maybe you're gonna let her walk out of here, but I'm not."

A mile long list of threats relating to future maiming formed in Beau's mind. But Perri's proximity to the door and his recall of the murky, fog-shrouded street shortened the list. "Stay away from her, Zamora. No more warnings."

"She's gone," he said, eyes on the door. "Who's going after her, Beau? You or me?"

As he turned away, he glimpsed the satisfied gleam in Mark's eyes.

Following the crisp clip of boots on cobblestones, Beau caught up with her on the unlit sidewalk that led up the hill to the hotel. When he grasped her arm, she all but collapsed against him. The eager way she came into his arms, clinging to him like grim death, head burrowed against his chest, convinced him that her being with Mark was some kind of quirky coincidence. "What is it, Perri?" he whispered against the top of her head, rocking her in his arms.

"Please, let's go to the hotel. I'll tell you there." She pushed back, her eyes searching the dark for his. "I feel so dirty. I need a shower."

His mind raced in rhythm with his heart. He'd seen enough movies, read enough books to know what that meant. He stepped to the curb and hailed a cab from across the street.

※

He got the story in bits and pieces as she paced, a bulky robe wrapped chin to ankle. A towel formed a turban for her hair. He wanted to hold her, but in deference to her agitated state, he endured the cat-like prowling. She finished her gut-souring story at the point where Mark had locked the door and walked her to the Laddie.

"He didn't notify security?"

"He mentioned it, then changed his mind. I didn't want to...pressure him."

Giving in to his need, he drew her onto his lap, tucked her legs against him and cradled her like a child. Inwardly, he cursed himself. Recalling her urgency for a shower, he prompted, "You're sure the bastard didn't hurt you? Is there anything you aren't telling me?"

She ran a hand up the voluminous robe sleeve. "Only my arm where he grabbed me. Who knows what he'd have done if I hadn't jerked away? If I hadn't found a place to hide?"

He watched her drift back to the scene, felt her burrow deeper into his arms.

"How did he know..." Her voice came from a distance. "He's been so quiet lately that I thought ...How did he know where to find me?"

"He's traveling with us, Perri, like I said." And following her all the way to Scotland showed commitment. "He was watching. That's why the bastards are called stalkers."

"Watching you and me. He knew when we split up."

He felt her shiver and fully understood the reaction. "Looks like it."

"I keep wondering why he didn't lock me in instead of only jamming the door where I couldn't open it. I almost feel he wanted to scare me more than hurt me. Like punishment."

Mark's pious eyes spiraled to the forefront of Beau's mind. "And you didn't recognize anything? His voice, maybe?"

After a contemplative moment she said, "He was . . . familiar in a way I can't . . . pinpoint. But he wouldn't talk to me. I only heard his laugh."

Beau's spine iced. "The bastard laughed?"

"When I threatened to call security."

"Don't you think it's strange that Mark showed up? That he just happened to see you, to know where you were? That he heard you banging the door when no one else did?"

She frowned, chewing her bottom lip studiously. "At first, I did. When the door opened and he was there— Whoever attacked me— I know it wasn't Mark."

Beau persevered. "It was dark, and he didn't let you hear his voice. You said you never really got close to the guy, except for his grabbing you. How can you be so certain?"

"The man who followed me into the shed smelled."

"He smelled."

She nodded, her cheek rubbing against his chest. "He'd been eating onions. And drinking. Smoking. When Mark came—"

She raised her hands to her face, pushed her fingertips against closed eyes. He waited, his gut convulsing with suppressed rage. Rage and runaway guilt.

"Mark smelled like dried sweat—golf course sweat. I'd recognize that smell anywhere. And like cigarettes, too. But he doesn't drink." Her brow pleated. "And I know from traveling with him that he doesn't eat onions."

"Anything else?" he urged carefully.

"Mark doesn't wear a ring. Whoever grabbed me held on so tightly, the metal bit into my skin."

Hope reared its head. "Which hand did he use?"

"I'm not sure."

She was favoring her right arm, where the bruise had begun to show. "Think, baby. Did his fingers wrap toward your body or away from you?"

After a moment she said, "Toward me. I kept feeling his knuckles against my ribs when I tried to get away. I'm bruised there, too."

The bastard was left-handed. The ring was probably a wedding ring, since people connected with golf seldom wore any other jewelry.

Her voice seemed to come from a distance when she surmised, "Maybe Mark is in on it, Beau. But he wasn't the one in the shed with me. The first one, I mean."

"It looks that way," he begrudged, then voiced the thought gnawing him. "It's my fault. I never should have let you go alone."

She shook her head. "I bullied you into it."

He'd let her down. He'd made a stab at getting security for her before she'd agreed to move in with him. After that, he'd thought he could take care of it. When reporting the Hilton Head incident to hotel security and local police had gotten no result, he knew he and Perri had been written off as transients. Seeing no sign of the sadistic bastard since

Hilton Head, he had lapsed into false security and dropped the ball. "No more," he swore. "Tomorrow you're moving into my room, and I'm getting twenty-four-hour surveillance."

She shuddered. "I hate that. It gives me the creeps."

He nudged the towel backward with his chin until he could kiss her slight widow's peak. "Sleeping with me gives you the creeps?" He nuzzled her throat. "If you promise not to drop the soap and bend over to pick it up, I promise not to make things hard on you."

She sat up, giving him a look that could freeze anti-freeze. "I'd hate living with a bodyguard." Snapping eyes marked her restored bravado. "All this proves my theory."

"What's that?" He'd known they'd work backwards to this.

"This is no way to live. Tonight—what's been happening with this creep all these months, is an omen. I should be home. She took a deep breath, as if gathering strength for her argument. "Home with Chelsea. I'm all she has, and I'm tempting fate."

"We had an agreement." It sounded lame, but the thought of this room, that course without her tomorrow— He refused to consider beyond that. "I'll be your bodyguard. I won't let you out of my sight." He tilted her chin, underlining his promise with his eyes. "I let you down before, but I'll make it up to you. This time you can trust me, Periwinkle."

Her eyes welled up too fast, burned too hot for him to believe the reaction had anything to do with his apology and vow. She squirmed out of his arms. Unable to read her thoughts, not knowing what to ask, he kissed her forehead and released her.

She opted for dinner in the room, then ate sparingly, silently, for the most part. Afterward, she made a brief trip into her room and returned wearing a long pink T-shirt with a Star Wars imprint and carrying a pillow. Wordlessly, she pulled back the bed covers, placed the pillow lengthwise in the center of the king-sized bed and climbed in. Hugging the demarcation line to her body, she murmured goodnight and closed her eyes. He watched her sleep for a while, watched the shallow rise and fall of her back, thanking God for the way the sickeningly weird and frightening circumstances had turned out. Perri was back in his bed.

So she was sick of the tour, blaming the lifestyle for what had happened tonight. He could relate. He loathed having no home, no roots, waking up in a strange town every week. Before he'd discovered Braden's true colors, High Meadow had been home; except for Nonna and Cal and Silky, that connection no longer existed. Perri was his home, his stability, his beacon in the night. But he was on unstable ground there, as she'd reminded him tonight.

She felt guilty over leaving her daughter, but for some reason she chose not to share, she was still strapped for money. His developing plan, if it worked out, could provide an answer for each of them, for them and Chelsea. If Perri agreed to it. But revealing the solution before he'd knotted the loose ends wouldn't be wise. If this strategy didn't materialize he'd start over.

Somehow, some way, he intended to give his boast of her being his wife legal validity.

Shrugging off his musing state, he took out the book he'd bought that afternoon, the one that sealed her scary fate when he'd gone into the bookstore instead of with her to the club shed.

He held the book, studied the cover. *Interpreting Character from Handwriting.*

In his computer case, he located the envelope containing the note he'd found skewered on his broken driver, months ago in New Orleans. He smoothed the paper beside the book and began his search for knowledge.

✳

Next morning, he practiced his short irons, testing his wrist, then deemed the last injection's magic held. He pulled his driver, watching Perri as she stood in the background, alternating between sipping coffee and leisurely applying sun block to her arched throat.

He had helped her transfer her things from her room to his that morning, pleased to discover she was still a minimalist. In his closet, she hung her few items of clothing. Her panties and bras claimed a meager space in the drawer that held his socks. She placed a bottle of Pantene in the shower and a tube of thirty-strength sunblock on the counter, along with Noxzema, Keri Lotion, Revlon mascara, blush and lipstick—Brandied Apricot. Her natural beauty needed no further enhancement.

Her possessions made scarcely a dent in the vanity space, compared to how her nearer presence jolted his awareness. While shaving, he caught a glimpse of her body when she edged back the shower curtain and reached for a towel...slender as a stem, graceful as a fawn, the round rise of her breasts sloping gently. Teased by the chilly air, her nipples jutted out of a dusky rose circle. Her wet pubic thatch glistened, the color of burnt honey.

Subtle stretch marks marring her brown belly and fanning over narrow hips filled him with a kind of awe. Harboring a strong desire to press his mouth to those marks, to trace their pattern with his tongue, he tried to picture her swollen, heavy with child. The scars were part of her now, residue of an event he'd missed. Next time. When she carried his child, he wouldn't miss a single touch, taste or sensation.

His eyes had worked overtime, savoring details the encounter that dark night on the beach had prevented. In that instant before the shower curtain closed again, his quick and keen vision had marked the indecision in her eyes, her mutual need. In his mind, that look had lingered.

"Get over here, woman, and earn your keep." He nudged a ball toward her with the toe of his shoe. "Tee that up." He wanted her close enough to smell her, to feel her heat.

She took her time replacing the cap on the sun block, then ambled over, hips swaying, with exaggeration, he thought. He trailed his gaze across the course, all the way to the sea, while in his side vision, she stuck a tee in the ground and placed a ball on it and stepped back—a different ball, of course, than the one he'd indicated. He took the coffee from her, sipped, then handed it back. He could swear she turned the cup to the exact spot his mouth had been before taking a drink, her gaze holding his over the rim.

He eyed the course again. Better that than the erotic pictures his mind toyed with.

"This is Pete's kind of course." A typical true links layout, windswept, built on sandy loam soil deposited over the years by the receding sea.

"How's that?" Courtesy, not curiosity, marked her tone.

"It's practically treeless, and since he can't hit the fairway most of the time, that's a plus. Pete's got a swing only a mother could love." He acknowledged a pang that ricocheted between guilt and regret. "He should be here. I should have forced a loan on him."

She cocked a honey-hued eyebrow. "He doesn't know the meaning of the word loan. If you let him, Pete Jacoby will bleed you dry, Beau."

Feeling she wanted to say a lot more, he thought of Pete's claim that she was jealous. Beau would call it intuition—street smarts—not jealousy. She had grown up knowing how to watch her butt, and she'd always been prone to watch his. Where that left Pete, he wasn't sure.

He took his stance over the ball. "He won't live long enough to bleed me dry."

He hit the ball and watched it fly, arch, descend, land and squirt forward. It ended up at a longer distance than his wildest dreams could have concocted at the previous tournament. With finality, he stuck the driver in the bag. "Let's go. We don't want to screw around with perfection."

"Perfection and modesty," she murmured, reaching for the bag. "Admirable traits."

Pushing her hand away, he made a move as if to shoulder the burden.

Panic shot into her eyes, ripped across her face. Her hands darted out, grasping, pulling.

"Don't you dare pick that up, asshole."

He laughed, fighting the urge to pick her up, swing her around, feel her against him, shock the hell out of the stodgy British. Drive Braden wild when he saw it on CNN.

"Then cut the sass, Periwinkle." He strode away, comforted by the rhythmic rattle of clubs as she followed in his wake toward the waiting candy mongers.

Reserved politeness marked the difference between the Scottish children who waited for Beau's candy and the American children who normally got the handout. From previous years, he knew if he didn't show up early on the number one tee they would let him pass without protest, then respectfully follow his round empty-handed. He had shown up early.

Enthralled by their Scottish brogues and their expressed knowledge of American golf, he signed caps, sleeves, programs, the backs of hands, and tiny, pale cheeks until his name was announced by the British official manning the number one tee.

As they tramped the second fairway, a manageable par four if the traditional northwest sea breeze stayed calm, Perri voiced what had obviously kept her quiet since the candy ritual. "What kind of magic exists between you and children, Beau?"

He had felt her eyes on him earlier, their opaque luster revealing nothing, other than close observance. "They like candy. I like them. It works out."

Rattling clubs rode the silence until she spoke. "It's not that simple. Kids can buy candy anywhere. There's a connection between you and them."

"Maybe." He shrugged. "It's an intrinsic kind of thing. They can tell I care, that I'm not patronizing them, anymore."

"Anymore." She seized the word, tone triumphant.

"The candy ritual started out as promotion, the idea of a hotshot publicist Granddad hired. That publicist is long gone, but the kids are still around. Usually, the ten minutes I spend with them is the highlight of my day." He smiled. "Before you came back, anyway."

Adroitly, she deflected his endearment, gaze measuring. "I never saw this in you—"

Had he heard skepticism or wonder? Either way, he decided to deal the whole deck. "Today—after what you said last night about needing to go home to Chelsea—I kept looking at those little girls and imagining they were her. Or trying to." He needed to see Chelsea's picture again, but thwarting his need, Perri had stopped wearing the locket.

They reached the spot in the fairway where his drive had landed. She unshouldered the bag, eyed the green and pulled an iron. When she spoke, her eyes held a beseeching look.

"Are you trying to sucker me, Beau? Just to get me into bed?" She evaluated the green, even though he knew she'd memorized the terrain at first glance. "You don't have to, you know. You don't have to live your life any differently than before I started working for you. Those groupies are still out there, ripe for the picking." She inclined her head toward the gallery as she handed him the iron. "Don't use my daughter to get to me, just because I'm convenient."

He took a practice swing, clipping what sparse grass grew in the sandy loam. "I gave up sleeping with groupies when Stephanie and I got engaged."

Her smile veered on the side of heavy. "Commendable."

"Yeah, well....Would you like the rest of the story?"

Her gaze trailed to the two pros and their caddies across the fairway. "They're waiting."

He hit the ball. It landed dead solid perfect, in possible birdie range of the pin. "I gave up sleeping with Stephanie the day you came on tour. You're it for me, Perri. Get used to it."

He took a bottle of water from a side pocket on the bag, uncapped it and drank with his eyes on her, then passed it to her. He watched her throat move as she drank. His heart and groin jerked out a lusty dance.

She capped the bottle and passed it back, her lips forming a speculative smile. "I think you staged that caper at the storage shed to execute the next part of your plan."

After pulling his putter, she shouldered the clubs and stepped out.

He fell into step, knowing what was coming. "Let's hear the rest of the theory."

"We've gone from separate hotels to rooms in the same hotel, to adjoining rooms, to one room. I don't know if I'm flattered or pissed because I've been manipulated."

"I love you, Perri. I'll love your daughter if you let me. Where does that fit in with your theory?"

For a fractured moment he thought she might cry, right there in the middle of the British Open. What the hell had he said that was so repulsive? But she finally gave him a pure Perri smile, a mix of reservation and devilment.

"I don't know where it fits, but you definitely don't need that publicist. I've almost bought your line, and I only just moved in."

Heady memory of having her in his bed last night ensnared him. As they walked onto the edge of the green amidst a smattering of applause, he felt her, as surely as if she'd touched him. Though it hadn't happened since the beach, he felt what it was like to hold her naked body, to be inside her, be one with her.

Perri lowered the clubs to the ground and sank onto the bag. Her eyes fixed his like beacons, as if she waited for a rejoinder from her earlier declaration.

He attempted to brush the dense fog away. "I'm gaining ground, all right. Now we need to get rid of that damned pillow."

"What we need is to win this tournament and get home, Beau. I'm too far from Chelsea."

"I'll win. But for the next four days, I have to go through the motions. I need your support."

She handed him a newly cleaned ball, one bearing her neat rendition of his initials. "Let's make a trade, buddy. My support for yours."

Whatever the hell that means. "Where? When? You name it, buddy."

He classified her smile as sad. "When the time comes."

Patience, he told himself. The importance of how he'd lost her trust, of what she expected of him to regain it, paled in his goal to comply. But he could see she was thinking, considering. Maybe starting to believe in him again.

Winning this tournament, if fate was kind and the cortisone kept working, would put him a step closer to the living legend he owed Braden, making the final break possible.

After that, life belonged to him and Perri.

✳

Hacked by archaic tradition that kept Perri from joining him for a beer to celebrate their brilliant first round, Beau passed up the smoky camaraderie of the men's grill for his locker. Opening it, he found a note hanging from an eye-level shelf, anchored by a box of Titleist Fours. He glanced around. Satisfied of his privacy, he retrieved the note, holding it carefully by the corners, eyes seeking out the signature. The pulse that had begun banging in his ear slowed, then revved. What the hell was this?

> *Beau. Made it over here after all—tapped Paula's Christmas fund for the airfare. I tee at noon today, so let's have a brew later. I'm at the Scottish Landing Hotel down the beach. It's not the Piersland, but it's got the Laddie Bar, so call me or come on down. I'll watch for you.*　　　　　*Pete.*

The paper trembled in Beau's hand. Déjà vu pounded a jackhammer rhythm in his head as he stared at Pete's left-handed scrawl. His mind raced to the graphology book back in his room, the frayed note, the hours he'd spent in deep study last night. Hours in which Perri slept fitfully, hugging a pillow, moaning with leftover fright.

Like a magnet attaching to steel, his eyes honed onto one word. Made. The note he'd found on his clubs had contained the same word in a vulgar phrase: Made her yet?

Remnants of a chilling passage from the book echoed dimly in his mind: When the second "point" of a capital M was...higher...than the point before or after it, it indicated...eccentricity. In both mind and nature.

His eyes sped down the paper, devouring, sorting. He zeroed in on the letter "g" in Landing. His recall held just enough clarity to nauseate him. A loop within a loop indicated extreme eccentricity at the least, mental disturbance, at the worst.

Was the writer—this writer—crazy? Sick? Dangerous?

He listened to the voices and laughter in the grill, some familiar, some not. If Pete was in Scotland now, had he been last night? Vague airline schedules, arrival times, filtered through his mind. Wanting to cushion Perri's trip, he had turned down a red-eye flight out of Chicago, one that ran every night. That flight, depending on when he caught it, could have put a jet-lagged Pete at Troon early enough for yesterday's practice, or delivered him for the first day's play.

Had Pete stalked Perri last night, followed her to the club storage barn, terrorized her, and then been scared off by the fight she put up? Beau could fathom Pete pilfering clubs, out of jealousy, maybe, or the resentment that had become evident lately. But staging that sick show in Perri's motel room, painting the foul picture on the pillow, the all-night phone calls, breaking into her room in Hilton Head? His mind raced backward. Pete had been at the Master's party. The motel scenario's time frame didn't fit.

Or did it?

Hands shaking, he folded the note and pocketed it carefully.

Upstairs, while Perri was in the shower, he placed the notes side by side on the bed. The comparison produced distinct copies in some letters, resemblance in others. Letter characteristics varied in the first note, as if the writer had lapsed in and out of an attempt to camouflage. Or was he a multi personality, writing as two people at once? The good twin warring with the bad?

One similarity remained constant. Beau searched for and found the book's interpretation: Words starting with well-defined letters, then slipping and sliding into hard to read, serpentine formations, show actual deceitfulness and possible criminality.

Beyond the bathroom door, the shower stopped. He heard the curtain slide back, close again, steel gliders whining on a metal rod. He pictured Perri's toned body, her sweet, tawny skin and classic face. Her helpless vulnerability. Missing facts, other than what she'd shakily shared, he tried to picture last night's narrow escape.

He looked at the notes again. Deceitfulness? Criminality?

Had Pete practiced yesterday? He reached for the phone and dialed the starter's desk to find out. For damned sure, until his suspicions were checked out, Pete would get nowhere near Perri. And Beau wouldn't be going to the Laddie for a drink. But he determined to consult a professional graphologist to confirm or allay his layman's interpretation.

Let Pete stew. Either he'd show his hand or put Beau's troubling hunch to rest.

✳

The first two days of the tournament sped by effortlessly, played out beneath untraditionally balmy skies. A storm threatened all through the

339

third day's play, then lived up to its promise with window-rattling gusto on Sunday, the final day.

Beau was tied for the lead with Colin Montgomery, the hometown favorite whose father had once been greens superintendent at Royal Troon. Knowing they'd be paired, creating a one-sided gallery, Beau had gone sleepless most of Saturday night, waking with a thudding headache. As he listened to the howling wind, an imaginary band squeezed his head, ratcheting tighter and tighter.

"Dress in layers, Perri." By noon the sun could be beaming, the winds calm. Or freezing rain could fall. Brits played through anything short of lightning. "You can peel if you get hot, but I don't want you getting cold."

He went to the closet for cords and a wool sweater he'd brought, just in case.

※

On the tee, Perri swayed a little in the gale as she passed him his driver. "Nervous?" In the morning cold, her voice trailed out of her mouth in a puff of steam.

"No way. I want to get back to the room and ply you with hot buttered rum. You'll be so grateful, you'll be all over me within—"

"From Anchorage, Kentucky, the US of A, please welcome, Mr. Beau St. Cyr."

Perri gave him a gotcha smile as the announcer's proper English voice swirled, echoed, and then faded in the wind.

Beau took the tee. After minimum set-up time, he took the driver back and down, then spanked the ball...too high. Wind snagged it. It sailed. The wind switched directions. The ball veered dangerously, then dropped onto the beach, mere inches short of the Firth of Clyde. He'd have to stand in the damn water to take the next swing.

Perri's audible groan brought polite laughs from a few gallery members.

Beau took his place beside her at the edge of the tee, smiling as a nearby camera cranked and Colin Montgomery, big as Goliath and twice as motivated, hit a low, screaming drive into the distance, center of the fairway.

Even in the morning cold, sweat oozed from Beau's pores, soaking his underclothes, his shirt, the hair beneath his clamped-down cap.

Now he was nervous.

They played score tag up to the three-par, eighth hole, the infamous "Postage Stamp," named for its tiny green surrounded by nasty bunkers and torturous dunes. Miraculously, Beau managed a two while Monty missed the green and then two-putted for a four. Beau went two strokes ahead.

In the next few holes, Beau went from leading to even, back to leading. As they approached the treacherous sixteenth, the soupy mist turned to slow drizzle, blowing horizontally, pricking his cheeks like tattoo needles.

"You okay?" He looked at Perri from the corner of his eye, hating knowing that even in the latest high-tech gear, she was cold, wet and miserable. Beneath the cuff of a stocking cap, her brow was a strange bluish shade. "Want my rain jacket?"

"I'm fine. How's your headache?" Her voice carried on a rush of wind, her reminder etching a jagged graph of pain through his head.

"No more problems. It's gone. My head, I mean. It exploded."

Her sympathetic eyes negated her laughter. "I guess you know there's a risk we'll be rained out."

And he'd win. By weather default. "Hell, I hope so."

She darted him a disbelieving look. "I never thought I'd hear you say that."

"I've never had so much to lose. I've been humbled." Winning posed the only way to retake control of his life. He wanted that, by hook or crook. But taking it back was a euphemism. He'd never had control. Braden had. That would change. Soon.

On the tee box, Perri turned the full weight of her intimidating gaze on him. "You can go two up on Montgomery and win this tournament right here, Beau." She kept her voice low, her tone intimate, as though they discussed more than golf. "Shut him out. All you have to do is birdie. The chance you can both do that is nil."

He eyed the hole, a par five whose green could easily be reached in three shots, making it possible to one-putt for the birdie she touted. Unless the wind was in your face. Like today. Unless it was raining. Nobody in his right mind would risk it. Today.

He made a pass at drying his face on a wet sleeve, whispering the detested words, "I'd better play it safe, let Monty be the hero. I'll lay up, hit on, two-putt for par." He offered compensation. "I'll get my birdie on the next hole,"

"You can bet your butt that's how Monty's thinking." Defiant determination had gathered in her eyes. "Birdie this hole and the next. Par the eighteenth, and go out in a blaze of glory." Her lips twitched in a tremulous, blue smile. "I'm in the mood for hot buttered rum."

Warmth spread up his neck and into his frosty cheeks. "This is asinine."

"I watched you make shots harder than this when you were fifteen."

Not in a blizzard. "I was showing off. Trying to get your pants down."

"Well, it eventually worked." Her smile turned sultry.

Woody reared his head. "Now who's running a caper, Periwinkle?"

"We need this win, Beau." She pulled the one iron from the bag and dug a dry towel from inside her water repellant jacket. She dried the blade and handle of the club, then blotted his face. Her fingers lingered around his mouth, tracing the outline of his lips with a corner of the towel. "Hit the damn ball, Beau. Show me you can. Again."

Drawing in a deep cold breath, he felt the pain in his head dissolve. He took the club and hit the ball long, straight, and far enough to challenge the law of physics.

"Nice." Smiling, Perri shouldered the bag and squished out in front of him.

His third shot, the one intended to put him in birdie position, flew over the green and landed in the bunker behind. Beau kissed his birdie goodbye.

Monty had played it safe. His fourth shot, a chip, landed on the green, hole high, not more than six feet from the pin. Easy one-putt, for a par, Beau surmised.

Perri's eyes big, round and luminous, leveled on his as she dried the handle of the sand wedge before passing him the club. "Never mind, buddy. You scared the crap out of him by going for it. He'll putt like a gorilla. You'll still win. We'll still celebrate."

Beau waded into the bunker like an automaton, purchased a stance in the soggy sand and eyed the flagstick. Visualizing. Perri stood on the edge of the trap, stone still. But he could hear her breathing. The gritty sound of the blade picking off and lifting the ball preceded the hollow clank of it dropping straight into the hole, hardly rattling the pin.

Beau's head jerked up in time to see tears spring to Perri's eyes. Her laughter got swallowed in the roar of a suddenly generous gallery. She offered her hand as he climbed out of the bunker, scraping wet sand from his face with the backs of his fingers.

True to prediction—or maybe a curse—Monty putted like a crazed gorilla.

Beau kept Perri beside him as he received the silver cup. He thanked all the proper people, starting with his high school and ASU golf coaches, running through his manager, the PGA and Colin Montgomery for making him work for the win. He told Nonna how pretty she looked in his High Meadow Farm television gallery. After crediting Perri with his miracle birdie on the sixteenth hole, he waited for her to grasp the handle of the cup and help him hold it aloft for the cameras. Then he lifted her, his hands at her waist, and kissed her wet mouth in private gratitude.

✳

For some reason he was unable to decipher, she wouldn't drink hot buttered rum, but she encouraged him. With hot tea, she matched him drink for drink, laughing with him when he got tipsy, and verbally replaying the whole round, including Monty's putts.

He waited for some indication they'd make love, that she'd be paying off her golf-course dare that had given him the strength to hit the ball, the determination to chip it into the hole. But somehow, taking him back to adolescence, Perri linked sex with integrity, and something was standing in the path.

Wearing the Princess Leia T-shirt and a pair of his wool socks, she curled up spoon-fashion, her head on his arm, her little ass pressed to his groin, a hand molding his to her breasts, in her adopted fashion. The extra pillow remained on the foot of the bed.

Beau lay in the dark, enjoying her freshly shampooed hair, her soft and hard warmth, the sleep-induced purr, her warm breath on his arm. He tried not to hate Braden for playing God, for depriving him of the last eight years with Perri, denying him the privilege of fathering her child. Somehow he'd make amends.

For now, he loved her; she loved him. That love would see them through.

CHAPTER TWENTY-TWO

Perri planned to leave Beau once they returned to Chicago. Although her quitting hadn't been mentioned while they were in Europe, she sensed his apprehension. He resembled a fox circling food in a ready-to-spring trap.

Sparse and difficult-to-time calls home had reaped no more news of Braden's antics. Still, she couldn't lose the feeling he was behind Chelsea's interview. Either way, she needed to be home. Discovery was only a matter of time. She needed to be there to protect her daughter.

Cohabitation was having a negative effect, however. The heady experience of sleeping next to Beau and waking to his sweet and docile morning nature, so like Chelsea's, was as addictive as breathing. In Scotland, a barrier had been lowered. She had undergone a softening that nipped at the edges of forgiveness, while the stalker's reappearance seemed to have sparked a fierce awakening in Beau. Never before, short of entering her, had he shown deeper, tenderer love. Comprehension eluded her, but she accepted the revered and troublesome change between them. Now time was running out. As Lake Michigan slipped past the window of the British Airways jet, Perri ached with dread, her heart as blue and roiling as the water.

Saying goodbye at baggage claim, going off on her own to find a flight to Louisville, had been her intent. But as she stood beside Beau, watching a red light blink their flight number above the baggage carousel, her determination waned.

"I need to call home. She eyed a bank of pay phones. "I won't be long."

He whipped his cell phone from his bomber jacket, agitated anticipation almost palpable. "Use this. Stay close to me, Perri. You can bet your friend was on that plane with us."

Knowing she had allowed herself to slip back into the comforting pattern of being taken care of, she suddenly felt caged. She took the phone and paced a few feet away, gathering resolve. But her gaze held to Beau's tall, slender frame, his masculine beauty and grace. As she watched, he fielded belated congratulations from peers and fans with an insouciant air that wrung her heart. He needed a haircut. He looked tired and anxious beneath the mock casualness.

Oh, God....Like a fool, she had allowed herself to fall more deeply, painfully, hopelessly in love with him. Enslaved by greed, she had invited his love in return. They deserved more than this jagged, ripping severance.

She turned her back and dialed. All depended on what Angie had to tell her.

"Not a word, honey." Angie clicked her lighter and exhaled sharply into the phone.

"The guy hasn't shown up again. You got riled up over nothing."

No. But at least the urgency was misplaced. "And Chelsea's all right?"

"She's fine. She missed a couple of days of the tournament because of the international time difference. She was pissed." Angie rattled her coarse, nicotine-ravaged laugh. A male voice sounded in the background, cushioned by a soap opera theme. "She caught on real quick, though, after Larry drew her a chart. She's sharp, Perri. Real sharp, I want you to know."

"I do know, Mom. I'm missing so much. I'm so ..." Torn. "...so sorry."

A moment's silence ticked over the wire. "I was only bragging, honey. She'll be sorry she's not here to talk. Lee and Nedra took her to lunch."

Perri sensed Angie shifting gears. Her tender tone indicated she had softened toward Perri's plight. Had Perri's reaction to the interview sparked a shared fear in Angie for Braden's tactics?

An inner voice urged her to announce she was on her way home. She risked a glance over her shoulder. Beau was directing his pilot to her green duffel. His clubs and oversized hanging bag, plus the taped cardboard box containing her new boots, were already on a luggage cart.

"I'll call tonight, Mom." From the Louisville airport asking for a ride home, formed in her mind, but not on her lips. "From Denver."

"Maybe she could talk to Beau then. She's all excited about you two winning."

Across the way, Beau shot her a beckoning glance as he signed autographs for a second crowd forming around him. "We'll see. I have to run, Mom."

When she joined him, he slipped an arm around her shoulder. "Everything all right, buddy? How's Chelsea?"

How easily the name now fit his lips. "Everything's fine. For now."

On the opposite side of the carousel, she spotted Mark and Pete, talking, laughing, their heads together. Pete's clubs and a sundry pile of bags lay at their feet. She watched them, intrigued, warily curious until Beau's voice nudged her out of her fugue.

"It's the new odd couple." Beau eyed the pair. "You know Mark caddied for him the last day of the Open."

She lifted her gaze to his, brown marble flecked with gold. Chelsea. Her throat tightened. She shook her head. "I didn't know."

"They made a damned good team. Pete won some money."

"I thought—"

"What? That Pete didn't show up?" His mouth tightened. "He managed."

"No. I knew he was there. But Mark's never... liked Pete."

His eyes clouded. "Maybe Zamora's not too picky when it comes to getting paid. Anyway, he's up to something, you can bet."

She couldn't picture the two of them as a team. She swallowed a bitter taste, not sure where Mark fit into the stalker incident, and still unwilling to blame him. "Is Pete flying with us to Denver? If he is, it's bad manners not to ask Mark, too."

"Pete hasn't been invited. So no reason to ask Robin Hood."

His grudging grin and tone fed her curiosity.

Beau pointed out the last bag to the pilot, making room on the luggage cart. "Let's go, bud." Grasping her arm, he steered her toward the door.

Curbside in the welcoming sultry heat, a limo waited to take them to the private air terminal. When they were sequestered in the back, the pilot up front with the driver, the glass partition closed, she pursued her hunch. "Is Pete pouting over having to pay his own way to Scotland?"

Beau shrugged. "I haven't talked to him since Quad City."

"That's odd." She cocked a brow.

His brief glinting glance turned to a smile. He jerked her braid, then smoothed it against her back with a gentle touch. "He'd have invited himself onto the plane, and that wouldn't work because I've got plans for you."

She retrieved the braid and trailed it over her shoulder, his nefarious look creating a stir in her lower middle.

"It's time I inducted you into the Mile High Club."

The stir became a whirlpool. "Your pilots would love that."

"They'd cheer, but if you're shy we'll close the curtain between us and them."

Irritation snaked up her spine, accompanied by pictures she tried to shove from her mind. "I'm sure they've seen it before. Or heard enough to feed their imagination."

His eyes quickened. He stared at her as if she'd sprouted horns.

She looked quickly out the window, raking her fingertips across her lashes, but not soon enough. He caught her chin and turned her to face him. His thumb caught a tear, then another.

"I didn't do it to us, Perri. Granddad did. And every word was a lie. But we'll beat him. We're survivors."

Gathering her in his arms, he kissed her wet cheeks, then her lips, his mouth issuing such a gentle, penetrating pledge that she found it hard to disbelieve.

✳

Beau played the Castle Pines course well on Tuesday, practice day.

In Wednesday's Sprint International pro-am, paired with celebrities John Elway, Mike Shanahan, and Patrick Roy, his performance sagged. He finished out of the big money, dejected and disgruntled.

"They're all millionaires, Beau," she reminded. "They don't need prize money."

"They're not the ones I'm worried about." He parodied a smile.

Perri had kept a careful watch, deciding his ailing wrist was not the culprit. Fear of losing had invaded Beau's game. His tense dread was affecting his swing, rendering his decisions and execution too conservative. He had lost his killer edge.

After play, he went to the practice range. Flailing ball after ball, he stared in the wake for as long as forty seconds—she counted from her cross-legged position on the ground—then raked a ball into position with the club head and lined up again. After the range session, he spent an hour on the putting clock until darkness fell. Witnessing his grace and soft touch there sparked memory of the kind of lover he'd been when she'd finally opened to him. Patient, gentle, thorough. She looked away, lost in memory.

Mostly, she kept still, enduring a silent ride back to the hotel. Once there, he stalked into the room and emptied his pockets of unused tees into a china bowl on the nightstand, sank with an exasperated breath and dialed the phone.

She stripped for her shower behind the partially closed bathroom door. Even through Beau's bitching, she recognized the reverent tone he reserved for Cal Johnson.

"The long game's fine—today. I hit sixteen greens in regulation, but I couldn't have putted if I'd been aiming at a manhole. Granddad's guru screwed me up royally." A pause. For condolences, she supposed.

"It's not the wrist. I've got to get rid of this center-shaft putter I'm using. I need you to find my old rear-shaft—yeah, the old Ping." He grunted a laugh. "No, I'm not drunk. If it worked in college, it'll work now. I think it's in my closet, top shelf. Dig it out. I'm sending the plane for it. Hell, yes, it's that urgent." Another silence, this one longer. "She's fine. She's great. A little homesick, maybe. A...family thing."

She heard him rise, imagined him pacing as far as the phone cord would allow. "She's gonna be hauling ass if I don't win this tournament."

Silence, then, "Money. Goddamned money. Do you believe that? I can fly a putter across the country, but I can't keep a caddie." Another pause, a wry, mirthless laugh. "I offered that—to pay her, win or lose. She's into money, Cal—but earning it. She hates charity."

An urge to laugh at his petulance or cry for his angst, tangled Perri's emotions. Quietly, she closed the door and turned on the shower.

He recovered his good humor in time for dinner with Justin Leonard. Perri sipped a pre-dinner club soda, listening skeptically to Beau airing his grief to Justin, whose team of local club members had aced the pro-am.

"The mid thirties used to be the prime age for golfers. Better college programs, stiffer competition on the Nike tour, and better equipment's changed all that." Beau gulped his Roy Rogers, eyeing twenty-six-year old Justin. Then his gaze shifted to the twenty-two-year-old Tiger having dinner with his entourage across the room. "Now the pros are hitting their peak in the early to mid twenties." He shrugged and took a quick drink, as if it were real alcohol.

"At thirty, you're not exactly over the hill, Beau," Justin cajoled, tone confidential.

"He had a bad day," Perri interjected, getting an empathetic smile from Justin.

"There's a world of golf off the course." Beau's tone took on finality as he settled against his chair. His long legs extended beneath the table, his knee striking an intimate connection with Perri's. "At my age, I've got years left to work behind the scenes. That's where I'm headed."

Justin took the bait. "Where's that?"

"Teaching, I hope. Kids preferably. They're the future of golf."

"You'd give up the tour to teach kids?" Justin challenged.

Perri stared at Beau, her heart threatening arrhythmia. Quit the tour?

A vein ticked in his temple. "I didn't learn from Arnold Palmer. A country club pro got me started, then my high school coach took over. You, too, I'll bet."

"Sure." Justin's smile turned skeptical as he posed the question forming in Perri's mind. "What if you crap out on the PGA championship next month? You'll be back to square one on the grand slam bid."

Beau smiled. "I'll win it, because I've got the world's best caddie. She practically whipped Montgomery's butt single handed to win the British Open." Finishing the Roy Rogers, he fished the long-stemmed cherry from the glass and passed it to Perri. His arm circled her waist as she chewed. "I'll win, and then I'm out of here...except for special events, maybe. But first we have to win this one." His fingertips caressed her ribcage. "Right, Periwinkle?"

She dropped the naked cherry stem back into his glass. "Right, bud. Starting tomorrow."

✳

On Beau's last hole the second day of the International, Perri stood scarcely breathing, watching him struggle to maintain footage on the testy side-hill. The ball that had squirted right off his driver now lay half buried in leaves and pampas grass, surrounded by scrub oak. Gingerly, he worked his way through the growth to the ball and spread his feet. With no club in hand, he took a practice swing that would have hung up in the branches had it been real. He swiveled his stance, pushed a pesky limb aside and held it there with a slender hip. He tried the pretend swing again. Better. He worked his feet, his hip.

She kept her eyes on the back of his head, concentrating on the tiny cowlick in his crown, drilling

positive thoughts into him. The majority of the
field had finished, scores tallied. This hole would
make or break his chances of getting into a playoff
for the cut.

From the fairway, Pete and Phil Michelson
watched with interest. Phil's caddie and Mark
Zamora stood in the background. Pete's bag hung
from Mark's shoulder. A now familiar eerie ripple
ran up Perri's spine.

Beau straightened to his full height. "Give me
my three iron."

Her heart drummed protest. "You're sure?
You've got to get the ball airborne enough to clear
the trees."

He shifted in the loose earth, dug in. He eyed
the distant green and the gallery clustered on the
hillside. "I'll go through the trees. I need the three
iron for length."

"It'll skid when it hits the green. Just jump on
the five." Now her voice pulsed along with her
heart. She glanced at her watch. "Your five minutes are almost up."

His hands fisted on his hips, gaze darting to the
fairway, back to her. "Cut me some slack, Perri.
This is a piss-ant tournament, not the PGA
Championship. The pressure you're putting on me
to win is doing a hell of lot more harm than good."

I know, my love. I know. This tournament
wouldn't matter in the end. After what she'd
learned when she talked to Angie that morning, she
had no choice but to go home. To leave Beau. If he
made the cut, she'd stay two more days. If not,
she'd leave tonight. The importance of earning her
percentage of another golf purse paled in the face of
reality.

She managed a smile as she pulled the five iron
and leaned forward to pass it to him. "Quiet, asshole. ESPN is listening. Let's keep this debate in
the family."

Mouth tight, he took the extended iron, turned the blade up to read the number, then handed the club back. "Okay, split the difference. Give me the friggin' four."

It took a moment to form the words. "We don't carry the four, remember?" Mindful of the Colorado altitude, the difficulty she'd have carrying the bag on the hilly terrain, he had practically emptied it that morning.

Leaving the stance he'd worked to perfect, he crossed to her in two giant steps, shoved the five iron into the bag with jarring force and jerked out the three. Their gazes clashed. He turned his back, stomped to the ball and reclaimed his stance. He pushed the pesky limb out of the way, angled a hip to hold it. Ready.

Don't move it again with your hand, Beau. Two strokes. Two he couldn't afford.

The limb wriggled. A fist of instinctive knowing formed in her stomach.

As if in a slow-motion movie, she watched his left hand sweep backward. Grasp. Shove. The iron arched, descended—Beau, don't!—and struck the ball.

She sucked in a raspy breath, deafening in the abrupt quiet; his head jerked up as he lowered the club. It struck his shoe, the sound echoing like a tree falling in a forest. They watched the ball land in the bunker fronting the green.

Pain and certainty shot into his eyes, waved across his face and tensed his body. He pried his gaze from hers to the pros, the caddies, and now a PGA official, waiting, watching from the fairway.

"Christ!" He snapped the word off like a dry twig.

She felt such love for him in that moment that her pain was surely as acute as his. She knew what it meant to make a mistake for which others suffered the consequences.

"It's okay, Beau. You can chip in from the sand—like the Open." She held out his sand wedge, eyes petitioning. "An eagle will wash out the two-stroke penalty."

His bile-laced laugh lay between them as he lowered his disbelieving gaze to the ground. She felt the tension coming off him in waves. "Kiss my ass goodbye in the Sprint International." His voice a grudging murmur, he handed back the three iron, took the wedge and trudged out in front of her, eyes riveted to the green.

His sand shot landed eight feet from the pin, earning a tense murmur and a sprinkle of applause. His one-putt brought a roar from a naïve gallery who believed they had watched the British Open Champion fight for, and win, a spot in the playoff.

Her stomach sour as brine, Perri trailed him off the green, eyes on Pete and Mark waiting at the top of the rise that led to the clubhouse.

"Hell of a birdie from that lie in the boonies, Saint." Pete's give-me-a-break grin failed to line up with his uncharitable gaze. "You made the playoff, so you'll make the cut. Tomorrow you'll come out of the chute bucking. Them that's got, gets. "

Mark's street-wise eyes locked with Perri's. Her chin came up, breath snagging.

The nerve in Beau's jaw pulsed. "Not likely with my two-stroke penalty."

Perri's rioting heart settled down and began to ache.

"Get outta here." Pete feigned shock. "You made a hell of an iron shot out of those trees."

"Cut the crap, Jacoby." Beau's voice turned steely. "You and Zamora saw me move the branch with my hand, but I'm about to rob you of the pleasure of reporting it"

With Mark's eyes drilling her back, Perri followed in Beau's strident wake.

℞

CHAPTER TWENTY-THREE

Braden's phone rang minutes after Beau walked out of the score tent, missing the playoff by one stroke, according to ESPN. Instinctive dread knotted Braden's stomach, while Winonna's dejected presence lay heavy as sea sand on his conscience. He lifted the receiver with a sweaty palm. An arrow prayer shot upward: Miracle of miracles, let the caller be Beau.

"Braden St. Cyr."

"Well, how'd you like Golden Boy's performance?"

A wave of acid welled in Braden's belly. "I... this is not a good time."

Winonna blanched, feeding off his tension, he sensed, for she could have no knowledge of the caller.

"You should respect our privacy on Saturday," Braden reiterated.

"Well pardon the hell out of me." The laugh. The one engraved on Braden's memory. "I wanted to say I guess you raised the boy right. He reported his own ignorance—the little two-stroke fuck up. He saved us the trouble of tattling."

Us? Braden switched the phone to his opposite hand, then swiped his palm on a thigh. He waited for a clue.

"It looks like your sexy little dupe's done a good job on him—got him playing with the wrong head in the game."

A profound analogy of history repeating itself. "Anyone can make a mistake."

Across from him, Winonna stirred, moaning subconsciously, Braden thought.

"Yeah, well, he made a big mistake in Scotland. Her ass was almost mine. He tell you that?"

Braden kept still. The crude phrase echoed in his mind. Pictures of Chelsea, of Perri's surprise that morning he'd wakened her in Beau's room, her tears when she'd read Christi's note, glared in behind his closed eye lids. "I told you that I don't—"

"Want her hurt. Yeah, I know. Hurting her's not what I had in mind." A lighter clicked, followed by a deep intake of breath. "And I'm running the show now."

"What do you have in mind?" He tilted his tone up at the end, trying, for Winonna's sake, to sound as though he were getting a sales pitch, not a threat.

"Scaring her. Driving the Saint crazy. It's working, and I'm getting off on it."

Braden heard voices in the distant background. Laughter. The caller's muffled voice, off stage, asked for a "brew." Was he calling from a bar? Locker room? A hotel room filled with—Caddies? Players? Demented golf fans?

He reached for reprieve from the evil on the other end of the line. "My last offer still stands. If you'll give me your address. A post office box will do."

"So that's what it takes to clear your conscience? Money wipes out a bad deed?"

"It would terminate the agreement. The one I made with you."

He laughed again. "Like you said, Gramps. Anyone can make a mistake." The line went dead.

Braden held on to the receiver, battling an urge to bang it against the cradle.

Winonna stirred, gasping a bit. "Who was that, Braden?"

Lately she was calling him that. Never "Granddaddy" anymore. Nor "dear." Just Braden. When she spoke to him at all.

"Some pesky salesman."

"What kind?" One auburn brow arched feebly.

"Insurance. He wants to sell me coverage on Beau's hands. He's a ghoul preying on the rich and famous."

Winonna's hand fluttered to her breasts, her breath rattling like coins in a beggar's cup. Her mouth pursed, vertical lines forming a starburst around thin lips.

"Let's have our toddy, Nonna." He dredged up a smile. "Maybe Beau will call."

She gave him the same kind of skeptical assessment Thelma Henslee had given him that day in her kitchen. The same judging look Dr. Calvin Johnson had leveled when he delivered the DNA test that proved what Braden already knew. She looked at him with the same scorn his attorney—the one who'd handled Beau's annulment—allotted when Braden instructed him to prepare the custody suit.

But what could Winonna know? Perceive? Imagine? Nothing. He had kept it all inside. Alone, he had struggled with his guilt and desires in order to hand her a neatly tied package, wanting to grant her a portion of her life's dream.

But racing time and death were beginning to take their toll on both of them.

✳

From the posh Castle Pines Golf Club, Beau took a ten-minute drive down Happy Canyon Road to Sedalia Bar and Grill. The roadhouse had become a yearly tour ritual. Golfers and caddies hightailed it there every night after play for greasy burgers, easy flowing Coors draft, and country-colored camaraderie with the locals. Once there, he stood inside the door, surveying familiar faces. A jukebox blasted LeAnn Rimes at PGA officials, TV crews, golf legends, rookies and hangers on.

At the bar, Mark and Pete hunched over bottles, heads together. Mark's attention appeared to be focused across the room, a wry smile splitting the shadows on his angular face. He spoke from the corner of his mouth, nodding toward a back table. Pete's laugh was too quick. Too loud. A heat wave swept from the back of Beau's neck down his spine.

He'd known Perri would be here. Known since he'd stomped away without a word or glance, leaving her outside the score tent with Teddy. Lonely as hell, feeling he'd lost something vital, he'd handed out candy and then endured his ESPN interview without mentioning Perri's name or adhering to his adopted MO of giving her credit. There'd been nothing to credit her with, other than not deserting his ass mid-round, when he'd adopted an attitude of belligerence and blame.

But he had every right to be pissed by her expectations, by the ultimatum she'd issued that night in the restaurant: Win, or I'm out of here. He was still pissed. Right now. But he wanted her more. Time to solve the issue.

Through a filter of smoke, she watched his approach, her gaze indifferent. When Teddy waved, he managed a nod. At the table, he stood staring down at Perri, while Teddy dragged up an empty chair, his only invitation to join them.

"I was waiting to take you to the hotel, Perri. What the hell are you doing here?"

She cocked a brow. "Waiting where? In the hallowed men's grill where women and caddies are off limits?"

His mind rejected a list of rejoinders. What could he tell her? That he'd needed time to cool off, to adjust to the most asinine error he'd made in nine years of professional golf? He kept quiet.

Teddy lit a cigarette and picked raptly at a ragged cuticle while Perri gazed into a glass of what appeared to be ice water sporting a used-looking lime. Willfully, his hand stole to the back of her chair. "Let's go outside."

"Thank you, but I'd rather not." She watched the dart throwers across the room.

He shoved his fingertips into his back pockets. "I wasn't asking you to dance."

Her head tilted, perfect little chin jutting, one brow arched. "You weren't asking me anything."

Teddy propped her feet in the spare chair, settling back, arms folded, her mouth working at banning a smile.

He waited for the pulse in his temple to quiet. "You're pissing me off, Perri. Let's go."

"I haven't finished my drink." She sipped, pinkie poking out.

He dragged her chair backward; it screeched against the wooden floor. Heads jerked up, faces brandishing curious frowns. Perri's eyes daring, she raised her hands, one forefinger crossed the other to from a cross. Teddy's reined-in laughter escaped.

At the bar, Mark's dusky, vigilant gaze bored in on the scene.

Beau caught Perri's arm and pulled her to her feet. Resignedly, she shouldered the backpack, reacting to the stares around her, Beau decided, rather than to his persistence. Instead of the scathing look he deserved, she awarded him a smile laced with just enough impunity to really burn his ass.

She kept smiling—at Teddy now, tolerant, apologetic. "It seems I'm being summoned." She leaned across the table to hug Teddy. "Thanks for the sympathetic ear."

Beyond Perri's shoulder, Teddy's brooding eyes met Beau's. "I'll be thinking of you, Perr. Keep me posted, okay?"

Beau puzzled that telltale request as Perri regally preceded him out the door.

❋

At the hotel, Perri left Beau checking the desk for messages and headed for the elevators. Upstairs, she dragged the partially packed, anvil-heavy duffel from the closet and wrestled it onto the bed. Eyes on the clock, she gauged her time.

Could she risk calling Chelsea before Beau appeared? Quickly, she reminded herself risk was no longer a factor. Within minutes, he would know all. Anxiety simmered like acid in her middle, while relief of knowing that urged her on.

From the bathroom, she heard a key working the lock. The door opening and closing sent a chill through her. She went out to greet him, then stalled in the center of the room, hands and arms laden with toiletries.

His eyes took in the duffel on the bed, the items she held, then locked with hers. He tossed a fat manila envelope onto the bed, rammed a hand into a pocket and added today's leftover tees to the cache on the nightstand. "So you're leaving and I'm the last one to get the word. History keeps on repeating itself."

She dumped her load beside the duffel, trying to ignore the clock. "I didn't want to tell you before today's round."

"How the hell could you tell me? I was still on trial."

Her head jerked around. "That's not true. My leaving has nothing to do with your missing the cut."

His gaze iced over. "Well, worrying about your leaving if I missed sure as hell went a long way toward just that."

The timbre of his voice—skating the thin line between hurt and challenge—made her ache. She closed her eyes for a moment, then rallied and began rolling the cosmetics in items of clothing,

362

stuffing them into the bag. "I won't fight with you, Beau."

He seized the duffel and dragged it across the bed, out of her range. His stormy eyes found hers again. "You're not quitting. Get over it, Perri."

She pounced onto the bed, lunging for the bag.

As though it were weightless, he pitched it onto the floor and reached for her. She scrambled backward. He tucked his body into a forward roll across the bed, ending up in front of her. She scrambled off, grabbed a handful of tees from the nightstand and flung them at him. They ricocheted off his chest onto the floor, clicking, clacking, rolling.

His fraudulent laugh coursed a quiver of dread through her body, her breath snagging on the look in his eyes. He was incensed, and yet...he wasn't.

She ducked under his arm, heading for the bathroom, but he was there, blocking the door before she could close it. She backed up, bumping into a wall.

"I have a plane to catch, Beau. I have to take a shower."

His eyes brooded, then reconfigured, like sun warming the Rockies. "Good idea." He stepped out of his shoes. Pulling his shirt from his khakis, he stripped it over his head and tossed it away. His gaze pinned hers as he undid his belt, his zipper, and peeled off his pants and Jockeys.

She turned her back, hugging herself. "I'm not doing this."

"Leaving me?" he said from behind, closer now. "You're right, Periwinkle."

"I'm not having sex with you. It won't prove anything." Except her love, her need, and that couldn't matter now.

He took a step, closing the distance between them, his arms resting loosely on either side of her shoulders, the heels of his hands braced against the tile wall. Only his breath on the back of her neck, the warmth rising from his rock-hard body, touched her. He smelled of the course, sun and grass, and day-old cologne. Desire rose from her core, thrummed through her veins. She hunched forward, fighting the urge to turn.

Arms banding her waist, he drew her up and against his pulsing hardness. His face lowered to the side of her neck, scratchy evening stubble stirring revered memory. She clamped her lips on the moan rising in her throat, focusing on his pure maleness, the muscles pressing the small of her back, their contrasting bodies, their like needs. Her mind pared away all but basic truth. He couldn't coerce her into making love with him, for she wanted him more than he wanted her. She ached with it. Ached to feel again the power of his unleashed need, to go beyond the secrets and lies governing their lives. She longed to sink into him, to enter a blue-hot oblivion where no reasoning, no judging or lack of forgiveness reigned. She turned within his arms. "This won't change anything."

"We'll see."

He lowered his mouth to hers, disclaiming her warning, his urgency eating away at her reticence. The kiss turned rough, wild, rousing the moan from her she'd tried to stifle. He responded instantly, hungrily, working the buttons on her shirt, freeing it from her shorts, pushing it and her bra straps off her shoulders. His hands fumbled for an instant at her back, then circled keenly to her breasts, seeking, finding, releasing the front catch on her bra. He filled his grasp with the weight of her breasts, kneading, thumbs grazing her nipples.

His hands. God she had always loved them. Harnessed power and skill. Gentleness. Within, a kaleidoscope of desire tangled with a sense of coming home.

Breaking a kiss, he hoisted her onto the vanity, spread her legs with a swift hand and moved between them. Eyes glowing like hot amber, he released the snap at her waist and worked the zipper down. A hand worked beneath her buttocks lifting; the other stripped her shorts and panties down her legs. He removed her sandals, letting them clatter, one, then another, onto the tile floor, wrapped her legs about his waist and moved in close. His body and his gaze seared her as he lifted her onto him and carried her out of the room. She clung, arms around his neck, her face buried there. No more protest or reason surfaced. No rationality remained other than want.

He lowered her onto the bed amidst his envelopes and her packing debris, then sat beside her. Her breathing quickened with the intent in his eyes. As though reclaiming her, his fingertips traced the dip of her waist, the flare of hip, his touch tapering onto her thigh and then between her legs, stroking, invading, penetrating. Need spread within her, like circles in a pond, ever bigger, until the pulse beat between her leg. His determined gaze held hers, as if blinking, glancing away, would break the connection.

Breath ragged, she rose onto her elbow, reaching, urging him down. He leaned to nuzzle her breasts, taking her into his mouth, his tongue circling, kneading, evoking a moan from her throat, an arch of her hips. Her fingers in his hair, coarse and resilient, guided his face up. She traced the contour with her eyes, her fingers and lips.

Stretching out beside her, he drew her to him, molding her breasts to his chest, their legs tangling. She closed her eyes as the feel of his hot naked skin fused them together. She had loved his body as a child, one too young to love that way, or to understand her craving, her strange unrest. She loved him, craved him that same way now, with nothing left to mystery.

Her body writhed, invited, begged, seeking the undulations of his, the familiar havens. He strad- dled her, caught her wrists above her head, and she grew still, pinioned by his knowing eyes. His hands stroked down her backside, grasped her buttocks and pressed her to his erection as his tongue skimmed her lips to thrust gently at the corner. Then his mouth took hers. It probed, peti- tioned, promised, as it fed the fire rising in her cen- ter. She worked her hand between them, down- ward, grasping, surrendering to the sensation of taste and touch to the moment's desire and need. He swept a hand along her thigh, fitted her leg around him, and entered her in slow, gentle, deep, penetration. All care fell away with the sensation of being filled by him. Sweet, sweet, Beau.

A feral groan rumbled from his throat as her legs parted to lift and tighten around his hips. He found a rhythm that she fell into, then matched thrust for thrust, surmounting the boundaries their past had erected, loving him more, even more, each time he entered her. Together and separately they climbed onto another plane, entered a mystic realm of using and being used, pleasuring and being pleasured. They had endured too many unfulfilled hours, days and nights. Too many desires had gone unconsummated. Within his arms, beneath his hands, his mouth, she shot to the brink almost too quickly, teetered, holding back, straining forward. Too far. Shattering, spi- raling down to lucidity.

She watched his chiseled features contort into a rapidly gathering climax that spasmed a wave across his face, through his eyes, and took him away. He finished with a shudder that rose in his throat as a deep groan against her mouth, and then his body ran slack. Satiated and defeated, she lay in his arms, their ragged breaths mingling, eyes melding across a pillow, as the imperfect world reformed around them.

For in a perfect world, the bedside phone wouldn't be ringing, fusing their bodies with a wire of tension. A perfect world would have allowed no lingering questions. There'd be no looming plane schedule to tear her from this bed. No torturous goodbye. She would fall asleep in his arms now and wake to discover Angie's call that morning had been only a bad dream. The phone rang on, shattering the hushed spell.

"Should we answer that?" he asked, voice husky and reluctant.

Her mind warred, tangled. "I know it's Mom. I'll call her back."

He ran a finger down the ridge of her nose, her throat, and circled a breast. Catching her hand, he pressed her palm to his lips, tracing the lifeline with his tongue, surely tasting himself. She looked away, her guard going up, rehearsing all she must tell him. "I'm going home, Beau. I have no choice." She eased back from his touch.

He smiled. "I'm not finished. I'm only regrouping. You'll change your mind."

Her smile felt as though it ripped her soul. She pushed up onto her elbows, chancing a glance at the clock. "I don't have long. I have to take a shower."

He drew her back down, a leg looping her thighs, his kiss playful. "See, you're already changing your mind. You remembered showers are my specialty."

She touched his mouth, pressed her fingers to her lips. "It wasn't only sex—what just happened. Not for me. You knew that, didn't you?"

Sitting up, he drew her astride his lap. "Don't talk in past tense, Periwinkle."

She eased off him, avoiding his eyes. The very bed beneath her seemed to suck at her, be drawing her down into an accumulation of decision and mourning. Suddenly too conscious of her nakedness, she rummaged in the duffel for clean clothing, and went into the bathroom, softly closing and locking the door.

When she emerged minutes later, damp from the shower, hair caught in a wet ponytail, he stood at the windows, his back to her, a forearm braced against the frame, his hand clenched into a fist. His posture and clean clothing over his sweaty body filled her with guilt. As she watched, resignedly, he flexed his broad shoulders, then moved a hand to the back of his neck, massaging the taut muscles her own hand had caressed minutes before. They had suffered enough. Too much. In truth lay the only path to freedom.

With purpose, she dug to the bottom of her bag, removing a flat, thin, rectangular object wrapped in tissue paper. She placed it on the disheveled bed, then resumed packing, eyes avoiding the tangled spread clinging to the edge, the wet splotches on the rumpled sheet. She heard him turn, felt him watching her.

"I can't believe this, Perri. You love me, I know you do. But you're leaving."

She worked silently. Soon he would believe. Understand.

He tried again. "Since you won't go on salary, how about endorsements?"

Her hands stilled. She met his gaze, jolted by the plea she saw there. "What?"

"I can't win every friggin' tournament. Even my sponsors don't expect that." He came toward her, his hands in his pockets, now, as though tethered. "But I can get you so many endorsements you won't care if I ever win again."

Her eyes stung. "There aren't that many endorsements in the world."

"We're talking mega money." Abruptly, his gaze took on a hawk-keen glare. "What do you mean there aren't that many? How the hell much money do you need, for Christ's sake?"

"There isn't enough in the world to make me not care if you win or lose, Beau."

"But you're leaving." Awakening dawned in his eyes. "So it's not the money. It's the son of a bitch who's been—"

"It's Chelsea. Someone is trying to take her away from me."

He gaped in a moment's stunned silence, concluding, "Angie."

"No. Someone as powerful as he is evil. Weeks ago, a man came around to Mom's—to Lee and Nedra's—asking questions about Chelsea. He said he was writing an article. That's why I told you I'd probably have to quit and go home."

His eyes quickened with recall, mouth tightening.

Her mind reeled back, then forward to Angie's news. "When I was pregnant with Chelsea I stayed with a woman in Louisville. Thelma Henslee."

He stared at her, seemingly baffled. "Why?"

She shook her head, trying to force her emotions and words into some order. "Someone's been there—to see Thelma—asking questions." Not a benign investigator, but Braden himself. "Gathering proof for a court case. I have to go home and fight him."

He seized on that. "It's Chelsea's father, right?"

"No." She reached for the tissue-wrapped article beside the bag.

"Just tell me who, Perri. I'll get it stopped. Give me a name."

"Braden St. Cyr." It tasted bitter on her lips. "Braden wants Chelsea."

He stared, confusion and doubt in his eyes. "Why in hell—He's crazy, I know that. But why Chelsea?"

She unwrapped the package and held it out to him, a portrait in vivid natural oil, framed in shiny brass. "This is Chelsea."

He took her offering, but his eyes held hers, searching, probing, before they finally lowered to the object he held. A chilled black silence surrounded them. Watching him she felt as if she were watching a familiar movie at warp speed: his expression raced through intrigue, disbelief, tenderness, passion. He settled on shock.

She touched a finger to the portrait, then caressed the cowlick in his own hairline. He jerked his head, pushed her hand away. Anger, not understanding, flashed in his eyes.

Give him time. "She has a second cowlick, Beau. In her crown."

He stared at the portrait, transfixed. "She's mine."

"Ours. She's seven, not five. I've never been with another man."

His fingertips whitened on the edges of the frame. His comprehending gaze lifted, at once brutal and tender.

"Chelsea is why I took Braden's bribe. Otherwise, I'd have thrown it in his face. I had had a test that came back showing damage, and with your family history—"

"I didn't even know—" He stopped, as if unable to voice all he'd not known.

"I was going to tell you, but Braden got to me first. Then I was too hurt."

"All this time you've been lying to me."

"Only about her age. And I haven't told you—"

"What? You haven't told me what, goddamn it?"

Her heart pounded while she waited to trust her voice. "She has patent ductus."

"Jesus, no," he moaned. He looked caught, suddenly stripped of bluster. Fear and dread rose in his eyes, emotions she hadn't known they'd ever share. "Is she dying?"

"She's stable for now, but I used all the money Braden gave me just to keep her alive. That's why I came on tour. I need money for her treatments and more surgery." She paced away from him, hugging herself, wishing, longing for him to hold her. She searched for words to reach him. "And then Mom told me someone had been asking Thelma questions." Now Braden knew. Beau knew. "I have nothing more to hide, no choice but to go home and fight. All along I've known in my heart that Braden was behind the questions. I've always been afraid—"

He whirled her around. "What the hell are you talking about? Afraid of what?"

"I've always known this could happen. I've always been afraid that if he found out about Chelsea, he'd try to take her the way he took you from your mother." At the mention of his mother, his eyes dulled, shuttered, as she'd seen in the past. "That's why I went to stay with Thelma while I was pregnant. The reason I took Chelsea on tour with me. To hide her from Braden."

"And me." He gave her a gimlet stare, his face carved with angry lines.

As she had feared, even as she hoped beyond reason to be wrong, she would get no help from Beau. "In my eyes, you and your grandfather were the enemy."

"Because you took his word over mine, and you were too damn proud to question."

"I have questions, Beau. Just as you have answers."

He seemed not to hear. "You've kept my child from me for seven—eight—goddamned years." He stared at the picture, stared at her, dazed. "No wonder I kept feeling like I knew her. Like I wanted to love her." His jaw jumped and writhed, as if dealt an electric jolt. "How could you do this to me? She's sick and she needs me. You played God, like Granddad. Only worse. You took away my flesh and blood."

"I meant to tell you, I wanted to. After that night on the beach, when you found her picture. But then we talked about Braden and you defended him."

He waited, mouth grim, arms folded, Chelsea's portrait tucked against his chest.

"I had my reasons for not telling you." Reasons that gave no sign of changing. "I've gone through hell. Alone. Because I couldn't trust you. Even when you knew Chelsea existed, and Braden was behind my leaving you, you never confronted him."

His hand plowed through his hair. "I know what I'm doing, Perri."

He was doing nothing. "Maybe so, but I don't. You talk a good story, but I kept waiting for you to give me a reason to trust you. You still haven't."

"Trust." He tasted the phrase, as if filtering it through his mind. "You can't trust me? Christ, Perri, I've worshipped you since you were ten years old. The only time I feel whole is when I'm wrapped around you, inside you, mixed with you. I've forgotten where my blood or skin ends and yours begins. What does that have to do with trust?"

Her eyes sought the tissue that had wrapped Chelsea's portrait, discarded, but not quite empty.

He took a long exasperated breath. "It's a matter of money, not trust. You left because you couldn't turn down the money. You traded your child's father for a friggin' bribe. But fate backfired on you, didn't it? So you came back and fleeced me again."

Anger fired her scalp, then bled to her face in a swift flush. She could hate him, now, and it would be best for each of them. But rummaging around in her emotions, she could only touch regret, as familiar as the pain in his eyes.

He shoved the portrait at her. She grasped it to prevent it crashing onto the floor. Jamming his hand into a pocket, he came up with a handful of change. He trickled it onto the pillow they had shared only a heartbeat, a lifetime, ago. From a different pocket, he produced a thick fold of bills, banded with a leather money clip.

"You screwed me royally, Periwinkle. You might as well get paid." He pitched the money clip with contempt. It landed on the tissue paper with a rustling sigh.

"Bastard." Her heart hammered; her chest heaved. She shoved the money aside. From the folds of tissue, she extracted a piece of creamy linen paper with frayed edges. She jammed the note against his hard stomach. "Who screwed whom, Saint Beau?"

℞

CHAPTER TWENTY-FOUR

What the hell? Beau looked at the yellowed parchment paper Perri shoved at him. A note. The recipient, Beau. The sender, Christi. Old. Opened and read so many times the fold was threadbare. Familiar handwriting nagged Beau's consciousness as he skimmed the page, the pulse in his throat rioting, his gut clamping like a vise. He read it again, disbelieving. Intrinsically, his gaze lifted to probe Perri's. Her face glowed hot, her eyes taking on a feverish glaze.

"So this is it. This is what you've been holding against me."

She reached for the note, but he held it back.

"Where'd you get it, Perri?"

She shot him a look of unvarnished fury, her glare close to cold hate. Her face leaked color as if whitewash had moved over her cheeks and down onto her throat. "I told you. Braden—"

"It's so old it's falling apart. Didn't that seem strange to you?"

Her face contorted with rage and grief. "Eight years is a long time, Beau. Eight lonely, scared, painful years of reading it over and over. That's why it's falling apart."

He read the note again, turned it over in his hand, ran his finger along the frayed seam. Musty with age, written by a ghost he suddenly felt closer to than ever before. An empathetic ache gathered, spread into a futile loneliness of his own.

God, Granddad. This time you've gone too far.

"You've been carrying this around all that time, holding a grudge. You never thought to question—"

"How could I when I was holding the answer in my hand? When Braden gave me the note, he confirmed everything Lee had ever said about you and me."

"Which was?" Somehow he managed to keep his tone even.

"He always told me I wasn't good enough for you. That's one thing he and Braden agreed on. Lee said you wanted one thing only and when you got it, you'd look for a new game." Her hands flew to her face, jerked down, fisting. "I loved you, Beau. I wanted him to be wrong. He wasn't."

"You didn't love me enough to verify this." He shook the note. It ripped slightly. She looked as if she watched the demise of a revered enemy.

"Beg you, you mean? Braden told me you'd found someone better suited to you. His words. Not mine. The note proved it."

She carried her bitterness like a shield, hiding behind her anger now, making any explanation, any vow, useless. "You've been had, Perri." Worse than he'd known or could imagine. "We both have."

He folded the note carefully, strode to the dresser, placed it inside his briefcase and worked the combination lock. Her voice turned him around.

"I'm questioning now, Beau." Her arms wrapped her waist. "Tell me who she was? When it started? Tell me when you realized I wasn't enough, and why you want me to think I am now."

Hurt welled up, choking him. "Too late, Periwinkle. You knew me well enough to trust—" A bitter laugh erupted. "Screw trust. We've established that as a lost cause. Let's just say you should have cared enough to ask me those questions eight years ago, instead of taking Granddad's word."

He grasped the briefcase and gathered the manila envelopes from the bed. At the door, he stopped and faced her. "If I loved you enough to forgive you for Chelsea, when I thought she wasn't mine, why didn't you love me enough to forgive me for what you thought I'd done?" She turned her back, meeting his gaze in the dresser mirror. Her silence provided his answer. "Get your ass in gear, Perri. Be downstairs in an hour. I'll have a limo pick you up, and the plane will take you home."

She frowned as though he'd passed sentence on her. "I don't want that. I don't expect it."

"Well, expect it," he snapped. "Nothing's too good for the mother of my child."

He watched his words meet their mark. She looked as if he'd struck her.

"Where are you going?" All of her bluster, most of her anger, had dissipated. Only grievous convictions remained in the shadows of her eyes.

"I've got business elsewhere. But when I'm finished, I'm coming for Chelsea, so get ready." He stopped, pierced with self-loathing when he saw the panic on her face. "I want to see her," he revised. To hold her. Love her. Make amends.

She shook her head, mouth grim. "Not yet. She doesn't know about you."

"Well tell her, or you can just let me show up, and I'll tell her. Either way, your little charade is over. I'm coming to meet my daughter, Perri."

After an eternity, she half whispered. "You have that right."

"And I'm taking it. On that, you can trust me."

✳

Nursing lingering shock and anger that tangled with relief and elation over Chelsea being his, Beau was well into his come-to-grips beer when he spotted Mark and Pete in the hotel bar. Survival instinct kicked in, taking precedent. He shoved off the barstool, seized the briefcase from the floor and crossed to their table, bent on bringing one more mystery to a close.

Mark watched him approach, while Pete's foggy gaze fastened in space.

Beau plunged into his spur-of-the-moment plan. "Can a guy get a sympathetic ear at this table?" He slipped into a chair, slumped back and crossed ankle over knee.

"Anybody can forget a rule and screw up, Beau." Mark clanked a coffee cup against Beau's glass. "You can't make every cut. Let's drink to your being human."

Pete lit a cigarette, ignoring the toast. He reeked of course sweat and liquor.

"I'm over that." Beau sipped beer, the scene running through his mind. "Perri couldn't take it, though. She's doing the cut and run. Can't say she didn't warn me."

Pete yawed in the chair, then straightened and focused, eyes narrowing as if examining Beau's news under a microscope. "Get outta here," he mumbled.

Mark offered, "Perri's got problems, or else she'd never leave a saint."

"You're sure as hell singing a new song, since I screwed up in Scotland."

"What happened in Scotland?" Pete slurred. His glass plopped on the table.

Mark shrugged dismissively, but Beau ignored the cue. "Some sick bastard's been on her tail, followed her to Scotland. I made it easy for him to get to her."

Pete's eyes glinted, then fogged again, while Mark's slitted, as he regarded Beau.

"Get to her?" Pete croaked.

"Long story." Beau shrugged, running a finger around the rim of his glass.

"Anyway, she's upstairs packing. Going home. She claims she's got big family problems, some legal fiasco." He drained the beer glass and held it aloft toward the bar. "Rotten deal, with the PGA Championship two weeks away."

"Gone, huh?" Pete grunted, his sentiments up for grabs.

"Gone." Beau easily read Mark's surprise, trailed by unmasked regret. A lot going on there still, but not what he had once believed. Or feared.

Pete's grin, loose and crooked, lacked a specific target. "Guess there'll be room on the plane now."

Mark's laugh held incredulity. "Tell us how you really feel, Jacoby."

Beau's nape burned. He leveled a gaze on Pete. "That's it? That's the extent of your sympathy?"

"You're a little hard to feel sorry for, Beau Jangles." The table tilted as Pete gripped it, hoisting to his feet. "See if you can get me a drink. Gotta see a man about a dog." He shuffled off, casting Beau a measuring glance over his shoulder.

Mark locked into Beau's gaze across the table. "I got him on the rebound, but in case you're wondering, I'm not getting engaged to the bastard."

Beau watched Pete narrowly miss a waiter bearing a drink-laden tray. "Why not? You two deserve each other."

"You gonna follow him, see what he's up to?" Mark nodded toward the lobby.

Beau took his time answering as they watched Pete veer in the direction of the men's room. "You'd make a hell of a movie director. You know that, Zamora?"

"Maybe he's on his way upstairs." He cocked a luxuriant, jet eyebrow. "To say goodbye, good riddance."

Beau shrugged. "I hope so. The gorilla I've had watching since we got off the plane from Scotland is posted outside Perri's door. He needs exercise."

Mark smiled, satisfied. "When did you figure him out?"

"Around the time you became his best friend." Beau risked a wry grin.

"Well somebody had to take the initiative." Mark returned the grin. "Knowing you, I'd say it was sooner than that."

Beau's mind back-reeled. "I got suspicious when his attitude changed—especially toward Perri. I retraced the relationship and remembered how he'd left her alone at the Master's party for so long, that first night the stalker showed himself. Then he slipped up a couple more times." His mind replayed the day Perri had seen Pete tampering with the clubs outside the plane. He pictured the graphology book and the handwritten notes in his briefcase. "I put the pieces together. I'm dotting the I's and crossing the T's as we speak."

"Don't bother." Mark settled against the back of his chair, running a hand through a glossy shock of shoulder-length hair. "The sick bastard's told me the whole story. Where I come from, we'd probably castrate him."

"It's your word against his." Plus, the matching handwriting on the notes.

Mark's hand stole to his waist, slender fingers working his shirt hem up to reveal a blue wire taped to his ridged, bronze stomach. "More or less." He lifted his armpit to reveal a small rectangular bulge. Through the shirt fabric, his fingers clicked a switch, his grin mocking any real merriment.

"What's in this for you?" Beau voiced the question that had nagged him throughout Mark and Pete's recent alliance. "Other than being in love with my wife."

As usual, Mark laughed at the word wife. "Hell hath no fury like a jealous saint." He shrugged. "I wanted you off my back. It's one of the twelve steps to sobriety."

"I guess I owe you," Beau begrudged.

"Then how about a job? I left some loose ends there that I'd like to tie up."

The relentless bastard was holding his course, just as Perri had claimed. "Perri's a class act, Zamora. She'd be hard to replace."

Mark lit a cigarette, waved out the match and released the smoke, smiling in that pious way he had. "Unfortunately, you'd know more about that than anyone, Saint."

Beau watched Pete emerge from the men's room on the far side of the lobby. Listing like a loose fence post, he looked around until he spotted a wall of pay phones, then headed that way, purpose in his disjointed stride. When he turned his back to the lobby, hovering over the phone he'd chosen, Beau moved in and stopped around the corner within earshot.

Pete's voice droned. "Bitch Beautiful is on her way home, according to Golden Boy. So you see, victory comes to the patient."

The past months reeled across Beau's mind. The aggravation of the ruined and stolen clubs, the graphic art left for Perri to find, the helpless fog he'd operated in until he'd gotten her close to him, the enigmatic way it had all kept happening, even after that. And here was proof of what he'd known but not wanted to believe.

Pete went on. "But you weren't too damn patient, best I recall. Seems like you wanted to change horses in the middle of the stream, huh gramps."

Beau's stomach muscles clamped down like steel bands on the bile rising in his throat. Even as he told himself it didn't have to mean what his gut instinct proclaimed, he surrendered to belief. To reality. His mind stole to Perri packing in the room upstairs, to Chelsea's picture on the bed next to the duffel, then to High Meadow, picturing the face of the man Pete addressed. Loneliness crept in like mist across a Kentucky bog.

"I did my fuckin' best to scare her pants off, but maybe I can't take all the credit for her blowing Dodge, since Saint Serious says she's got legal problems. Bet you and some gaggle of lawyers know about her legal problems, huh? Guess there's more'n one way to skin a sleek little cat."

A snide laugh curdled Beau's stomach. Wait, he told himself. Hear it all.

"Guess you and me are outta business, so go ahead and send that check you've been harping on. But you probably want to send cash—better make that a money order," Pete rambled on, giving the name of a hotel in Michigan, the next tour stop. "I don't wanta be greedy. Whatever it's worth to you. But if it's not enough, I'll still be calling the shots. I'm guessing you wouldn't want Golden Boy to know about our little deal." Another pause, a begrudging laugh beneath his breath. "Blackmail's a dirty word, Mr. St. Cyr. I'll try to forget you brought it up. Say goodnight to the old lady for me."

The receiver clanked in its cradle.

Beau dropped the briefcase and walked out of hiding into Pete's path.

"What the f—" Pete staggered back against the phone, then righted himself, a blustery grin on his freckled face. His gaze darted around the lobby, an unfocused plea in his eyes. "Whatever you think you heard, Beau—"

"I know what I heard, Jacoby." He'd carried the suspicion long enough to make it viable, but hearing the proof filled him with disappointment that tangled with his rage. He seized Pete's belt and jerked him up close, thigh to thigh, chest to chest. "Never call Nonna the old lady again."

Squirming, Pete laughed feebly. "That's it. You're pissed off by that?"

Willfully, Beau's body advanced, slamming Pete against the phone cubicle, gratified by the look of pain shooting across his face. "Is that what this was all about, Pete? Pissing me off?"

His shoulders sagged. "It's a long story, Saint. I doubt you'd get it."

"I get it, all right." But until five minutes ago, nothing could have convinced him Braden was involved. "You wanted me to squirm, and you succeeded. I hope it was worth it, Peter, because your pro tour is over, once Dean Beaman hears the story. He's in the hotel, so let's go up and visit."

Pete strained backward, but Beau held on, gagging on the soured breath that came rapid and shallow now.

"The commissioner will laugh," Pete chided, eyes scornful. "I've covered my ass. It's your word against mine. I'll tell him the little bitch led me on."

Beau grasped the neck of Pete's shirt and twisted. "What about the stolen equipment? How about the pilfered bag, the smashed driver with your calling card on it? Did Perri entice you to do that?" His mind seized on the Masters, Perri's swim in Rea's creek. "There were snakes in that goddamned creek, Jacoby."

Pete's nostrils flared, eyes wild as those of an unbroken horse. "Your granddaddy," he rasped. "He put me up to—"

Beau silenced him with a look. Braden wanted Perri gone, but given his penchant for St. Cry legend, even he wouldn't stoop to sabotaging Beau's game. He had stooped much lower by agreeing to—or instigating—terrorism.

Pete's darting mind registered in his eyes, as though he'd read Beau's thoughts. "Your granddaddy's a pro, Beau. He'll never admit a thing. You'll be running to the commish with a sour grapes tale."

With a shove, Beau released him. Pete danced backward, running a bony finger inside the collar of his hand-me-down shirt. Beau retrieved the briefcase, fished out the notes, one signed, one not, and clasped them in his fist. Memory crowded Pete's eyes.

"You didn't quite cover your skinny ass, Jacoby." Beau inclined his head toward Mark who lounged against a far wall, watching it all, a satisfied smile on his face. Beau found gratification in the dread that leaped into Pete's eyes. "Looks like your new best buddy is ready to take an elevator ride." He grasped Pete's shoulder, turned him and shoved him forward. "Let's go. Friend."

He thought of including Perri, letting her witness Pete's confession, then thought better. She was safe, the main objective accomplished. Safe and out of his life. Again.

Score another round for Braden.

CHAPTER TWENTY-FIVE

Silky Johnson opened the door to High Meadow with a startled expression. She took a brief look at Chelsea, then pulled her gaze up to Perri's and groaned, "Law, chile. My boy, Calvin, Jr., done tole me the truth." She stepped onto the front veranda and eased the door closed, her seen-a-ghost expression evolving into joy. Dark, knowing eyes glistened in an unlined face. "Ump ump um. Now that I see with my own eyes, what can I say, 'cept thank you, Lord?"

"Say nothing just yet," Perri murmured with a conspiratorial smile. She leaned to graze the woman's cheek with a kiss, feeling comforted. "How are you, Silky?"

Knees creaking, Silky knelt, and took Chelsea's hands. "Fine. Just fine."

Chelsea's amber eyes, wide with question and awe of her surroundings, swept upward, seeking a mother's clarification. But with satisfaction, Perri noted Chelsea didn't shrink from the stranger's advances.

Silky shook her head, her pewter hair catching the sun. "Mr. Beau. Mr. Beau." She whispered homage, as though he were there. "This precious, beautiful child."

Smoothing Chelsea's hair, Perri ventured, "Do you suppose Cal could show her the horses?" She had spotted him outside the barn when she'd driven the long lane from the county road to the house. "I have business with Braden—if he's here." Her heart revved with the words. She swallowed hard. "And then I'd like Chelsea to meet Beau's grandmother...if she's feeling well enough."

"Miz Winonna needs some tendin' to, but I'll see to it, you can bet."

"And Braden?"

A frown ridged Silky's brow. "He's here all right. Does he expect you?"

Surely he must expect the inevitable. "No. But he'll see me." She placed her hand on Chelsea's shoulder. "Go with Silky, honey. Her husband is Mom's friend. He'll let you pet the horses."

"And ride," Chelsea added, and then she informed Silky, "I've never done that," as she engaged her tawny hand with the plump, black one Silky offered.

"Well, I don't know about riding," Perri hesitated.

Silky placed the tips of her fingers on the brick porch and gave her body a grunt-accompanied hoist. "We got one just her size. You don't worry 'bout a thing, little mother." At the steps, she turned. "Mr. Braden's in his study. He's having a bad day, but you go on in, Perri, honey. We got to get this settled while there's still time."

A curious Beau-like expression filled Chelsea's eyes as Silky led her away.

The house, quiet as held breath, felt overly warm, stale air secreted a medicinal odor within the flowery aroma of room spray. Perri stood in the marble entry at the foot of the sweeping staircase, gathering determination, grasping her bearings.

From somewhere down a dim corridor to the left, a frail female voice called, "Silky? Who was that at the door?" A pause in which Perri felt pulled, guilty. "If I have callers, I want to get dressed, don't you know."

Remembering Beau's increasing concern for his grandmother, Perri eased Winonna's voice to the back of her conscience, postponing that part of her mission. From aged memory, she made her way along an opposite corridor in the direction of

Braden's study. When she stood in the wide entry, each jagged edge of emotion suffered within the room came glaring back, but the faded shabbiness time had rendered surprised her. Or had Braden's domain always been faded? Worn? Flaws invisible to young, unsophisticated eyes that had seen only through Beau's tales of intimidating grandeur?

A head of silver-streaked sandy hair showed above the desk chair that angled to face an open window overlooking the putting green and stables beyond. It framed as well, Silky and Chelsea as they ambled toward a waiting Cal. He waved with gusto while holding the reins of a young bay. As Perri's mind embraced the Pegasus in the airport, along with Chelsea's fascination with the sculpture, something eased in her heart.

Braden swiveled the chair to face her, his elegant fingers draped over the leather chair arms, as though holding on. "Her resemblance to Winonna—to Beau," he corrected, "is...striking." While his voice held the cultured Southern quality Perri recalled, it was as dry and abrasive as sandpaper. Not a glimmer of acceptance or welcome showed in his unflinching stare.

Uninvited, Perri crossed the room. Slipping into the chair she had occupied eight years ago, she grieved for the ingenue she'd been, reliving the residue of pain, certain only of a fragment of her present. She was home to stake unequivocal claim to Chelsea.

The mission reconfirmed in her mind, she collected resolve and addressed Braden. "I'm through hiding the fact Beau fathered Chelsea." She saw a brow quirk, involuntarily, maybe. "But she's my child. Nothing you do—or try—will change that."

His mouth and eyes hardened. "From a biological standpoint, that's true."

Her heart rapped in her ears. "I carried her. I gave birth to her. I've raised her. She's my child."

Braden's gray eyes narrowed, his wince easily detectable. Yet, he let her argument lie. He opened a desk drawer, fiddled with something hidden from view and then lifted an oversized bottle cap to his mouth, tilted back his head and finished off the contents. Covertly, he dabbed his mouth with the back of a manicured hand.

Though unsure of the nature of the advantage he'd forfeited, Perri seized it.

"I know you've been having me investigated, and I know what you're up to. But you won't find me as easy to deal with as Beau's mother. I'll fight you, Braden." No more would she address him as Mr. St. Cyr or sir. He deserved neither formality nor respect. Her trembling hands grasped the chair arms, her throat threatening to close. "Unlike her, I'm not afraid." She rejected disquieting visions, her eyes trained on him.

Braden closed the desk drawer soundly and rested against the back of the worn leather chair, his hands laced at this belt buckle. "You should be afraid, considering the undesirable circumstances you've left her in to go gallivanting like a gypsy."

The accusation rang familiar. "Just how undesirable her circumstances are is not for you to say." She took a different bent, one she'd lain awake wrapping her mind around. "I'm willing to share Chelsea, but I'll never give her up. If you insist on a custody battle and I see I'm losing—" She voiced the promise she had made to herself. "I'll take her and run."

He rallied, sitting forward in the plush chair. "I'm prepared to offer you—"

A rod shot up her back. "You don't have enough money to offer me."

His trim brows torqued. "Then you've had a change of priorities, I see."

She stifled rebuttal. "You bought me off once, but with lies, not money. You deprived me of having and giving love, and you cheated Chelsea out of a father. That's done. You've seen your last victory over me."

His mouth contorted as though he'd sipped sour milk. "I believe I showed you proof of Beau's preference for another woman."

She fought against drawing a stabilizing breath, declaring, "Beau denies that note." Had he? Not with words, but with his eyes, his anger, his denouncing silence.

Braden blanched, his hand darting to the drawer, then coming away empty. He grasped a letter opener from a marble jar and used it to draw phantom circles on an ink blotter edged in gold-embossed leather. His fingertips drained as white as his face. "He's seen it then. The note?"

The tremulous quality of his voice piqued her curiosity, but she tabled the question for now. "You meddled in our lives. If he was unfaithful, you should have allowed me to discover it. Or given him a chance to tell me."

The words rang hollow as her mind replayed Beau pocketing the note two nights ago, still without explanation. He'd walked away with the tool she'd used all these years to wring hate and anger from a situation that could have been dealt with so differently.

"I was pregnant with a damaged baby, and I was scared—too naïve to question then, but I'm wiser now. I spent your bribe to save Chelsea's life. I've been on tour to make more money for her next surgery. I don't see that as giving you a legal advantage. I'm not a run-away mother." Suddenly, a solution she hadn't seen before unfolded behind her eyes. "But now that I don't have to fear naming Beau as her father, I'll get legal aid. No court anywhere would take my child when they hear what you've done." She hoped the dagger she shoved deeper was sharp enough. "I have nothing to fear now that Chelsea is common knowledge."

Braden shrugged off her threats like a duck shedding rain. "Common knowledge? If you mean Silky and Cal—"

"I mean Beau, damn it."

What did she see in those steely eyes? Dread? Fear?

"I spent eight years hiding Chelsea, thinking of you and Beau as a team. The note sealed my convictions. With your record of child stealing, I knew you'd have no qualms about doing the same to me." She paused, forcing her gaze to his, holding it with difficulty. "You and Beau aren't a team. You're all alone in your scheme."

Beau's own threats regarding Chelsea echoed in her head. He intended to stage his own campaign for custody. If she'd correctly interpreted his anger, he'd be crusading against his grandfather, as well as her. Surely no court would grant him reprieve for cheating, for not questioning Braden's deceit, letting her struggle for years, caring for and loving Chelsea alone. Only she had been weak enough to consider granting Beau a reprieve, and she had miraculously managed to pull back from the brink of insanity.

She left the chair and paced to a different window. Arms hugging her waist, she gazed at the wing that housed Beau's quarters, reliving her wedding night. Knowing she was pregnant with their wounded child, she had loved Beau too much to seek his comfort that night. Later, devastated by his rejection, she'd harbored too much hurt and pride.

She turned back to face Braden. "Did you think Beau and I would never talk? We know what you did, lie by sordid lie. It's too late for us to be together. You accomplished that, but you're no longer the master of our fate. Mine or Beau's."

Chelsea and Cal had moved from the stables to the putting green, and childish laughter floated through the open window. As though the sound was magnetized, Braden swiveled the chair for an instant, then jerked back to face her. He wore an expression she neither could nor wanted to identify. "You're assuming a lot and guessing the rest. I've heard nothing from Beau about your confession."

Eight years of silence, in which she and Beau each had lost, skittered across her mind. "That's his way. He's a master at silent suffering. It gives him the advantage."

She watched doubt form in Braden's gaze, then suspend to acceptance.

"Why?" she demanded, no longer capable of quashing the question.

Glaring, he appeared defensive, then flustered. "Excuse me?"

She paced, stopped and stared at her obscured reflection in the leaded glass of the armoire bar. Without turning, she addressed Braden's image. "Why did you—do you—hate me? I'm not blue blood, but from what Beau says, neither are you, so neither is he. We loved each other once." The painful fact of loving him still, longing for him, jerked her around. "He and I and Chelsea could have been a family—your family. I don't know what stigma I carry that keeps you from forgiving me, but you stole the life Beau and Chelsea and I would have had together, and I'll never forgive you for that." She strode to the desk and braced on the heels of her hands. "I deserve to know why."

After what seemed an eternity, time in which she willed an answer, he said, "Sit down," all stridence gone from the command. "You do deserve that much."

Wary of the qualified concession, she took the chair, breath snagging. The pulse in her throat

A Risk of Rain

rioted with hope for an end to her craving for closure.

Again Braden's hand pilfered the opened drawer, but came away empty. He pushed back from
the desk, crossed to the armoire, opened it and
stared in as though memorizing the contents.
Except for a background of Chelsea and Cal's voices mingling on the heavy summer day, silence filled
the room. Eventually Perri heard glass clink
against glass, a faint splashing sound. She glanced
at the grandfather clock in the corner.
Midmorning. Before her stood proof of a man living
with deceit, negating any exclusive pain she had
believed she and Beau shared. Awaiting her
answer, she forbade herself concern for Braden's
feelings.

"Once I hated only your father, but I was in love
with your mother."

The curious words came from behind her. She
swiveled in the chair to see him staring out the window.

"I suppose you know all about that. My name
was probably a household word after he was fired
from Owl Creek."

"You had an affair with my mother?" Her tone
revealed her surprise.

He sipped from the exquisite crystal glass, then
stared at the whiskey. Warm. Brown. The color of
Beau's eyes, and Chelsea's. "No. She never knew.
I was in love with her...lusty... eauty. Compared
to—she was vivid and alive. I took that as a come-
on at first." His voice snagged. "It wasn't. I envied
Lee, a drunk, with a woman like that. He figured it
out and we had words. I hardly think you didn't
know."

She hadn't, but now she saw it clearly, it reverberated like shock waves. "Lee wasn't around long
after he got fired. And Angie refused to talk about
it." Perri had sensed the anger though. She voiced

her thoughts. "Lee's termination brought the divorce to a head when Angie refused to move again because he'd lost another job." Ironically, he had settled in Anchorage and started the nursery.

Braden grunted a begrudging laugh. "Your daddy is a drunk, Perri."

That much was true. "I'm not my father. I was fourteen when that happened." Her mind ran through the years after, years when she'd gone from girl to woman.

He glanced at her over his shoulder, then came to lean against the desk, focusing somewhere beyond her. "I nursed a fierce grudge against him. As you became more involved with Beau, I felt mocked and my vendetta deepened. Seeing the two of you together ate at me. Knowing Beau would rather be with you than breathe—never mind play golf—I got the idea Lee Hardin was behind it. That he was trying to get to me again through you."

"I'm not my mother," she said softly. "Yet you punished me for your lust. And you sent Beau to school in Europe." She had officially begun to love him then, and to wait. "You deprived yourself and his grandmother to punish me."

He took a hearty drink, coughed. "I aimed at your father, through you."

Her memory drifted back. "He wasn't that kind of father." Had Lee ever known her feelings? Ever cared? The houses they occupied had been small, cheap construction. She knew he'd spent every moment at home, drunk or sober, harassing Angie, then coercing her into bed, then trying, often failing to finish what he'd instigated.

"From the time he was hired—against my advice—he and I disagreed on how the Owl Creek course should be maintained." Shrouded in memory, Braden's voice held a resigned intonation. "I wanted him fired long before he was, but the rest of the board wouldn't agree. Aside from Beau, in those days Owl Creek was my life. I had fought for years to lure a major tournament to the club and finally managed to get the PGA Open scheduled." He took a drink, clinching his eyes as he swallowed. "That year, when the course reopened in the spring, the wrong chemicals were applied to the greens and we lost them. The tournament rescheduled on a Louisville course, making me a laughing stock, ruining my name in golf. At the time, I feared the scandal would taint Beau's name as well. Knowing my feelings for Angie, Lee swore I tampered with the chemicals in order to get him fired. To get rid of him." He shrugged. "That proves how little a man of his...caliber knows about sacrificing for priorities, but that's another story. I took the stance that he was drunk when he treated the greens. He was fired, and I resigned from the board because they had failed to listen to me in the beginning, thus avoiding the whole disaster. I've hated him—and you, his flesh and blood—since that day."

"And my mother?"

"I never managed that, but I look at you and see her." His mouth hardened.

She stared at him in near disbelief, her interior churning. "You played God with my life—with Beau's—because of your wounded pride."

"Interesting that you recognize that flaw so easily." His words were sardonic, his tone empty.

Even as she struggled not to accept his meaning, she heard herself say, "No matter how you tricked me, what you led me to believe, I should have fought for what I wanted—fought for Beau." For Chelsea's sake.

"Just as I should have turned a blind eye to Angie. I should have hung on at Owl Creek and fought for my honor." He took a pull of scotch, grimaced. "Hindsight is wasted. Your grudge has lasted only eight years. I've lived with mine for fifteen."

She summed up his disclosure. "And now you want Chelsea."

Frowning, he sipped, eyeing her over the glass. "Not for the reason you think."

She rose with finality. As she moved toward the French doors that led onto the lawn, the putting green beyond, he straightened from leaning on the desk. For the first time, she noticed the stoop of shoulders once broad and firm enough to intimidate a young girl. Don't care. He didn't deserve her empathy or pity.

She watched Chelsea lining up a ball, grasping a putter shaft that came to her chest, while Cal squatted behind the hole giving cues. Perri tried and failed to push aside a wave of loneliness washing over her, an ache for what might have been. "I want Chelsea to know her great-grandmother...if Winonna is willing. That's why I brought her with me today. I have no right to deny her heritage, even though unfortunately it includes you." Once more she reached for resolve. "Her heritage also includes me. If you threaten that, my warning stands. I'll take her to the end of the earth to beat you."

He shoved away from the desk, leaving the empty glass there. "Winonna doesn't know...that Chelsea exists. She knows nothing about...what's gone on." Petition filled his voice, his rigid posture and corrugated brow indicating his concern.

Perri grasped the carved iron door handle, opened the door and motioned for Chelsea. "Your secret is safe with me. I wouldn't know how to begin to tell her about the hell you've created."

※

Winonna's room was cheery with the sun flooding in from the window facing the grape arbor. But the flowery aroma Perri had detected upon entering the house, more pronounced here, couldn't mask the stench of death. At the sight of the pink-haired, lace-draped woman propped in bed against a bank of satin pillows, plastic tubes trailing from her nose, Chelsea's body sagged against Perri's thighs.

The expectant and knowing expression on Winonna's wan face assured Perri that Silky had confided in the old woman, prepared her. Winonna held out her hand, inviting them into the room. Busy with a water pitcher at a dresser draped with a yellowing antimacassar, Silky beamed. A large, silver-framed portrait of Beau topped the dresser, as though guarding the profusion of prescription bottles scattered there.

Chelsea's attention had gone to the portrait, like a kitten to goldfish.

Aware of Braden's hovering presence, Perri advanced to the bed, a hand on Chelsea's shoulder. Winonna patted the mattress. Perri sat, drawing Chelsea up beside her and into the shelter of an assuring arm. Bound by useless tradition, she asked the obligatory question whose obvious answer must go unspoken.

"How are you, Mrs. St. Cyr?"

Thin lips tugged, never accomplishing their aim. "Tolerable. Just tolerable." A palsied hand fluttered over the tubes stringing across the fine linen to an oxygen tank beside the bed. "I'm sorry ...for this, dear."

Perri's throat pained. She felt unsure of protocol or how best to proceed. Unable to anticipate Braden's reaction to her sudden appearance, she had withheld from Chelsea the preparation Silky had bestowed on Winonna. "This is Chelsea. Sweetheart, I'd like you to meet Winonna St. Cyr." Her words emerged too formal, strained.

"Such a pretty name...Chelsea," Winonna crooned, taking a tiny hand between hers, liver spotted and gnarled. "Your daddy calls me Nonna. You must call me Grand Nonna."

Chelsea's head darted up as if yanked by a string, her eyes seeking Perri's. Lips frozen against a smile, heart melting with relief, Perri nodded. "That would be nice."

"You know my daddy?" Chelsea's awe-edged voice floated on the quiet.

"I surely do, darlin'." Winonna chortled. "Your daddy is my truest love."

Behind them Braden shuffled. He rattled change in his pocket, cleared his throat.

"That's him, isn't it?" Chelsea looked toward the dresser. "In that picture."

Winonna's eyes sought Perri's, then her watery gaze hardened as it moved past Perri's shoulder, seeking Braden. Her mouth drew harshly, trembled, ran slack. A spot of spittle formed at the corner. "It surely is your daddy. I can tell you all kinds of stories about him when he was a little boy—just your age, darlin'. Would you like that?"

Nodding heartily, Chelsea leaned forward to embrace Winonna, ignoring death, filling Perri with gratitude that her sense of right had triumphed over pride.

✳

Richard Braden St. Cyr, III. With savor and care, in triumph known only to him, Beau signed and passed the legal document back to his attorney. While the attending attorneys gave the agreement final perusal, Beau took visual inventory around the conference table. With his new partners' business skills, his own teaching and financing ability, no reason existed for their endeavor to fail.

Yet the jarring, grievous news from High Meadow that morning overshadowed his satisfaction. Throughout the day's negotiations, he'd concentrated on keeping the wobble out of his voice as memories surged, blinking to clear his welling eyes without making his new partners uncomfortable.

The celebration champagne-lunch at Scottsdale's palatial Phoenician Hotel had been a heller. Ironically, with today's new beginning, an era of his life was ending. Turning down dinner, he shook hands around the table, left the frigid, air-conditioned office, and drove on streets oozing asphalt like prehistoric tar pits, across the Valley to Carefree where he stood on the barren, rocky hilltop and surveyed the desert. The land pulsed, hummed with a hushed, rhythmic chorus of crickets and the lonely cries of parched winds, the faint rat-a-tat of a woodpecker maiming the saguaros. In the twilight, a distant pack of coyotes howled mournfully. Other than High Meadow at dawn, Beau had never witnessed such serenity, such potential for peace, but High Meadow, too, was now part of his past. Standing there within the walls of the half-completed house he now owned, he'd never been so conscious of the slide toward night. The distant mountains grew gray, and the sky fell away from him, receding every moment into deeper shades of blue.

This place and Chelsea would be his future.

Throat aching, suddenly realizing he was no longer captive to his pride, no longer accountable for other people's feelings, he let tears for Winonna roll. He had given up too many women in his life. Too many women, too much hurt, but he would hold on to his daughter. At this moment, in this place of promise, he would begin the quest he had watched Braden fail. He would heal the precious wounded, not with control, but love.

❋

"Dust to Dust. Ashes to ashes. Death, where is thy sting? It is here, Lord, victorious in the hearts of those who loved Winonna Claire St. Cyr. And who among us gathered here could not love a creature so gentle? Be merciful, Father. Grant them peace, for she is at peace at last."

With a will greater than his grief, Beau's arm stole around his grandfather's shoulders as Braden sat hunched in the pew crying quietly. In unison with his concession, Silky's warm, heavy arm hooked into Beau's. She laced her fingers in his and squeezed as the priest continued.

"We return Winonna to You, to pleasure heaven as she pleasured earth. Not for seventy-six years, a mere whisper in eternity, but for all infinity. We pray only for Your comfort to those who mourn her."

Gripped with sorrow that warred with a sense of relief, Beau filed past the open bronze casket in the company of his extended Cajun family, whose gathering had delayed the service by days. Finally making his way from the church, he noted the pitiful size of the remaining congregation, as fitting in his grandmother's death, as in her life. He paused at the bottom of the church steps to wait for his mother, who in his honor, had risked Braden's undiminished wrath. She hustled up to him in a too-hot black silk dress, a flowery scent preceding her. Even in her early fifties, she maintained the show-pony characteristic Braden disdained as having hooked Beau's father.

"Thanks, honey." She sounded breathless, her voice raspy from Scotch and cigarettes. "With the old lady gone, I don't have a lot of friends in that church."

In those few words, she disclosed more than he'd ever been told of her brief tenure at High Meadow. He managed a smile. "They're mostly strangers to me, too."

As was she, this woman who'd appeared out of their sketchy past an hour before the service. In that hour, she had lamented their estranged relationship, revealing that she had agreed with Braden's demands that she not contact Beau until he was in his teens, to prevent his being torn.

Beau Jr.'s uninsured death had left her penniless, and she had another child, a half-brother Beau had never seen. She had taken Braden's bribe and complied with his terms. By the time Beau reached his teens, she'd been unable to penetrate the wall that formed between them. Today's confession had scraped the first layer off Beau's scabbed-over resentment, but multiple layers remained.

His gaze stole from her pretty, prematurely wrinkled face to a far corner of the churchyard. He'd forgotten how damn verdant this place was, every shade of green in creation. Standing in soft, late afternoon sun, wearing a white blouse beneath the black dress, pearls, flats, her free-falling hair held back with barrettes, Perri resembled the nubile ingenue he'd so deeply and hopelessly fallen in love with. Emotions tangling like grape vines, he reminded himself that the woman waiting to pay her condolences had risked conceiving and giving birth to his wounded child.

His mother's spike heels mired in the soft churchyard as he steered her in Perri's direction. Perri reached out when he stood close enough to touch, but her hand dropped before making contact.

"I'm sorry, Beau." Her eyes glistened, and her nose had been rubbed red with the Kleenex crumpled in her hand. "I know how much you loved her." Her lips wavered, as though forbidden to smile. "And she worshipped you."

He nodded, unable to do more for a moment. "I know. It hurts that I never got to see her again, because I was angry with Granddad...and too damn busy arranging my own life." The way her eyes clouded prompted his next words. "Silky said you've visited every day since you've been home." Having talked with Winonna every night since Chelsea appeared in her life, had convinced him that her knowing another St. Cyr child existed—

"flawed but flawlessly beautiful," his grandmother had called her—had allowed Winonna to draw her final labored breath. "Thanks, Perri. What you did meant a lot."

Her turn to nod, her throat moving noticeably. "I didn't know her well, but she always treated me ..." She sucked in her bottom lip. Beau felt the threat of her tears creep into his own throat.

"...treated you like since Beau loved you, you deserved some respect?"

Perri's head jerked up to meet the eyes of the woman who'd spoken. "Always."

His mother gave a soft, sad laugh. Again, Beau's arm went on a rampage, this time circling her trim waist. "This is my mother, Perri. Christine St. Cyr." Christ! Chelsea's grandmother. A new dilemma to deal with. "Mom..." At least he hadn't choked on the word. "This is Perri." He'd almost said Hardin, before recalling what he'd discovered in Braden's safe in the pre-dawn hours. He purchased firmer footing, advancing into and embracing his future. "Perri and I have a daughter. She's almost...eight. Right, Perri? Her name is Chelsea."

Christine looked from him to Perri and back, doing quick math behind her artfully made-up eyes. Her smiled chastised kindly. "Mercy! Talk about keeping secrets."

Beau smiled and nodded, not unpleased with what he saw in Christine's gaze. "Perri's a master, all right."

Chin hiking, Perri folded, then unfolded her arms and offered her hand. "It's nice to finally meet you, Mrs. St. Cyr."

"Call me Christi, sugar. Everyone does, don't they, Beau, honey?"

"Everyone, Mom."

"What?" The lush lashes shadowing Perri's cheeks flew up, exposing wide eyes.

"Mom's name is Christi. She wants you to call her that." His pulse hammered.

Awakening, clear and bright as dawn on a Kentucky meadow, leapt into Perri's mascara-smeared eyes. "Christi," she whispered, tasting, swallowing, digesting reality. "I'll...call you that," she managed. "Thank you."

Were tragedy not gnawing his gut, he would have savored vindictive satisfaction, but revenge proved to be anything but sweet. Eight goddamned years she had suffered, just as he had. One more elusive piece had been wedged into the sordid jig-saw puzzle that was gradually depicting their life.

Her gaze shifted to his. He locked her in. Unguarded relief, and lustier emotions she lacked the skill to hide, flooded her eyes. His loins grew heavy in shameless disregard for his grandmoth-er—who'd always claimed life was for the living—lying within the church. If Perri or his mother looked—hell if the whole congregation looked—they'd know how much he wanted Perri. Always had. Probably always would, no matter the cir-cumstance or who was to blame for what had passed between them.

As if reading a script, his mother gushed, "Imagine me a grandmother! Chelsea, you say? I'd love to meet her—if that's all right." She looked to him for confirmation.

"We're working on that." Catching Perri's quick frown, he took his mother's arm. "We need to be going to the cemetery." Behind Perri, the family lined up to file into the waiting black limousines. Braden was already tucked inside the lead car, his door ajar, beckoning to Beau. Involuntarily, Beau's fingers tightened on his mother's arm. "You can ride with me in my car, Mom."

"I don't know, honey. That might not sit well with your grandfather." She held back while Perri watched her with the rapt attention of an empathetic understudy.

"It's a new era. A decade too late, but here at last." He kept his eyes on Perri. "Wait for me in my car, if you don't mind, Mom. I need to talk to Perri for a minute."

He waited until Christine was out of hearing distance, mindful of Perri's anxious glance. "The stalker was Pete," he announced. "You won't have any more trouble."

Her eyes quickened with mirthless satisfaction. "How did—"

"It took awhile, but I figured it out. Then Mark confirmed it. He'd been hanging out with Pete, hoping for a confession." Recall of Pete's face, the defeat in his eyes when he'd been officially expelled from the tour, played through Beau's mind. "I think I knew a long time before I even let myself suspect."

"I'm sorry, Beau. He was your—you thought he was your friend."

"There's more." He answered her curious expression with, "I overheard him talking to Granddad. They were in it together."

"Oh, God," she gasped quietly, one hand going to her mouth, brows knitting, raw regret in her gaze. "That has to hurt doubly."

He shrugged granite-heavy shoulders. "It's an era of revelation, it seems."

Her eyes misted over. "Beau, about the note. If I'd only known Christi was your mother—" Her voice broke. "The paper was so old, just as you said, but I thought—it looked like fine bond, like paper someone you would love—"

"That someone was you. The note was god-damned old. Used."

Grimacing, she regrouped, "Braden split your parents, too, didn't he?"

"He tried. They loved each other enough not to let him."

"Unlike us, you mean?"

"Is that what happened? We didn't love each other enough? Or was it pride?"

"Why didn't you tell me? When I showed you the note?" No accusation, only question seasoned with a pinch of defeat.

To him, the fact the infamous Christi was his mother was now insignificant. A different issue chewed his gut. "If we're finally into asking why, why weren't you more honest about the note, instead of holding it against me all these months? Hell, for years. You must have liked being one up on me. Liked seeing me beg? If not, then why?"

Lifting her chin, she met his eyes without an outward flinch, pride intact.

"Braden did a number on us, Periwinkle. But we let him when we believed him."

"I know."

She looked away, watching the mourners descend the steps until he broke the silence with the question foremost on his mind. "Why didn't you bring Chelsea?"

The name brought her head around. Apprehension skittered across her eyes. "She'd never understand. She's too young." And too fragile, her eyes proclaimed.

In a firm, final voice, he said, "I've got some things to handle, then I'll be over."

She opened her mouth as if to speak, then silently hugged her waist, frowning.

"Make sure you and Chelsea are there."

Pulling away from the curb, he watched Perri get into Angie's old Cutlass, close the door and then rest her forehead against the steering wheel. As he spied on her apprehension, pity nipped at his heart. Memory and instinct cautioned him against weakening. He intended to have his daughter. An

hour at graveside, a wake at High Meadow, a show-
down with Braden, then his relationship with Perri
would meld into the new era. For better or for
worse was anyone's guess.

CHAPTER TWENTY-SIX

Braden had hoped he could count on Beau respecting his feelings enough to postpone their inevitable confrontation, but when the last mourner's car pulled down the lane and Braden gratefully retired to his study, Beau appeared. Dressed in scuffed loafers, faded Levis, his vintage bomber jacket, he took the chair Perri had occupied a week before. The stoic, chilled-whiskey gaze he leveled doused Braden's hopes.

Braden broke the ice. "I saw the Hardin girl at Nonna's service."

"Her name is Perri. I wish I could say she came because she loved Nonna, but you never allowed love between them. She was there out of respect for me."

This was going to be worse than he'd imagined, worse than he'd let himself dread. "I see you're wearing your traveling clothes."

Beau slipped his hands into the jacket pockets. "Right." Solemn. Final.

"The PGA Championship is a week off." Braden faked a smile. He'd counted on Beau remaining at High Meadow until the last minute, practicing at Owl Creek, working out on his own state-of-the-art putting green. Hurriedly, he changed his approach. "I'd rather not be in the house alone tonight. It's too...soon."

"I'm headed for Scottsdale. I'm buying a home there." He measured Braden, eyes masking whatever churned in his head. "I'll ask Cal to stay with you. In fact, he and Silky can move into my rooms."

Braden's spine iced. "Scottsdale." He knew his double shock showed.

"Desert heat's good for heart conditions." Beau quirked a brow in false speculation. "Or is that asthma it's good for?"

Senselessly, he countered. "Nonna was the only one with a heart condition, son."

"Chelsea has one. But you know that. Right, Granddad?" Auburn lashes lowered onto chiseled cheekbones as he thumbed through a group of papers on his lap, made a selection, and held it in his hand like a weapon. "Were you going to wait until the legal work was done to tell me I had a daughter? Or were you hoping to get hold of her behind my back, rather than go to court, since you're used to doing battle with women?" Anger, repulsion Braden found hard to assimilate with Beau, marked his tone.

Braden opened the drawer, took out the new, more powerful medication the doctor had given him. He splashed some into a glass he kept handy. "Facing you in court never entered my mind, Beau." He raised the glass to his mouth, lowered it. "I saw no reason to bother you with the investigation or custody suit until—"

"To bother my game, you mean. Bottom line, right?"

"Well—yes. You should be grateful for that." How much would this curt, hard-edged, vindictive stranger have to vent before they could drain all the cankers, air them and get back to basics? He rolled the glass in his hands, then took a sip, needy of relief that was taking longer each day. "I see you're angry. That makes it unanimous. Your grandmother found some notes I'd made and cornered me on my plan to get custody of Chelsea." He replayed the scene in his mind. "She wasn't speaking to me when she died."

Beau's mouth tugged on a derisive smile. "It took fifty years for her to see you weren't God, huh, Granddad? What goes round comes round."

406

"Considering what I've been through these last few days, Beau, I think you—"

"Now that Nonna's gone, I'll never spend another night in this house." Beau pitched the paper he held onto the desk, as though it had turned to a sheet of molten steel.

Braden's eyes riveted on the document—the annulment that was supposed to be in the safe. If the ground had caved beneath him, he couldn't have been more stunned, more frightened. On top of the annulment, Beau slapped down a note of some kind, a heavy, sloppy, unfamiliar scrawl. Next, a second note, smaller, tighter handwriting on aged linen notepaper. Easily, instantly recognized. Then a legal agreement of some sort. Beau fanned the papers out in haphazard order on the desk.

"I'll give you a minute to look these over." Beau's voice was too quiet, detached. He left the chair and strode to the door that overlooked the putting green, shoulder braced against the frame, fingertips jammed into his back pockets.

Hands palsied, Braden laid Christi's note on top of the annulment contract, no further perusal needed for either. Gut on fire, heart hammering, he examined the first note. Innuendoes and threats. Only the caller could have written it, which meant Beau knew about Braden and the man. But how much? What? With dread spreading like cancer, he laid the note aside, picked up the legal agreement, leaned closer to the light and read. The scarcely believable words and Beau's signature wavered on the paper.

He prayed for mercy he didn't deserve. "You've entered into a joint venture in Scottsdale?" Incredulity crammed his tone. "Why Scottsdale, for God's sake?"

Beau eyed him, then returned to the chair. "It's a year-round golf Mecca."

"It's a hellhole." He couldn't corral the challenge.

Beau shrugged. "Four months out of twelve, maybe. Air conditioning makes it perfect for what we have planned."

We? He tabled that question. "Which is?"

Once lenient eyes accused him of stalling. The paper was clear. An upscale golf school for kids. Luxurious accommodations. On course as well as classroom instruction.

"The deal is done." Beau's tone underlined the last word. "This is my last tour season. I'll try my damnedest to get you the grand slam, since that's your life's goal. You should know, though, all depends on whether I get my last cortisone injection, so maybe you should pray for a lenient doctor. Then pray my head's on straight for four days in a row, because you won't get another shot at me, Granddad." He leaned forward, forearms resting on the worn arms of the chair. Pale lamplight masked his eyes, belied innocence he'd never possess again. "I overheard your conversation with Pete Jacoby."

What in hell was this? "I've never talked to him." Still, his gut flared.

Beau's laugh cut deep. "You didn't even know who you teamed up with? Christ, Granddad. It could have been a maniac even sicker than you and Pete. You had me working my ass off to win against a stacked deck, and you're telling me to practice more." New rancor sharpened his tone. "You didn't give a damn what happened to Perri."

Pete Jacoby—Beau's best friend. The bastard was the caller. Braden tried and failed to claw out of the nightmare. Lifting the annulment papers, he ventured, "How did you find—how'd you get these?"

"I had a hunch. Last night, I took the key off the ring on your nightstand and opened the safe." His eyes dared Braden to challenge his cunning.

"You sleep soundly for someone who must have one hell of a guilty conscience." He cocked a brow. "Or maybe you have no conscience."

"Beau—" What between here and bloody hell was there to say? "She was bad for your game. She got your randy Cajun blood up. Your father was the same—always wanting the wrong women."

Beau's look resembled pity. "She wasn't good for your ego, either, since she was Lee Hardin's daughter." He leaned forward, the pulse in his jaw rioting. "I also found the phony pre-nup." He plowed his fingers through his hair. "Here's another bottom line. Perri and I have a child, just like I wanted when I married her. But we aren't a family. Because of your obsession for control, we may never be a family." His throat wobbled. "I love you, Granddad, but you stole eight years of our lives, and I'll never forgive you for that."

Gripped by déjà vu for an instant Braden saw an eerie image of Perri in the chair, heard Chelsea's laughter from outside the window. He pushed back from the desk and moved to the bar, splashed one finger of scotch into a glass and gulped it. He held on to the edge of the armoire, waiting for the excruciating fire to go out.

Beau spoke into the quiet. "Perri's afraid of you. Afraid for Chelsea."

Perspiration rivered down a ribcage. "Perri's been here, Beau. She brought Chelsea to see—to see Nonna. We talked. I fired the investigator, called the lawyer dogs off." Only pride had kept him from telling Perri, setting her mind to rest. And Beau's.

Beau seemed not to hear, or not to believe. "Don't keep threatening to take Chelsea from her like you took me from my mother, because I'm not dead. And to get Chelsea away from Perri, you'll have to go through me. I doubt you want that. You're an old man, now, all alone with no way to take care of a little girl. Your case wouldn't even get before a judge."

Beau rose, gathered the papers. Braden reached out in ignored petition.

"Beau, I wanted her for your grandmother. I hoped a child in the house might keep her alive."

Beau's eyes measured, judged. "Instead, your scheme may have killed her." He turned to go.

Braden crossed the floor swiftly, heading him off. "The custody suit is over. Perri and I made a trade, son. She said she'd be willing to share Chelsea if I'd call it off."

Eyes empty as a blind man's, Beau murmured, "She said that, did she?" A strong hand on Braden's shoulder moved him aside. "Then she's a hell of a lot more generous than I feel at the moment."

Slumped against the doorframe, Braden listened to Beau's footsteps fade along the corridor. Then silence, until he heard the subtle whine of the front door opening, the certainty of it closing on the last of his dreams. Mocking silence echoed within the walls of High Meadow.

Just as Beau had said, he was an old man, who had defeated only himself.

※

The car that turned down the street, flashing a path of light across Angie's yellowing lawn, could have belonged to anyone, but knowing, Perri whispered against the coconut fragrance of Chelsea's fresh-from-the-shower hair. "Here comes your daddy, sweetie."

Like Perri's chest, Chelsea's little body tightened, then ran supple as she scooted to the edge of the porch swing the two of them occupied. She smoothed her nightgown, Perri's commandeered Star Wars T-shirt. "He drives fast, Mom." Her observation held commendation rather than reproach.

Perri found a soft laugh to offer. "He's in a hurry to meet you. Are you nervous?"

She spared Perri a brief glance in the gathering twilight. "Are you? You said he's nice."

Perri stroked her daughter's back, throat aching. "He's very nice, honey. Wait and see."

Beau's Astin Martin pulled to the curb, and he was out, almost before the powerful engine quieted. The heavy door closing, his jaunty steps on the concrete walk blended with a locust chorus rising from the hackberry trees. Perri's hand gripped the chain supporting the swing as he stepped onto the wooden porch, his physical presence as forceful as a blow.

"Sorry it took so long." His eyes, disbelieving, rejoicing, accepting, took in Chelsea in the T-shirt, then sought Perri's. "Is it too close to bedtime?"

"We'll make an exception." The knot in her throat broadened, tightened. She should have asked Angie to oversee this meeting and taken Angie's place at the movie. But that would have prolonged bringing to a head threats Beau had made in Denver.

He crossed to the swing and knelt, his hand curiously coming to rest on Perri's knee. "Do you know who I am?" he ventured softly, getting a tentative nod from Chelsea.

"Hi, Daddy." Though the greeting was bold, the delivery was tentative. Shy.

"Hi, Princess Leia." His voice was thick, a little husky.

Chelsea indulged him in the game. "I'm Chelsea. It's Mommy's shirt."

"I thought it looked familiar." Aiming his infectious smile at Perri, his hand cautiously enfolded his daughter's. "You're as beautiful as your mother, sweetheart."

Perri's heart surged, then settled into a sharp ache as Chelsea spared a smile, revealing a gap in a row of teeth in transition. "Mom calls me sweet-heart, too."

His soft laugh could have come from his soul. "Your mom and I sometimes think alike."

"She says I look like you, and I think so." Chelsea touched his hair, drew her fingers onto his cheek, brought her hand to rest on his shoulder. Perri had watched her love him from afar, through the magic of television. Now Chelsea's dream was coming true. "Are you nervous?" She cocked a brow, Beau-style. "If you are, it's okay, 'cause me'n Mom are, too."

Beau's amber eyes darkened, shone. "I'd probably feel better if I could hold you."

Perri looked away, then back quickly when she felt Chelsea's hesitance. At last her arms circled Beau's neck. Perri's knee felt suddenly cold when he took his hand away to draw their daughter into his arms. She swallowed furiously, clinched her eyes, opened them and swiped furtively with the back of her hand. She wouldn't let him see weakness he could use against her.

Chelsea broke the embrace to seek Beau's face. "Feel better?"

He turned his eyes on Perri, his smile a perfect read. "It'll do till I get hungry again."

Chelsea giggled. "You're funny. Mommy said you were, and she's right."

His brows arched, accenting his cowlick. "She talks about me a lot, does she?"

"She didn't used to, but she does a lot now. She said you—"

"Daddy doesn't want to hear what I said, Chels," Perri scolded mildly, no longer able to keep quiet. "He wants to know about you."

Beau rocked onto his heels, muscular thighs straining inside the Levis. His face glowed with familiar, once-revered devilment. "Sure Daddy does. What else did she say, Chels?"

412

Perri tried to rise, but his hand was back, on her thigh now, holding her in the swing. His eyes centered on Chelsea, distracting her from his man-handling. Pissed, yet touched, Perri settled in for whatever just dues Beau deemed necessary to erase eight years of omission.

Chelsea chattered on. "She said you'd be scared I wouldn't love you, 'cause I didn't know you like I do her, but it's not your fault that I don't." She looked to Perri. "Right, Mom?"

Perri nodded, her smile a parody. "You'll find she has a wonderful memory. Daddy."

"As infallible as her mother's." Gentle malice infested his grin. He got to his feet, eased Chelsea closer to Perri and fitted his big body in beside them. His arm unfolded across the swing, circling the back of Chelsea's head, painfully close to Perri's shoulders. With his foot against the floor, he gave the swing a gentle nudge. "What else did Mom say, sweetheart? Did she by any chance tell you how much I love you?"

Chelsea's head bolted up. "How'd you know she told me that?"

"Lucky guess." He gave the swing another, bolder shove, arm touching Perri now.

"You didn't have to worry, though." Chelsea's hand, with newly polished Angie-pink nails, came to rest reassuringly on Beau's thigh. "I already loved you—you know from watching TV all the time? I picked you for a daddy 'cause you give away all that candy."

Helpless with grief and regret of the wasted past, Perri lowered her face into her hands.

Beau's arm closed in, his fingers snaking along her neck, curling to stroke her throat as he spoke softly. "I picked you out, too, Chelsea."

This time she curved her little body around to stare into his face. "When?"

"In my dreams. I can't wait to get into bed every night and dream about you." He patted his lap. After an instant's indecision, Chelsea climbed onto him, rested her head against his chest.

"Where's Angie?" Beau stroked Chelsea's cowlick as he lazily propelled the swing.

"The movies." Like quicksand, weariness pulled Chelsea's voice into a mumble.

"She wanted to stay and watch. But Larry dragged her away."

"Larry," he said speculatively. "He's the bad guy, right?"

Chelsea stirred in restless protest, inducing Perri's reply. "He's a real saint."

"Glad to hear it."

They sat silently, Beau gently rocking the swing as evening settled in. In a vacant lot across the street, a soccer game broke up, called by darkness. Chelsea's questions, mostly about Beau's life on tour, and his answers droned on until Perri heard drowsiness creep into Chelsea's voice. Beau's perceptiveness surprised her.

"Sleepy?" he murmured.

"I don't want to go to bed." The answer came sharp and quick.

"You don't have to." He nuzzled her ear. "But if you fall asleep, I've got you. Okay?"

"Okay."

Gradually, the night grew still, except for Chelsea's soft breath. Perri's mind helplessly toyed with sketchy flashes of lost moments like this, of ghostly might-have-beens. Aching, she finally broke the silence she knew Beau could stretch to infinity.

"I'm so sorry about your grandmother. Are you okay with it?"

"Sometimes I wonder if I ever knew her. Her illness turned her to a porcelain doll that Granddad built a wall around." He lowered his mouth to

Chelsea's hair, taking a deep breath. "I never knew my mother, Aunt Ginger or Nonna, but I loved them all." He looked at her, the look a magnet that drew her eyes to his. "I only knew you, but he ended that, too."

"You've finally talked to him." She knew, from his kicked-in-the-stomach demeanor.

"We had it out. It's over with Granddad." He gave a quiet, deprecating laugh. Faint lamplight filtering through a window highlighted a vein ticking in his temple. "I'm no longer an indentured legend in the making."

Could she believe that? That he'd actually break from Braden? She reminded herself his freedom, how he chose to live his life, no longer concerned her. Except for Chelsea's welfare.

A car slowed at the stop sign on the corner, then cruised through without stopping. A breeze ruffled Perri's skirt and bathed her brow. As if part of the wind's kiss, Beau's hand stole to Chelsea, smoothed back her hair without disturbing her sleep. Perri watched, mesmerized.

"She is beautiful, Perri. She's sweet and sensitive, and you've taught her to love."

His tenderness wedged in her throat. "Actually, she came to the world that way."

"I wish I'd been there."

Had she wished the same less than a million times? "I'm sorry. Jesus, I'm so sorry." Spoken at last, the words exorcised some, not all, of her guilt. "I did what I thought I had to do. Seeing you with her now hurts so much."

His fingers feathered her neck, a touch as light as imagination, mocking the jolt in her loins, in her heart.

"I'm not blaming you, Perri. I'm through with that. I want to make up for lost time."

Warning flags waved in her mind. She shrugged away from his touch, keeping her voice low. "I won't give her up. I'll fight you, Beau. It won't be good for Chelsea, but I'll fight you the same as Braden."

He shifted in the seat, then he rummaged around inside his jacket. Drawing something out, he passed it to her. "I don't want to fight you, Periwinkle, and you'll never have to contend with Braden St. Cyr again."

She unfolded the paper, a legalized document the darkness prevented her from reading. A custody agreement. But she assumed she knew the wording, his intent. He wanted her to surrender legally and quietly. "I won't sign this."

She cringed at his bitter chuckle. Chelsea stirred in her sleep, murmuring incoherently.

"Ironic you'd say that, since you didn't sign it." His hand moved to her back, fingers arching to massage either side of her neck, as though he knew how badly her head and heart ached. "This is our annulment you thought you signed. It's forged. What you signed was a phony pre-nup Granddad concocted as soon as he heard we were married. In the heat of the moment, I guess you thought it was the annulment. He got me to sign by telling me you'd asked for it. Then once he had my signature he—or God knows who—forged yours."

Her mind whirred like a speeded-up movie reel. Pain. Anger. Disillusionment. Then it highlighted love that had refused to die. "Then we're..."

"We're married, Periwinkle. You and me." A finger circled the bone at the top of her spine. "As married as we were on the Louisville courthouse steps almost nine years ago."

She stared at the paper as though she could see the name in question. "You're sure?"

"I'd know your signature anywhere. I saw it on enough charge slips during our Nike year." His tender smile tempered the words. "We're married. How do you feel about that?"

She drew her feet into the swing and circled her shins with her arms. Resting her chin on her knees, she stared across the darkness to focus on a street lamp a block away. His question reverberated in her head. Married. Married with a child. The annulment, their estrangement had all been a shameful, agonizing ruse from which she would never recover.

"Suddenly Mommy is speechless," he said softly. "Chels would be amazed."

A scalding tear shoved through her lashes. Another emerged and spilled over. She dabbed discreetly with her forefinger.

"Want me to go first?" To her lingering silence he offered, "You said the tour's no place for a child. Right? Well, I'm leaving. The Championship will be my last tournament."

"It doesn't matter, Beau. Tour or no tour, I won't give her up."

"You want to hear me say it, don't you?"

Did she? At least she'd know what she was facing. "Yes."

"I'm opening a children's golf academy in Scottsdale. I'm buying a house—"

She stiffened, ready to protest, but he held up a hand. "You can see it first. If you don't like it, we'll find a different one. But you'll like it. Chelsea can have a horse, and there's a private school, and a bus will stop at our door. The Mayo Clinic is minutes away with the best heart doctors in the country." He caught her chin, forcing her to look at him. "I want our daughter, Perri, just as I said in my typical asshole fashion, but I want you with her."

"Beau, this is—" Too soon. Too tempting. Too fragile. "We need time." She lifted the paper in her hand. "Time to think about this."

"I've thought about it nonstop since I found it. I want a home, Perri. Carpools and braces, bills and taxes and PTA." Chelsea stirred, protesting his

417

exuberance. He adjusted his timbre to intimacy. "I want all the things I've never even seen, other than in books and movies. I want to play husband and father to your wife and mother."

She shook her head. "Too much has happened." And it was happening again. "Too many scars." Too much he didn't know, so much she couldn't seem to sort out or find the courage to reveal.

"Nothing has happened, baby." His hands cradling her face, he drew her forward, their bodies forming a steeple over their daughter. "It was all a cruel, sick joke. We never stopped loving each other for a minute. I'm leaving the tour, Perri, like you wanted. Just be glad."

"I never asked for that. I said that I—"

His look quieted her. "Surely you want a home, too, for Chelsea. We're getting a second chance, so let's take it."

Images whirled in her head. "I don't know— There's been so much pain, and now you're telling me it was all a joke. I need time...."

He pressed his brow to hers, murmuring, "Fine. I'll give you time. A week. Meet me in Mamaroneck for the Championship. Caddie for me. I'll stand a hell of a lot better chance, maybe my only chance, if you're there."

Oh, God! Caddie? The remainder of his words came out of a fog.

"Let's go out in a blaze of glory, Periwinkle, to prove to Granddad we can do it, but not for him, for us." His grip on her chin stilled her head from shaking in denial. "And the academy will reap the benefits of a grand slam-winner and a grand-slam caddy, if you want to teach, too." He gave her time to absorb his petition. "Will you do it?"

"I . . . can't."

He went rigid. "Why the hell not?"

In his lap, Chelsea jerked, moaned. Shaking her head, Perri pressed a finger to her lips.

His voice dropped to a husky whisper, insistence intact. "I want you and Chelsea with me in Mamaroneck. I need you. Don't say no."

"I know what it's like to need someone."

He gave her a black-layered look. "You're punishing me for something I didn't do."

"God, I know," she moaned, aching. "I need time to get over that."

"Do you love me?" His tone and gaze drilled her. Getting no answer, he threatened, "Maybe I'll wake up Chelsea and ask her. She's not jaded enough yet to lie."

Her eyes drifted to their daughter, supine on his lap. "I love you more than my next breath. But I can't do what you ask."

He gathered Chelsea more closely in his arms, swinging with her now as though they were alone, as though Perri's refusal had constructed a wall between them and her. She rose and walked to the far end of the porch. Behind her the rhythmic whine of the swing quieted, followed by the screen door scraping open. She turned to see Beau disappear inside the house, Chelsea in his arms. Longing to share, imagination surging, she stayed her ground. This was Beau's time with his daughter, too long overdue.

It seemed eternity passed before he returned and, without ceremony, took her in his arms. "I've never loved you more than right now. That's what she does to me."

His words echoed eight years of mirrored emotion. "I'm glad."

He ran his fingers into her hair, the heels of his hands pressing her temples, lifting her head, holding her firm. His kiss, gentle and absolving, held that same sweet warmth she never stopped craving. With his mouth, his tongue, the very air he breathed, he stirred her soul until longing and need evolved into silent denial, and she backed away.

At the foot of the steps, he turned to her. "You won't change your mind?"

"So much has happened. I have to have time...."

He looked at the sagging screen door before holding her away from him, seeking her eyes. "I'll think about that while I face the toughest test of my life. Alone."

His footsteps echoed on the walk, the street lamp outlining his lithe body. He paused to stare at her across the car top, their eyes fusing in the darkness. She stepped back into porch shadows. He didn't pull away from the curb until she'd gone inside and turned off the light.

✳

Even though it was evident Beau would make Friday's cut, Perri could scarcely bear to witness his pain the camera close-ups so clearly revealed. She reached for Chelsea's hand, bringing it to her lips, startling them both when a hot tear splashed there. Chelsea rose to her knees on the lumpy sofa, slipping an arm around Perri's neck, a tiny hand patting her shoulder.

From the opposite end of the sofa, a scolding frown creased Angie's face.

"Watching Daddy play golf always makes you sad, huh, Mom?" Chelsea leaned around to seek Perri's eyes. "Is it 'cause you wanta be there? You can, Mommy. It's okay with me and Mimi." She looked at Angie, who nodded, eyes misting, nose glowing rosy.

A chasm of guilt formed in Perri's chest. Chelsea was too young, too fragile to be burdened with sorting out Perri's mistakes. "I want to be with you, sweetheart, but I miss him."

"It's his sore hand, right? That's why you're crying." Chelsea issued a piteous smile.

Perri nodded, sucking in her lip, biting hard. "I can tell it's hurting him." She felt it.

"But he'll win, won't he?" Her voice soared anxiously.

Perri stroked her hair. "Maybe, Chels, but...I don't think so."

"Perri," Angie reprimanded gently, then urged in a theatrical whisper, "Don't worry her."

Perri's tears flowed freely now, blotting out Beau's form bending over a too-long, probably impossible putt. Across the room, Larry left the worn Lazy Boy to pace like a panther before the open front door. When the gallery's moan signified Beau's errant putt, he headed for the kitchen, mumbling expletives.

"Larry's worried, too, huh, Mimi?"

"He's thirsty, princess. He knows Beau's the best."

Perri stroked Chelsea's sweaty hand. "Let's keep our fingers crossed."

Chelsea's eyes clouded. "I want him to win, so he'll pass out candy."

"Oh, honey...." Memory running rampant, she drew Chelsea onto her lap and pressed her mouth to her hair. "Daddy always, always passes out candy. Even if he loses."

※

When Beau walked off eighteen on Saturday afternoon, Chelsea rushed into his arms.

He had discovered himself no longer alone when he made the turn at nine and spotted his family in the massive gallery on the number ten tee box. Once he'd convinced himself they were no illusion, the hellaceous pain in his wrist gave way to thundering in his chest. Nimble and coursewise, Chelsea's hand locked in hers, Perri had somehow managed to stay in his sight the remainder of the round.

He scooped Chelsea up at last, felt her legs lock about his waist while the gallery and a murmuring herd of show-pony groupies watched. Burying his face in her wind-tangled, sweat-dampened hair, his eyes sought Perri's over a bony little shoulder. He held out an arm and Perri moved beneath its shelter while media cameras hummed in the foreground.

"Hey, buddy." Empathetic eyes gazed up into his. "Nice round."

"Right, Periwinkle. Second worst in my career."

She frowned. "What happened to the injection? I thought you had one more to go."

"Seems there's a spot of infection setting up, so I'm having a go at it on my own, more or less." He faked an English brogue, then smiled wryly. "Mostly less."

But he was still in the pack, stalking glory. He heard clubs rattle, felt Mark moving up behind him and eased Chelsea back to the ground. When she reached up to possessively hug his hips, he swayed a little, from joy rather than pressure. Son of a bitch. As often as he'd watched Lehman, Love, Norman, Watson, greeted this way, the feeling was head and shoulders above what he'd imagined.

"I have to talk to you, Beau." Perri brought him back, her eyes like thunderheads, her smile turning tentative.

"You bet, babe." He jostled her against him, the other hand on Chelsea's head as he turned. "Mark, this is—"

"I'd have never guessed, Beau Jangles." Mark's priest face broke into a devil's grin aimed at Perri. "Nice surprise, Perr." He tousled Chelsea's hair. "Hey, red. Wanta help me hand out candy? Looks like your Daddy's got his hands full."

Chelsea's embrace fell away from Beau as if he'd grown thorns. She shot him an apologetic glance, slipped her hand into Mark's and accompanied him to the waiting children.

"Well-adjusted child," Beau murmured against Perri's brow.

"I tried."

"You succeeded."

She closed her eyes, and he kissed her there, sampling salt and mascara, ignoring the crowd surging around him, the camera's grind. "Come with me to the score tent. I need support when I sign this piss-poor card."

"Can it wait?"

Her urgency intrigued and plagued him. "The hell with PGA tradition. It can wait." He urged her aside, into the shade of the bleachers, signaling the media for privacy. Getting it, he drew her into his arms and claimed her with a possessive kiss, the way he'd wanted to for nine holes. He kissed her again. Make that nine years. "Whatever you have to tell me, Periwinkle, let's just say it's behind us."

"It isn't." Her hands wavered over her lower body before her arms wrapped her waist.

The solemn set of her mouth prompted, "My mistake. Tee off."

"I wanted to caddie for you—I still want to, more than you can possibly know."

He shrugged. "Zamora's fired, then. He'll be the first to understand." Drawing her further beneath the bleachers, he nuzzled her salty neck. "With you bagging and Chels in the gallery, I'll shoot a perfect par tomorrow and make double history. But we need to get to bed early." He gave her the seductive grin he reserved for her, honed from their childhood.

She eased back; her hands in the bends of his arms. "I'm pregnant with your baby."

It took a while to get his mind around it, but his heart latched on instantly. He heard himself laugh, saw the consternation go out of her eyes before his gaze migrated downward to her almost concave stomach. "You're pregnant?" His memory shot into reverse. "How the hell do you know? The Denver fiasco was only ten days ago."

"It happened that night on the beach."

He knew he was supposed to act reverent, or awed, or in some damned way she could record in their baby's book. But as he recalled their hunger that night, his smile raged with a will of its own. "We weren't exactly thinking birth control, huh, Perri?"

Her face rosied, eyes sparking. Before she could lose that glow, he said, "God works in mysterious ways, I guess." For some asinine reason, he couldn't stop smiling. "How long have you known?" Without sharing the news with him, another loss they could credit to Braden. But who was keeping score anymore?

"Just before the British Open."

"Then you knew that night in the restaurant, when you told me you'd have to go home."

She nodded. "I stayed with you as long as I could, but I was afraid."

Her gaze strayed from his and he turned to seek its target: Chelsea holding candy court, her hair flaming, its luster secondary only to her smile.

He urged gently, "Afraid you'd injure the baby, or afraid the baby was already injured?" He watched Chelsea, taking in every nuance, every gesture, searching for the flaw he knew was there beneath her perfect surface. "Were you thinking of an abortion, Perri? Is that why you didn't tell me?"

"Never," she swore. "I was thinking you'd never make the break from Braden. That once you and he knew about this baby, I'd be fighting for two children instead of one."

His thumb caressed her chin as he attempted to convey understanding. "And you were going through that all alone, like before."

She shuddered slightly in the hot, humid confines of their hiding place. "I almost made the same mistake twice. I almost didn't tell you, Beau. My mind played all kinds of crazy tricks. I thought of taking Chelsea, going somewhere and starting over. And then when you told me that we're still married..." Her eyes closed, and she appeared to drift onto a sea of memory, frozen there, before they opened, her gaze locking his. "I'd been on my own so long, making my own decisions, that it's become an obsession. And it's hard to believe that you've broken with Braden."

"Do you or don't you believe it? Bottom line." If not he would convince her.

"I've chosen to believe it." She smiled, but looked troubled, indecisive. "I can have an amniocentesis, if you—"

"What would that prove?" His pulse quickened to match the one rapping in her throat.

A thread of fear coursed through her eyes. "Whether or not the baby is...all right."

"It doesn't matter, Perri." He pulled her against him, one hand smothering her words against his chest, the other snaking between their bodies to stroke her abdomen. "If I knew we'd have our baby only a month, a day, or even an hour, it would break my heart, but it wouldn't change my mind. I want a chance to go through it with you. I want to make it up to you." Against her ear, he whispered, "I need to hear you say you aren't afraid, that you want that, too."

"I have so many scars," she whispered back. "You'll suffer from them. I'll make you miserable."

"Then I'll die miserably happy. Tell me you aren't afraid, that you believe in me, Perri."

She sought his eyes. "I love you with my heart and soul. Can we start there?"

"We've got the tee, buddy."

✳

When she lay in his arms that night, spent from their lovemaking, he kissed her mouth, nuzzled her bare breasts and worked his way down to her stomach. Her hands stole to his hair, fingers stroking, pressing him close, arching against him.

"Let's see now," he murmured against her silky skin. "Perri, Chelsea, and Baby Beau."

"What?" Her voice told him she was slipping over the brink of contentment into sleep.

He nuzzled the curly mound at the apex of her thighs. "Just adding up my score card."

His cheek against her stomach absorbed her soft laughter. Turning her, he fitted her backside against him, then curved around to whisper into her ear.

"I just realized, Periwinkle, that win or lose tomorrow, I've already won the grand slam."

THE END

Forbidden Quest by Dar Tomlinson

Carolyna Sinclair suffered a vagabond lifestyle in her disastrous first marriage. Seeking stability, she works to establish an interior design clientele in Savannah's historical district and views her fiancé, politically motivated architect Hugh Masters, as the man to help bring order to her chaotic life. Yet Hugh's staid characteristics that she finds assuring also leave her troubled, and give her a feeling of settling, rather than soaring.

Cally begins to question her engagement when she meets Paul Michael Quest, a caramel-skinned Jamaican immigrant-artist searching Savannah for the mother who abandoned him at birth. Intrigued by Paul Michael's mission, his warm-coffee-colored braids and musical voice, she is haunted by the unconditional love in his eyes.

Forced to examine her traditional Southern beliefs and elite lifestyle, Cally must choose between family heritage and Paul Michael's love, which fulfills her, challenges her beliefs, and infuses her with passion, enabling her to believe true love can cross cultural and racial barriers.

Designer Passion by Dar Tomlinson

Seven years after her husband disappeared, Holly Harper is struggling to save the failing ski apparel business they began together, when a handsome chauvinistic investor named Chess Baker arrives to save the day, so long as he can have controlling interest in the company. Their tempestuous relationship is exacerbated by the return of Holly's husband and an insider trying to sabotage their business.

Broken by Dar Tomlinson

Zac Abriendo had it all: A wife, a son, and a job he
loved. His world was grounded in a deeply rooted
commitment to work and family that spanned gen-
erations. His days were spent on the Gulf shrimp-
ing with his father. His nights were divided
between computer classes at the local community
college and his duties as a father and husband.

All that changed the day Carron Fitzpatrick
walked into his life.

Carron was everything that Zac wasn't. She
was rich. She was white. She was cold and calculating. She would stop at nothing to get what she
wanted. And she wanted Zac.

**Dar Tomlinson was born in Ranger, Texas, grew
up in Oklahoma, and got married before she
graduated from high school. She spent the next
twenty-five years raising two sons, working as
an interior designer, and filling spiral notebooks
with an on-going novel. In 1983 she settled in
Denver, Colorado with her husband and devoted
herself to writing full-time. She now divides her
time between homes in Denver and Scottsdale,
Arizona.**

GENESIS PRESS. INC.
315 3rd Ave. N.
Columbus, MS 39701

www.genesis-press.com
Toll free for orders: 1-888-463-4461